DEAD ENDS

Also by Tony Moyle

'How to Survive the Afterlife' Series

Book 1 - THE LIMPET SYNDROME
Book 2 - SOUL CATCHERS
Book 3 - DEAD ENDS

Sign up to the newsletter
www.tonymoyle.com/contact/

DEAD ENDS

TONY MOYLE

Copyright © 2018 by Tony Moyle

All rights reserved. This book or any portion thereof may not be reproduced or used in any manner whatsoever without the express written permission of the publisher except for the use of brief quotations in a book review or scholarly journal.

First Published: July 2018

ISBN 9781717744067

Limbo Publishing, a brand of In-Sell Ltd

53 The Sands
Ashington, West Sussex RH20 3LQ

www.tonymoyle.com

Cover design by Lucas Media

For...

Myra D, Erica R, Emma T, Richard C, Di D, Brian E, Dave E, Kieran W, Gerald M, Sue M, Ian H, Louise M, Nick D, Carmen M, Colin M, Beth M, James M, Tom D, Simon J, Emily R, Pru L, Karl H, Russell C, Tegan T, Steve J, Faye S, Paul S, Steve D, Dave C, Sarah S, Ben W, Chloe H, David M, Michelle H, Barry C, Jack V, Wayne P, Vicky W, Nicky P and Simon Capel.

"Without your positive encouragement there would be no afterlife" T.M.

dead
/dɛd/

adjective
adjective: **dead**
    1: no longer alive.
    ◦lacking emotion, sympathy, or sensitivity.
    ◦devoid of living things.
    2: complete; absolute.

ends
/ɛnd/

noun
noun: **end**; plural noun: **ends**
    1: a final part of something, especially a period of time, an activity, or a story.
    ◦to emphasise that something, typically a subject of discussion, is considered finished.
    ◦ a person's death.
    ◦ (in Biblical use) an ultimate state or condition.
    2: the furthest or most extreme part of something.
    3: a part or person's share of an activity.
    4: a goal or desired result.

Notes from Book 2 - Soul Catchers

(Note: Contains spoilers)

An eleven-year-old Chilean boy places a flower at the foot of a gravestone. It's John Hewson's. On the reverse is a patiently chiselled message, 'God Protects the king.' John's mother confronts the boy, David Gonzalez, believing he is responsible. He explains that he's investigating John's death and she reveals that he wasn't killed in a car crash after all. His death came as a result of a single bullet wound to the chest.

In Hell the demons call a council of creatures. Senior demons are summoned to explain how John's soul has escaped from the metal box suspended above level twelve. Between Primordial, guardian of reincarnates on level zero, and Brimstone, operator of the Soul Catcher, they formulate a theory. John triggered the Limpet Syndrome again, releasing a second part of his soul and drawing a previously removed part from Nash Stevens, a rockstar that John once possessed. The two oppositely charged parts of his soul attract each other, leaving the neutral part free to wander.

Asmodeus sends for Laslow, who was last seen shooting John in Limbo. Laslow, once carrier of Satan's soul, confirms that John had become angrier towards the end, proving that the positive part of his soul left first and the negative second. The message 'Newton's third', which was burnt on the inside of John's box, is a reference to revenge.

David Gonzalez reviews a list of names under the heading Newton's Third. The first name is Laslow's. When David reaches Limbo to confront him he finds his decomposed corpse nailed to the white funnel.

Other than the souls streaming into Limbo, and a rather disturbing boisterous soul called a 'shadow,' the only survivor of the massacre is the Clerk. He explains how Heaven's Soul Catcher was turned off and how Limbo, along with twelve neutral jurors, were used to decide on the final destination for all souls.

On level zero, Sandy Logan, former politician and current plastic pigeon, has worked out what Emorfed is. At a pass over event, where the reincarnates finally let go of life, Sandy identifies a shrew suffering from a form of Tourette's. The shrew is what remains of John, his positive and negative personalities struggling to live with each other. Sandy and Ian protect John from the demons and concoct a plan.

Victor Serpo, formerly Agent 15, has escaped to Canada with the remaining samples of Emorfed, which he sells to the highest bidder so the recipient can escape their emotional pain. A strange, unregistered patient turns up. It's his old boss, former Prime Minister, Byron T. Casey. Although Byron was shot by Laslow, his body was healed at the peak of the solstice and Satan took up residence in his body. Using an apple, Byron explains how the soul is split into three parts with each part being managed by Hell, Heaven and a potential 'third way', a place for neutral souls that lack a god. Byron convinces Victor that his Emorfed patients must be killed to stop the shadows, a by-product, from infecting Hell.

David visits Donovan King to seek therapy for his premonitions and his complete lack of emotions. Donovan knows what 'God Protects the King' means. It refers to a mysterious historical figure called Baltazaar who lived in Phoenician times. Donovan reveals that Herb, Nash Steven's old manager and Emorfed victim, has killed himself. This makes David suspicious and he travels to Herb's funeral to find out more. There he bumps into Nash Stevens who freaks out about how much David knows about John Hewson.

On the island of Bryher in the Scilly Isles, Violet Stokes, former head of the animal welfare group JAWS, and Fiona Foster, the reporter who broke the Emorfed story, are raising their two adopted children. One is an eight-year-old boy called Scrumpy, who's obsessed by pirates. The other is Grace, a pale white-haired girl with an amazing affinity for science. She's the daughter of Faith, who still suffers from her exposure to Emorfed.

Victor and Byron start assassinating Emorfed patients. In Monaco they come into contact with Baltazaar, who has taken up residence inside the old preacher Donovan King. Byron and Donovan create a terrible geological storm as they battle over the fate of the Emorfed clients.

In Hell, Sandy and Ian enrol a group of strange volunteers to help them steal Faith's soul from level twelve. They include a sociopathic cat, a racist spider, an evangelical ox, a gibbon who plays practical jokes, and an extremely slow sloth. Meanwhile, the senior demons, including the reclusive dark matter demon, Mr. Noir, seek out John on level zero. Sandy and Ian succeed in finding Faith's soul and unleash the shadows to fight on their behalf by infecting all the murderous dictators on level ten. Sandy also persuades the lesser demons, led by Fluffy and Red, to start a rebellion against the senior demons who are forced into retirement on level zero.

David follows Nash to the Scilly Isles where he befriends the boy Scrumpy and gains employment on their farm. Through Victor's connections Byron learns of David's location and starts to plan his next move. Nash, fearful of who David is, informs Baltazaar of their location through prayer.

Mr. Brimstone heads to the library to help find more information about John. John's book is massive and contains more than fifty lives, but the front cover has been worn away, withholding who John really was. Brimstone discovers a new sapling growing beneath the two oak trees, a sign that the 'third coming' has arrived. A new book, laminated and blank, suggests this new neutral god is eleven years old.

A battle erupts in Hell between Brimstone, the six reincarnates and the shadow souls. In the melee Faith's soul is sent back to her just before the heart is removed from the Soul Catcher, stopping it working and sending a small ball of metal out into space. The shadows also kill John on Sandy's command. In Limbo, the Clerk watches as the walls slowly expand from the increasing volume of souls arriving but not leaving.

Back on Bryher, Byron and Donovan descend on the farmhouse determined to kill David, who they believe is the third coming. David meets Grace for the first time and recalls how a girl of her exact description was involved in John's car crash. Byron kidnaps Scrumpy and takes him to the next island. David pursues him in Grace's high-speed red tractor. When he finds Scrumpy he swerves to avoid Grace in the road, just as John had done so many years before. It transpires that John's death was a premonition of what would come to pass.

Baltazaar confronts David before setting fire to the tractor and forcing David to trigger the Limpet Syndrome for a third and final time. A small ball of metal ascends into the air. It arrives in a strange world covered in meadows of white grass in the shadow of a giant red sun. Grace, who has the power to stop time, escapes with Scrumpy in his boat. Byron, not convinced that David was the 'third coming', follows the girl, who manages to escape. It's clear to Byron that the 'third coming' isn't a 'he', but a 'she'.

In Hell, Sandy has taken over management of Hell while Ian and the other reincarnates have been banished to level zero. Brimstone warns Sandy that souls will eventually evolve. While the senior demons watch their very first pass over a voice speaks to them invisibly from the air. It's John's.

CHAPTER ONE

LIFE

In the beginning there was a bang. Apparently it was big. Not that anyone was there to witness it. The discovery of said 'bang' came more than thirteen billion years later when a bunch of scientists pointed some complex equipment into space and confidently pronounced that the microwaves were behaving strangely and making funny whooshing noises. Technically, if it was a 'bang' it was not precisely at the beginning. A bang can't happen in a vacuum. Something must have existed beforehand to trigger all the commotion normally associated with any explosion. Difficult to start a firework display without the crucial element of an actual firework. Maybe it wasn't a bang, or big, or even at the beginning? Let's start again.

Near the start of space and time, but definitely not at the very beginning, there was probably an event which may have been big, but was certainly noticeable billions of years later when overconfident scientists predicted, due to nothing more significant than the length and volume of microwaves, that there might have been a bang. Or possibly a minor cosmic burp. That's the problem with science, you have to sit on the fence until all possible evidence is available.

Scientists want us to believe that the 'bang' came from something called the singularity. An object so small you'd struggle to see it through the world's most powerful microscope. Yet this infinitesimally dense speck, surrounded by total nothingness, contained every observed and unobserved object in the universes. Just remember that the next time you're packing for a holiday and convince yourself it's physically impossible to get everything inside your suitcase. Everything that was, currently is, or ever will be in the future existed inside the singularity.

Everything.

The view out of your window, the chair you're sitting on now, and even the complex chains of organic matter contained inside the bottom that sits on it, were all crammed inside. It would stretch most people's imagination just to think of fitting your arse, chair and living room inside an invisibly small single point of ignition, but then consider the billions of stars, associated celestial bodies, and multiverses that were also contained within it. And you thought the story of Adam and Eve was far-fetched.

Non-religious types often cite the illogical and whimsical nature of faith as an explanation as to why God doesn't exist. How can anyone build the Universe in seven days? It's irrational to believe that Moses parted the Red Sea with nothing more than a chariot and a first-class prayer, or that Noah crammed two of every animal on a vessel no bigger than a canoe. Noah's story looks reasonably safe if you consider that all of Noah's animals, and the rest of existence, were inside the singularity. If we believe in science, that is. Belief isn't just about fact, it's also about who you believe in.

There is one aspect of the Big Bang theory that scientists do agree on. None of them has the first idea where the singularity came from or how it got there. They agree it was there because they've got lots of graphs, and how can you argue with a beautifully intricate Venn diagram? Whether the singularity produced the gods or the gods produced the singularity isn't important. It was so long ago even they can't remember.

LIFE

What scientists can validate is that the singularity got bigger. Expanding outwards, it produced material: dark, light and some other stuff in the middle no one has come up with a convincing formula for yet. Over time, and with a nasty cold front weather system in attendance, this material started to cool and collect under immense pressure to form subatomic particles with interesting names like strange quark and gauge boson. These clumped together to form larger particles until, with the moral support of gravity and other such forces, these larger objects eventually coalesced into planets, solar systems, galaxies and the Universe.

The Universe is impossibly big. This isn't a statement based on some overly complicated dissertation from a professor with too many letters after their name and a brain the size of a space hopper. Just look out of your window. See if you can spot the edges? Didn't think so. Anyway, if it wasn't huge it would be called a tiny-verse instead.

And there wasn't just one of them either.

As matter and energy spewed rapidly into the expanding space, the fifth force dragged the competing energies into different regions. Oppositely polarised particles pushed and pulled against each other, squabbling for position around a central point. Four unique Universes formed, three in rotation around a fourth one that sat in the middle like an intergalactic cosmic fidget spinner. In a tiny portion of that central universe, orbiting around a star with eight brothers and sisters, floated a planet that John Hewson once called his own. This central Universe was responsible for the creation of the human race. John could no longer be counted amongst their number as he was currently residing in uncategorised forms in two of the other universes, some light years away from each other.

As the universes cooled and expanded, conditions were created that allowed the formation of organic matter and complex molecules. With the extension of time these molecules evolved into simple living organisms. Each of these simple life forms possessed the potential for a living spiritual force that developed in tandem with the physical form like an unseen virus. The soul. As the physical host developed the ability to produce sentient capabilities, so the soul evolved its capacity to collect energy in the form of electrical signals.

Why humans developed these sentient responses more quickly than other creatures isn't entirely clear. What is indisputable, however, is that each soul's host demonstrated characteristics unique from each other. The human drive for survival and advantage manifests itself in the properties of the soul within. All of them had the basic capacity for sustaining charge, attracted by and sourced from three competing universes that span around the cosmos, holding the energy suspended, for now, inside its own unique organic vessel.

All but some.

Some souls evolve.

And just as Darwin documented in his work on the evolution of species, evolution is only possible as a consequence of a mutation.

The peripheral universes were, until recently, designed as a resting place for three unique forms of energy that only existed inside souls. One attracted purely positive energy, one negative and the last neutral. None of them were currently performing their cosmic responsibilities with any aplomb.

Following a bout of vandalism from a mob of dead dictators, egged on by a bunch of mutated shadow souls, Hell's Universe had lost the use of its Soul Catcher, a mysterious machine with the ability to suck souls towards it. Heaven's Universe had turned their Soul Catcher off more than a millennium ago to farm Emorfed, the recycled remains of souls, capable of suppressing human emotion by removing all but the neutral elements of the soul.

LIFE

And in the thirteen billion years prior to a small ball of metal landing on its surface and getting nosy, the final Universe was known only to gods, the only visitors since the singularity burst and started all this nonsense.

All three exits for the soul were now celestial dead ends. The soul had only one route after death. A place known as Limbo, located in the Earth's mantle under the surface of Switzerland. It would soak up these souls with the same exuberance a piece of crusty bread does with gravy after a nice roast dinner. Something would have to change. If it didn't, the consequences for the human race would be catastrophic.

*****

Perching on the edge of a vast chasm, a small ball of silver metal basked in the frenzied glow from a deep red sun far closer to the limits of an orbiting planet than Einstein would recommend. Solar flares leapt from its surface like great pink salmon escaping upstream for the breeding season. The flares licked the translucent surface of this unknown world with the fervency of desperate window-shoppers on the first day of a sale.

The liquid metal within the ball swirled within the confines of itself as if its eyes were repositioning to analyse the next feature of the landscape. A sense of order and uniformity oozed from every natural landmark from foreground to horizon. The chasm below the ball was the only topographic feature without a monotonous sense of conformity. The excavation of whatever lay there had all the hallmarks of a hurried and slapdash mugging. No attempt had been made to return the landscape to its original state, no regeneration to mask what had been done there. It was difficult for the ball to judge the size and scale of this deep quarry because, number one it was a ball of metal, and number two it didn't have eyes. Which really didn't explain why it knew a large hole was stretching out in front of him.

The football pitch was always a good unit of measurement. Everyone loved using it to measure anything that was bigger than…a football pitch. Nothing was ever described as a third of a football pitch, but many objects were calibrated in sizes of multiple football pitches. Uncertain as to the basic measurement of any type of pitch that involved any ball-based competition didn't stop the ball reflecting in his mind that the quarry was at least ten football pitches big. Which also didn't really matter as only it was conscious of the comparison, given that no other living thing appeared to occupy the world it found itself in.

Its awareness switched directions. In an anatomical sense this meant his sight was now where his butt had been previously. Only landmarks with angles absorbed his perception. In the foreground a field of white grass waved casually at him as it was battered by the geothermic conditions swirling around the planet. In the background a set of perpendicular mountains queued patiently for some unseen geological audit. Trees, of which there were few, were similar in design to those drawn by an Etch a Sketch or a very peculiar child. Not a curve was present in any of them.

The ball rolled forward towards the grass, an impulse unthought and unprovoked. Although it demonstrated many of the characteristics that might suggest it had fallen off the production line of an automotive factory, there was something unmistakably 'alive' about it. Its senses were as uncomfortable and unfamiliar as they would have been if they were scattered unabated as a cloud of blue electricity. The only difference now was the physical and tangible feel to its existence and a complete lack of the emotional perception notorious with the experience of being a soul. The life swimming within was palpable yet devoid of any sense of who or what it was.

LIFE

Life was unaccustomed to this harsh new kingdom. No birds flew in the orange-tinged sky. No animals grazed amongst the chalky-ridged plains. No water ran across the countryside carrying wriggling fish or writhing sea critters. Those trees that had had the temerity or bloody-mindedness to set down roots might just as well have been produced by a machine whose only job was to make unimaginably boring fake plastic trees. Life and death normally meandered the passage of time with the same predictability that night follows day. Here neither had made an appearance for some considerable time.

Until now.

The sheaths of white grass, where the ball had arrived a short time ago, seemingly aiding both his size and movement, were getting noticeably bigger. Their accelerated growth was evident in both height and width, towering over the small ball of metal in minutes. When they'd achieved a suitable girth and grandeur, the two dozen or so thin, square sheets of white translucent pulp resembled a procession of printing paper lining up to feed a giant, overproportioned photocopier. A few of these sheets flapped in the wind, desperately trying to stay in shape. Uncertain as to the final end point of the growth that appeared to take them by surprise, each one spontaneously started a process of rearranging their simple square forms.

As they squirmed and wriggled, a series of ripping noises echoed off the walls of the square mountain range, as they removed themselves from the roots that had bound them to the ground. Ten feet tall and wide and as thin as cigarette paper, each sheet began to fold itself into elaborate patterns. No two objects followed the same instruction manual, yet every move was assured in its accuracy of turn and crease. Acrobatically they jumped, flipped, rolled, crimped and squashed their bodies to form an array of interesting origami characters.

LIFE

As the troop of newly formed paper creatures nodded in appreciation of the colleagues on either side of them, one took its place at the head of the crowd. The ball watched with fascination. It was the most interesting thing to happen since it had arrived. Which wasn't difficult given the competition was a hurriedly dug hole and a tree with square fir cones.

The two dozen arrivals were mostly humanoid, although here and there a few had clearly made some hideous folding error or simply mistook their brief. Standing at the front, a character with a chiselled torso and way more neck than necessary addressed the crowd.

"Ok, does everyone know what's going on?"

The ball made an imperceptible shake in the form of a metallic swirl. None of the paper army noticed it was there, but their shaking heads seemed to agree nonetheless.

"I'm guessing we've been summoned," replied a short, stubby figure with half a paper finger in the air. Where the other half was was anyone's guess.

"Exactly," said the leader. "It's been a long wait, but finally it's happening."

"What is?" said another who'd had trouble perfecting the folds around its facial features and had ended up with one eye, three ears and a droopy bottom lip.

"When our world welcomes inhabitants, only then are we created to manage them," said the leader.

"What inhabitants?" said another voice.

"I'm sure they're around here somewhere, it's a big planet after all. Before we go look, let's see if everyone is present and correct. Roll-call time."

The leader strolled uneasily down the ranks of his platoon with the watchful eye of a sergeant major. Not wanting to fall below his own standards of scrutiny, he stopped occasionally to converse with one or two of its soldiers.

"What's happened here, then?" it said halfway down the row.

"Something went a bit wrong halfway through, sir. Around step nine in my instructions I think one of my squash folds went a bit wrong."

"A bit wrong," repeated the leader.

"Yes."

"You were aiming for humanoid, weren't you?" probed the leader.

"Aiming for, yes, sir."

"Yet what you've ended up with is more of a swan effect, wouldn't you say?"

"I thought it was more like a goose," it replied before a sharp-edged stare cut it off. "At least I didn't end up like that one."

The leader followed the direction of the swan's beak to a long, flat object closer to the ground. Bending its knees for the first time, the leader crumpled its body down to where it assumed it might achieve an element of eye contact.

"Don't ask," came a muffled response.

"I'm going to," replied the leader.

"Ok, you're the boss."

"What good are you going to be at managing the potential influx of souls if you're folded up as a paper aeroplane."

"I panicked," came a voice from beneath the cockpit area. "Everyone seemed to know what they were doing. All I could think of was this."

"How long have you waited for this moment?" asked the leader, quite aware of the answer to come.

"Oh not long, really, it's hard to…"

"A few billion years, isn't it?" prompted the leader accurately.

"As long as that! It's so easy to lose track of time," said the plane.

"And you've been so very busy," replied the leader sarcastically. "What with all the competing priorities you've had existing as a blade of grass since the dawn of time."

"Sorry, sir."

"You had one job."

The leader returned to its position at the front of the group. Half of the two dozen had produced decent enough humanoid figures, although each with a variety of personal creativity thrown in for good measure. The remainder ranged from elaborate napkins to paper fortune tellers used by young girls in school playgrounds to allocate different colours and numbers to unsuspecting friends.

"Clearly some of you are going to have to start all over again."

A muffled response came from one of the misfits.

"Forgot the mouth, did you?"

The Sydney Opera House nodded.

"It's very hard to refold a second time," offered the swan, who was actually rather pleased with what he'd managed. To go from eternal blade of grass to goose, or swan, at the first attempt was a miracle.

"Enough," shouted the leader as the din of argument grew. "The refolding will have to come later. We have been summoned because, after an extreme period of waiting, we have received a guest. As servants of the afterlife we must account for those that arrive here. Spread out and look for it."

"What will they look like?" said a skinny character whose head was about the same length as his body.

"Who knows? There haven't been any before, have there? If you're asking me to guess I'd suggest you look out for something unnatural. If it's got curves, that's a start," said the leader.

The ball did its best to show off how perfectly round it was.

"What about the small ball of metal that rubbed past me this morning? The one who's currently standing over there by the big hole," said the paper aeroplane, who had the advantage of seeing through most of the legs.

"Excellent work," said the leader.

On its signal the troop formed what they hoped was the right formation and marched, waddled, tumbled or hovered across the meadow towards their target. The ball stood its ground through no other instinct than this was likely to be more entertaining than staring into a shoddy crater. The leader stooped down and placed the ball of metal into his palm and raised it in the air for the creased necks to crane themselves a decent view.

"Is that it!?" said someone under its breath.

"I believe so," said the leader.

"It's not what I was expecting," replied another.

"No, nor I."

Everyone with heads nodded. The plane retracted its flaps.

"Welcome to Neutopia," said the leader, clearing his throat assertively. "The resting place for souls of a neutral disposition. We are the Accountants. It is our job to manage you."

There was a pregnant pause as everyone waited in anticipation for the sign of a response.

"Not very chatty, is it?" said the swan.

CHAPTER TWO

ENDGAMES

Glaciers don't tend to be in a hurry. They are by nature slow responders. Tens of thousands of years may pass when the only obvious progression in their appearance is the acquisition of a few new wrinkles desperately in need of some geological face cream. None are sprinters, but some move more quickly than others. In the battle for world speed records, the Jakobshavn Glacier in Greenland is the ice age equivalent of Usain Bolt. It's not unheard of for it to move as fast as forty-five metres a year. That's almost the same speed as a sloth.

The Aletsch Glacier, stretching out in a southerly direction from the Jungfrau mountain in Switzerland, is positively pedestrian in comparison. When its notable life events are measured in generations and a time-lapse photographer would struggle to produce results in a lifetime, it can't be accused of being in a hurry. As it had done for tens of thousands of years, its mouth sucked the three peaks of Jungfrau, Mönch and Eiger with the ferocity of an octopus strangling a fish. It's a view that has been largely unchanged since the end of the last ice age.

Until now.

Much had been spent to commercialise Jungfrau, the highest peak in a wall of mountains that separated the glacier from the Swiss Plateau. Tourism had been cultivated with the same loving care afforded to the herds of cows grazing on the lowland pastures. Tunnels had been dug. Miles of rail laid. Gaudy attractions constructed. You could ride a large, yellow blow-up ring through the snow or go on a massive zip wire ride as long as you paid extortionate amounts for the privilege. All of it designed to distract you from noticing the massive glacier you'd originally come to see.

Millions had been spent, confident in the knowledge that the gravy train would flow for as long as the people were conned into believing the experience was genuine. They were as high as they could be in the Bernese Mountains: whether they actually looked at them was irrelevant. The majority of the general public only cared about buying T-shirts with pictures of goats on clifftops, or the ability to take a selfie to prove to their friends they were there. Job done. Kerr-ching.

What the Swiss tourism department couldn't predict, given the safe bet of a mountain being the highest in a region on any given morning, was that one morning it wasn't. Not only were the general public now ignoring the creature comforts of the Jungfrau theme park, with its shops and restaurants, but they were also finding it difficult to locate. Which wasn't surprising since a bloody big, metal dome was casting a shadow over peaks unsheltered since geological forces pushed them there several eons ago.

Baltazaar, still squatting resolutely in the physical body of preacher Dr. Donovan King, tilted his Panama hat to shade his eyes from the sun's glare reflecting off the metal. The curved wall of Limbo was no more than fifty metres from his vantage point, perched less than comfortably on the summit of the mighty Eiger. A wide grin was trying desperately to relocate his ears.

Limbo was not normally this obvious. The cavernous, metallic sphere, built to process the neutral souls of the world, once occupied a point a thousand metres under the Alp mountains where no inquisitive human might accidentally stumble upon it. It had served the same purpose since the dawn of religion itself. When the system only catered for processing negatively or positively balanced emotions, something had to be done with the 'abnormalities'.

Baltazaar had been the co-architect of the solution. Rather than wait for the afterlife to evolve a third option for man, a place where logic, not love or hate, ruled, they would bring it here. They would build Neutopia on Earth and manage it on their terms. Satan was all too happy to act as his accomplice. In his desire to control the energy of souls, the essential fuel that stoked the furnaces of Hell, not only would he co-operate, but he'd also fall right into Baltazaar's trap. Building this structure would require Satan to use a human body, a trap that would be almost as hard to escape from than Limbo itself.

Limbo was not always this grand. Only one small ball bearing-sized sample of Celestium was needed to stimulate the engorged object currently above surface and blocking out a vista untarnished for thousands of years. If Baltazaar was responsible for placing Limbo here, he was not solely responsible for its current expansion, although he welcomed the turn of events with glee.

Celestium was a unique substance for many reasons. Firstly, it was a heavy element alien to Earth's universe. Secondly, it was the only known source of the fifth force, an interaction yet to be discovered by humans and responsible for, amongst other abilities, drawing souls around the cosmos. Without the fifth force souls do not travel to their predetermined destination. And the closer the source of this power, the more likely a soul will be drawn to it. Limbo was on Earth, so all souls were initially pulled here. Thirdly, if unmanaged, Celestium not only pulled souls towards it, it also absorbed them. And sometimes them it.

As Limbo's token sample of Celestium drew every ejected soul to it with the increasing rate of human deaths, so it expanded. In normal circumstances these souls would eventually be processed and sent on to their final resting place, easing the metal's expansion outwards. Souls were redirected to Heaven or Hell by firing them away from Limbo at a pace so rapid they connected with a different source of Celestium before Limbo could pull them back again.

But those other sources no longer existed. This was the last and only place they could go. As the stream of souls from millions of humans entered on a weekly basis, the bulbous entity swelled like a teenager's acne. It would not stop. Baltazaar had failed to neutralise human will power with Emorfed, and the next best thing was to destroy the whole species entirely. Who would stop him? David had taken the bait and triggered the Limpet Syndrome for a third and fatal time. The third coming was no longer a threat and the Devil was licking his wounds, always one step behind.

It was only a matter of time before Limbo's Celestium expanded exponentially to consume all living things before the weight of it triggered a 'big crunch' followed by a second big bang and the renewal of the universe.

*****

Only two countries in the world have no capital city. One is Nauru, a rock island on the Equator with less than ten thousand inhabitants. It has the honour of being officially the least visited country in the world. It has no capital because in truth it can't be bothered to name one, and if it did, tourists might come and make it not 'the least visited country in the world'. Paradises are generally places without tourists. They just make it look untidy and have a habit of attracting fast-food restaurants.

The second country in the world without a capital city is Switzerland. The reason for this is quite different to Nauru's. They don't have one because for hundreds of years they haven't been able to agree which city it should be. This in itself shows a useful insight into the historical nature of Swiss values. A nation divided by region, language, culture and a spectrum of deeply held beliefs about which is the best cheese in the world. This argument alone could keep factions busy debating for the whole of a parliament's life. The answer of course is Gruyère.

All of this is not to say that people who live outside of Switzerland don't know where the capital city is. We all think and believe it's Bern. It certainly demonstrates most of the essential features of a capital city. It's big, contains many functions of government, and features on maps with a square rather than a circle. Everyone believes it apart from the people who truly matter, the Swiss. For thousands of years they've done things very differently from the rest of us. It would be easy to criticise them as being odd. But unlike most other countries, they don't tend to have a propensity for drama, cause wars for no particular reason, or get involved in other people's business. They would do, if they could only agree on it.

Unlike Nauru, whose main attractions included a few discarded rusty Japanese guns and a limestone rock formation in the shape of rolling pin, Bern did have locations of note. Some of the more notable tourist attractions included a statue of a man eating a baby and a small hole filled with big, brown bears. Other countries might have campaigned against these archaic and offensive absurdities and had them removed. Not in Switzerland. Consensus was the name of the game here, at least it would be if they could agree on it.

This was reflected in the way the country did its politics. There were seven people on the Federal Council, all representing different parties and interests. Their business, or at least discussions around topics that might eventually lead to business, took place in the Federal Palace, a feature of Bern which had led other countries to conclude it must be the capital city.

The Federal Palace was an impressive structure built in the early nineteenth century, but in a style of a much older building. Its domes dominated the skyline and its interior chiselled masonry swept through long chambers and vast, open hallways. It was as beautiful as it was noisy. Several studies in recent years determined that the background noise in the debating chambers was the equivalent of a washing machine on an eternal cycle. The jury is still out as to whether this was a contributing factor for all the indecision or not.

The Clerk fidgeted uncomfortably in his leather chair. It felt alien against a body that had only experienced small, plastic chairs three sizes too small for his backside for as long as either buttock could remember. The room, a plush modernised corner of the Federal Palace, featured a long, buffed-glass table and several identical leather chairs. The lighting was false and irritating, like a bag of torches had been set off in a bunker. There were no windows in the room, and the atmosphere was agitating at least one of its two occupants.

The other person here seemed only too happy to endure it. Rogier Hoffstetter had spent most of the last hour pacing around the table. The Clerk thought this might have been an unconscious reaction to having previously experienced the discomfort of the leather chairs. It was hard to know how long they'd been there. The lack of solar or lunar clues, and the Clerk's unfamiliarity with the outside world, added to the suspension of time. It also didn't help that Rogier kept repeating himself.

"Right, let's go over this again," said Rogier, further wearing down the threads in the cream-coloured hessian rug. "Who are you?"

"Clerk," came the incongruously exasperated response, given he was the type of person who normally adopted an almost impenetrable positivity.

"And what has happened to my mountain, Mr. Clark?"

"It's not Mr. Clark, it's just Clerk."

"Clerk who?"

"I don't have a second name, or a first as it happens, I'm just the Clerk."

Rogier screwed up his face in confusion.

"I understand you have football players who also only go by a single name, if that helps," added the Clerk kindly.

"I'm guessing that's not the reason, though."

The Clerk shook his head.

"How is it possible you have no name?"

"Because people have, for as long as I can remember, called me the Clerk, therefore I answer to it."

"But how long is 'for as long as I can remember'?"

"What century is this?" asked the Clerk pertinently.

"It's the twenty-first of course!"

The Clerk used his fingers to count but ran out of digits. "Longer than I thought."

"Surely at most, if the reference to time is centuries, you only need fists not fingers to count it. No one can live through more than two."

"You'd think so, wouldn't you?" the Clerk chuckled. "I think you probably have more pressing questions, Prime Minister."

"You're right, although I'm not really the Prime Minister. It's convenient to use that expression in the company of international audiences but we don't really have them in Switzerland."

"What do you have, then?"

"My official role is President of the Swiss Council. We make decisions based on a seven-member Cabinet and rotate the presidency every twelve months. It's just my luck that this should all happen on my watch. Whatever 'this' is."

"Let me go over it for you one more time," said the Clerk.

ENDGAMES

Of course the explanation wasn't easy to take in unless you had an extremely broad mind and the ability to embrace concepts that were not only difficult to accept, but also until recently you thought physically impossible. The Clerk chose to slow down the rate of information and use really small words.

What had happened to his mountain? Limbo had happened. A place hidden away from the consciousness of mankind for generations was currently expanding outward at an alarming speed, consuming as it went anything in its path. The expansion could only be the result of one thing. Souls. No other substance or energy was attracted to the fifth force. A force that only Celestium possessed.

"The fact that this foreign metal substance attracts souls is one thing, but if it's been there forever, why and how is it expanding like this now?" asked Rogier, interjecting once again.

"Why and how are very different questions," said the Clerk. "I can only answer one of them. There have always only ever been three sources of Celestium in the multiverses, I assume only one of them is left, or functioning correctly."

"But you said you were an expert on endgames. That is why we brought you here. How can you be an expert if you don't know why?"

"Sometimes in life you just have to accept what is happening because you can see that it is. Knowing why isn't going to stop it. All the signs tell me the endgame has begun, but the outcome of the end is still in play, it is not predetermined."

"How do you know all this?"

"Because I helped set the rules of the game. What's important now is how we play them."

"But it's not a game, is it? A large part of my beautiful country is now under a metal sphere and before long the general public will stop calling them the Alps and start calling them the Dome."

"Then we must win the game, Mr. President. If we don't it's not just your country that will be affected. Every country is in danger."

"But how can we stop it?"

This question had long loitered uncomfortably at the front of the Clerk's brain. The answers were not palatable. Souls had to go somewhere. If not Limbo, then where? It was not within his power to fix the other Soul Catchers, and nor did he have the means to communicate to anyone who might. The only alternative was to find a way to stop the movement of souls themselves. It was an option with potentially unintended consequences. It meant forcing the soul itself to evolve, which might create problems larger than the one they were currently wrestling with.

Unless they did nothing.

They let the endgame play out as intended by higher authorities than science and religion. They accepted the uncomfortable truth that humans could not put off the inevitable path of their uncontrolled existence. They accepted the proposition that humankind was ultimately responsible for its own fate. Their collective actions had sent them careering unstoppably to this moment. It could never be stopped, only delayed.

Not on his watch.

"There is one way we might stop this," said the Clerk.

"How?"

"We need a way of communicating to the whole world with one simple, unambiguous message. A megaphone that can talk to the whole planet."

"There are plenty of TV programmes we can get you on," said Rogier.

"No, it has to be bigger. It can't just focus on one national broadcaster. It must traverse language barriers and cultural interpretations. It must be global. The souls come to your country from every corner of the world and we must get the message to every one of them."

"What if we spoke at the United Nations? That would be relayed to every country simultaneously."

"Perfect. Let's go."

"I'm afraid things in my country don't work like that. First we must get approval from the Federal Council, and once that's agreed we have to request an audience at one of the UN council meetings."

"How long will that take?"

"Let's hope it doesn't take as long as the decision to remove the Bern bears."

"How long did that take?"

"We're still discussing it: we have been on and off since the sixteenth century."

The Clerk didn't express it, but based on his calculations of Limbo's current expansion he thought it unlikely the Palace would still be visible in sixteen days.

CHAPTER THREE

PATIENTS AND PASSENGERS

The West Cornwall Hospital in Penzance had all the aesthetic appeal of a council estate that had just given birth to a crematorium. Not that it mattered. None of the patients admitted were in the slightest bit bothered by any architectural awards it might have won. All hospitals tended to fit into two categories when it came to appearance. They were either dilapidated Victorian buildings constructed in a time when dourness was in fashion, or they were spectacularly overdesigned greenhouses, modernised to convince any unsuspecting visitor of the illusion that nothing unpleasant could ever possibly happen within its hygienic interior.

The truth, of course, is that no one likes being in a hospital, whatever it looks like. Even doctors aren't that keen. At least they know they've got a high probability of leaving in the same mode of transport they arrived in, and more than likely in the same twenty-four-hour window. Patients and visitors can't be so certain. When it comes to patients, clearly the nature of their condition or symptoms will have a major impact on their time of exit and state of existence. Although even the knowledge of having a minor ailment does nothing to stop the universal fear of being there.

The mere fact that you entered with a trivial ingrowing toenail in no way detracts from the irrational and media-inspired fear of what might befall

PATIENTS AND PASSENGERS

you once you've entered the building. Hospitals are, by design, full of ill people. Ill people have a habit of infecting other people. They're also full of old people. Old people have a habit of being much closer to death than birth. Death brings disease and diseases spread. But there is one other condition that hospitals are saturated with. Fear. And that spreads fastest of all. No, hospitals are not places you visit for kicks. Not even the hardiest of extreme sports enthusiast would pick it out as a 'thrill ride'.

There is one group of people that frequent hospitals who deserve most of our sympathy. Doctors get paid. Patients are hopefully cured, or scare themselves better as a consequence of the perpetual horrors that act as a catalyst around them to speed up the healing process. Visitors, on the other hand, get nothing at all out of the endeavour. The best-case scenario for the hospital visitor is the discovery that the person you went in to see isn't dead. Fortunately, on most occasions, they aren't and the rest of the experience is just bitterly disappointing.

It probably started before the front door. The car park has already removed any coinage you might have concealed about your person and is fully prepared to humiliate you further by insisting on you parting with a week's salary for a parking stay not long enough to even locate your loved ones, let alone to identify if, in fact, they're still alive. This is because they've been hidden from you inside an insanely complicated rabbit warren of wards and corridors, and all the signs have been written in hieroglyphics.

The situation will not improve when you're on the premises. The kiosk will invitingly tempt you with hot refreshments, most of which have been brewed inside a tumble dryer and priced in the range of Gambia's national debt. Only one person will work at the kiosk, despite there being several thousand customers, and their suitability for employment will be based on their

PATIENTS AND PASSENGERS

deep-rooted dislike of humans and an inability to count to eleven.

Without doubt there will be an old crone mesmerisingly mopping the same square of lino floor with the energy of a slow-moving glacier. No one is entirely certain whether the 'crone' officially works there or not, because no one has lived longer than the time she's been cleaning the same area of floor. Any misguided attempt to ask the crone for simple information regarding the hospital, like where the toilets are or what year it is, will be met with the sort of confusion toddlers exhibit on the discovery of a cat flap.

Most visitors will spend only a fraction of their visit with the person they came to see. This will in part be due to the confusing layout of the building, a deep desire not to spend time in close proximity to other ill people, and a fear as to what to say when they do find their sick relative. By law, hospital conversations only focus on the following information: the quality of the food, how they feel, how they felt yesterday, how they think they might feel tomorrow, what medication they're taking, whether they've been forced to defecate in a device that looks remarkably like a plastic frying pan, when they might get out, whether any of the other patients are friendly, and whether they've eaten enough grapes.

No one teaches you how to behave as a hospital visitor. People just know how to do it. But not all visitors are necessarily best described as people.

Byron T. Casey stood in front of the automatic glass doors of the West Cornwall Hospital. A variety of different characters had already successfully navigated through them with apparent ease. None of them appeared to offer up any secret word or motion to signal the doors to open, but still some invisible power detected the person was there and did it anyway. Byron was technically not 'all there'. His body was definitely in attendance, but a significant part of him was some light years away, probably in residence on the tenth level of Hell enjoying a nice sponge bath. That significant part of Byron had been substituted in his physical body with the soul of the Devil himself.

When the coast was clear and no one else could be accused of triggering the device, Byron shuffled forward a little. The doors slid open. He waited, expecting them to close rapidly in an attempt to catch him out. Nothing happened. He strolled forward and into the building, where he noticed the doors compliantly shut together behind him. Byron stood in the reception area baffled as to the purpose of this invention. Were human beings incapable of pushing open a door? Had human society become so lazy that the very act of getting into a building had become overly taxing? Were doors that frightening? There was only one person who thought so. The very person Byron had come to visit.

Byron stuck out like a sore thumb. His red velvet suit, slightly singed around the bottom of each trouser leg, clashed horribly against the magnolia-painted walls and crisp, white uniforms. Soot marks over the top of his bald head looked like a horribly unplanned addition to a sophisticated and illegible tattoo that consumed the back his neck. Fellow visitors, who were already startled and disillusioned by the experience of the car park, gawped at his attire and mildly irritated facial expressions. Byron approached the reception desk with purpose.

"Hold on a minute, lovey," said the gaunt and pale-looking receptionist anticipating a question that Byron had never considered asking.

He stood awkwardly for much longer than a minute, desperate to say 'Do you know who I am?' but deciding, by the vacant and stressed appearance of the woman, that it wasn't worth it.

"How can I help you, lovey?" she said, not attempting to look up from a computer screen which had her hypnotised.

"I've come to visit a patient. Victor Serpo."

"What department is he in, my love?"

This was the third reference to love in the space of three responses. What was that about? Did she really not know how totally inappropriate it was to suggest that emotion to the Prince of Darkness. Was it too much to ask for a bit of anger and aggression?

"I've no idea what department," Byron replied truthfully.

"I can't find him without more information, I'm afraid."

"He was admitted with a large portion of his left foot in his hands: does that help?"

"Accident and Emergency," said the woman.

"I would say it was both," replied Byron, not aware she was referring to an area of the hospital.

"Down the corridor, through the double doors, take the second corridor on the left, head down to the end and it's the first door on your right. Don't forget to sanitise your hands before you go in."

"Sanitise! What are you insinuating? I might not be a 'local' but that doesn't mean I'm unclean."

"I'm sure you're not, lovey: infection control, that's all."

Given his unique ability to create havoc and rain down pestilence on all and sundry, he wasn't convinced that a bit of hand alcohol was going to help with their infection control strategy.

"Thank you," he grimaced coldly.

"Aren't you going to take him something?"

"Yes. I'm bringing him hope and fear in equal measure."

"Unconventional. I was thinking of something to cheer him up. There's a kiosk over there."

Byron made a brief stop at the kiosk in order to conform with some bizarre ritual he didn't fully understand, before retracing the directions given to him by the receptionist. The route was occasionally blocked by a poorly parked trolley, occupied by an even more poorly parked body. A bustle of white and green coats demanding attention swerved past him in their quest for some vital piece of hospital equipment. Intrigued, but in no way influenced to rush, Byron paced calmly towards his destination until a room on his left caught his attention.

The prayer room.

It wasn't significantly different from any normally functioning room other than, to recognise its importance, someone had stuck a sign on the door denoting it as such. Curiosity got the better of him. It was empty. Other than a few books of religious significance and a cross placed centrally on a table, it had all the spiritual instincts of a centipede.

'This was what they did,' he thought. Humans cared little for religion until mortality stalked up behind them and blew on the back of their necks. Then it mattered. Then they needed a prayer room. A place for panic-stricken wretches suddenly aware of their own fate and desperate to justify their purity to an entity whose own existence they doubted when they pulled up in the car park, or worse in an ambulance. To cement this pointlessness, signs around the room signified that it was a multifaith one. In case God was busy, or ignoring them, the fall-back position might be Allah, Buddha, Shiva or, at a push, Zeus.

Byron knelt down in front of the table and placed his hands in the requisite position. Eyes shut, his mouth transformed into an ironic smile.

"Having fun?" he breathed into his hands.

If Baltazaar was listening, he wasn't showing it.

"I'm aware of your intentions, you have played your hand, Baltazaar. But you have absolutely no idea what mine are. You've had the upper hand for much too long. It's time we raised the stakes. Watch your back. I'm coming for you."

Fifty-year-old knees, once owned by a far heavier individual, creaked like an old floorboard as Byron lifted himself to his feet. In an act of spite and childishness he raised a finger towards the cross and aimed a quick burst of heat in its direction. It slumped in molten cross form on the table. He left to continue his search for Victor.

At the door of the Tintagel Ward he extended his arms and squirted a large dollop of alcoholic foam into his hands before bursting through the doors with the gusto of a hospital porter. To his surprise most of the patients appeared to be elderly, which made it much easier to spot the middle-aged figure of Victor Serpo. Byron floated forward, his hands held out in front of him with an offering that bulged out of a brown paper bag.

"I thought you might come," said Victor. "What's in there?"

"Grapes," replied Byron.

"I thought you were more of an apple guy."

"I was advised that everyone always brought grapes, not sure why? Can't see how grapes are any better at accelerating the healing process than any other fruit. I can go back and get you an avocado if you'd prefer it."

"No."

"Suit yourself."

Byron twiddled his thumbs. It wasn't easy to learn the etiquette that came naturally to other human visitors about the ward. When all you really wanted to do was tell the patient what you wanted done next, even if you had to accept that one of their feet had only recently been reattached to the leg, it was hard to know what question came after the grapes.

"How's the....foot?" asked Byron tentatively, pointing at two long bulges under the blanket.

"A little unresponsive. They tell me it'll get better, but my shoes won't fit anymore."

"It could be worse, most of this lot," he said, pointing out some of the other invalids around the ward, "probably won't make it through the night."

This remark, said rather too loudly, had the effect of agitating the patient in the bed next to Victor's.

"Death! I can see death. He is here. Nurse!" came a desperate voice from the elderly gentleman sporting a number of delicately placed tubes about his body.

"Victor, you seem to be in a ward for more, how can I put this, elderly specimens."

"They ran out of beds. It's amazing I got…"

"Nurse! Help me. I feel weak. He's come for me," continued the neighbour, whose wizened stature was barely noticeable under his bedsheets.

"Why are you here, Byron?" said Victor.

"Because we are running out of time and…"

"Nurse. Nurse. Hurry. Death is coming!"

"Excuse me a moment," said Byron standing and approaching the man who was half-encircled by a shabby green curtain.

"You called," said Byron to the man hidden behind it.

"Nurse. I need the nurse."

"I think you said 'death' was here and I couldn't help but pop my head around the curtain and wish you luck. If it's all the same to you, I'm trying to have a quiet conversation with my colleague there," he added, pointing to Victor who was covering his eyes. "If you'd like me to speed up the process of death, just keep wittering away like an imbecile, being rude and interrupting my train of thought. I can make it very quick, you know."

Byron's eyes slowly glowed orange like a long draw on a cigarette.

"NURSE!"

"Yes, Mr. Jenkins," came a voice from the bottom of the ward.

"I think I've soiled myself," he replied.

Byron returned to his own patient. "If I wasn't on a deadline I could have a lot of fun here."

"You'd be the only one," said Victor. "What do you want, Byron?"

PATIENTS AND PASSENGERS

"What I always want from you. Your loyalty and your talents. It's time to be proactive. Baltazaar has the advantage and we need to wrestle it back. What he expects us to do is intervene in the destruction of mankind."

"Aren't we?"

"No."

"But I thought you said we had to win the battle against the extinction of mankind before the battle of the gods began."

"That all depends on who you consider to be 'we'. They will win the first battle, and we will be prepared for the second one."

"I don't get you. Who will?"

"Grace will. She won't do it out of love or hate, she will do it because it's logical for the human race to survive. How she manages it isn't important. She's a god now, she'll figure it out. Whilst she struggles with that, you and I will be preparing to outsmart her and Baltazaar when the final show down begins."

"Ok. So what's the plan?"

"You're going to assassinate God."

A few patients, including Mr. Jenkins, peered above their bedsheets and wished for the mobility necessary to make it to the prayer room.

"You want me to kill God! Is that even possible? You've seen what he can do," whispered Victor.

"Easy for a man of your talents. Think of the kudos, think of the money. The man who killed a deity. You'll be made for life. Film adaptations, talk show appearances, books, you'll never need to work again."

"But why?"

"Because, for one thing, he's an arse. I'm meant to be the evil one, yet he's currently doing a more effective job of it than I am. Plus, if there is no Baltazaar, then the only fight will be with Grace, and I don't think she's got it in her. After all, she's only eleven."

PATIENTS AND PASSENGERS

*****

Escape from the Scilly Isles had been swift. Only Violet and Fiona had refused to leave. They'd made their home on the island for more than a decade, most of it in secret. They at least had some reason to stay. Having been incarcerated in her own body for the whole experience, Faith had no such attachment. Nash had only been there as an excuse to see Faith and now that she was returned to him, he saw no reason to remain. Grace's whole identity was shrouded in a rational dissection of what made most sense, and staying didn't. The one who struggled most was Scrumpy.

The islands were entangled with his own sense of identity. The freedom and adventure was all he'd ever known, and boy, did he love it. To be ruler of your very own kingdom, free from the responsibilities that most eight-year-olds had to contend with, was an immense privilege. The place was, simply, home. If he had any roots, subconsciously attached to a life that preceded his adoption, he certainly wasn't aware of it. The islands were all he remembered, all he needed. And now he was leaving them behind.

The only other constant and relevant connection to him was Grace. Yes, he'd miss his adopted mothers, but they didn't share the inexplicable bonds he had with his sister. After all, she was as different from him as it was possible for a person to be. She was clinically logical and computational with her ability to manipulate her understanding of all things scientific, while he was consumed by the love of all things inexplicable.

More than that he had no desire to explain them. Nothing became more worthy of exploration once you knew all about it. A cave had no sense of adventure if you knew what was in the shadows. No sea worthy of navigation if someone had got there before you. And there lay the fascination. Grace was inexplicable, even though she herself understood what most could not. The islands might provide adventure, but not eternally. A lifetime of observation could be assigned to Grace and you'd still not have scratched at the surface.

The Scillonian pulled out of the harbour for its three-hour journey to the mainland. Anxiety levels were still high. Every action that hastened their escape should have brought more calm, but the knowledge of what was potentially following them didn't play by the rules. It didn't respect boundaries or distance. Whatever space you put between you and it, it would never leave you. It stuck to the skin like a musty smell or permanent marker. They might get further away, but they would never be truly safe. It was all part of a larger puzzle doing cartwheels inside Grace's head. But this puzzle could not, for once, be solved alone.

"Mr. Stevens," said Grace, staring vaguely out of the window as the harbour wall ducked behind the headland.

"I suppose it should be Dad," said Nash, who was still adjusting to the idea it had taken him eleven years to discover he was a father. Given his previous lifestyle as a rockstar, a highly promiscuous time, it was perfectly possible Grace was not the only one.

"Mr. Stevens," replied Grace, ignoring the request, "tell me about John."

"Why do you want to know about him?"

"I feel a connection to him. The young Chilean boy who came into my bedroom, that was John, wasn't it?"

"Yes, I'm sure it was," replied Nash, rotating his coffee mug round and round in its saucer.

"The Chilean boy...John...told me that I'd been there at the car crash that caused his death and then an hour later I witnessed it for real. It was like he'd predicted his own death," said Grace.

"John's a rather complicated character," replied Nash. "Grace, what is it you want to know?"

"What I want to know is what I am. I've been working on that puzzle my whole life, and I think John might hold the answer. Tell me what you know about him."

Nash had been a father for less than a week, yet he found the awkwardness of a child's question as natural as someone who'd done it for years. Nash explained all that he knew about John. How they came to be shackled together, how he'd joined John in tracking down Ian Noble, a man reincarnated as a pigeon, and how they'd been partially separated by Donovan King's exorcism. It was on the retelling of this part of the story that Grace barged in.

"I have seen the man you describe," said Grace. "I'm pretty sure it was the preacher that caused the Chilean boy's death in the tractor. I overheard him say the boy was the third coming, a god even."

"You're sure it was Donovan King?" said Nash, bamboozled to why, of all people, he would be on the islands and involved in what they had got themselves into.

"No, of course not. I don't have all the evidence, so I can't be totally certain. What I do know is a storm formed above Tresco as I sailed away with Scrumpy, and it was not a natural phenomenon. It was too localised, too instant."

Nash scratched his head. He was out of his depth, and had been ever since a concert had gone horribly wrong all those years ago. When they'd decided to leave the islands most of his instincts informed him to run away. Now all of them were. But where? Where was safe? They were being hunted by all manner of dangers, some known and some not. And very possibly they were mostly hunting Grace.

"If all you say and all I heard is true, the evidence points to only one conclusion," said Grace. "I already know I have the ability to alter time whenever I feel like it and I can understand science way beyond some that have studied it all their long lives. I was born with a neutral soul due to the Emorfed in my mother's bloodstream. I was conceived by you, while John was in possession. It would appear you're not the only one I should call father."

Nash spilled the coffee mug that he'd been constantly fiddling with through the whole of their conversation. Was there no way he'd ever shake John out of his life? Her evidence seemed sound but it wasn't the only conclusion the pair of them had reached. Before they had a chance to speak it, Scrumpy burst up to the table and broke their concentration.

"Come quick. I've just seen an old man with a wart on his face that looks like a kettle!"

CHAPTER FOUR

ABSOLUTE POWER

Power and paranoia are comfortable bedfellows. The more power you gain, the greater the paranoia rises at the thought of losing it. It can take a single innocent question or misplaced action from those around you to trigger the powerful into a murderous rampage. It has happened to the best and worst of them down the years.

Than Shwe, the one-time leader of Burma, was so sure he was going to be assassinated he went to radical ends to avoid it. One morning he decided to move the whole capital city to the middle of a jungle where there was no electricity or running water. Nicolae Ceauşescu was so convinced the Romanian people were plotting against him that he banned Scrabble, deeming it too intellectual and a way of transferring coded messages. However, Saddam Hussein went to extreme lengths to ensure his survival. Every day he would have multiple meals prepared in several different cities so no would-be poisoner would ever know which one he was going to eat.

This behaviour should come as no surprise. All dictators share a collective wobble of personality traits that includes narcissism, a history of cruelty against their people, and a shared sense of grandiosity. And one other thing is common amongst all individuals who have held absolute power: a day will come when it will be gone. More than likely through a bloody uprising of the people they oppressed.

Sandy thought his reign over Hell would be different for one simple reason. He was already dead. Any attempt on his life would only, he hoped, bring him back to where he was. What he did fear, though, was something worse than death. The shadow souls he had control over were not the easiest mob to influence. Each was a fused mass of negative and positive emotions whose behaviour patterns were driven by whatever feelings were nearest to the surface.

Sandy had focused on giving them what they wanted in return for keeping him in power. But he needed a more convincing deterrent. Given the nature of these malevolent entities, only one remedy could neutralise them. They existed because they had been splintered away from the rational neutral element of their original form. Emorfed ripped out the shadow souls from the host, leaving a human without emotion. Only Emorfed could repair the damage.

It was no surprise to him that the shadows had destroyed the Soul Catcher. If no route existed to return the shadows to their hosts, there would be no way to neutralise them. If Sandy was going to secure control he needed to find a substitute. In a situation like this there was only one advisor worth talking to.

"Brimstone," chirped Sandy from his propped-up imperial throne.

Visually not much had changed on level twelve, Sandy's centre of power. The long, stone table still featured prominently through the centre. Thrones, encrusted with the elements of the prior occupant, were still in position around it. They were no longer filled by the uniquely constructed senior demons, but by the plastic vessels of former dictators, each having surrendered any remaining logic as a consequence of meeting a shadow soul. The strong metal boxes still floated in space above their heads on the ends of long chains.

Mr. Brimstone was the only remaining senior demon to survive the enforced exodus to level zero.

He had stood alone against the uprising, desperate to save his precious Soul Catcher from the fate that befell it.

"What is it?" said Brimstone as he clumped his three-foot-square stone body to the side of Sandy's throne.

"I don't think that's how you address me, is it?" said Sandy sternly.

The maniacal dictators chuckled at the abuse their former keeper was receiving. General Tito even flicked Brimstone a two-fingered salute in confident rebellion.

"What is it, Master?" repeated Brimstone.

"NO! The full title. If you remember I have recently added to it."

"What is it…" Brimstone sighed. "Master of Hell, Lord of the dead, Ruler of all reincarnates, Conqueror of the afterlife and Mightiest of all pigeons."

"Now that wasn't hard, was it?"

"Actually…"

"Enough. You said to me recently that 'souls are good at evolving': I want to know what you meant."

"I meant that by your actions you have destroyed the last known Soul Catcher, which means souls will be flooding into Limbo and causing it to expand. You see, the human soul is like a lungfish, very difficult to kill."

"Lungfish?"

"Clever little critters. You can bury one without air and moisture for six months and when you dig it up it'll just grin at you and swim off."

"So, you're saying that souls will find a way to survive."

"Of course. They always do."

"What's your best guess?"

"I don't have one. You can't predict evolution. Evolution happens because of mutations. Do you think anyone predicted that a giraffe would grow a long neck?"

"As Sandy Logan, Master of Hell, Lord of the dead, Ruler of all reincarnates, Conqueror of the afterlife and Mightiest of all pigeons, I demand that you stop it happening."

"Ha, I can't stop it. You can't stop it. I'd be amazed if anyone can."

"But I'm all-powerful!" said Sandy, standing up on his plastic pillows and fluffing up his chest as best he could to look threatening.

"Sorry, I think you've confused yourself with a god."

The dictators around the table whispered to each with lowered voices, behind raised hands.

'What were they talking about?' thought Sandy. Were they planning to overthrow him? Was his inability to stop evolution seen as a weakness? He needed that deterrent to stamp his authority.

"Brimstone, I want you to send the lesser demons down to level zero and bring me the oldest of all the reincarnates."

"What for?"

"I need a deterrent," he whispered.

"I don't see how half a dozen plastic geriatrics will be much use against these boys."

"Not in plastic form, no. But they do have something inside them that might work."

"You can't just force them into pass over, it doesn't work like that," replied Brimstone, cottoning on to the pigeon's plan.

"Just do it or I will send you for therapy with Mr. Silica again."

A small, shadowy sandstorm bristled with energy in the throne to Sandy's left. Without further comment Brimstone removed his apron, to protect his ego from any flack the lesser demons might aim at him, and strolled calmly to the lift to descend down to level one.

*****

Not much had happened in the ten minutes of silence between the Accountant's introduction to the metal ball-bearing and now.

"What do we do now?" said the origami swan quietly.

"We need to start building," said the leader.

"How do you know?" said the paper plane.

"I just know, right. It's all in here," he said, pointing to a head that looked more like a paper hat than a high-functioning intelligent brain.

"Hold on. Fifteen minutes ago you were nothing more than a blade of grass swaying in the wind, and now miraculously not only do you appear to be in charge, which no one approved, by the way, but you're also supremely confident that we need to build something!" said the swan.

"Are you questioning my authority?" demanded the leader.

There was a brief moment of visual confirmation.

"Yes," came a group of answers.

"Oh. Ok. Well, let me put that to bed straight away. I am Accountant A, and 'A' always comes first. I know I am 'A' because my instincts tell me I am. They also tell me we need to build."

"But why?" asked a crumpled colleague whose teeth had all been folded inside out.

"I don't know why, do I!? As you said I was, until recently, a blade of grass. Team, are we really going to have an existential crisis this early in the development of our species? I don't know why I know, because that would make me question who I am and why I'm here. I personally would like at least a few more years of life to build up to those questions, rather than down tools at the first sign of uncertainty."

The Accountants analysed each other's reactions to see what the general opinion was, only to find that no one appeared to have one. Behaviours and opinions clearly took more than a quarter of an hour of existence to form.

"Right, then. As I said, we need to build."

"But build what?" said the swan.

"What's your name?"

"How should I know?" replied the swan.

"You don't know! Isn't it obvious?"

The swan stared blankly at him as if Accountant A was suddenly conversing in an alien dialect. Eventually he shook his head.

"Does anyone here know their names?"

The rest shook their heads, although some just copied what the swan had done as a sign it was the correct response in this situation.

"Right! It seems I'm the only one here that has any idea what our job is. I will assign you names in alphabetical order. You will be Accountant M," he said to the swan.

"Can't I be Accountant B?" he replied.

"No."

"Why not?"

"Because clearly Accountant B would be the second in command if anything should happen to me, and as I don't know which of you is the most sensible and trustworthy, I'm not willing to assign it yet."

"That's discrimination," said Accountant M.

"Absolutely. Were you under the impression this operation was going to be run by a committee?"

"Not anymore," grumbled M.

"Plane, you'll be Accountant J," said Accountant A.

"So he gets a better rank than me," said M. "In what way is a plane more competent than a swan?"

"He's not asking me difficult questions."

Accountant A continued to assign his troop into rank. Most nodded thankfully at their new names and assignments. The Sydney Opera House got 'Z', even though he'd made some speedy and subtle refolds in order to demonstrate his potential. This had resulted in him transforming from a notable Australian landmark to an undefined landmark with several legs. The metal ball watched with fascination. Was all of this palaver for his benefit? If it was, he felt he should show as much interest as a malleable ping-pong ball-sized metal object could.

"Ok. Now you have names," said A, "it's time to build."

"I hate to ask, but what are we building?" asked M.

"A Soul Catcher," said Accountant A, matter-of-factly.

There was a long, pregnant pause.

"What's one of them?"

CHAPTER FIVE

EVERYWHERE AND NOWHERE

The change in Hell's management structure had a profound impact on almost everything. The lesser demons, of which there were thousands, were adjusting to a life of leisure and free time. The jobs they'd previously done no longer needed doing. Either the shadow souls had taken over their duties, or it just wasn't required anymore. The Soul Catcher was broken and no souls had arrived for a considerable period of time, which no one could measure, as time had never been an easy concept to tie down. It might have been a millennium or just as easily a couple of nanoseconds.

Those inmates that resided on the lower levels of Hell, souls that occupied plastic vessels imprisoned behind their own private prisons, were no longer being stimulated. Stimulation used to involve having a variety of objects designed to inflict pain forced into sensitive regions of the body or having distressing mental dramas played out inside their heads. Now they sat around wondering vacantly what they were supposed to do next. What was worse than the stimulation? Boredom.

The only area of Hell that wasn't discernibly different from a period now widely referred to as B.S. (before Sandy) was level zero. It still housed all the reincarnated souls, who at some point had suffered from the Limpet Syndrome and as a result were forced to spend the afterlife housed in a plastic vessel in the shape of an animal. But they were no longer alone. Now another species also lived there. Namely what was left of the senior demons, most of whom had adjusted favourably to their new surroundings.

"Who's up for some yoga?" asked Mr. Fungus, a creature whose anatomy was mainly constructed of interesting fungal varieties, far more suited to this environment than the pits of fire and cold stone he'd been used to.

"Yoga! What's that, then?" asked Mr. Gold.

"It's a relaxation method that the ox taught me. It's supposed to help reduce stress through meditation and stretching."

"Too right," replied Mr. Aqua. "I'll be great at that."

"Under no circumstances is anyone to do yoga," demanded Asmodeus.

In Satan's absence Asmodeus had been the previous custodian of Hell, until a quite surprising revolution had been masterminded by an overambitious pigeon, a few dozen dead dictators, and a new species of soul who only knew how to do chaos. However long the period since B.S. was, all of it had disagreed with him. The environment, with its fake landscapes designed to deceive the inhabitants into believing they were really on a beach or hopping through a glade when they were in fact sitting on various forms of injection-moulded plastic, was disagreeable.

The behaviour of the other demons, with the exception of Primordial who'd always lived here, was also disagreeable. Yellow-bellied surrender monkeys, the lot of them. Rather than work tirelessly on finding a way to take back their positions, they had instead decided to act like they'd been enrolled in a five-star health farm. They were integrating with the reincarnated species with alarming regularity. Conversing with them was one thing, forming a tug of war team was quite another.

EVERYWHERE AND NOWHERE

The element that Asmodeus found most disagreeable was the pigeon. It made his skin crawl to think of Sandy marching about on level twelve dishing out orders and changing everything he'd so tirelessly manoeuvred into place. And what frustrated him most was he didn't have the first clue as to what to do about it.

The reincarnates were, for want of a better word, tame. Level zero had always been a necessity rather than a plan. As such, the creatures housed there were never subjected to the normal physical and mental torment normally instigated on souls with the misfortune to arrive in Hell. They were left to erode at their own pace. If a demon suddenly revealed a cattle prod or pitchfork, most of the population here would just watch passively to see what would happen next. They were more than happy to welcome their new neighbours as long as they didn't disrupt their way of life. The only exceptions were six characters who had recently returned from a rather difficult incident at the Soul Catcher.

There was one other significant inhabitant of level zero, although he wasn't certain it was accurate to describe himself as an inhabitant, or indeed identified himself as being completely in level zero. Following a brief stint trapped inside the plastic vessol of a shrew, with only the positive and negative parts of his soul for company, John Hewson would now describe his position as everywhere other than being inside a shrew.

"Ahem..." said John. *"Can I bother you for a moment?"*

"I'm not talking to you," said Mr. Noir, in the disgruntled voice of a child who'd just lost a game of rock-paper-scissors. *"I've told you I don't interact."*

"Yes, I get that. I'm just struggling not to, as I seem to be everywhere where you are, which seems to be level zero from what I can make out. Do you have any idea as to what I've become?"

EVERYWHERE AND NOWHERE

"A bloody nuisance," shouted Asmodeus, who found the constant interruptions of a creature he could neither see nor touch as another disagreeable aspect of living here. "Give it up, John. You're just refusing to accept the reality that you're finally and properly dead. Done, finished, passed on, deceased, extinguished, kicked the bucket, dancing with the cosmic maggots…"

"I've been dead many times before, and at no time did it feel like this."

"Denial. That's all it is!"

John went over the sequence of his recent life and death events to see if there was any truth in the accusation. Life had definitely come first, but certainly hadn't been a one-off. If Brimstone was to be believed there had been more than fifty of those. John, the fifty-first version of whoever he was, had been alive for about thirty years until a well-placed bullet forced him to give it up. His soul had endured a rather one-sided and unnecessary trial in Limbo before being shot across the multiverses to Hell. From there he'd gone back down to Earth to possess Nash Stevens, only for his soul to be exorcised by a mad Irishman with a stutter. That's when things started to really fall apart. And for 'things' read John himself.

The positive part of his soul had been grafted onto Nash, whilst the other two parts returned to Hell to spend a limited time in the vessol of a small girl. After that it was into Byron and the shenanigans with the election, Emorfed and a final showdown with Laslow in Limbo. The two remaining parts of his soul were imprisoned in a metal box suspended above level twelve until a voice had encouraged him to escape.

He'd triggered the Limpet Syndrome, severing the last two parts of his soul in half, and the negative part drew the positive part from Nash. Between them, they'd managed to send his neutral portion back to Earth inside the body of a newborn baby. The other two elements struggled to live with each other inside a

EVERYWHERE AND NOWHERE

plastic shrew. He'd lost touch with the neutral part of his soul after that and couldn't be certain as to its fate. But then what?

When the shadow soul had attacked him at the Soul Catcher, releasing his soul out into the open, everything changed. The characteristic cloud of electric blue gas just didn't appear, or if it had, he wasn't aware of it. As he left the plastic vessol he just kept expanding outwards, getting thinner and more distant all the time. Was that denial? Bloody weird, but definitely not delusional.

"Ok, so if I'm dead how come I have so many questions? Answer me that. Surely non-existence is like the stuff on the other edge of space, just nothingness. No time, no mass, no nothing!"

"I can't hear anything," said Mr. Gold, who'd always refused to accept any evidence that Mr. Noir was anything but a figment of their imaginations, and wasn't going to change his mind just because people suggested Noir had multiplied. "Let's yoga."

"Do you want me to get the ox?" said Asmodeus.

All the demons shook their heads in recognition that a conversation with Abe the ox was a powerful deterrent for almost anything.

"All I want to know," said John, *"is who I really am."*

"Then go to the library and leave me alone to work out how to dislodge a rather irritating pigeon," said Asmodeus.

"I can't go to the library, I'm stuck here," said John.

"You really don't get it, do you?" said Mr. Noir running out of patience and hoping to put a stop to the incessant questioning. *"You are everywhere."*

"I don't get it."

"You've passed over into a completely new state of matter. You've evolved, moved over to the other side, if you will. Like me, you can be anywhere, whenever you want. If I focus I can be in cell 78901 on level seven where a former bank manager is contemplating when

EVERYWHERE AND NOWHERE

they're going to come back and lob arachnids at him again as he's getting bored. If I want I can watch Mr. Brimstone coming down the lift from level twelve, or watch with interest as a plastic lion tries to convince a spider that he won the Nobel Peace Prize twice in the same year."

"You mean...I can go...anywhere?"

"ANYWHERE!" snapped Noir. *"Sadly, I'll also be there doing my best not to interact with you."*

"But how do I do it?" asked John.

"You have to concentrate on your own existence."

"Like meditating?"

"I suppose so."

"Come and join the yoga class," replied Mr. Fungus enthusiastically.

Asmodeus threw a polypropylene stick, which struck him in the groin region with a spongy thwack.

John tried to shut out the stimuli. Focusing on your own existence was tricky when you didn't know who you were in the first place, but the more he shut off the voices around him, the more he started to connect to his conscience. The blurry vision of level zero was starting to clear like the window wipers of his soul were removing the existential bird poo of the Universe. The more he focused, the more the vision expanded.

As John concentrated on himself, the wider his sphere of vision became. The extension brought more awareness of other regions, creatures and activities. Imagine being able to hear every human being on Earth talking at the same time. The din would send you mad unless you were able to turn it off. It was no wonder that Mr. Noir didn't want to interact. It was an essential imperative to keeping yourself sane.

"I can see all of Hell, just by focusing," said John in both amazement and concern.

"Told you yoga works," said Fungus, rubbing his crotch from the earlier impact.

"There you go. Well done," said Noir. *"Now shut up!"*

"Hey, I can see Mr. Brimstone. I think I'll go and have a chat before heading upstairs to give Sandy a dose of his own medicine."

Asmodeus's ears, which totalled six when he was wearing his more scary persona, pricked up. "I may have spoken too soon. Of course you're not dead, John. Now, what are you planning to do to Sandy?"

*****

The Federal Council had been in session for several hours, and the only obvious decision that had been made was how many of them wanted tea and how many wanted coffee. Throughout this wrangling the Clerk had sat around the table fascinated by the lengths that people would go to to avoid the important. They were supposed to be discussing the motion of averting mass extinction, yet they'd not even agreed on an agenda yet.

The seven other people around the oval table were a representative spectrum of the wider Swiss demographic. Three woman, four men; left, right and centre of the political persuasion; some old and some young; and creeds from minorities and majorities. The system could not be accused of inequality or nepotism. It could, though, be accused of prevarication. It appeared that fairness was not a good barometer of speed of action.

"Ninety metres," said the Clerk solemnly as the council continued to ruminate over agenda items.

"What is?" said an elderly politician who had earlier been introduced as Anna Brandenburger.

"That's how much of the Alps you've lost since you agreed to having four coffees, two teas and a hot chocolate with whipped cream."

"Mr. Clark, we do not make decisions in this chamber on the basis of some random old man with a theory. Where's the evidence?"

"It's just Clerk, by the way, and if you'd like the facts I can take you to see it: the longer this conversation takes, the shorter the journey will be. Are you familiar with the phrase 'fiddling whilst Rome burns'? If you wait until morning then you'll probably be able to see Limbo from the top windows of this building."

"It's true," interjected Rogier, "I have seen the problem for myself."

"We'll have to vote on it?" said a smart-looking young man with a middle parting so well cultivated you could open a railroad down the middle.

"Are you really suggesting, Leon, that we have to take a vote on whether or not you believe that I have seen it?"

"Rogier, you know the system: we vote on everything, once we have debated it thoroughly of course."

Over the next hour a series of opinions were bandied around the chamber like a bunch of schoolchildren were deciding on who should be 'it'. The discussion was clearly not going to be based on any evidence, which Rogier had produced through a series of photographic handouts containing a number of rather pointless red labels indicating a massive metal object poking out of a mountain range. No, this debate was all about personal agendas and who people thought was currently winning the argument.

Each of them seemed to flip and flop to different views, not wanting to be siding with the minority opinion. After everyone, except the Clerk, had said their piece, one of them rang a small bell in the middle of the table. They all got up from their seats, some more delicately than others, and headed over to a small cubicle set in an alcove to the side of the room. There they queued patiently one behind the other to take their turns to cast their votes on small scraps of paper. Once all had done so they returned to the table, where minutes later a smart-looking employee with a ruffled white collar approached.

"The vote on whether Rogier Hoffstetter's claim that a large, metal sphere is protruding from the Alps can be believed was as follows," said the employee. "Three votes for no and three for yes. Mr. President, you have the casting vote."

"I wonder how I'll vote," said Rogier sarcastically. "Yes!"

"Motion is passed," announced the employee, retreating to the door, but staying in range. It wouldn't be long until he was back again.

"One hundred and twenty metres," said the Clerk.

"Now that we have a consensus on the issue of Limbo, we must press on with what action we should take," said Rogier to the council.

"As the member for the Green Party," said Leon, "I say it is a natural phenomenon. It should be left exactly as it is."

"The Alps are a protected natural wonder: does that not also concern the Green Party?" replied Rogier.

Leon decided not to answer.

"Why should we trust him?" said a thin-looking black man with small, round glasses, who was waving a finger at the Clerk.

"Because, Jan, we have no one else who claims, as he does, to have the answers. I have spoken to all our scientific experts and they simply have no reasonable explanations."

"As a Christian Democrat my members would be most concerned at this meddling in religious matters. If God intends for this outcome, then we should not stop it."

The Clerk had heard enough. Quite out of character he stood up and smashed both fists onto the table.

"Ladies and gentlemen, this shit is real. It goes beyond party politics and personal ambition. It is not a

EVERYWHERE AND NOWHERE

green issue. It is not a religious issue. It is not a moral issue. This is simply an issue of survival. If you do not act then the human race will be lost, permanently. I know this because Limbo and its contents have been my life's mission for longer than the brown bears have been stuck down a hole in your city. Longer than this country has had inhabitants, in fact."

"That's just not possible," replied Anna.

"Shut up, you old crone!" snapped the Clerk. "It is quite simple. We must get a message out to the world. The message must be heard far and wide. We must help humans evolve or they will become extinct. You must agree to request an audience at the United Nations, and it must be now."

Seven pairs of eyes scanned the other occupants of the table.

"Well, we'll have to debate and vote on it," said Jan.

"Two hundred metres," sighed the Clerk.

CHAPTER SIX

LONDON CALLING

The Accountants listened intently to Accountant A's description of the Soul Catcher he wanted them to build. Maybe it was the complexity of its functions, the conceptualisation of how it might look or the immaturity of their thirty-minute lifespans, but none of the others had the first idea what he was talking about. It was the equivalent of asking a newborn baby to understand the techniques for making macaroons and then telling him to make a batch.

"I'm a bit lost," said M, with a swan-like paper wing in the air.

"Why is it always you?" said A.

"Not sure."

"Is anyone else struggling with the concept?" said A.

The whole platoon raised whatever appendages were mobile enough.

"Urgh," replied A, almost giving himself a paper cut as his hand hit his forehead.

"What's it for?" said M.

"You mean you want to know what a Soul Catcher is for!?"

"Yes, exactly."

"A soul catcher…" he replied extremely slowly and hoping for a sudden light bulb moment. "Isn't it fucking obvious!"

"Nope."

"Oddly enough…it's a machine for catching souls."

"I know that, I'm not stupid, you know. What I meant was, why do we need a machine to catch souls?"

"Accountant M, look around you and tell me what you see."

The entire group of Accountants followed M's lead and scanned their surroundings. The silence was deafening. Not a noise could be heard around the barren landscape. The world they occupied had been almost completely untouched. Other than the quarry, the vista was immaculately designed as the creator had intended. Every angle was pure and straight. Every stone mathematically perfect. There was logic everywhere, including in the evolving intelligence of this paper army.

"It's all very regular, isn't it?" said M.

"Oh you noticed that. It's the living embodiment of a beautifully neutral world. A place constructed at the dawn of space and time to house the souls of all those who demonstrate no emotional values. It was closed off to those souls, but now it is open again. Who knows how many more will come, but it is our purpose to prepare nonetheless."

"Right, I see. You're expecting more small balls of metal, are you?"

"Not really. The ball isn't a conventional soul. It's part of the machine."

"And what does it look like again, this machine?" asked Accountant J, whose tail fin was pulsating nervously like a high-rise building in an earthquake.

"Square. I only want to see angles, no curves. There will need to be a large box for collecting the souls, a long shaft extending out into space and a computer terminal so that we can see all the souls inside and those on their way," replied A, pointing to a spot to their left and up to the translucent barrier above them.

"Sounds impressive," exclaimed M, "I only see one potential downside to what is otherwise an extraordinary and inspirational objective."

"And what's that?" sighed A.

"What material are we supposed to make it from?" huffed M, correctly reapplying the team's focus to a barren and untouched wilderness.

"Improvise."

"With what?" asked M.

"Your minds."

"My mind is logical. I don't think it does improvisation. Isn't that more of a creative thing?"

"God! M, you're more inquisitive than a four-year-old."

"Then it would appear I'm a quick developer."

"You're a pain in the arse."

"Can't you just give us some instructions. I don't need much. Just some diagrams showing us how to put it together will do. Maybe with some letters assigned to holes in the materials you want us to use and a picture of one of us standing next to it to determine which way around it should go. I don't need words, just pictures."

The collective nodded in agreement.

"Really? What am I meant to write these instructions on exactly?"

"Paper. I think we have plenty of that."

Unintentionally, Accountant M had lit a flame of inspiration inside his leader. There was a limited selection of easily workable materials in this world and even fewer tools to craft them with. But there did seem to be plenty of white grass. Miles of meadows stretched out as far as the paper eye could see.

"Right. I want you to harvest the grass. Pick as much as you can and bring it back to this spot."

"Isn't that murder?" said Accountant D, who, other than being one of the highest-ranked amongst them, was significant because he had three arms.

"Definitely not. They aren't alive. We are because the ball rolled past us."

"If I hear any of them squeal I'm stopping immediately," said M.

"Fine. They won't, that is unless the ball here decides to go for a little roll."

The metal ball had enough to occupy it, including the revelation that it was responsible for this eccentric new species. He thought two dozen of them was more than enough to begin with.

"And what's all the paper for?" asked J.

"Papier mâché of course."

*****

There were many places that Nash Stevens could have decided to take his new family, but each option had reasons both for and against. Gloucester Road had way more of the latter than the former. It wasn't exactly unknown to the authorities. The building had remained empty since Herb, Nash's former manager, had moved to a care home. Since then it hadn't been rented out or renovated. It had more than a little resemblance to the house of Miss Havisham from *Great Expectations*.

Large dust sheets were still draped over much of the furniture, although this hadn't discouraged the dust from finding a home elsewhere. The internal hubris, so contrasting with Herb's own character, was still visible underneath the dusty veneer that had accumulated in the decade since any humans occupied it. The antiques were still around every corner, the expensive art still hung from the walls. Nash crossed his fingers and hoped they'd cleared out the fridge in the process of laying the place down to rest. Herb was not known for keeping fresh ingredients in it even when he lived here permanently.

The building no longer belonged to Herb. Dead people don't tend to have a lot of use for them. To Nash's great surprise the house and its contents had been left to him in Herb's will after he'd passed away. The five people who attended his funeral had a twenty percent chance of being the recipient. Herb's mother was in her eighties and a permanent fixture of

Scotland, and most of his other associates were either physically hampered or still whacked off their tits by a lifetime of drug abuse. His mother could be counted in both camps these days. It can't have been a difficult decision to leave the property to the one person Herb knew had a better than evens chance of living to the end of the month. Not everyone, though, was pleased with Nash's choice to come here.

Faith had only visited the property once before and it had coincided with her abduction and forced exposure to Emorfed. Much had changed in her life since then. Twelve years under the control of Emorfed's shadow, unable to feel or demonstrate any emotions, had robbed her of her most vibrant years. As a seventeen-year-old she had fallen in love with the idea of dating the famous and enigmatic Nash Stevens, lead singer of one of the country's most popular rock bands. Now, almost unknown to her, she was a mother to her own child, surrogate to another, and Nash had given up all trappings of fame and fortune.

Nash no longer personified the danger and mystery that first seduced her. He struggled to fit his increasingly large body into skinny jeans, was going grey, and his idea of excitement was staying in to watch a box set. The glamour had been replaced by middle-aged normality, outside of the fact that they were being hunted by the afterlife of course.

On the conveyor belt of life things change before you've even noticed, and it affects everyone in different ways. Faith's adoration for Nash had waned, even though he had spent a decade or more trying to protect her. But from what? Was he protecting her from external dangers or from the degradation of his own image of her? When the shadow had descended over her soul, he imagined its return would put her back unaltered. But it hadn't. The passage of time had not just changed her appearance, it had changed the essence of who she really was.

"Nash, the washing-up needs doing!" hollered Faith from the kitchen, at the exact moment Nash had eased his body into Herb's favourite chair, having just completed her last command.

"Can't it wait?"

"No," came the sharp response.

Nash struggled out of the comfort of his chair and returned to the kitchen like an obedient hound.

"And once you've done that, you can start working on the other jobs."

"Other jobs, my sweet?" said Nash innocently.

"The bins need taking out, that toaster needs fixing, the radiators need bleeding, the drains are blocked, Grace's bed is still broken, the bathroom needs grouting, and the chimney needs cleaning."

"Just those," he said casually.

"For now."

"I'll get on to them. I was thinking…" he said, looking for the right time to raise the subject, "…after I've finished all of those jobs, we might…you know… when the kids are in bed of course…have some…adult fun?"

The corner of Faith's mouth curled up in disgust at the idea. Her frumpy, floral-patterned dress expanded as she made herself look bigger and more unattractive. Her hair, once blonde and well cared for, drooped limply around a face that hadn't seen a blusher for several months. Her head moved slowly left to right as if a reflex had been triggered in the back of her head like the switch on an Action Man figure.

The awkward moment was broken by an eight-year-old boy filling a rucksack with whatever contents he could salvage from the fridge.

"Just off out," he said nonchalantly.

"Ok, Scrumpy, see you later," replied Nash, still preoccupied by the outcome of his poorly delivered sexual advances.

It was only by observing the doubling volume of Faith's eyes and her dumbfounded expression that

Nash realised what was happening. He quickly followed the boy to the front door.

"Scrumpy, where are you going?"

"Exploring," he replied, looking a little confused by the question.

"For what exactly?"

"Who knows? That's the whole point of exploring, you don't know what you're going to find until you go. Otherwise it would be called finding, not exploring. Who knows what treasures and adventures are out there? It's a whole new world of possibilities. Dragons, wizards, goblins, unprotected caves, fairies with mystical powers, a magic fountain…"

"Drug dealers, gang members with really sharp knives, the homeless, weirdos and paedophiles," added Nash.

"Paedophiles?" replied Scrumpy, trying to work out what the last of the list of dangers was. "People who really like bikes?"

"That's not what they are, I'm afraid," replied Nash. "London isn't like the Scilly Isles, Scrumpy. You can't roam around on your own, it's just not safe."

"So when can I go out exploring?"

"When there's a suitable adult to accompany you on a well-planned excursion where all of the risks can be assessed. We can go to London Zoo at the weekend if you want."

"How is that an adventure?" he asked, looking crestfallen.

"They have a gift shop."

Scrumpy's face was not impressed.

"There's loads of other things to do there," added Nash quickly trying to save the idea.

"Can you roam around interacting with all the animals, or climb up the cages, or visit it after midnight, or pretend to be a lion tamer or…"

"No. You can stand in line and wait to see some of the animals from behind wire fences, or wait for an expert to talk about one of them, or buy overly priced food from a branded and themed restaurant."

"I'll pass," said Scrumpy. "How am I meant to entertain myself?"

Nash considered this for a moment. What were eight-year-olds supposed to do? He only knew one, and it just happened to be the one dressed head to foot in camouflage in front of him. The only other eight-year-old he'd come into contact with was himself more than three decades ago. That eight-year-old was mainly interested in guitars and Saturday morning television.

"Television?"

"What's that, then?" asked Scrumpy.

"What…you don't know what television is!?"

"Nope."

"It's the flat thing in the living room that we tend to stare at in the evenings. It projects pictures. You can watch films or dramas or documentaries, anything you want. I bet they have some great programmes about pirates," he said encouragingly.

"So it's a bit like watching an adventure without actually leaving the house."

"Exactly."

"Sounds rubbish."

"We all have to adjust," said Grace, as she descended the staircase which ended in the hallway near the front door.

"Your sister is right. The situation is not easy on any of us at the moment. What do you do to occupy yourself, Grace?"

"I invent or think," she replied.

"There you go, Scrumpy, what about that?"

"She's brilliant at those things. I don't do thinking, it takes way too much energy. I'm all about the doing," he said honestly.

The three stood on the paisley carpet runner in a stand-off of views and differences. Four sizes of coats hung limply from the hatstand that hugged the space between the wall and the door. The springs of the letter box creaked and then snapped shut as a white envelope landed on Scrumpy's toes, who was still holding the door handle, waiting to open it. As all eight-year-olds would, he ignored the letter. Not his business after all.

"More junk mail," Nash muttered.

There was no address on the letter, just a name. Grace.

"This was hand-delivered," said Nash silently. "They know where we are."

"You're so lucky, Grace. I never get anything," added Scrumpy, oblivious to the significance of the letter arriving here.

CHAPTER SEVEN

THE PRIEST OF BYBLOS

In a corner of St Stephen's Tavern, Byron nursed a Bloody Mary while Victor nursed his newly attached left foot. It functioned much like it had before, but would never again look good in a flip-flop.

Even though the pub was in close proximity to the Houses of Parliament and a regular swarm of tourists, it was as empty as ever. The scarcity of patrons might be a side effect of having two men inside who would scare even the most hardened football hooligan. Or it was possibly empty because it was only quarter past eleven on a Tuesday morning. Or more likely it was to do with the fact that it was just a shit pub. The worn leather upholstery spewed out the internal foam from beneath it and the drinking glasses had a frosted quality from too much cleaning.

Victor was the first to break the silence.

"We always appear to end up back here," he said awkwardly, not really knowing what to fill the silence with.

Byron didn't respond, continuing to analyse the contents of his drink with the assistance of a wilted piece of celery.

"They'd probably go bust without us," Victor chuckled.

Silence wrestled back its advantage again, until Byron chose to break it.

"Limbo has advanced more than I'd expected," he said, opening up a newspaper on the centre of the cigarette-scorched table top. A photo of Limbo

THE PRIEST OF BYBLOS

enveloping a large section of the Alps was featured on a double-page spread with the headline 'Armageddome'.

"Clever," replied Victor on seeing the headline. "I thought you said Grace wouldn't let it happen."

"She won't, but perhaps she hasn't learned the truth yet as to her own role in all of this. We might need to give her a little nudge."

"That involves me, right?" said Victor knowingly.

Byron slid a white envelope across the table.

"Once you find her, which I'm sure you can, make sure she gets this."

"What is it?"

"A version of the truth."

"But not the whole truth," added Victor.

"Only what she needs to know to help her save mankind. Where to go, what to do, and who she is. I have conveniently omitted any advice as to what to do after that," he said with a smirk.

Victor wondered how pleased Agent 12 would be to get another visit from his former colleague. It wouldn't be difficult to apply the right pressure in order to identify where Grace was. There was no question of him not following Byron's orders, but there was something Victor wanted to know about this important young girl.

"How is Grace a god, if you don't mind me asking?"

"The same reason I'm one."

"And how's that?"

"Because my soul isn't like yours. It evolved differently."

"I didn't know that you had one."

"Some might say the same of you, Victor!"

"Fair point."

"A god is a being whose soul has developed as the result of a mutation. My soul does not weigh twenty-one grams like yours, and it is not made up of three different parts. My soul only has the capacity for malice, pain, suffering, fear and malevolence. It can only manage negative emotions."

"How did it mutate?"

"How should I know? I wasn't exactly aware of it at the time."

"But how does it make you different?"

"It means my soul can keep an organic host alive for longer and will only ever be drawn to the Soul Catcher in Hell, where it can be sent back here again if it so wishes. Over the last two thousand years that hasn't been possible because I have been forced to share digs with other souls like Laslow's or bodies like Byron's. Plus it's more fun down here, more humans to corrupt."

"Is it only gods who have the ability to keep a body alive for longer than intended?"

Byron looked at him suspiciously, "It sounds to me that you're fishing for a way to become immortal, Victor."

"The thought had crossed my mind. I can't spend all the money I'm going to make assassinating God if I'm dead, can I?"

"I'm not going down that path again, it's nothing but trouble."

"You've done it for someone before?"

"In a manner of speaking."

"What do you mean?"

"Back in the old days, when humans were less complicated, I used to offer people deals in order to remove their souls from them early in exchange for something they wanted. On one occasion it backfired on me and I have been trying to make up for it ever since. Someone fought back."

"Who?"

"The Priest of Byblos."

*****

THE PRIEST OF BYBLOS

Throughout human history there have always been gods. Some of them have lasted longer than others, but all fade eventually. It's perfectly rational to understand why human beings have always sought a higher power to explain the extraordinary. How else would an early human population come to terms with a bolt of lightning striking the ground or a mountain erupting with lava or even the pattern of the sun and the moon with no information to direct them to any other conclusion than that an invisible man was responsible.

Humans believe in such things because they fear what they cannot explain for themselves. It's no different from their belief in the existence of ghosts. Strange how people rarely claim to see one of those when they're in a large group in a well-lit room. Ghosts are introverts, it would appear, and aren't big fans of the light. Gods, like ghosts, allow humans an acceptable, if unexplained, hiding place from their own ignorance and fears. It's an essential part of what makes humans, human.

It doesn't explain, though, why there have been so many gods down the years. If gods act as a crutch to support their inability to make peace with the inexplicable, why do they need so many? Isn't one enough? Unless their collective view of gods is wrong. Does a god have to be central to a religious doctrine, or is that just a set of crazy rituals they've manipulated to suit their own purpose for so long that no one really understands why they need to do any of them anymore? Maybe gods exist irrespective of what we think or do. It all depends on what you know about gods, doesn't it?!

*****

Down the years the Devil had become accustomed to being double-crossed. It had happened often enough for him to be permanently on his guard. It wasn't that he was particularly gullible: it was only possible for

THE PRIEST OF BYBLOS

others to take advantage of him because of his single-minded addiction to satisfy his insatiable hunger for mischief. The opportunity to make the life of humans uncomfortable was always too much of an incentive for him not to take the bait. The first deceit had been the most damaging. It had landed him in the position he still occupied today. Manacled to planet Earth and forced to walk amongst the humans.

When Baltazaar and Satan had agreed to remove the final piece of Celestium from Neutopia, in order to plant it on Earth and develop Limbo, he'd well and truly fallen into Baltazaar's trap. Someone had to take human form in order to complete the task, and Baltazaar had persuaded him that it would be a good career move as he'd have the chance to continue his manipulation of the locals. It wasn't made clear to him that it might be a permanent transition. Baltazaar remained in spiritual form and Satan was stuck with limbs.

Confined to an earthly body and unable to return to his own dominion, the Devil wandered the land looking for opportunities to mislead or tempt unsuspecting humans. Often this would manifest itself in offers of wealth or power in return for some hidden sacrifice by the foolish and fallible human. This usually involved them handing over their soul and being forever destined to remain negative as a consequence of their greed.

The simple corruptibility of man meant the Devil yearned for suitable adversaries who might make a game of it. Someone who would compete with him on an intellectual and spiritual level. Could the human race provide someone with the credentials to test him? Candidates came and went, swiftly dispatched without so much as a shot on target. Each victory was as hollow as the last and increased his thirst for stimulation and challenge. It eventually came as he walked the Middle East a thousand and more years ago.

THE PRIEST OF BYBLOS

It was an encounter that changed the fate of humankind forever.

In a barren and barbaric country, ravaged by war and famine, he observed a destitute holy man dressed in peasants clothes and propping up the walls of an ancient city. When the Devil first met him the man was already in advanced years, and only referred to himself as the Priest of Byblos.

The Priest had been banished from the city and in his desperation to survive was forced to seek charity from the travellers that entered it. In return for food or water the Priest would offer a prayer for the traveller's safe onward journey. Very few accepted.

In poor health and aware that death was fast approaching, the Priest feared most of all what would greet him in the afterlife. Disguised as a market trader, the Devil stopped at the archway in the walls of the great city and offered the Priest a vision of his future in return for a sacrifice. On this occasion the Devil was not interested in the man's own soul, as he was too old and unlikely to survive the winter. Instead, the old man would exchange Satan's foresight for the soul of his youngest son.

After much consideration, but driven by his own selfishness, the Priest agreed, but with one condition. After seeing the vision, the Devil would grant him twenty-four hours to spend with his son before his own life ebbed away and his son's soul was exchanged. The Devil agreed.

The Priest was shown all that would come to pass. He witnessed in horror as his soul travelled through the newly constructed Limbo and was processed once it was there, before experiencing the final, blistering journey to Hell and a resting place amongst the cells of level one. When the vision came to an end, the Devil revealed himself and smiled weakly at his victim. Another human had been defeated by the sharpness of his malice without so much as a minor counter-attack. What the Devil had shown him was a lie. At that time in history Heaven was still a legitimate destination for a man of faith. It was all part of the despair the Devil so enjoyed sowing in the minds of the weak.

For the holy man the vision wasn't quite what he'd hoped for. Devoutly religious, he'd spent his entire life preaching messages of hope and forgiveness. He'd falsely constructed a paradise for the righteous, and encouraged his subjects to keep faith that their sacrifices in life would finally be rewarded after death. It appeared from the vision that all he'd believed in was false. Not only would this affect his own destiny, it would be the fate of every man, woman and child.

Not on his watch.

There would be twenty-four hours available to help his son escape the fate the Priest had burdened him with. He entered the city, where his son lived in a palatial home with every luxury money could buy. His son had disowned his father many years earlier, unable to agree with the Priest's principled views on how he should live his life. The father begged his son to listen to his advice before describing all that he'd seen. In their final moments together the Priest sought forgiveness for his unbendable faith in the creator he'd resolutely believed in. He beseeched his son to work tirelessly to cleanse any religious thought from his mind, now and for the rest of his life.

The key, the old man said, was to remain rational and logical and attempt to balance positive and negative emotions, therefore avoiding the fate of an afterlife in Hell. He directed his son to leave behind his material excess and run away. The longer he could hide from the Devil, the more time he had to manage the balance of his soul. But he could not run forever. One day the Devil would catch up with him, and then he must be ready.

If he evaded the Antichrist long enough, the son was told to preach a message of personal responsibility and warn others of the trick that might meet them in the

THE PRIEST OF BYBLOS

afterlife. In the meantime the Priest would do what could be done to rectify his own mistake. It was the last time any living human saw him.

When the Devil arrived at the city gates the following day at the time agreed to receive what was promised, the Priest and his son were nowhere to be seen. Furious, the Devil visited the son's house to find it empty. In his anger the Devil burnt the city to the ground and swore to hunt down the Priest and his son. Using his unique ability to communicate with human souls, he reached out to both of them.

"You may run, but you can't escape death. Deals with the Devil shall not be easily broken. They will follow you through this life and the next."

The son did more than just escape capture. For years he travelled from village to village, region to region preaching a new message contrary to the many other pilgrims that walked the land. Just as the original disciples had managed before him, the messages gathered momentum. People were energised by the controversial and progressive nature of their central themes. Cast away the doctrines of an everlasting life and live for now. Be fair and logical and restrain from acts of anger or excessive pleasure. Focus on what you can do for yourself, not what can be done for you by others. The more people that noticed, the harder it was to keep under the radar from more powerful ears.

As thousands converted to this new religion and lived life to its messages, so their souls changed to reflect it. Not all were left neutral, but those that were arrived in Limbo after death with no obvious path. The more these neutral souls arrived, the more it enraged God. How could these mortals turn their back on His love and power? How could they believe the words they were hearing without evidence to back it up?

Finally, after decades of searching, Satan finally caught up with the Priest's son to reclaim what had been promised. The man, now in his late-forties, stood upon a hilltop beside a small stone cairn in a country

THE PRIEST OF BYBLOS

of dust and sand. The man welcomed Satan with an outstretched hand.

"Where is your father?"

"I thought you might have the answer to that," said the man.

"He has disappeared from my view and has not yet passed over as his vision showed."

"Good for him."

"Bad for you," said the Devil. "You owe me your soul."

"And I willingly give it to you," he replied.

"Why are you not frightened?" asked the Devil.

"Because you may take my soul, but it no longer belongs to you."

"We'll see."

Satan raised a hand and extended a skinny finger in the man's direction. Twenty seconds later all that remained of him was a pile of soot and ash and a cloud of electric blue energy.

CHAPTER EIGHT

EXCESS

When is enough, enough? The more you get, the more you want, an ever-increasing circle of desire. Once the floodgates open it's hard to hold back the tide. The lesser demon's very existence was based on being told what to do. Slaves do their duty. No rights, no views, no values and no ambitions. Now, a species that was never equipped for self-determination was living with no rules at all. And it was causing problems.

It had been a while since Mr. Brimstone had last visited the lowest regions of Hell. He'd been far too busy rushing around completing ludicrous tasks for the 'master' that included building a bird bath completely from gold leaf, destroying all the modern art with any reference to Satan, and banning left-handed scissors. At the same time level zero had been transformed into a nirvana of sin for a group of demons with no self-discipline to moderate it. Casinos, nightclubs, sporting attractions and opium dens had all been built to keep them happy. But they appeared nothing of the sort.

Brimstone stood in the doorway of the lift watching agog at the sight that greeted him. His eyes expanded so much that very painful lines of lava seeped down his cheeks like tears. A deep sense of sadness flooded over him to see what had become of his world.

To his left a full-scale brawl was in progress. Punches were being landed on faces, and a variety of feet were being used to kick other bodyparts with strange and unintended results. A stone demon's legs

EXCESS

were currently lodged in the thigh of a demon whose anatomy was made of mercury. Undeterred, he was still punching it in the back of the head, even though each strike went through and back out again. All this commotion was being played out around a poker table knocked to its side in a hailstorm of plastic casino chips.

To his right, half a dozen demons lay in a variety of contorted positions in a hastily constructed beer garden, either unconscious on the floor or vomiting into plant pots. An overweight demon made of hawthorn bushes and wearing an ill-fitting black suit had just thrown a patron through the double doors of a bar called 'The Twilight Alehouse', where he landed in several pieces on the ground.

In the foreground, trying to maintain order from an unruly group holding placards, were two demons with fake beards and official-looking hats. The placards featured a variety of strange demands, most of which had been written over the top of previous requests. 'We want more chocolate!' and 'Where's my holiday!?'

All around them thousands of incarcerated souls stood behind the iron bars of their cells watching avidly.

"What is going on here?" demanded Brimstone.

"Oh, Mr. Brimstone, am I happy to see you! They're just never satisfied. They keep demanding more," replied Fluffy, a cotton demon who, with his friend Red, had led the first rebellion against the senior demons.

"It's Hell down here," added Red. "Crime is through the roof. We've got a possible obesity crisis and an epidemic of sexually transmitted diseases."

"How?" replied a bemused Brimstone. "You're all asexual!"

"I know," said Fluffy who appeared to be walking uncomfortably. "Disgusting, isn't it?"

"How do we stop it?" asked Red.

EXCESS

"I'm not sure we can," said Brimstone. "Sandy is responsible for this and only he can be held to account. I suggest you take your placards up to level twelve and let him know."

"But what about all the shadows? They'll destroy us," said Red nervously.

"Revolutions can't exist without sacrifice."

"He's talking about you," said Red, pointing to Fluffy.

"You ungrateful shit."

"What are you going to do, suffocate me with your wispy hands?"

The two exchanged shoves and pushes like two drunks trying to co-ordinate a fight while balancing on a wobble board.

"STOP!" shouted Brimstone. "Can't you see what you've all become. You wanted freedom but you couldn't cope with it. You're not built for it. We all have to accept what and who we are. Don't get me wrong, I was all up for a change in the system. We had Fascism but this hedonistic mess is even worse."

Both demons stared at their feet.

"Somehow we will sort all this out, but for now I have a job for the two of you."

"You can't oppress us. We don't do jobs anymore. It's part of our charter," said Red, confidently pointing out a stone tablet standing on a plinth nearby.

"How would you like me to set fire to one of your ears?"

Red placed both hands to the side of his head and found he needed to shout his response. "WE CAN MAKE AN EXCEPTION FOR YOU!"

"Go down to level zero and find the oldest of the reincarnates and bring them up to level twelve. Take a couple of shadows with you as bodyguards if you need to. And hurry up."

Fluffy and Red moved awkwardly towards the dried-out lake and the trapdoor that could be found at the bottom, avoiding as they went the anarchic chaos

EXCESS

swirling around them. A few random objects, like a chair and a stein glass, were just some of the projectiles hurled at them as they went.

"These creatures are designed to follow," said Brimstone under his breath. "They only respond to fear."

"Brimstone."

Any lesser demon that wasn't already unconscious or drunk immediately stopped what they were doing. They were only used to voices in their heads, not ones that came unattached from bodies.

"What can I do for you, Noir?" said Brimstone.

"It's not him, it's me."

"Who's me?"

"John."

"I didn't know you did jokes, Noir. Very good, though. Have you been practising? I've got one. How many lesser demons does it take to change a political system?"

"What! No, it really is me, seriously."

"I've been to the library, I saw his book burn. He can't exist anymore, that's how it works."

"What about evolution?"

Brimstone hated it when he was right, particularly when it meant he didn't know what to do or say next. It was true that he couldn't predict how evolution would happen, but he still wanted to know, "Prove it."

"The first time we went to the library together I tried to save a boy destined for the fire. It caused a paper cut which you had to seal up," replied John, remembering an experience only he and Brimstone would recall.

"Fuck!" said Brimstone, quickly shaking his head at a group of demons who saw his remarks as a command and had started to hump each other.

"Brimstone, I need your help."

"Again! Why me, John? Why can't you ask someone else for once? I'm not your personal assistant, you know."

EXCESS

"Maybe not, but at the moment you're the closest thing that I have to a friend."

"Ha. You can stop trying to butter me up. I'm not and never have been your friend. I am interested in one thing and one thing alone: putting all this back the way it was."

"And that's why you and I need to be friends. I can help you, but you must help me first."

Brimstone was not suffocated by allies. Satan was away and currently not answering calls. The senior demons were on solitary confinement and the lesser demons had all lost their minds in a sauna of addiction and overindulgence. Who else was there?

"What do you want?"

"I want to know who I am."

"You're John. There you are, done. Now how can you help me?"

"But I'm not John, am I? He was the fifty-first version of someone else. I'm tired of saving everyone else at my expense. It's time for me to know the truth."

"The truth is I don't know. Your book is gone and the cover was worn down so I couldn't read who it originally belonged to."

"There must be a way to find out."

"Why is it so important to you?"

"Because I feel empty. I can't make sense of the world or my place in it."

"John, have you ever heard the story of Sisyphus?"

"It's a type of wort cream, isn't it?"

"No. Sisyphus was the king of Ephyra. The gods punished him for his craftiness and incessant deceit. They made him push a vast boulder to the top of a hill, but every time he got close to the summit it would roll back to the bottom. Endlessly he was, and possibly still is, pushing that rock back up the slope."

"And the moral of this story is…"

"You are Sisyphus. I mean not literally of course," he added in case John saw this as an answer to his original question. "The interpretation of this story is that absurdity arises from mankind's attempt to extract meaning from a meaningless universe that offers only a life of toil and inevitable death. It's a lesson I must remember to teach the lesser demons."

"You're saying that life is meaningless."

"I'm saying that truth can only be found if you rebel against the passive resignation to a certain fate. You are who you are, John. You're not what you were or what you might be. You are you. Maybe it's time you just accepted that simple truth and gave up the search for greater meaning. It's a forlorn search that will send you insane and will always leave you wanting more."

"Perhaps it's time I rebelled, then. I can't live without knowing."

"Which is good, because you're still dead, whatever you've become."

"Someone must know."

"Only the Almighty can tell you that."

"Maybe it's time to ask Him, then."

*****

"Anyone down there?" shouted Red through the open trapdoor.

Neither of them fancied going down for fear of not coming back again in the same condition. Some distance below them out of a thicket popped a head. After the head came a stretched neck, ideal for peeking unnoticed from bushes. Engorged black eyes rolled in its plastic skull from the momentum of a jaw that chewed on a mouthful of plastic leaves.

"You there," said Fluffy. "Come here."

Without the slightest concern the white llama lifted its body from the undergrowth and strolled forward, continuing to nibble at tasty morsels as it went. Its body was as plump as its neck was long.

"You're a bit fat for a llama, aren't you?" said Red.

"Although you might expect me to be toned, I am in fact just very big-boned," replied the llama.

EXCESS

"You're in a blow-up plastic vessol, you haven't got bones, you weirdo," said Red. "You must have wind."

The llama continued munching, ambivalent to the stain being placed on his character and accusations of a possible flatulence problem.

"We have a job for you, llama. The master requires the oldest of your number to present themselves to him for a special…award," said Fluffy, not entirely sure why Sandy had made the request but certain it wasn't going to recognise some great achievement.

"Where the plastic creatures roam, mountains soar and rivers foam, you want me to find the oldest of our kind, to satisfy a pigeon's mind," sang the llama.

"What's wrong with him?" whispered Red to Fluffy through pursed, barky lips.

Fluffy shrugged his shoulders.

"Why all the rhyming?"

"I'm just a llama that likes a bit of drama. My poems are a source of relief….although my name's not…Keith," said the llama, struggling to construct a decent couplet on the spur of the moment.

"What is your name, then?"

"Lloyd…and I quite like Pink Floyd."

Fluffy demonstrated the universal hand movement for 'crazy'. Neither of them trusted the llama to do the job well, but if it meant they could go back to the relative sanity of level one, all well and good.

"Lloyd, will you do what we've asked?" said Red.

"Of course, it could be worse," replied Lloyd.

The two demons watched the llama disappear from sight from their lofty vantage point out of the trapdoor and remained nearby to await the volunteers.

When the llama reached the desert biome, where he knew most of the others would be gathered, he arrived midway through a game of five-a-side football being played out between demons and larger mammals. A rather unenthusiastic crowd were doing their best to understand the offside rule while debating how this entertainment was way less exciting than a good pass over. Even though the demons were winning, Asmodeus was actively demonstrating his displeasure by standing some distance away with his fingers in his ears.

"Sir, I have a request from a guest," said the llama.

"What do you want?" replied Asmodeus, taking one finger out of a lughole.

"Two heads appeared, one had a beard, and asked me quite nicely to search precisely for a geriatric made of plastic."

"What? Talk normally or I will have to bite you."

"It's a heavy curse, but I'm compelled to talk in verse," replied Lloyd.

"Is every creature here broken?!" bellowed Asmodeus in frustration. "Let's take this one step at a time. We'll use simple questions and you can just nod, ok?"

The llama nodded theatrically.

"Two demons came through the trapdoor."

The llama nodded again.

"Looking for geriatric plastic? They want old reincarnates, correct?"

Again Lloyd nodded.

"What for?" added Asmodeus, forgetting the system completely.

"An award will be presented by those that are frequented by a pigeon of great power...who I've heard needs a shower."

"A decent poem isn't just about sticking words together that rhyme, you know."

"It's not poetry, it's rap," said the llama.

"Well, it definitely rhymes with rap."

The llama looked at him impassively.

"There are lots of other forms of verse, you know. You could try free form, haiku or even a well-conceived limerick."

"Really?" said the llama, relief revealed in his face. "I thought poems always had to rhyme."

"Not at all."

"Let me try a limerick."

"Do you have to?"

"There was a pigeon in Hell, who made a nasty smell. The demons recoiled from the thought that he'd soiled all over the place that they dwell."

"Anyway…I wonder why he wants the oldest," said Asmodeus.

"To be clear…" exclaimed Lloyd. "I have no idea."

Nearby, another group of misfits were paying almost no interest in the football and slightly more attention to the unconventional poetry session. One of them in particular was being as nosy as ever.

"We're the oldest," coughed a voice from within the crowd.

Sadly, Asmodeus knew who'd spoken. He'd become rather overfamiliar with him.

"Of course, me first…and then this lot," said the lion as he encouraged the others to nod in affirmation.

"How could I have guessed?" said Asmodeus. "Strange how you, Roger, are always the best, oldest, quickest, cleverest, please add the adjective of your choice."

"I'm just uniquely amazing," replied Roger. "Get over it."

Asmodeus had no idea what Sandy wanted with the oldest reincarnates, but he didn't like it. Maybe he was going to torture them? Maybe he was going to keep them captive? On reflection all of these options appealed to him as it meant they wouldn't be down here, being annoying. Clearly the best outcome was for him to be up there and them to remain down here, but as this wasn't a viable alternative right now he'd take what he could.

"I totally believe you are Roger. I think you, the spider, ox, gibbon and sloth should definitely volunteer."

"What about me?" said Ian.

Ian was a one-time accomplice of Sandy's. They'd fallen out when Ian had tried to protect John from

EXCESS

Sandy's ever-increasing cruelty. It was a rejection that still hurt. All he'd ever wanted to do was make Sandy proud of him, to demonstrate he was capable of more than accidents. He hoped that day might still come.

"I think there are more than enough pigeons on level twelve just now. I don't want to create an obvious succession plan. Primordial, I wonder if you'd be kind enough to escort the others to the exit so they can fulfil our master's request," said Asmodeus, rubbing his hands together.

Primordial was a good choice of chaperone as he was the only one the lion really feared. Like a pitch marshal, only lacking the fluorescent jacket, he escorted the five creatures from their seats. All except the sloth. No one was entirely certain if he was still alive. Had he passed over without anyone noticing?

"I wouldn't wait for him, it could take a while," said Vicky the spider sarcastically when Primordial gave him a jab in the ribs.

"I'm."

"Plan A?" said the Gibbon.

"Not."

"I'll start on the webs," replied Vicky.

"That."

"Let me strap him down, I'm amazing at that part," said Roger.

"Old," said the sloth before noticing that they'd strapped him to the back of the ox and he was already on his way, travelling ten times faster than he would have done otherwise.

CHAPTER NINE

THE UNITED NATIONS

It had taken three thousand metres of expansion before the Federal Council had narrowly agreed to the Clerk's recommendation. The consequence of this needless delay was that Jungfrau was no longer a tourist attraction, unless you happened to have recently died and were one of a million balls of blue electricity rumbling around it like the contents of a tumble dryer. Significantly less fun than the zip wire experience previously in place there.

Once all the arrangements had been made to speak at the UN Assembly, Rogier Hoffstetter and the Clerk travelled to New York City, home to the world's most complicated and elaborate debating society. It wouldn't be easy for either of them. The United Nations is, like most formalised bodies, awash with formalities and procedures.

Special sessions of the council can only be convened in matters of urgency or national security as long as you jumped through lots of hoops. Firstly, the General Secretary needs to be informed, then a majority of the Security Council have to agree, and finally the other one hundred and ninety-three members have to be given fourteen days' notice to attend. With these formalised and uncompromising processes it would be extremely difficult to see how the UN could successfully intervene in the event of an imminent nuclear war. It would be all over before somebody had seconded the motion.

THE UNITED NATIONS

Despite the speed with which Limbo bludgeoned itself further into the world, time was still on their side. Armageddon wasn't in a hurry, it would seem. This looming danger had more than a passing resemblance to global warming. Almost everyone agreed it was happening, but they also believed it wouldn't happen for a while so there was plenty of time to grab lunch and do some more research.

In the vast debating chamber four hundred pairs of eyes, connected by two hundred pairs of headphones, waited patiently. Emergency sessions weren't rare, but they were tediously boring. Whatever the topic was it rarely affected all the representatives in the room. Normally it was about some local dispute about one nation over fishing the sea, or the threatening behaviour of a neighbour awash with rumours that they'd developed some level of extinction event weaponry, only for it to transpire it was actually just an elaborate hoax.

Unless the key speaker happened to mention your country directly, you could pretend to listen or even have a little sleep. Which in reality meant the same thing. A delegate's induction training included a detailed seminar on how to sleep whilst keeping just a fraction of their eyes open. It must have been an effective course because they were all brilliant at it.

This session would be the same as all the others. Standing at the front of the room some lanky president, of some backwater country that no one cared about, would drone on about some triflingly unimportant motion, using deeply complicated highbrow vocabulary to prove just how important and clever he was. In turn, the translators would struggle to translate 'asinine' into Swahili, and because there was no equivalent word they'd just make most of it up. By the time the speech got through to each delegation's ears most of it was completely different than originally intended. Like a massive game of

THE UNITED NATIONS

Chinese whispers. Which was unfair on the Chinese who understood better than most.

The formality was that if you requested a session here, your leader had to personally make the case for action. The UN Assembly was no place for the general public or diplomatically uninitiated. If the Swiss had gone to the great trouble of requesting all these people to gather, then the message would have to be delivered by Rogier himself.

Standing at the rostrum in the centre of the world's most powerful people, he was suddenly transported back to a secondary school assembly. Every day a pupil would be chosen at random to read a passage from the Bible in front of the whole school. There they all were, hundreds of his peers, waiting, some praying for him to slip up. All they needed was for you to say something ridiculous so they could mercilessly remind you of it for the next nine years. The baying crowd got their reward when a thirteen-year-old Rogier confused the word 'Gentiles' for 'genitals'.

Sweat started to squeeze through the pores of his forehead. Shivers vibrated up his back under his brown nylon jacket. The air was evacuated from his throat by an invisible suction pump, rendering his mouth dry and incapable of coherent speech. The nerves came in waves at the very moment in his life which would define him and his leadership, for better or for worse.

"Mr. President, ladies and gentlemen, distinguished guests, I speak to you today in humble gratitude that the council has honoured our request for this special assembly. Switzerland and the Swiss people have always prided themselves on their independence and their strong sense of freedom to choose to remain different. You may think our country acts like every family's long-lost relative, aloof and distant, but we acutely understand our place in the world. That place is part of a global network of nations, dependent on

THE UNITED NATIONS

each other and connected at every level of society and government."

The delegate from Djibouti let out an unconscious yawn as if the pressure in the room had just dropped several bars.

"My country may be famous for chocolate, Army knives and cuckoo clocks, but as a nation our combined talents go further and wider than you might imagine. Today those talents and resources have been stretched to breaking point and we can no longer act independently. Not only can we not act alone, but also we can no longer ignore the threats that exist to other neighbours and our family of nations. A spectacularly dangerous event is unfolding in the heart of our nation. If it continues unabated it will endanger everything the human race holds dear. What is unfolding is a potentially calamitous phenomenon."

The translator from Suriname looked panic-stricken. It wasn't the possible nature of the threat that had created the anxiety. Taki Taki, the creole dialect language used in her country, had one of the smallest vocabularies in the world. It was made up of just three hundred and forty words. The limitations of the Suriname dictionary meant several words and phrases had multiple meanings. 'Give me a hug' and 'set fire to my toes' were only discernible if you delivered the words with the precise vocal twang. The number of people who'd got it wrong on Valentine's Day was legendary.

After a brief pause to compose herself, the last sentence of Rogier's previous statement 'potentially calamitous phenomenon' was translated to her delegate as 'flip-flop black miracle'. The Suriname delegate didn't seemed bothered and continued to practise his talent of sleeping whilst nodding every half-minute or so.

"The abnormality of which I speak is currently dominating the central region of our once breathtaking countryside. A gigantic, metallic dome has germinated

THE UNITED NATIONS

like a seed in the land and has now expanded beyond our capabilities to control it," continued Rogier.

The translator from Suriname's head hit the table, sending a dull thud around the circular auditorium. She turned off the radio feed to her headphones and decided to just make it up as she went along. It wouldn't be the first time.

"This alien structure is expanding every day by several miles. Soon it will start to devour our borders and enter the concerns of other nations sitting around this room. We have canvassed every known expert to help us understand and solve the crisis. All but one have failed to offer any clear explanation."

Rogier had thought long and hard about how to introduce the Clerk to the gathered global diplomats. The truth would not help their case. Explaining to them that a man of indescribable age and no obvious qualifications, had suggested he was an expert on endgames and purported to have been involved in setting the rules of Armageddon, would have been a difficult thing to sell. They'd come up with an alternative.

"Ladies and gentlemen, I know it is quite against the procedures of this assembly, but I would now like to introduce you to the only expert who has given us any useful insights as to how we might stop its advance. Mr. Clerk is Chief Scientist at the Institute of Near Extinction Prevention Technology."

It was only pointed out to him in the minutes leading up to his speech that this fake government body formed the acronym INEPT.

"Mr. Clerk has an important message that must be broadcast across every country represented in this room. Failure to do so will result in the end of our world and our species. We must act now," demanded Rogier, clenched fists hitting the rostrum, shaking a few dozen of the collective from their slumbers.

The Clerk stepped forward to take his place in front of the green and white marbled background. Above his

THE UNITED NATIONS

head three figures sat on a raised platform like VIPs watching the performance from the luxury of the royal box. They were probably important, but the Clerk wasn't one for airs and graces. A dapple of blue and cream leather poked through the fog of human bodies. Each one was a seat that lacked a person capable of passing his message on to their people. Not a single country could be missed.

"Who is supposed to be sitting there?" said the Clerk with a pointed finger.

This was definitely against protocol. The auditorium was accustomed to listening, not answering. A few embarrassed diplomats, in seats that straddled the empty ones, fidgeted uncomfortably until the Clerk's hard stare forced them into action.

"That seat belongs to the delegate for Djibouti," replied the man.

"Where's he gone?"

"Toilet?" replied the man with a shrug.

"Well, go and get him," said the Clerk sternly. "And anyone else not here for that matter."

"You want me to go to the toilets and knock on all the cubicles and ask if any of the occupants will declare themselves to be the delegate from Djibouti?" said the man irritably.

"Yes."

"Do you know who I am?"

"I don't care if you're the former President of Saturn. Go!"

The Clerk tapped the rostrum impatiently until the delegate finally got up and edged himself carefully past his colleagues like a late arrival at a cinema showing. The man who sat in the centre of the platform behind the Clerk's head leant forward to speak.

"Mr. Clerk. The UN doesn't work like that. You can't just command our delegates to do as you please. This platform is for communicating to them, not directing them."

THE UNITED NATIONS

"I once worked in a place very similar to this. It was circular like this one. It had a dock in the middle and a very similar platform where three characters sat in judgement. The central character in that theatre sat where you do. He, like you, had too much power. The place I speak of is the source and reason for us being gathered here today. Soon it will occupy this very building, unless everyone does their duty. I don't care about old-fashioned and pointless procedures, things change," snapped the Clerk.

A rather embarrassed delegate returned, still tucking his shirt into his trousers. He waved apologetically to a man he'd never set eyes on before. When there was no cream and blue to be seen, the Clerk cleared his throat.

"Mr. President, esteemed delegates and, most important, people of the world. I stand before you today with no allegiance to any country or culture. I have nothing to gain personally and no axe to grind against any other. I am not a politician and never plan to be one. Yet I have witnessed events beyond your comprehension. The message I bring to you today is extremely important and very simple. Don't die."

The faces in the crowd stopped presenting bored and tired expressions and replaced them with ones of utter bewilderment.

"Let me explain. The metal dome, that I'm sure many of you have seen in your daily newspapers, is Limbo. It is a place built to collect and process the souls of human beings. But it no longer processes them. It is expanding because the system is broken. There is no forwarding address for any of us. At this point some of you may be thinking that you don't believe in religion and it doesn't affect you. Fine, ignore me. See for yourself what it's like to be suffocated by a mass of souls jammed tightly around you. Your religious persuasions are also irrelevant. I don't care if you identify yourself as a Muslim, Christian, Buddhist or Jedi. All our souls are destined to arrive in Limbo, unless we stop dying."

THE UNITED NATIONS

"How can we just stop dying?" said the President from behind the speaker's shoulder.

"In truth, we can't stop our flesh dying. But we can stop our souls doing likewise. The process is called the Limpet Syndrome. It is known to happen naturally, but extremely rarely. It can only occur if the human in question has a strong enough reason to remain on Earth to rectify a wrong or finish an outstanding deed. Yet it is an unconscious reflex in all those who have triggered it in the past. Now I am giving every single person in the world the motivation to do likewise. If we do not, then the metal sphere will continue to grow until it replaces our planet."

"But how do we do it?!" shouted one of the older delegates, likely to be one of the first to be forced to try.

"When death comes, in whatever form or guise, your soul will be ejected from your body. A few seconds is all you'll have before the power of the fifth force will connect to it and you'll soon be whizzing through the air unable to put the brakes on. In those vital few seconds all of your emotions and will power must be focused on your own personal survival."

"And then what?"

"You'll force your soul into a process of reincarnation. A word of warning here. It's likely to be whatever organic life form you were last looking at the moment before you died."

"Can't I just choose to be a shark?" said another delegate.

"No, it's pot luck, I'm afraid," replied the Clerk.

"There must be another way," said the President. "Can't we just nuke this Limbo thing?"

"No. Atomic weapons would be useless. Limbo is made of a substance which may well have even stronger properties."

"I think it's time we talked through the narrative of a UN Security Council Resolution," said the President.

"Why?"

THE UNITED NATIONS

"Because that's how we agree on actions, Mr. Clerk."

"If I told you we were about to be hit by a huge asteroid from space, you lot would sit around for hours voting. I wonder if that's what really happened to the dinosaurs," he said sarcastically.

"Process is process, Mr. Clerk. Are you done?"

"Not quite. Remember these two words. DON'T DIE!"

The Clerk stood down from the podium to an atmosphere of surreal silence. Normally a speaker would leave to a standing ovation or a hearty round of applause. The auditorium was too stunned by the contents of the speech to offer anything but quiet contemplation. The Clerk wasn't bothered. He wasn't in it for the plaudits. As long as his message got through to the people, then the first of his jobs was complete. It wasn't the only job he'd have, though. Saving mankind would only be step one.

Rogier and the Clerk exited the chamber and navigated their way through press galleries and passageways until they reached a private office that had been booked for them. Once they were there Rogier exhaled so powerfully it was as if he'd been holding his breath for the entire experience.

"Thank God that's over," said Rogier, pouring himself a glass of water but wishing it was something stronger.

"Over," replied the Clerk. "This is not over."

"Not over? But we have done what we set out to achieve."

"All we have done is pass on the message. If all goes our way people, will listen and act as I have instructed. After that the endgame moves to the next stage."

"What next stage?"

"Limbo isn't expanding by accident. Someone wants to destroy mankind. They're not going to stop because of us. Emorfed was the first attempt and this was the second. It will continue. A great battle is on the horizon and we must be ready."

"How?" said Rogier, scanning the room to identify a liquor cabinet to steady his nerves.

"We must build a coalition of nations to fight that battle."

"Against who?"

"Gods, I expect."

*****

When Grace had finished reading the letter she placed it on the living room table and sat quietly in thought. The rest of the room evaporated into the ether as the nuggets of information settled into place like dusty pieces of a jigsaw. Nash and Scrumpy waited patiently for her to reveal what the letter contained. When it was clear she was in no hurry to do so, Scrumpy's patience disintegrated.

"What does it say?"

"Many things," replied Grace.

"But have you won?" asked Scrumpy.

"Won what?"

"Don't you remember? Whenever we used to get mysterious letters like that back in the Scilly Isles it would always say that Mum or Mom was the lucky winner of some amazing prize and all they had to do was travel to a meeting and spend all day talking to a man in a suit and watch a presentation about some scheme before collecting whatever it was they'd won. Strangely they never went. Such a waste."

"I've definitely not won anything," said Grace impassively. "It was from Byron."

"And..." said Nash, who had never formerly been introduced to his partner's father on account that Byron had initially threatened to shoot him, and latterly because he was quite possibly back from the dead.

THE UNITED NATIONS

"Byron is clearly not who you remember. He has been possessed by the Devil and now has more than a number of challenges he wants my help with."

"So that's what he's become," said Scrumpy who'd spent a limited time being held captive by him. "He should have stayed as a pantomime villain, he'd have been better at that."

"As an ex-politician some might say most of them always have been," added Nash. "Why you, Grace?"

"For the reasons that were left unspoken when you and I talked on the boat back from the islands. There's more to me than just a neutral soul. This letter proves it. My soul is a mutation. And if you own a mutated soul you possess powers that others don't. These powers would be seen by most to be omnipotent."

"What's impotent?" asked Scrumpy.

"Very different from omnipotent," replied Nash. "It means Grace is god like."

Although smarter than the average eight-year-old, Scrumpy hadn't paid much attention in his English classes, as for most of the time he'd been sailing a dinghy around a bay rather than being in them. He'd spent even less time in R.E. which he'd incorrectly translated to mean 'Recess Exploration'.

"Wow, are you really a god!"

"No."

"Do a miracle."

"No."

"Go on."

"No."

"Please, just a little one. Turn the TV on without touching the remote," said Scrumpy, scanning the room to identify a suitable test case.

"TV turn on," said Grace.

The television came to life two seconds later.

"That's literally the most amazing thing I have ever seen in my whole life," said Scrumpy, bursting out of the settee and waving his hands at the thirty-eight-inch wonder.

THE UNITED NATIONS

"Scrumpy, we have voice-activated controls. That's not a miracle, anyone can do it. TV turn off," said Nash to prove his point.

Scrumpy reversed back into position in a bodily heap of disappointment.

"Grace, tell us what else it says," added Nash.

"There is a war coming. The human race is under threat and only I can stop it. Heaven and Hell have become dead ends and all human souls are massing in a place called Limbo. A way must be found to stop it or Limbo will expand and consume the Earth. Byron wants me to go to Switzerland to stop its progress. He's a little loose on the details, however. He also states that I must draw Baltazaar out into the open."

"It would appear you aren't the only one attempting to stop it," said Nash, rummaging around in an antique piece of wooden furniture down the side of his chair and removing today's paper. "Look."

On the front page the headline stated in capital letters, DON'T DIE. The accompanying black and white photograph showed two men that none of them recognised. One was old and shrivelled, the other lanky and well groomed. Grace took the paper in her pale white hands and started to absorb the details.

"I don't know who they are," said Grace, always disappointed when knowledge was not complete enough for her to process it.

"What do we do next?" said Nash.

"I'd like to be taller," said Scrumpy looking at Grace. "If it's not too much trouble, oh mighty one."

CHAPTER TEN

GLUE

The small, metal ball watched as an endless chain of origami creatures harvested, moved and deposited the white grass into a huge mound. Tirelessly they worked without breaks or quarrel like a family of eager worker ants. Throughout this process Accountant A continued to motivate their work levels, occasionally assessing the quality of the materials farmed and the size of the pile. After what seemed an age he raised his hand in a stop sign.

"I think that should do it."

It was impossible for the small ball to quantify how much of the grass had been collected as it was definitely smaller than a football pitch, but the hill wouldn't have looked out of place in a small builders' merchants. It was the ball's opinion that there was certainly enough to build a Soul Catcher. After all, he'd seen one before, although he wasn't sure how.

"That's a good job, platoon. I'm very proud of your attitude," announced Accountant A.

A number of the troops gave each other congratulatory slaps on back, producing a sound reminiscent of someone reading a flick book.

"What now?" said Accountant M, one of the only ones to abstain from all the backslapping.

"Now we complete the machine," said A.

"How, exactly?"

"We put all the grass together in the shape I described to you earlier," replied A.

"Let's try that, shall we?" said the paper swan.

GLUE

Accountant M wobbled over to the pile of grass and returned holding two individual blades. He held them aloft in all directions as if a magician was checking with his audience that no illusions were being surreptitiously used to trick them. Theatrically he brought the two blades into contact with each other before removing them again. He repeated this a couple of times to double-check there wasn't some secret way of attaching them together that he wasn't aware of.

"Nope," he replied categorically.

"I knew that," said the leader, not wanting to lose face, but being slightly discouraged by the demonstration.

"What is this papier mâché you talk about?" said Accountant Z, who had been of little help in foraging for grass due to the restriction that, although he had plenty of legs, he still had no arms.

"I believe you put paper and glue together, which allows you to mould the mixture into an object. When it dries it goes solid," replied Accountant A, going on instincts alone.

"What's glue?" asked Accountant J who had just landed gently on a landing area, having been extremely useful in the logistics of the great grass collection.

"It's a sticky substance that fixes things together," said Accountant A confidently.

The platoon fake nodded as if they immediately knew what he was talking about.

"I'm no expert," said M, "but I think I've worked out the flaw in your plan."

"There's no flaw, we just need to find a glue substitute."

"And where are we going to get that from? Don't tell me all that grass cutting was for nothing," replied M indignantly.

"Of course not. What about spit?"

"What about it?" said Accountant D.

"It's sticky, isn't it? Right, everyone start spitting."

GLUE

Spitting is, and always will be, a disgusting act on many levels. Firstly, someone else's enzymes being projected from their mouths are a sure-fire way of spreading disease. Secondly, in order for it to be done successfully it is impossible to spit without making the world's most disgusting noise. It's a noise that no one would ever think about having as their mobile phone's ringtone. It's a guttural sound with the tonal quality of sandpaper being tortured. Thirdly, on a purely etiquette level, it's not an acceptable way to behave.

None of this was really that important in the circumstances because, as a race that still hadn't made it to its second day, not one of them had ever done it before. Hard to be offended by something you've never tried or seen. Also, as it happened, it didn't come that naturally to them. Most of their behaviour was still being learned and that process only comes from instinct or watching other people. This created a chain of imitations as one Accountant watched the next attempt and fail to produce what was required.

A few of them coughed. One dislodged a kneecap from too much exertion. Several passed out completely. One produced what can only be described as confetti. After multiple techniques and attempts had been tried unsuccessfully the leader called them to a halt.

"Not spit, then. There must be something here that would work."

The ball felt he knew the answer. If only he had a way to communicate it to them. He fidgeted on the spot. Rolled back and forward. Lifted slightly into the air, but none of them noticed. Maybe a form of charades would work? He rolled across the soil to the feet of the leader. After a short pause to ensure it'd been noticed, it trundled off into the distance.

"Where's he off to?" said A.

"Papier mâché-related boredom?" replied M.

GLUE

"About-turn, march," ordered Accountant A, as the troop without question filtered into order and quickstepped after it.

The ball stopped at the base of the nearest tree. Its trunk was square with sharp edges on each corner. Branches angled out on all sides with small, purple postage stamp-sized leaves bristling at their ends. To make the point of its advice, the ball moved around its circumference a couple of times.

"It appears he wants us to notice the tree," said A.

Accountant M approached, still carrying the two blades of grass he'd tried to fuse together earlier on. Gently he held the two blades on either side of the trunk and let go. They floated down to the ground with no sign they might miraculously attach themselves together on their way to, or on, the ground.

"Trees aren't sticky, then," replied M with the air of a science professor.

The ball, realising that light suggestion wasn't working, took matters a step further. It dashed off away from them and then, with more velocity than it looked capable of, shot forward into the tree. A light, tingling sensation vibrated through its metal. The tree remained unaffected. The ball repeated the action more fiercely than before.

"Is it trying to commit suicide?" said Accountant J.

"I'm not entirely sure," said A, "but it is a strangely captivating sight."

"You wouldn't use a tree if you wanted to kill yourself. You'd lob yourself off the cliff into the quarry, or spend hours picking tiny white blades of grass for no apparent reason," said M, adding a subtle dig that didn't go unnoticed.

"Careful, M, I won't tolerate insubordination."

The ball continued without pause. The metal inside it was now dizzy from the repetitive nature of head-butting the tree, but not without reward. As the ball struck the tree for about the thirtieth time, a crack appeared in the bark and a small line of liquid ran down the trunk.

Accountant A wiped his hand across the excretion and rubbed it between his fingers. "It's sticky."

*****

"Why did you volunteer us, you idiot?" said Vicky, her eight legs strolling carefully through the stench of the swamp biome.

"Lions don't listen to insults from spiders," said Roger.

"What about from ox?" said Abe.

"Nope."

"I assume you have a reason for putting us back where all the danger and terror is, though?" said Vicky sarcastically.

"Obviously," said Roger without a moment's pause. "I have this plan I've been working on. It's so good, I almost surprised myself."

"You've not got a good track record," added Elsie the gibbon, who was travelling at the back of the convoy scheming up pranks to play on the sloth who was still strapped to the back of the ox.

"Yes, I have. I'm a genius. Name me one mistake I have ever made. Just one."

"You threw yourself out of the window and came back as a lion. You tried to use kung fu moves on Mr. Brimstone with almost zero effect, and…" reeled off the spider, who was soon cut short.

"They were all wins. W…I…N…S," he repeated confidently.

"Is there anything you've ever failed at?" said Elsie.

"Of course not. I'm Sir Roger Montague, the third Earl of Norfolk. I'm a legend in my own lifetime."

"Although you're dead," added Vicky. "So you could say you failed at staying alive."

"No, I'm not done with life yet. I'm just working on other projects."

GLUE

"Of course you are, you narcissistic fruit loop," whispered Vicky.

"So what's this amazing plan of yours?" asked Abe inquisitively.

"I could tell you, but it's fair to say that none of you have the capacity to understand it, so I'd be wasting my time," said the Lion gently padding his plastic paws in between the thicker patches of bog.

By the time Gary the Sloth had formulated his riposte to this overt bragging some fifteen minutes later, they'd reached the rope ladder and the moment was gone. Red and Fluffy were waiting for them at the top. A rope was lowered to secure the ox who was the only one who couldn't climb up unaided. Gary was now attached to an ox who itself was attached to a rope. The five animals reached the dried-up lake and were immediately interrogated.

"Right, I need names and birthdates," said Fluffy.

"I don't take orders from filthy demons," said Vicky.

"Then I suggest you turn around and go back the way you came. If you want out you have to answer my questions."

"I'm not sure any of us, other than the lion, want out," said Abe.

"Sir Roger Montague, the third Earl of Norfolk. I'm the oldest here!" shouted Roger, answering the initial question before the others could ruin his yet unannounced plan.

"But what's your birthday?" asked Red.

"4th of July."

"Yes, but what year?" probed Red.

"Nineteen Eighty-Four," added Roger.

"You're not the oldest then, are you? I mean..." added Red before being cut off mid-sentence.

"B.C.," replied Roger with a grin.

"Did they have earls in those days?" asked Fluffy suspiciously.

"I wouldn't be stood here if they didn't, would I?"

GLUE

"What about you?" said Fluffy to the ox. "Name?"

"My name is Abe, God bless you."

"You don't look old enough to get in here. Your plastic skin is still smooth and shiny."

"I definitely am old enough."

"What's your date of birth, then?" said Red, assessing the Ox's body language for any potential deceit.

"7th of October...." The ox paused as he tried to calculate the appropriate year he should give. "Eighteen Seventy-Six."

"So how old does that make you, then?"

Standing in the background, the lion was holding up the claws of both front paws in an attempt to trigger the ox's response and save him from being refused entry.

"One hundred...and...twenty...sorry...thirty... one...no...two," said the ox with a final nod.

"Go on, in you go, but I'm keeping my eye on you," said Red.

"You next," said Fluffy, looking at the sloth whose head was upside down and hanging off the side of the ox's abdomen, "as you appear to be together."

"Gary."

"Age?"

"I'm just warning you that if you're in a rush and don't want any of us to pass over before he gives you the answer, you might want to skip this one. I can vouch for him," said Vicky.

"You all need ID if you're getting in, ok," replied Red abruptly.

"It's your funeral."

"Age?" said Red again.

"Two."

"Well, that's not old at all," said Fluffy.

"Hundred."

"Oh that's better."

"He's not done," said Vicky helpfully.

"And."

GLUE

"And what?"

"Thirty."

"In you go, then."

"Eight," finished Gary as the ox trotted off to join the lion.

When it was established, often falsely, that all five of the animals had a combined age of over six thousand years, they were all allowed entry. The spider had lied the most. At best she thought she might be about thirty, but had squared the number to get as close to the lion as possible.

"Head over to the lift and Mr. Brimstone will escort you up to level twelve," said Fluffy.

In the distance a glowing and steaming dwarfish block of rock was leaning against the lift shaft that stretched up into the void and through the ceiling. When he saw the gaggle of misfits approaching, he exhaled desperately.

"Not this lot again," said Brimstone before they reached him.

"They weren't very popular down there. I guessed this was going to happen," said John.

"They've all got a screw loose."

"Maybe that might play into our hands," replied John.

"I'm listening."

"What's Sandy's state of mind like at the moment?"

"It would be best described as insanity with a hefty dollop of paranoia."

"They're not going to help the situation, then, are they?" said John.

"No. And actually nor will you. I have an idea."

"Go on."

"When we get up there I want you to talk to Sandy directly. He'll think it's the voices in his head, and when he asks me if I can hear it I'll deny it."

"Brilliant."

Mr. Brimstone shifted the metal bars of the lift to one side as the creatures approached. "Why you five?"

"I keep asking myself exactly the same question," replied Vicky.

"Everyone get in."

They squeezed into the small cube. Brimstone commanded the ox to press number twelve on the panel as there wasn't enough room for him to stand on the small box he normally used to reach the highest button. The metal cage gave a little jolt before it trundled slowly up through the levels.

"No hard feelings," said Roger.

"For what?" said Mr. Brimstone.

"Kicking your arse with all my amazing kung fu!" replied Roger.

"Let's just agree not to talk to each other, shall we?" said Brimstone, clear that there was no one in the universe who might successfully argue with the lion other than Primordial.

After several minutes of travel the lift came to a halt at its uppermost floor. Brimstone pulled the doors apart and exited first, glad to be out of the overcrowded space. The animals followed swiftly. Around the vast table the assembled plastic vessels turned their chairs to face the new arrivals. Not one of them was pleased to see who'd arrived. Least of all Sandy.

"Brimstone, these aren't the oldest, they're the most damaged. That's not the same thing."

"I'm told they passed all the checks done by the lesser demons."

"What checks were they, then?"

"I think they just asked them for their birthdates."

"There are many ways to identify the age of something. I'd have preferred it if they'd cut this lot in half and counted the rings," said Sandy, and stormed along the centre of the table towards the group with the ferocity of a marching band.

"You know, you really should learn to respect your elders," said the lion, tongue nowhere near his cheek.

GLUE

"In a way you five have done me a favour. Not only will I be able to construct my deterrent, I'm also going to get rid of the five most irritating residents of level zero," said Sandy with a dark chuckle.

"What exactly are you going to do with them?" asked Brimstone.

Sandy flew over so he was out of earshot of the dictators and shadows.

"I'm going to force them to pass over," he whispered, although not altogether effectively. "What's left of them will be the same as Emorfed, which I will collect and use to control the shadows. They will never disobey me if I possess the only compound that defeats them. I'll be able to rule forever."

"And how exactly are you going to force them to pass over."

"Reincarnates have never been punished the way other vessels have for fear of something going wrong. Punishment has always been administered in order to degrade the soul within. All we need to do to speed up the process is to break out the torture weapons."

"I command you not to hurt these creatures."

Sandy looked around nervously for the source of the voice. "Who said that?"

"Said what?" replied Brimstone innocently.

"You didn't hear it?" asked Sandy.

"Hear what?"

"The voice, just then."

"You mean this one," added John.

"There it goes again. You must have heard it that time," said Sandy, looking at everyone in turn.

The animals had heard it. But given the recent news that each of them would soon be sporting a variety of sadistically painful medieval devices designed to speed up their own destruction, they didn't seem too keen to acknowledge it. So they just shook their heads and waited to see what would happen.

"Who's there?" demanded Sandy. "Show yourself."

GLUE

"I can't show myself, Sandy, because I am the ghost of John Hewson sent to haunt you for eternity!"

"Ghost, is that even possible?"

"Whooooooo," said John, getting into character.

This was not helping reduce Sandy's paranoia. It was bad enough to have the constant anxiety that Osama bin Laden might lead a revolt against you, without the added stress of a former adversary returning from the dead, if indeed that was at all possible based on what he'd learned about being dead.

While Sandy was dealing with his own internal issues, the lion had signalled for the group to follow him. They were now edging closer to the perimeter of the level. Around them was the window, a huge, transparent barrier that separated them from the universe outside. Roger had been through it once before, only to be returned to Hell's Soul Catcher immediately after. But that Soul Catcher was no longer working.

"Where are you lot going?!" shouted Sandy.

"I'm still talking to you," said John, splitting Sandy's attention and forcing him to cover his ears.

"It's time for my plan," announced Roger to the others.

"You'd better hurry up and tell us, I think Sandy has noticed we crept off," said Vicky.

"Jump," said Roger.

The gibbon did a little hop in the air.

"No, no. Jump through the window."

"But that'll just bring us back again," said Vicky who had witnessed it for herself.

"It can't, though, can it? There's no Soul Catcher."

"So we'll just end up floating in space for eternity instead: brilliant," said Vicky disparagingly.

"That's not what happens to Emorfed, is it?"

"But we're not the same thing, are we, you plastic idiot?"

"Come on, it's now or never," replied Roger.

"What are you basing this plan of action on? Have you done a risk assessment, or researched the possible outcome?'

"No, but I've never been more confident in my whole life than I am now," added Roger.

"That's almost impossible," said Vicky.

In Sandy's confused anxiety a group of shadow souls had picked up the reins and were bearing down on the reincarnates. Soon they would be captured and the moment might not present itself again.

Roger took two steps backwards and leapt at the barrier with the confidence of an experienced pole-vaulter. The lion suit filled with space and flew off like a balloon. His soul floated in suspension for a moment, and then shot off towards a group of distant constellations. Importantly this appeared to be in a direction further from Hell. The others weighed up the alternatives of staying or risking it, and en masse followed the lion.

CHAPTER ELEVEN

THE PENNY COLTRANE SHOW

Times Square Television Studios buzzed with the twittering voices of one hundred and fifty ticket-holders patiently waiting for the intro music to start. Every day a new audience filled the studio to watch yet another adrenaline-fuelled encounter between members of the general public with their strange personal grievances to air. Why they felt it necessary to do this on national television was anyone's guess. But still they came.

There were those that sought only the notoriety of their fifteen minutes of fame. Those that wanted to humiliate a family member or friend for their own personal revenge. And those that were frankly too stupid to fully comprehend what was going to happen. Yet still they came. Boxes of applications and emails arrived each day at the production company offices, each topic judged based on an ever-increasing scale of shock and sensationalism.

Penny Coltrane's programme was not the only show in town. Every channel had its own version, each competing in a cut-throat race for ratings and advertisement revenues. It was no longer acceptable to show run-of-the-mill stories like 'my boyfriend's secretly taking drugs' or 'I'm ashamed to show people my third nipple'. That was way too old-school. The bar was much higher these days.

THE PENNY COLTRANE SHOW

Penny had learned from her predecessors that nothing was off-limits. The more controversial and ridiculous, the more likely she was to air it. Threats of litigation or death just made her more motivated to proceed. As a result tickets were rarer than Yeti droppings.

The lights faded and the chattering crowd immediately hushed to silence. A middle-aged woman with several facial piercings and deep black mascara sat seemingly petrified in a chair centre stage. The familiar walk-on music played out over the PA system, and Penny entered from the shadows of the left-side curtains. The audience spontaneously leapt from their chairs and offered chants and violent screams. It was like a lion had walked out into a Roman amphitheatre and was about to butterfly a Christian or two.

The powerful lights illuminated the stage like Gotham City's bat beacon. It was nearly matched in intensity by the pale and gaunt woman that sat sweating anxiously in the seat, wondering what on earth possessed her to think coming on the show was a good idea. Camera three followed Penny's movement as avidly as the audience, before zooming in for the show's introduction.

"Kirsty says that her relationship has hit bumps in the road," Penny announced in a calm and friendly voice. "Kirsty, what's happened?"

Camera three swivelled back to the isolated woman. Microphones descended from the ceiling like drones.

"I've been with my partner for nearly four years, Penny, and we have two lovely children."

A picture of two toddlers flashed almost subliminally on the TV studio's branded backdrop, having the desired effect of setting the audience off into collective audible sympathy.

"When I first met him, Penny, he was everything I wanted in a man. Big muscles, charming, blue eyes, a great sense of humour, his own pickup truck and only three or four facial scars. It was love at first sight,

THE PENNY COLTRANE SHOW

Penny. When he proposed to me it was all so romantic. He took me to my favourite restaurant…"

"Lovely, which one, Kirsty?"

"Burger King. The tables are bolted down so he had to move to one side so he could get down on one knee. Everyone was cheering and clapping. Then he asked me to be his wife. It was so romantic," said Kirsty in a deep-toned and scraggly American accent throughout. Occasionally she would pause between words to see if she actually knew which ones to use.

The crowd murmured impatiently. They'd been expressly promised shocking revelations, fights, swearing and the dismantling of furniture. After two minutes, which was precisely thirty seconds longer than the average human being was willing to wait for anything these days, they'd witnessed none of it.

"Great, so what's wrong?" said Penny, sensing the changing mood in the room.

"In the last few months he's started acting strangely. He's just not the same person I fell in love with," replied Kirsty, breaking down in tears.

Penny rushed forward like a reality television version of Florence Nightingale.

"I'm sorry, Penny, it's still so raw," wept Kirsty, wiping her tears with her blouse.

"It's alright, Kirsty, love, the pain will go away if you talk about it," said Penny, internally counting up the surge in viewing numbers.

"His behaviour is starting to worry me. The other day, when we were out having a walk, I caught him sniffing another woman."

The crowd mainly gasped, although a lone man's voice was heard saying, "What's wrong with that?"

"It's like he can't stop his instincts. Then later, on the same walk he stopped in the middle of the park and…it's hard for me to say it, Penny…he squatted down and did a big, steaming poo…right there in front of everyone. He was so proud of himself. He ran around everyone, smiling and jumping up and down."

THE PENNY COLTRANE SHOW

The audience reacted without the aid of the prompts being offered from behind the camera on large pieces of white card.

"The worst time is at night. He acts like such an animal, Penny."

"Some people would say that's a good thing, am I right, ladies?" she asked the audience, who responded with predictable mob agreement.

"I just want to know why he's changed," wept Kirsty.

"You deserve the answers, my dear. His name's Brent, let's find out his side of the story."

A German Shepherd bounded out onto the stage to a chorus of boos. The dog made an immediate beeline for Penny's crotch, a big, pink tongue flopping out from one side of its jaws. The host gave it a hard stare and it instinctively turned itself nimbly around and jumped into the vacant seat next to Kirsty. The chair itself was large enough to fit an oversized human arse, but struggled to contain the dog's larger than usual mass.

"So, Brent, why do you feel the need to sniff other women when you already have a lovely fiancé and a beautiful family?"

"I just can't help myself. I've tried to stop but something deep inside me just loves sniffing crotches."

"You disgust me," snivelled Kirsty, turning away from him.

"How long have you felt this way, Brent?"

"I think it first started when I became a dog. Definitely didn't feel like it before."

"And how did that come about?"

"I was listening to the radio on the way to work and this news fella came on. He said that if you were about to die, you had to really focus on...um, not dying. Well, I was so distracted by the weird stuff he was saying that I completely missed my turning and drove straight into a pet shop at about seventy kilometres an hour. Next thing I know I'm this cloud of electricity looking down at the puppies in the shop. I think that was probably the start of it."

*****

Scrumpy pressed the standby button and the stupid, attention-seeking idiots instantly vanished into the glass screen.

"It'll never catch on," he said to himself, jumping to his feet.

In the hall stacked up on high were several rucksacks bulging at the seams. Nash was in the kitchen writing a letter, and Grace was sitting on the stairs already wearing her hat and coat.

"Are you ready, Scrumpy?" she asked.

"Too right. I can't stand it here with all these walls."

"Where's Mum?" asked Grace, as Nash left the letter on the kitchen table and turned off the light.

"She doesn't fancy another adventure. I begged her of course, but her mind was completely made up. I said we'd phone regularly to make sure she knew we were safe. Hurry now, we don't want to keep our taxi waiting."

"Shouldn't we wait to say goodbye?" asked Scrumpy.

"Too painful, best we just leave the note."

"You haven't told her at all, have you?" added Grace.

"Of course I have," replied Nash.

Grace placed her fingers to her lips and everything around them froze. The hands on the landing wall clock quivered in position, desperate to return to the monotonous journey around its face. Grace strolled to the kitchen, removing a pen from her jacket pocket as she went. She opened and read the letter before making a variety of editorial changes and resealing it. People always wrote a version of what they wanted to say, but never what was really happening. Grace thought her mother deserved to know exactly what was going on, not a sugar-coated story. She returned to her original position and took the pressure of the clock's seizure.

"That was strange. Did either of you feel that?" asked Nash.

"Did your stomach rumble as well?" said Scrumpy.

"I think it's time we went," said Grace. "There's much to do."

"But where are we going?" asked Scrumpy.

"To take a first-hand look at Limbo," said Nash.

"No, we're not. I've changed the plan. Doing exactly what Byron wants us to do seems illogical to me. He tried to kill all of us, remember. Why would we do what he wants? Plus the evidence points in a different direction."

"Where?" said Nash.

"The United States."

"But I've made all the arrangements. The flights, accommodation, transfers…"

"Have all been duplicated," replied Grace. "Let Byron think we are doing what he wants while doing something completely different."

"But why the US?"

"Because we need to find this guy," she said, holding up the black and white newspaper clipping of the Clerk.

CHAPTER TWELVE

KEYBOARDS AND CUBICLES

In the centre of a patch of red, dusty ground, adjacent to what used to be a rather plentiful grassy, white meadow, was a monstrosity of paper and tree sap. A large box, about the size of a garden shed, dominated the centre and a long, hollow girder stretched through the top out into the air, gently teasing the translucent barrier that surrounded the planet. Hastily plastered to one side was a second box with no obvious function. The visible front face of this second box was constructed from a square piece of dried tree resin, and beneath it was a series of keys made from shiny, square pebbles. Each one was engraved with a different letter of the alphabet or strange symbol.

Accountant A stood nearby this shoddily constructed control panel proudly assessing their achievement. Even by his lofty ambitions they'd built what was required more quickly than expected. It was quite possibly the first time in history a building project had been successfully completed before the deadline and under budget. It was probably also the first one that was designed by an origami alien race with nothing more than a field of grass and a couple of square trees. The big question was, would it work?

"Was it what you wanted?" said Accountant M, staring at the object with contempt rather than pride.

"It's magnificent," came the reply.

"Is it?"

KEYBOARDS AND CUBICLES

Accountant M waddled around the machine one more time to gauge whether the full majesty of their exertions had passed him by. Papier mâché boxes with chimneys coming out of the top didn't really float his boat.

"How does it work?" asked Accountant J, who, with the ability to fly, had been instrumental in fixing the chimney in place. More than once he'd flown a little too close to the barrier and had to make a number of emergency landings.

"The chimney collects the souls from the other side of the barrier, which sucks them down into the collection chamber," said Accountant A, pointlessly indicating the only significant parts of the contraption with his finger. "Then we can see who's in there on the screen of the computer terminal."

"And are you expecting them just to fall down the chimney?" asked M.

"Obviously not."

"Then how are you expecting them to get there?"

"An energy source," replied A.

"But it's not doing anything," said M. "It's less active than a sloth. What are you expected it to be powered with, happy thoughts?"

"Something much more powerful than that. Something which was naturally here until it was stolen. A substance that was only recently returned to us."

"What?" said half a dozen Accountants at once.

Accountant A pointed to the silver-coloured ball who'd spent much of the last few days running painfully into trees. It was the only one apparently both willing and capable to tap the sap from the trunks. As a consequence everything had a shaky, duplicated look about it and the ball had wondered for a while why they needed to build two Soul Catchers.

"What's that got to do with it?" asked Accountant M.

"It's made of Celestium, which is the source of the energy we need."

"Magnetic, are they?"

"What?"

"Souls," said M.

"Celestium isn't magnetic and nor are souls. It omits the fifth force, as long as it's housed in the right place."

"And a papier-mâché box with a chimney is recommended, is it?"

"Not as such. I don't think it's ever been tried before, actually."

"Perfect. You're saying all our efforts might have been a waste of time."

"You had a lot on, did you? Look, experimentation is crucial in invention."

"And fancy words are crucial in bullshit," whispered M.

"We shouldn't question whether it works or not until we've finished it."

Accountant A gently picked up the ball of metal in its crisp, folded hands. The resin screen was lifted off to reveal an empty compartment attached to the side of the larger structure. He gently placed the ball inside and replaced the front. The ball was just visible through the yellow-tinted screen. A square stone pebble had been hastily carved with the word 'GO' on it. He pressed it. Nothing happened.

"Shock horror," said Accountant M. "We've put some random metal in a paper box and pressed a stone with the word 'go' on it and nothing happened! I can't understand why. So much of what we've done in the last week makes solid scientific sense."

"Sarcasm does not suit our species," replied A.

"What are all these buttons anyway?" asked M.

"It's a keyboard."

"But what's that button for?" said M, pointing out an odd-looking squiggle symbol.

"It's a shortcut for the word 'and'," he replied passively.

"What's the point of that? Is it really a time-saver to press one key instead of three."

"Three times quicker, Accountant M. As a species we're all about the productivity."

"Ok, I'm alright with that, but if we're really trying to be more efficient, why don't you make that squiggle key a shortcut for 'Welcome to Neutopia, we're the Accountants, good afternoon how are you?'"

Accountant A ignored him partly because he wasn't accustomed to being wrong and partly because his colleague was starting to get on his nerves.

"What's that one for? It looks like an 'a' key with a massive tail."

"It's for sending email."

"What's an email, some sort of shelled mollusc?"

"No. Maybe there's another sequence of buttons you have to press," continued Accountant A, trying to move the conversation on. "Let's try this one."

Accountant M moved towards the control panel and without force picked up the 'GO' button from the console. "It's not even attached to anything."

Sometimes in life you have to accept that what you desperately want to believe in might actually be false. This isn't a comfortable journey for the most seasoned and experienced academic, but it's even more challenging if you've nothing else to fall back on. If the only option in your mind is the one you've been driving towards, where next? Accountant A had been created for one specific purpose. The notion and design of what needed to be done had been lying dormant inside him for longer than the reality of life itself.

It had to work. There were no alternatives. What was the point of the Accountants if they weren't here for this? Were they supposed to identify a different vocation in a world with less potential than a small asteroid on an inevitable trajectory towards a red dwarf? Sometimes in life you have to ignore the obvious setbacks and redouble your efforts, or hope that a mysterious ball of metal gives you a leg-up.

Inside the box, feeling a lot warmer but a little isolated, the ball thought about their predicament. It was clear to it that the machine would only come to life in the same way the grass had. The energy of life had initially come from him moving up against the blades of grass; maybe the machine would be the same. It rolled up against the yellow screen and gave it a little knock.

Accountant A lifted the screen away in response and watched as the small ball of liquid metal rolled over all the stone keys, leaving a light metal trail like a cybernetic snail. The result was instant and surprising. The small, inanimate pebbles started to shine with a pale blue glow as if life itself was trying to force its way out to the surface. After the ball had finished with the keys it moved on to the screen and finally the interior of the box. Once each element of the controls had been galvanised, the whole device started to shake gently like an old engine desperate to work and avoid a trip to the scrapheap.

The Accountants watched in amazement as the machine gasped for air. The walls of the papier-mâché box contracted and expanded and, although cracks started to appear in their handiwork, the structure remained solid. A number of the Accountants with larger surface areas were knocked to the ground as a massive sonic boom ripped through the area. A column of energy pulsed through the chimney and burst out into the atmosphere.

"It's working. It's working!" shouted Accountant A, doing a rather embarrassing and quite spontaneous dad dance.

The Accountants clapped, although they had no idea why. Most of them were still baffled as to the general purpose of the machine and their own involvement in building it.

"What's happening?" asked Accountant Z, who still hadn't got around to fixing his disastrous anatomy, and had many more legs than he did eyes. Which was none.

"We've finished it," said M, slapping Z on the back. "What now?"

"We wait for all the souls to arrive," said Accountant A.

Expecting an instant influx, the Accountants lifted their heads to the sky like a band of amateur birdwatchers.

*****

"What progress have you made, Victor?" said Byron over the telepathy network.

It wasn't a conspicuous way of conversing. Victor would never know when Byron would suddenly get the urge to contact him. Which meant he could be doing any number of other things at the time of the call. It wasn't as if telepathy came with a 'do not disturb function'. It also wasn't prudent to talk out loud to a voice in your head when you were in a crowd of people. It had the tendency to create a great deal of unwanted attention and anxiety in those close by. None of these situations was apparent to the caller, of course. Patience wasn't a virtue that the Devil had ever cared for. If he called, you'd be wise to answer.

"What do you want?" whispered Victor.

"Why are you whispering?"

"You've caught me at a bad time."

"Oh, I'm awfully sorry, Victor," replied Byron sarcastically. *"What was I thinking? It's not as if the end of the world is coming. Oh yes, it sort of is."*

"It's just that I'm on an aeroplane."

"So?"

"Have you ever travelled in economy?"

"No. I have jet-propelled feet, it doesn't really seem necessary."

"If you had, you'd know that in an economy seat they sit you nine millimetres from two complete strangers, who, on this occasion, are in desperate need of a diet plan. I'm currently sandwiched between multiple layers of blubbery bread...and I'm talking to myself."

"Go to the toilet, then."

"Can't it wait?"

"I'll ignore you said that."

Victor nudged the portly man in the seat to his right who was either asleep or dead, two perfectly satisfactory outcomes of being forced to fly economy on a transatlantic flight. The gap between the man's legs and the seat in front would be best measured by a nano gauge. Victor's instincts told him to shoot the man quietly in the ribs and roll his dead body into the aisle. Sadly, international airlines rather frowned upon members of the public carrying weapons on-board so he'd left his behind. Where he was going he could buy a new one from almost any street corner with nothing more than a smile and wadge of fifties. The only other way out to the aisle was to wake the man up. He nudged him more forcefully.

"Hey, buddy, what do you want?" said the man as he rediscovered consciousness.

Victor pointed to the illuminated cubicle sign. The man cajoled his body out of its cheaply upholstered cocoon and Victor got a clearer view of the elderly man.

"Do I know you?" said Victor, who'd always had a good memory for faces.

"No, I don't think so, buddy," he replied before his attention span ran out faster than a goldfish's. "Hey, wow, look at the view out of the window. You can see Yellowland. Betty, come and see this."

A decrepit old woman, so thin she'd struggle to get wet if she ran around in a shower, dragged her arthritic body out of the seat across the aisle from them. She

KEYBOARDS AND CUBICLES

removed her sunglasses, revealing eye sockets that were several shades darker.

"I think you'll find it's called Greenland," said Victor under his breath.

"Wow, Greenland. I thought that was a fake place where Santa lived. Imagine the possibilities for tourism."

"Get a photo, Bobby," demanded the woman whose arms were almost snapped off by the weight of an oversized Nikon camera sporting every add-on that money could buy.

"Excuse me," said Victor, keen to get as far away from the pair as possible. It wasn't the first time he'd met this couple. They were certainly easier to deal with when they occupied separate cells in London's underground sewer network with only several hundred pigeons for company.

Victor entered the cubicle and locked the door.

"What was that all about?" asked Byron.

"Just some irritating tourists."

"Are you on your way to Switzerland?"

"No. Change of plan. Grace is going to America."

"What? Didn't you give her the letter?"

"She received it alright. It seems she's ignored your advice."

"It appears I underestimated her. If she's not following my information she must have gained her own."

"They certainly planned to go to Switzerland initially. Even kept their tickets booked as a deception. I followed them all the way to the airport before I realised what they'd done. Booked myself on the next available flight."

"It's the Clerk. She thinks he's the key."

"The Clerk?"

"A former employee. I read an article last week that he's been to the UN to send a message to the world. It would appear he's encouraged everyone to trigger the Limpet Syndrome on death."

"Isn't that a good thing? Won't it stop Limbo expanding?"

"Possibly, but it won't be all he wants. He's been meddling in the affairs of gods for too long now."

"What do you want me to do?"

"Kill him. Forget about assassinating Baltazaar for now. It's about time he and I had a little meeting anyway. Go for the Clerk and continue to follow Grace."

"Understood," replied Victor and the call was over.

As he stood up to leave the toilet he realised his gun was not the only thing he'd left behind before reaching the airport. His medication was also banned. A queue of fellow travellers watched in anticipation as the cubicle door opened and shut three times in quick succession.

CHAPTER THIRTEEN

UNSTOPPABLE FORCES

Every footstep dislodged a new avalanche of sand and slowed his progress. The dune was in constant flux, as the contents of its mass struggled to assume a constant state. The wind, responsible for constructing the landscape, whipped the sand particles into clouds that clogged in the throat. A gecko skittered erratically along the surface, stopping frequently to feel the vibrations of its prey on the ground, only to be deceived by the nearby boots striking the sand.

When Byron eventually reached the top of the dune, the isolation of the desert stretched far and wide around him. In a world overcrowded with people, this barren environment was one that civilisation had yet found the inclination to spoil. No matter which point of the compass you faced, humans and human activity were noticeably absent. Life itself struggled to find a foothold, only the exceptional survivor, such as the geckos or the odd scorpion, even tried.

Across the landscape small waves of wrinkled sand queued up patiently to crash onto unseen shorelines. Other dunes bravely stuck their heads into the open to be battered into submission by the unforgiving elements. The airborne sand made an eerie sound as it whistled through the barren contours, occasionally joined by the cackle of a solitary bird circling high overhead. Although the last recorded drop of rain struck earth here some months ago, the sky was recruiting a temporary crew of eager, grey clouds.

UNSTOPPABLE FORCES

Byron wiped the trickling beads of sweat from his brow and removed his jacket to use as a makeshift rug. It wasn't the first time he'd been here. In his past, long before he'd made use of Byron's body, he'd travelled extensively in this area. There were few regions of the world he'd yet to explore. Evil wasn't localised, it fed off human weakness, and that was everywhere. Everywhere except here, where very few humans had ever stumbled.

It had not always been the case.

There was a time when people came here to avoid him, a ridiculously naive ploy by those who lacked any true understanding of what he was capable of. There was nowhere he wouldn't go to get what was rightfully his. No hiding place from fate, no escape from the inevitable. But for him, this place did not hold happy memories.

On the adjacent dune, a hundred metres away, a figure waved at him casually. It wasn't a surprise. After all he'd recommended the meeting. But not the location: that was Baltazaar's to choose, and he knew how much it would wind Byron up.

It had always been a challenge to work out the optimum distance that could be maintained between them safely. It had to be far enough away to avoid some catastrophic weather pattern and close enough so they could hear each other speak. Over the years they'd got the distance down to a T, unless one of them saw fit to shorten it in order to prove a point through the ensuing devastation.

"Enjoying yourself?" shouted Donovan, as he used his signature Panama hat as a makeshift fan, wafting the air across his weathered face.

"No," replied Byron loudly. "Not really."

"Didn't think so."

"I see you're still squatting in the Irishman," added Byron, referring to the bodily shell that Baltazaar still occupied.

"I'm quite attached to him."

UNSTOPPABLE FORCES

It was an expression that gave more away than he intended. It was no longer a choice for Baltazaar. He'd typically maintained a spiritual form on Earth in his long involvement in the lives of humans. But once he'd discovered John's existence, it had been necessary for him to take human form. That was the only way to bring things to a satisfactory conclusion.

"You know why I brought you here, don't you?" asked Donovan.

"Because you're a piss-taker."

"It was here, wasn't it, when he played you for a mug?"

"You can talk. It wasn't just me he fooled, was it?"

"But you lit the fuse. You had to challenge them, didn't you? You had to demonstrate your control over mankind. It was only a matter of time before one of them beat you."

"I wasn't beaten. The game is still a draw. It's currently heading into extra time. Which is fortunate because not even the Germans are as good at penalties as me."

"I'm afraid that all depends on the referee, which just happens to be me and I'm extremely corruptible."

"Don't we know it? You know your plan is failing, don't you? Limbo's pace has slowed and humans all over the planet are avoiding their ultimate death."

"I know," replied Donovan bitterly. "I had a remarkable conversation with a salmon only yesterday. It's a setback, that's all."

"Once Limbo stops growing, he's going to come out to meet us. Right under our noses he's been scheming the whole time."

"He's just a human," growled Donovan.

"A human that you made immortal. Good move!"

"The Priest of Byblos is only immortal if he stays in Limbo. And I only did that because you felt compelled to offer him a deal. Without that, none of this would have happened. People would still fear and love us if it had not been for your lack of foresight."

"But I caught up with his son, I took his soul and cast him into the fires of Hell."

"But did you? You've not been to Hell since his arrival, have you, so you have no way of verifying that."

This truth hit Byron with more force than one of Donovan's thunderbolts. He had no proof as to what condition the son was in. No way to certify he was being suitably punished. His intended destination was a metal box on level twelve where all undesirables were placed. Without comment he made a mental note to check in on what remained of his subjects, to find out its conditions, if that was at all possible with the chaos that appeared to be in progress there.

"And now, the Priest has used this opportunity to seek out his fate. To complete the final part of his strategy and we have no way of stopping him."

"That's why I've sent Victor to take care of him, once and for all."

"And then what? When the world is overrun by talking animals and both our realms have been starved of energy, what then?" said Donovan, almost desperately.

"Then we return to this spot for one final battle, just you and I," said Byron calmly, avoiding any reference to Grace.

All successful battles relied on having better intelligence and superior planning. What Byron knew, that Donovan didn't, was that Grace existed. As far as Donovan was concerned, the third coming had been avoided when David had passed on. All Byron needed to do was manipulate Grace to his own ends. Granted, it hadn't worked so far, but Victor would soon change that. All Byron had to do was work out how.

"And in the meantime?" asked Donovan.

"I suggest you ready your forces," replied Byron.

*****

UNSTOPPABLE FORCES

All Sandy had wanted was a deterrent. Was it too much to ask? Just something to protect his power from the fragile alliance with chaos. Of all the outcomes he'd considered, none of them had included his deterrent jumping out of the window and disappearing into space. And it had not gone unnoticed by his unruly subjects, who had questioned each other as to why Sandy had invited the animals here in the first place.

"He doesn't look very happy with you, does he?" teased Brimstone, pointing to Mr. Silica who was bristling with blue sparks.

"I can explain everything," chirped Sandy.

"Accept me!" said John.

"John, you don't exist. I saw your end!" shouted Sandy.

"Who are you talking to?" said Mr. Brimstone, keeping up the conspiracy.

"It's John!"

"I can't hear anything. Maybe this is the evolution I spoke about. Maybe souls can come back as ghosts," he lied again.

"I'm all-powerful," chirped Sandy, not altogether convincingly. "Nothing can stop me."

The dictators, filled with human malice and a heavy dose of shadow steroids, moved into a small huddle on one side of the table. After a brief confab they seemed to come to a unanimous conclusion. Their leader was showing weakness. Every single one of them knew how that felt. They'd either been on the receiving end of it in their lifetimes, or had in fact been the deliverer of the treachery. They knew what power was. You could smell it. It was a sort of metallic odour that forced you backwards to hide in your pathetic place. Unless you stood up to it and fought back.

This unique smell of power was no longer coming from Sandy's plastic shell. It had dissipated, seeping out of him as consistently as his odd paranoia. It was time for change. Not all of them were initially willing to overthrow their master, but they were soon convinced when the majority of the rest were in favour. Slowly they advanced on him, blue fire burning in their eyes, Mr. Silica at their head, heir apparent.

"What are you doing? Back off or I will destroy you," shrieked Sandy.

"You and whose army," growled Silica, backed by those who Sandy had once set free.

Murderous dictators could be useful allies, but it would be wrong to call them loyal and dependable subjects.

"Mr. Brimstone, stand down unless you want to join him?" said Silica.

"Consider me stood down," he replied almost instantly.

"You brought this on yourself, Sandy," added John.

"Indeed you have," replied Silica, proving that Sandy was not the only one who could hear the strange voice in the air.

Sandy was torn between the irritation of discovering that the voice in his head was real after all, and the soon-to-be end of his reign. Survival instincts took over and he attempted an airborne escape. It didn't last long. Silica had soon wrestled him to the ground and surrounded the purple pigeon with a cloud of sand and energy. The throng of dictators swooped in to add their own dose of retribution, punches and kicks distorting the plastic of his vessol. Death was not their intention, it was a fruitless endeavour and there was a much nastier option.

"Lower a cask," hissed Silica to the others.

Soon one of the thick, metal chains, that was suspended in the air, was being lowered to the ground.

"You're only here because of me!" screamed Sandy as he was pigeon-handled towards it. "This is not the end, you'll get what's coming to you."

"He's right, you know," added John, as the box with Sandy inside was slammed shut and returned to the air.

"Really! Who's going to stop us now?" hissed Silica, all six inches of him.

"Ian."

"Ian! Don't make me laugh. He's less effective than a handbrake on a canoe. If that's the best you can do, bring it on. I've already eaten him once."

*****

Primordial and Asmodeus were taking one of their regular strolls around the forest biome. It was mainly in silence, occasionally broken by one of them offering a new idea to help remove them from their current predicament. The ideas became more outlandish the further they walked. They'd contemplated everything from kidnapping, all-out war, breeding a race of shadow-eating plastic dinosaurs, and schemes for removing level twelve completely and propelling it into space.

"Maybe we're coming at this from the wrong angle," said Asmodeus.

"What do you mean?" asked Primordial.

"Well, we're thinking about it from the viewpoint of a demon, not a pigeon."

"That's all I've got. I've never been a pigeon before."

"Maybe we should ask one."

"No. Not, Ian. He's an imbecile," pleaded Primordial.

"Surely it's worth a try?"

"I'd rather pickle myself in acid."

Since the other animals had left, Ian had taken to spending time in his own company. Friends had never been easily made. Back in the days before he'd become a pale white pigeon with different coloured eyes he had even tried to find a girlfriend. Modern technology had taken some of the fear out of talking to the opposite sex and allowed someone with Ian's social irregularities a platform. He'd set up an online dating profile and been liberal with some of the truths about himself. After all, creating regular disasters and having a propensity to break things was not a set of attributes likely to appeal.

Even then interest had been minimal. Women appeared to have a unique ability to read a profile and construct a completely different picture of the individual in their head. That, or they were put off by the photograph of a scrawny dude with ghostlike complexion and two different coloured eyes.

Sandy was his one and only friend in life, although it was wrong to label it as such. Ian now knew that Sandy's interest in him had always been for his own gain. Once that had come to an end he'd been jettisoned like a piece of rubbish. If only Sandy had recognised his real qualities. Loyalty, honesty, modesty, and a genuine gift for catastrophe. Maybe it was just best he stayed out of everyone's way. He couldn't be blamed for accidents if he wasn't around.

The best place for this, he thought, was the tall stone pillar where he and Sandy had once taken John to protect him from Primordial. The canyon biome was already underpopulated, and from the lofty heights of the tower he could avoid bumping into someone or something. At least that's what he thought. As he sat sulking to himself, four heads appeared over the tower's stone overhang. Three of them were owned by the same body.

Primordial oozed over the lip of stone and reconstituted himself into the pile of filth that was so uniquely him. Asmodeus landed softly on the ground, propelled to the top by the winged lion that made up the bottom section of his more frightening state. Wisely he soon mutated back to the more angelic version.

"So this is where you got to," said Primordial.

"I'm trying to stay out of people's way," said Ian.

"But why?" asked Asmodeus, offering a fake question that anyone who'd met Ian knew the answer to.

"I'm a failure. Everything I do goes wrong. I just want to be on my own."

"You're just feeling down because Sandy rejected you. You're not on your own there. We were all double-crossed by him."

"I just wanted to be useful. To show off my talons."

Both the senior demons were drawn to the pigeons' toes until they worked out his mistake.

"You mean talents," said Asmodeus knowingly.

"See, I can't even get that right."

"There's no point sulking about it, though, is there?" said Primordial.

Ian shrugged.

"You're not going to let him treat you like that, are you?" added Asmodeus.

"I thought I might."

"No. Where's your backbone? There must be a way we can help you get your own back," explained Asmodeus, another in a succession of people pushing their own agenda at his expense.

Ian's expression suggested otherwise. It wasn't just blank, it was decidedly opaque.

"Any ideas?" asked Primordial hopefully.

"What can I do? He's always been smarter than me. I'm just an idiot in a pigeon suit," replied Ian.

"Everyone has their own unique strengths and weaknesses."

"Not me. It's only weakness. My ideas never work. Good intentions always backfire. Catastrophe follows me like the string on the end of a kite."

"It might just be that your weaknesses are in fact your strengths," said Asmodeus.

"Yeah right," said a confused Ian. "How would that work?"

"Because it's random," said Asmodeus as a revelation smacked him between the eyes. "We've been struggling to formulate a plan to remove Sandy because we've been trying to think too logically. Every idea we've thought of has had faults, reasons why it wouldn't work. But what if we didn't have a plan? A plan can't have faults if no one knows what it is," said Asmodeus.

"I don't get it," replied Ian.

"No, nor do I," added Asmodeus. "But that's the sheer brilliance of it."

"Is it?" replied Primordial, not quite on-board.

"Yes. Think about it. The shadows are driven by chaos. They don't have a plan, but they've still been pretty successful. We have to match chaos with chaos. And who's more chaotic than Ian?"

"No one springs to mind," replied Primordial.

"But what if I get that wrong?" asked Ian.

"It won't matter. You can't get it wrong when we have no idea what is right. If you just go on instincts then catastrophe will follow."

"Yes, but to who? It'll probably backfire and all land on me."

"Look, do you want to show your talents or not?" replied Asmodeus, not wishing to face up to the last question as part of his new devil-may-care attitude.

"I think so."

"Right. That's settled, then. What are you thinking about right now?"

Ian's mind was currently thinking about how many kestrels you could fit in the average-sized handbag. He thought it was about three. It didn't seem immediately relevant to their situation.

"You really don't want to know," suggested Ian.

"Ok, but if you were going to take on the shadows, how would you do it?" asked Asmodeus.

Ian did his best impression of mustering up his intelligence. A synapse collapsed at the effort. Chaos, he felt, was something that came naturally to him only when other people were around. There was little internal shame at causing yourself discomfort if there wasn't an audience to ridicule you for it. The larger the crowd, the bigger the embarrassment. But was it possible? Was there a way he might actually help for once? A voice, that he took to be his conscience, thought so. Must have been its first day at the office.

"Let them all out," he offered.

"Who?" asked Asmodeus.

"Everyone. Every single soul trapped here. I need a crowd."

"But it would be pandemonium!" said Asmodeus.

"I think that's the point, isn't it?" replied Primordial.

CHAPTER FOURTEEN

HEAVEN SENT

In theory, Roger's plan had been brilliantly conceived. He knew from past experience that the Soul Catcher in Hell had been broken. A small, metal ball had risen angelically from the heart of the machine before gravitating out into space to some unknown location. After that moment all activity from the device had stopped, to the delight of the shadow souls and the dismay of one Mr. Brimstone.

Shortly after this event, once they'd been rehoused amongst their new senior demon neighbours, they'd all witnessed the pass over of one rather cantankerous walrus. It had taken much longer than anticipated, which many had put down to the added pressure of performing for a new audience for the first time. The senior demons had got rather bored of all the waiting around and had, on several occasions, attempted to speed up the process through a combination of childish insults and gentle prods to the poor creature's abdomen. If anything, that appeared to extend, rather than shorten, the process.

When eventually the walrus made his final bow, the residual remains of his soul seeped out from its plastic vessol and the spectacle was as captivating as it always had been. The environment was illuminated by the energy of the last passing of life, and the light blue electricity dispersed out through the window and into the cosmos. Somewhere out there it would be collected, but no one for certain knew where.

HEAVEN SENT

Like Sandy before him, Roger had worked out, through his own observation, and conversations he'd overheard, the likely destination for this substance. It was being farmed and reused. The shadows were the ultimate example of the truth. One day this recycled energy would be used on humans to kick out the emotional portion of the soul and leave in place what remained. There was only one place where it could be collected. Only one place likely to have a sibling Soul Catcher.

Of course, theory and practicality were quite different art forms. Roger certainly hadn't predicted the excruciating velocity in which his, and the other creatures' souls, were being smashed around the multiverses like the world's longest tennis rally. There was nothing uniform about their journey. They had whizzed past and through almost every major galaxy, some on more than one occasion, and this roller coaster ride wasn't even close to ending.

Theory had made a rather short but compelling case in Roger's mind, and it didn't need much convincing to reach the conclusion it was the best idea he'd ever thought of. The basis to this brainwave was that if the Soul Catcher in Hell couldn't pick them up, then where else would they go? Their journey was currently giving them the answer. The challenge for the Soul Catcher in Heaven was that it was set to pick up neutral energy sources. And, although they certainly had traces of it, they also still had a streak of the other energies, too. Which meant the power of Limbo was also in play.

The fifth force was driven by, and an intrinsic part of, Celestium. If the metal was housed in the right instrument, then it omitted the fifth force and drew soul energy to it. Where there were two sources of this energy it was normally the case that the nearest would connect to the soul first. In principle, because the other universes rotated around Earth's central universe, Heaven was closer to Hell than it was to Earth and should be the natural end point. As long as the source was set to the right polarity, of course.

Roger felt certain that if he maintained the right attitude, practicality would catch up with theory and he'd be proved right yet again. A fact that the others would never hear the end of it.

After they'd covered more distance than the light omitted from most supernovas, their pace started to slow as they felt themselves approaching a patch of space so dark and suffocating that nothing could escape it. Every emotion was compressed inwards, combining and fusing into an ever-decreasing volume. The discomfort was over remarkably quickly, squeezed as they were through a cosmic sieve and released into a much more comfortable location.

Galactic peace was soon disrupted by a new force catching up with them like the hook on a fisherman's rod catching a mackerel. They were being reeled in to an unknown destination. A series of voices, cracked and distant, were fighting for attention as they approached a translucent barrier and a familiar white nozzle reached out to consume them. One by one they were sucked through it and deposited with a squelch into a bulbous glass chamber.

Then all was quiet.

*****

Wormwood was settling in for another in an endless procession of disappointing shifts. Through habit he'd punched in as usual, not that anyone was ever going to check. What was there to check on? The job was as one-dimensional as a catwalk model's personality. The sequence of his day would be as it always was.

Come to work.

Punch in.

Check the machine was still working.

Watch a steady trickle of light blue energy flow out of the bulb.

HEAVEN SENT

Ensure that it flowed along a complicated series of tubes, through a device constructed to instigate the process of condensation, until it collected in a large, sealed vat.

When the vat was full, which at his last guess happened at the end of most decades, turn the tap at the bottom and collect the contents.

Realise that you last turned the tap about three weeks ago and it probably wasn't worth checking today.

Sit down in bitter disappointment that there was nothing else to do today.

Spend the rest of the day contemplating how many angels you could fit on a pinhead.

Punch out.

Go home.

At the last count this was how the last one hundred and fifteen thousand, four hundred and eleven shifts had gone. Each one exactly the same. There were no teammates to share the monotony with. This was not a job that required support or management intervention. Wormwood was the only angel responsible for their Soul Catcher, a job previously both fulfilling and varied. How he used to revel in welcoming those positive souls to Paradise.

Back in the day they had an elaborately choreographed ceremony to make newcomers feel at home when they first received their vessels. Speeches, instructional demonstrations, a highly complicated dance routine and personalised bouquets were all perfectly co-ordinated like the opening ceremony of a major sporting event. How he missed it. Now there was just him and an extremely slow filling vat.

None of this tradition was necessary anymore because his job had been reassigned from welcoming committee to glorified recycling manager. Only remnants of souls ever reached him and even that was an event in itself. Maybe two or three reached the Soul Catcher in any given time period, although it was hard

HEAVEN SENT

to say exactly as they took so long to process it became a skill to identify individual samples.

It hadn't just been Wormwood's job profile that had changed over time. His character had been gradually affected, too, like the slow movement of a continental drift. Everything was now a chore. If pessimism and bitterness were Olympic events, Wormwood would have more medals than the historical achievements of all European countries combined. Even though the repetitiveness of existence had caused his change in outlook, any suggestion of changing it would be met by an equal level of animosity.

Wormwood stretched out his tall, muscular frame along the copper oxide-afflicted chaise longue that faced the machine. He squirmed uncomfortably to readjust the position of the stumpy wings that drooped out of his shoulder blades. They'd never been used for their intended purpose, but apparently it was poor manners to have them grafted off. Then, as he'd done countless times before, his eyelids clenched together and his head collapsed backwards for the remainder of his shift.

Before the grip of sleep took him on some disappointing dream sequence, he was woken by four bursts of noise, one after the other. When he looked up to identify the source, four electric blue clouds were whizzing around the inside of the Soul Catcher pretending to be in a complicated game of chase me. He stood up and approached the machine. This wasn't normal, and he was very familiar with what normal looked like. Placing his ear against the glass, he was certain he heard a pathetic little roar.

"Great," he said in a tone of voice that suggested it was anything but.

It had been such a long time since a situation of this nature had occurred that most of the emergency manuals were still written in an old style of language which few truly understood. Wormwood opened a drawer in a white-painted cabinet and removed a dusty

HEAVEN SENT

manual. As he opened it several pages floated down onto the overgrown grass beneath his feet. After much page-turning, he stopped and started to read the instructions out loud.

"Placeth yee vessolith yonder fennel." He sighed and reached for a small torch on a cord that was attached to the side of the cabinet.

Into the distance he turned the torch on and off in a stream of indecipherable code and waited. After what seemed like an age a tall, blonde female turned the corner between two white-domed houses, each with a cross sticking out of the top. Across her arms were a stack of flaccid bodies, arms and legs hanging on either side.

"Wormwood," she said as she arrived. "Did you have to bother me?"

"Apparently so, Muriel. I'm overjoyed about it, as you can see."

Muriel's hair caught in the breeze and flicked around her face as she moved mesmerisingly towards the Soul Catcher. She attached one of the vessels to the valve and gave Wormwood a nod.

"Presseth thine lever and mindeth yee digits," he said, following the book's guidance as best he could.

Nothing happened.

The four souls continued to fly around the sphere with the certainty of a sunrise.

"Disappointing, but unsurprising," he said.

"What does the computer say?" asked Muriel.

Wormwood moved towards a glass screen where four solitary entries were listed on the left-hand side. Each name was written in a strange type of font and flashed red intermittently.

"What luck," said Wormwood depressingly. "They're abnormal."

"I'd say anything arriving here is pretty abnormal, Wormwood. Do you need me to get the 'special' selection?" she said.

"Nothing would please me more," he replied, his mouth curled into a grimace. The wrinkles, evident in his face most days, were multiplying like they'd been soaked in water.

While Muriel disappeared to collect whatever was meant by 'special' selection, Wormwood continued to stare dejectedly into the mists of the Soul Catcher. How could they be here? It had been the equivalent of a thousand years since the last one reached them, and now there were four. It was beyond comprehension and, more importantly, the well-heeled laws of physics.

When Muriel eventually returned she was carrying a menagerie of animal suits each made from a fine silk, beautifully sewn in gold thread. Vessols weren't plastic here, much too bulky and uncomfortable to wear for day-to-day purposes. It was very difficult to go jogging wearing plastic: it led to awful chaffing around the crotch area. No, silk was the best option in these parts. It was easy to collect and versatile to work with. Here souls had always been free to do as they chose. Back in the day there were whole shopping centres dedicated to the tailoring of new collections for all possible occasions.

Souls had their outfits for day-to-day use and then a series of others for special events. Santa outfits for Christmas, ones with elaborate fascinators for annual hat day, and special loose-fitting, tracksuits for jogging in. But no one tended to go with the 'special' selection unless they were about to attend a very special fancy dress party.

Muriel attached the first of these unusual all-in-one costumes to the valve as before and signalled to her colleague, who once again 'pulleth the lever'. The silk expanded as the first soul entered its new abode. Quite unlike the plastic versions, which had a habit of flying off the valve with the pressure placed upon them and careering off into the distance, these ones placed the recipient calmly down on the turf.

HEAVEN SENT

Abe looked out at the new world around him. A vast city of white-domed, single-room houses stretched out in every direction. On the top of each of these was a selection of religious symbols highlighting the faith of the occupant. Stars of David, crosses, crescent moons, and nine-pointed stars were just some of the examples he could see.

On the horizon a towering wall encircled the edge of the city. Crawling above it, desperate to break through, a thick infestation of brambles topped the wall like natural barbed wire. A rainbow crossed the city overhead, but its colours were dull and jaded. Abe was convinced that he saw the indigo portion flicker off for a moment only for it to return once the owner had put another coin in the meter.

In the centre of the city, raised up slightly on a hill, was a white structure whose roof perched upon a series of columns. A dimly lit beacon projected out into the sky which had an autumnal feel to it. Light grey clouds ran across the horizon, late for appointments with low-pressure systems.

Abe noticed that the two figures watching him wore differing levels of frowns. They didn't seem at all pleased to see him. He walked forward to greet them and found his body moved easily in its brown silk skin. Two small horns protruded from either side of his head and the material under his belly sagged a little, just as it always had. Although he couldn't see them, he swore he felt two wings sticking out of his shoulder blades. Significantly, and happily from Abe's point of view, there was no sloth tied to his abdomen.

The male character attempted to move his body around like he was wearing an invisible hula hoop: he swayed his arms weakly in the air, a depressing one-man Mexican wave. He mumbled incoherently some forgotten chant until the whole proceedings got too much for him.

"It's no good. I can't remember any of it, and what's more, I frankly can't be bothered to," exclaimed

Wormwood, having tried to re-create the welcoming dance but failing dismally.

"Is this what I think it is? It is, it really is. Oh, bless the Lord. I never gave up on you, I knew you'd come for me," said Abe, falling to his knees and burying his head in the overgrown lawn.

"What are you doing here?" said Wormwood. "It's not that I'm not pleased to see you. Actually, it is that I'm not pleased to see you. You've ruined my ridiculously pointless schedule."

"My prayers have been answered. I never imagined that *He* would be a disciple. God does work in mysterious ways."

"Who's *He*?" spat Wormwood.

At that very moment the next soul filled the silk vessel which Muriel had just attached to the nozzle and a lion expanded in front of them.

"Him!" said the ox in reverence.

"That's a lion, not a disciple. Disciples tend to be fisherman, tax collectors or carpenters."

"You should see my collection of ornate spoons, they're magnificent," said Roger, shaking out his golden fabric and smiling at the realisation that he, too, had a pair of wings. "I love self-improvement."

Once the remaining souls of Elsie and Vicky had been removed and placed in their gibbon and spider silks, respectively, and Wormwood was satisfied that most of his task list had been returned to normal, the inquisition began.

"Explain," said Wormwood, bicep-laden arms resting defensively on his hips.

"Transfer," said Roger.

"We don't do them."

"Holiday."

"Not been popular here since the Middle Ages."

"Sabbatical."

"Four random reincarnates, previously assigned to Hell, are not allowed to go on sabbaticals."

"Ah, that's where you're wrong," said Roger, never in doubt of his own self-confidence. "There's five of us."

"Four," repeated Wormwood grumpily, having quickly counted in case he'd missed someone.

"The other one's not here yet," added Vicky. "I knew he was slow, but who'd have thought that his soul would be sluggish as well?"

"I literally can't wait for his arrival," lied Wormwood. "Heaven's so unbelievably busy at this time of the millennium."

*****

"I-Spy with my little eye, something beginning with S," proposed Accountant J.

"Sky?"

"Guess again."

"Is it by any chance…Soul Catcher?" said Accountant M.

"Yes!"

No one chose to play I-Spy. It was only ever played as a last resort, a filler for boredom when no other options were available. It was predominantly played on long car journeys before the invention of mobile phones and mini-DVD players. And because of that, the following argument will almost never be heard.

"Mum, I'm bored."

"Stop complaining, your father's trying to drive. Why don't you watch a film or play games on your phone."

"Urgh, it's sooooo boring! Can't we play I-Spy instead?"

"Certainly not. Too much I-Spy is bad for your eyes. You need a rest from it."

"Please, Mum."

"You know the rules. We have a strict one-hour-a-day I-Spy limit."

HEAVEN SENT

Much to the Accountants' annoyance they'd built a huge, but currently inactive, Soul Catcher before they'd had the good sense to invent television. Since the collective euphoria of seeing the Soul Catcher come to life, nothing interesting had happened. Nothing. There was an expectation that a flood of souls would be winging their way to the machine in order for them to have jobs that were meaningful and life-enhancing. Instead they'd watched mournfully as regular pulses of energy shot out into the sky and returned empty-handed.

It's hard to live happily when you can't fulfil your purpose. They were Accountants without so much as a spreadsheet to pore over. There was nothing to count. They'd considered diversifying into auditing, but having started counting up blades of grass, someone suggested I-Spy might be more entertaining. They were wrong of course, very wrong.

The question remained as to whether the machine actually worked at all. Just because sound and light came out of it didn't mean it was effective. Sound and light came out of a toy gun but it wasn't likely to win any duels. And if the machine didn't work, the situation was even more depressing. It meant they'd built it needlessly. In that situation there would be nothing for it to 'catch' other than the attention of passing UFOs.

"Your go," said Accountant J.

"I spy with my little eye, something beginning with A," sighed Accountant M.

"Oh, that's a tough one."

"No, it isn't."

"Um...air."

"Can you see air?"

"No, but I know it's there."

"Which would be the correct answer if we were playing I-Know rather than I-Spy."

"Fair enough. Um...Acute angle."

"No, that's two As anyway."

"Give me a clue."

"They're sitting all around you contemplating suicide or desperately trying to refold themselves into more acceptable forms," said M, specifically looking in Z's direction, who had repeatedly attempted to refold himself since the machine came alive. It hadn't gone well. Once you've folded paper once or twice it's almost impossible to remove the creases. His current form was best described as a scrunched-up ball of paper.

"Oh, this is a really hard one. I don't know. Give up," said J.

"Accountants," answered M coldly.

"Good one, I'd never have got that. Who's next?"

"I think we've probably exhausted this game for now. We'll have nothing left to fill eternity if we carry on."

Accountant M waddled over to the console where Accountant A was still desperately staring into the screen.

"Sir, the troops are getting restless."

"Are they?" said A, turning his head to discover most of his platoon were lying dormant on the ground. "They look alright."

"Did I say troops?" replied the swan, "I meant me."

"Patience."

"You said that last time. Maybe we should face up to the fact that all of this was a complete waste of time."

"I won't accept that. Remember your place, M."

"Have you tried any of the other buttons," he said, pointing to the console.

"All of them in multiple combinations."

"Perhaps you should ask the ball what we should do?" said M, mainly joking.

It was better than nothing. Accountant A typed in the shortest message he could think of. Help. The screen blinked back at him before a message started to type a response.

HEAVEN SENT

'I thought you were meant to be helping me!'

"I wasn't expecting that," said A.

"Type something else," suggested M eagerly.

He typed, 'Why?'

'Because only one part of me is here.'

"What do you think that means?" asked M.

Somehow, Accountant A had always known that for the machine to work it would need an energy source and it would have to come from a piece of Celestium. The world had been on standby ever since the last traces of the substance had been dug up and stolen from the quarry just over in the distance. He'd also expected that the only way the Celestium could return here was with help from a soul. But not part of a soul.

'Who are you?' typed Accountant A.

'David...SYNTAX ERROR – John,' came the confused reply.

"That's odd. I didn't know our computer could overrule itself."

"Don't ask me," said M. "I'm still getting over the fact that it works at all."

'Where is the other bit of your soul?' typed A as part of his further enquiries.

'God knows,' came the reply.

*****

John felt that Sandy's demise had an unsatisfactory conclusion about it. He'd been on the end of both Sandy's harm and his help over the years, but no one deserved the fate he himself had once suffered. The metal boxes were the cruellest of Hell's devices for delivering discomfort. The solitude and loneliness of them had the effect of driving you insane as you fought off the voices that you brought with you, and some that seemed to appear from nowhere.

The memory of his own experience sent a convulsion through the air, as his undefined mass made the light from torches bend more than normal and fiddled with forces that weren't supposed to be interrupted. Because he filled all the space in between the 'stuff' he was as much in the prison cell as Sandy was. He could see him lying in the middle of one, curled up in the foetal position and cowering from unseen horrors.

John had heard a variety of voices on his many visits to Hell. One particular voice came to him on his first entrance to Hell. He'd always believed it had come from his father, or at least the father he thought he'd had at the time. Knowing now how complicated his many lives had been, there were potentially fifty others who might lay claim to that title. He was clear that anything related to those people had been used to manipulate him for the good of others. That voice had said, quite clearly, as if the orator was whispering softly in his ear:

"Find the way."

And he had, although it was still unclear where it was taking him.

A second distinct voice had spoken to him during his time in the box. It had offered him the advice which had led to this current chain of events. It had uttered exactly the same words that Baltazaar had given him during his exorcism, so it was easy to believe that's whose voice it had been. But it couldn't be.

Baltazaar was only able to speak to the positive part of his soul and at that time it was briefly attached to Nash, until the Limpet Syndrome had released it. If it wasn't Baltazaar who spoke, and it wasn't his father, who had been influencing him? And, given how long he'd been here, why had he heard it so infrequently? After all this time there were still so many questions. He was tired of pushing the heavy rock up the hill for the amusement of others. It was time to discover the truth.

"I can't decide if things here have improved or not," said Brimstone, watching Silica getting comfortable in the mightiest throne, home to many owners' butts in his history of working Hell.

"Same smell, different depth," replied John.

"I thought you were meant to be helping me put all this back the way it was," huffed Brimstone.

"One step at a time. Sandy won't bother anyone for a while and now all we have to do is figure out how to deal with this lot."

"Any thoughts on that?"

"Yes, I do."

"And?"

"I just whispered something into Ian's ear."

"Ian! You have met Ian, haven't you? The walking catastrophe with fewer noticeable skills than a beetroot."

"Of course. Everyone needs their chance to shine."

"What did you tell him?"

"Find the way."

CHAPTER FIFTEEN

DON'T DIE

How long would it take for the average person to go clinically insane if they were on the receiving end of the same question asked repeatedly? An hour, half, six minutes? It would be a lot quicker for most of us than it was for Grace. She wasn't equipped with the right genes for irritation. It washed over her like a rock at the bottom of a waterfall.

He'd asked her at the airport.

And on the flight.

Again on landing at JFK.

In the taxi.

At the hotel reception.

In the hotel room, and about a hundred times in between.

Always the same question, and Scrumpy was not in the slightest bit perturbed by the lack of a sufficient response.

"What's it like being a god?"

Eventually Grace tried to answer.

"Difficult to say. It is what it is."

"No, it's not, it's amazing. Can you move stuff by just looking at it?"

"I'm not a Jedi."

"Can you turn anything into food?"

"Not that I'm aware of."

"Can you bring people back from the dead?"

"I think time will tell."

If Scrumpy had found London bemusing it was nothing compared to the intensity of New York City.

DON'T DIE

He'd never seen so much glass. It was like the city was running a secret competition to see how much of it each building could use without falling over. There was almost as much glass as there were people. Millions of them, tightly compressed into an area equivalent to St Mary's, the largest of the Scilly Isles. The most intriguing quality of these people was their almost total lack of fear.

On the journey from the airport to their hotel they'd encountered this quality head on. Their distinctive yellow taxicab had swerved, and sometimes aimed for, quick-paced pedestrians whose reaction had been a mixture of total oblivion, overexuberant hand signals and a crescendo of colourful language. He'd learned a number of interesting new expressions as a result. Douchebag, numbnuts, and shitbucket were just three of the expressions he'd stored for future use. After all, he wanted to fit in.

Grace, unsurprisingly, had been unfazed by the whole experience. This was just another place full of illogical and impatient people with nothing more important in their lives than getting to work on time or picking a fight with the next man. None of the world made sense to her, so all of it looked very much the same. Plus she had way too much on her mind to let things like this distract her.

There was no proof to say the man in the photograph was still in New York. And that in itself had put Grace into shutdown. When something remained unclear it was a puzzle. Puzzles would consume her energy. Pieces of information flew around in her brain until they made the correct conclusion. Anything else was a distraction. Which included Scrumpy's inquisition.

Lacking the right level of detail made the conclusion a hypothesis, and that had to be tested to confirm its validity. If the man in the photo had left the city, there was no way to tell where he might have gone. And only picking up the trail here would give any clues to it. Grace had worked out that the other man in the picture was Rogier Hoffstetter, and he at least was still in New York. It had been confirmed by Grace's analysis of his social media feeds.

Nash, Grace and Scrumpy walked down Third Avenue, doing their best to avoid the onrushing human traffic or being identified as foreigners. As they strolled, something caught Scrumpy's eye and he dashed to his right. Of all the things he'd expected to see in this giant, alien city, this wasn't one of them. It had transported him out of this monstrous field of metal towers and concrete walkways to the heather on the hilltops of Bryher, where he'd watch them scurry and hop timidly amongst the gorse bushes. But here they were in the city. Rabbits.

These ones didn't have the freedom of their British cousins, trapped claustrophobically inside tiny metal cages, eyes begging for the observers through the window to release them. The pet shop's window would be the only view they'd know until that miracle occurred. Scrumpy placed a hand to the glass and a tear welled in his eye in mutual sympathy for those on both sides of the glass.

"Can we get one?" said Scrumpy to Nash as the other two joined him at the window.

"It's a little impractical. How would we get it home?"

"I don't want to take it home. I want to release it."

"These aren't wild. I can't imagine what they'd think of Central Park with all the joggers and sunbathers. They wouldn't survive in this environment for a week."

"But look at that one, he's so sweet with his little white tail and floppy ears."

Nash followed Scrumpy's finger and made eye contact with what was a rather dejected specimen. The rabbit fixed its stare on Nash, a technique it had learned from those that had previously been picked out as suitable pets, and did its best to look desperate.

"I'm sorry, Scrumpy, we have more important things to do today," he explained, taking Scrumpy's hand and encouraging him to continue towards their intended destination.

There wasn't much further to walk. When they saw the distinctive red pillar crossed by a solid yellow awning, they knew they'd arrived. Six hundred and thirty-three Third Avenue, the location of the Swiss Consulate.

Inside, shiny, black quartz tiles reflected the light from neon bulbs positioned around the entrance room. A rope barrier criss-crossed its way up to a series of cubicles, where smartly dressed staff waited to hand out visas or answer citizens' questions. How many Swiss nationals lived or visited the city was perhaps measured in how quiet it was inside. The three of them joined the short queue and waited to be called.

"How can I help you?" said a smiling lady from behind one of the desks.

"We were hoping to find these men," said Grace, presenting the woman with the black and white newspaper cutting.

"I'm afraid I only do visas," replied the woman.

"You just said, 'how can I help you?'," replied Grace.

"I know, but..."

"Can you tell us where we can find them, then?" asked Grace again.

"It's a figure of speech," she added.

"You mean a lie," corrected Grace.

"I'm sorry?"

"You said, 'how can I help you?', but you meant 'I'll only help you if you need a visa.' So why don't you just say that, if that's what you mean?"

"Because I didn't know if you needed a visa or not."

"I don't."

"I know that now, but I didn't before did I," replied the woman, getting quite agitated under the interrogation.

"Do you know who these two people are?" asked Grace, changing tack.

"Well, yes…"

"So, you can help us, then," added Grace.

"I didn't say that."

"But you do know where they are?"

"Yes. No. Maybe."

"It can't be all of them, can it?"

"Yes, I know where they are. No, I'm not at liberty to tell you. And maybe I'll call security."

"How would I make an appointment with Mr. Hoffstetter?"

"That depends. Are you a head of state, government official, diplomat or major celebrity," she said ironically, given that a pre-teenage girl was standing in front of her.

"No."

"Shame," she said, motioning to the next person in the queue to come forward.

"I am a god, though," said Grace casually.

"Security!"

Grace placed her finger to her lips and converted the two onrushing security men into statues. If she wasn't going to get co-operation she'd have to take matters into her own hands. At the back of the room a solid wooden door prevented unwanted intruders from the heart of the building. A fingerprint recognition system was attached to the side panel and the finger of a doorman, frozen next to it, was very easily borrowed.

Grace headed up the main stairway to the offices on the first floor. It was her instincts that no president would want to stare out of the ground floor, and the risks of injury would be greater closer to the pavement. Upstairs a series of old-fashioned, glass-fronted offices led off from the corridor. In one of them, at the other end, she found who she was looking for.

Rogier and the Clerk were standing hunched over a large world map spread out over a conference table. A couple of miniature UN flags on cocktail sticks had been pierced into certain countries. In particular, Suriname, Djibouti, Nauru and Switzerland. On a pad next to it a list of countries had been struck through with red ink. Grace replaced her finger on her lips and the conversation in the room continued as it had done before she'd made her way upstairs and into their company. It soon stopped when they realised their number had increased by one.

"Where did you come from?" said Rogier in shock.

"The door," said Grace accurately.

"But you're not supposed to be here," said Rogier, reaching towards his mobile phone.

"There's no point calling them. I can disappear as quickly as I arrived."

The Clerk sat down in his chair, his bones already aching from the exertions of leaning over the table to consider the state of their meagre coalition. He analysed the young, single-minded girl in front of him. White flesh and hair, light blue irises that almost shone. He smiled to himself at the familiarity. "What's your name?"

"Grace."

"And how did you get in here?"

"I walked in," she said.

"Why didn't someone stop you?" demanded Rogier.

"They couldn't," answered the Clerk before the girl could respond.

"Why not?"

"Evolution," replied the Clerk.

"I have two companions downstairs that are most likely being cavity-searched at this very moment," said Grace. "I'd like you to send for them. One is a middle-aged man and the other an eight-year-old boy with frizzy hair and way too much energy."

"It's fine," said the Clerk as he caught Rogier's expression of disbelief. "They're not dangerous."

Rogier picked up his phone and rang his bodyguards. Soon Nash and Scrumpy were escorted up and plonked into seats around the map table.

"Why are you here, Grace?" asked the Clerk.

"I've come to find you."

"Me? Why me?"

"Because I have questions."

Grace proceeded to outline the sequence of events that had brought them here, what she knew about herself, and what had been told to her by Byron. She also highlighted the conclusions she'd made as to who she was and what her purpose had been. Even though some of it was too far-fetched for Rogier to accept, all of it was delivered factually and without omissions. Once she'd finished speaking everyone fell silent.

The Clerk stood up and paced the room.

"What am I?" asked Grace, to split the silence.

"You're the third coming," said the Clerk.

"The what?" asked Rogier.

"A god will come who has only neutral interests to govern all souls with that predisposition. I assumed it would be David, but clearly I misinterpreted the situation."

"A god! That's impossible," said Rogier.

"Nothing is impossible," added the Clerk.

"Yes, it is," said Scrumpy, interjecting for the first time. "I can't eat an entire blue whale in an hour, can I?"

"It's theoretically possible."

"Sail across the Atlantic Ocean in a box of matches with no oars?"

"That would depend on the size of the match box, wouldn't it?"

"Ok, what about if I wanted to be Henry the Eighth?"

"That's impossible."

"But you said…"

"It was a figure of speech," replied the Clerk.

"We came here because we want to help you," said Grace.

"You can't help me, I'm afraid. My time is drawing to an end and soon I will have to face my demons."

"Then we are here to help mankind."

"That you can certainly help with. The message 'don't die' appears to be working but we cannot hold back the tide forever. One of the dead ends must be opened."

"Dead ends?" asked Nash.

"Yes. Every soul must be placed in the afterlife somewhere. There are theoretically three possibilities. Limbo's expansion proves that none are still open."

"But how can we open them?" asked Nash.

"You can't, but it's possible she can," replied the Clerk.

"How?" asked Grace.

"By making the ultimate sacrifice."

Grace knew exactly what he meant. The exact details of her destiny had been clear to her the moment she witnessed and understood the changing nature of the storm that gathered over Tresco when they sailed away on Scrumpy's boat. The concept did not frighten her as it would a normal human. There was logic in what had to be done if the wider human race was to survive.

"What is your role in all this?" asked Grace.

"I'm responsible for it. I sowed the first seed that grew into mankind's disaffection with gods and by doing so instigated Baltazaar's desire to punish us. He first attempted to achieve it using Emorfed."

"I helped John Hewson stop that," said Nash. "He borrowed me for a while."

"So, John Hewson was the last of the twelve, too," said the Clerk. "I never recognised him, although his vessol choice was his own."

"I'm the physical manifestation of Emorfed," said Grace. "Nash is my father."

"As is John," added the Clerk, reflecting on his first impressions of Grace and why he'd felt such immediate comfort.

"What are the maps for?" asked Scrumpy who'd lost interest in the adult conversation and was poring over all the countries of the world.

"We have been trying to raise a coalition," replied Rogier.

"It's not going very well, is it?" replied Scrumpy rather too accurately.

"No."

"The people of the world are wrapped up in their own self-interests. Their reaction will come when it's too late to repair. Time has run out. If we can't raise a coalition of nations we must look to bolster our defences through other means."

"What are the troops for? Isn't the 'don't die' policy enough?" asked Nash.

"No," replied Grace. "The troops are needed to take on the gods, a distraction strategy, I would think."

"Exactly," replied the Clerk.

"A distraction from what?" said Nash.

"From Grace's battle with the other gods."

"NO!" shouted Nash, bursting out of his seat and advancing on the Clerk who had moved to pacing in front of the window. "She's done enough. I will not allow her to be put in further danger."

"But she is Nash. She's already in danger. It's her very purpose for being alive."

Suddenly the pane of glass directly behind them shattered. A bullet, aimed from the building across the street, accelerated through the room and into the small of Nash's back. He fell forward into the arms of the Clerk.

"NASH!" screamed Scrumpy.

"Everyone down on the floor," shouted Rogier as further bullets ricocheted into the room. Everyone hit the deck.

DON'T DIE

Grace put her fingers to her lips and the room froze. She moved towards Nash.

"Nash, remember. Don't die."

CHAPTER SIXTEEN

VICTORY

While time was at a standstill no further danger would befall those that Grace had left behind in the Swiss Consulate. What mattered now was finding those responsible. There was no rush. Time would be reset only once she'd discovered who had pulled the trigger. The bullet's trajectory, through the first-floor plate-glass window, then Nash's flesh and finally the wall, suggested the shooter was across the road and slightly above them. The view across to the other side of the street suggested two possible culprits.

The thirty-storey glass skyscraper to the right-hand side was built almost entirely from windows and offered a million opportunities to line up the shot. It's foreboding nineteen sixties' frame loomed overhead, mocking her optimism. Hundreds of office workers were confined like poultry hens behind floors of glass, kidnapped by their swivel chairs and the unstoppable disease of capitalism that beamed out of luminescent screens. A shorter wing of the building with a flat roof jutted out from the third floor and infiltrated part of the pavement.

A blonde-haired head was just visible, presumably lying on the concrete roof facing towards her. His body was frozen in position, unable to retreat and unaware of those who would soon be in pursuit. In his hands something conspicuously black clashed with the lighter-coloured surroundings of the rooftop. This information was enough to set Grace in motion. As she retraced her earlier steps through the building she

VICTORY

stopped to borrow a pair of handcuffs that were hanging from a security guard's belt. Outside on the urban stage all its actors had been placed on pause as an unscheduled game of musical statues was in full swing. Drivers were in mid-gear change, cyclists in half-rotation around their pedals, a dog with a leg cocked against a fire hydrant in mid-urination. At times like this the world was hers to mould.

Anyone with even an ounce of greed or envy in them would immediately be corrupted by this level of power. Banks would have been plundered, people abused and future outcomes changed. In the case of Grace it was just a useful talent only used in the most important situations when all other options had failed. Stopping time came with responsibility. She had no evidence as to the side effects that might arise from such a power. She certainly wasn't prepared to damage anything in pursuit of her own personal gain. That part of the deal had always been unspoken since the beginning.

The discovery of her ability had occurred by accident when she was five years old. In an attempt to quieten the already vocal three-year-old Scrumpy, she'd gently placed her finger to her lips to suggest calm, and calm she got. Scrumpy's incessant chatter stopped with every other noise. Along with it the wind ceased blowing, the rain stopped falling and the Earth welcomed her to a lonely stage. Over the years, through experimentation and intrigue, she'd discovered she could stop and speed up time, but never reverse it. She'd tried only once.

One time too many.

As a young girl, fascinated with scientific exploration, she'd attempted to understand how a fish was able to breathe underwater. She would lift her goldfish out into the air to examine its gills and to test how long it might survive outside its familiar aquatic environment. Not long was the answer. Each time she would keep the fish out of water for a slightly longer period. Unsurprisingly, this eventually led to the untimely death of the fish. She attempted to bring the fish back to life, not because she had any affection for the creature, only to repeat the experiment and continue her desperate quest for knowledge. The result of dabbling with time to achieve this resurrection had unusual consequences.

Her original shimmering blonde hair was shocked to pure white as colour ran for cover threatened by some invisible fear. In each house on the island of Bryher every single light bulb blew simultaneously, plunging the island atmospherically back to the eighteenth century. It troubled her to lack the know how as to why pausing time or speeding it up was so easy, while reversing it had such dangerous outcomes. The only plausible explanation was that the future could be changed, but never the past.

She weaved across the normally busy Third Avenue and up into the building in front of her, easily gaining access to the second floor via an old-fashioned iron staircase on the exterior of the building. As she accessed the building through a fire escape, a number of people were in the midst of a retreat, their faces frozen with fear from what had just been a startling noise from the roof above their office. These terrified mannequins, each heading in the opposite direction than she was, led the way to the perpetrator like a line of breadcrumbs. Up another fire escape that led to the roof, and there he was. Leaning up against the stone lip of the roof, still clutching his firearm, a bullet in mid-exit from the chamber.

The man's arms were presented to her perfectly, already close enough together to allow the handcuffs to be placed around them with ease. Once she was satisfied his escape had been prevented she placed her finger to her lips and the bullet, after some delay, burst out of the gun with a muffled thud. It was the last bullet he would be able to fire.

VICTORY

Anyone with even a minor sense of humour would have found the sight of an armed assassin, utterly bewildered as to how his hands had instantly become shackled, completely hilarious. A sense of humour was Scrumpy's thing: Grace didn't even find the sight of a man falling off a skateboard funny.

"What's happening?!" shouted Victor, trying and failing to release his hands from the cuffs and dropping the gun to the floor in the process.

"I need to talk to you."

"Grace! I just saw you over there."

"Yes, and now I am here."

"How did you do that?"

"Lots of practice," she replied.

"I was trained by the British Government for two decades and even I couldn't have been that stealthy."

"Did they teach you how to stop time?"

"I must have been ill that day," he replied sarcastically. "Wait until Byron hears about this. He's been desperate to work out how you managed to escape from Bryher when he set your house on fire. This explains it."

Victor sat on the ground refusing to struggle from his predicament. He knew how handcuffs worked. The movies might show people easily wriggling out of them, but the truth was, unless you chopped your hands off or someone opened them, it was impossible. Struggling was pointless: the only muscle capable of helping him out of the situation would be his tongue.

"Your move, Grace."

"Why did you do it? Why did you shoot Nash?"

"Because he jumped up in front of the other guy as I took the shot. Collateral damage. If you put yourself in danger, then danger has a habit of biting you."

"You killed a good man. Scrumpy will be devastated."

"I don't care. We must all face death. Nash has been closer than most over the years. It was just his time."

VICTORY

"We'll see," replied Grace, thinking about what she whispered to him shortly after she put her finger to her lips. "Why do you do it?"

"Why do I do what?"

"Follow him. The Devil. What good has he done you?"

"Money, and lots of it."

"And this time, to kill the Clerk, what has he offered you?"

"Nothing as such," said Victor. "He protects me."

"Does he? What about your little problem?" said Grace. "What has he done to help you with that?"

Victor's steely determination in the face of his captor took a turn. How could she possibly know about his OCD? Although he'd been in her general area, they'd never even spoken. To his knowledge no one could have told her that information, few people knew the truth, and most of them had been shot for doing so.

"How do you know?"

"Byron can talk to you even when he's not here, can't he?" said Grace.

"Yes."

"And you know why, don't you?"

"Because he connects to the negative part of my soul."

"And you know he can't speak to me because I don't have that part."

"What of it?" Victor replied curtly.

"But I *do* have the neutral part in me."

"And...so do I," exhaled Victor deeply, suddenly aware of his and Byron's mistake.

How did they miss it? Byron had never even raised the possibility that she might be able to communicate to almost anyone on the planet, while neither Byron nor Baltazaar could return the favour and eavesdrop on her. She could enter his thoughts, explore his experiences, deduce his deepest weaknesses, and there was nothing Victor could do about it.

VICTORY

"You know it's not your fault, don't you?" said Grace calmly.

"I don't know what you're talking about."

"Yes, you do. You can't hide it from me. You feel responsible for her death, don't you? Although you followed your orders to the letter, the result cost her her life."

"Yes," he whispered solemnly.

Early on in his career, when life was simpler and destinies had yet to be written, Victor had been involved in a raid on the house of a Russian diplomat who was blackmailing a key member of the British Government. The Russian held incriminating evidence about a business deal being struck to secure a long-term energy supply for the British Power Board. The Minister in question had offered several bribes and favours to a corrupt and powerful oligarch in order to lower the contract's costs.

Unknown to the Minister, his cellphone and emails were all being tracked and recorded before being used to blackmail him. The Secret Service were called to break into the diplomat's house in London and steal any evidence that could be used to damage the administration. If they failed, the exposé would shake the Government to its foundations and tarnish the future career of a highly regarded rising star. The mission was successful in retrieving the evidence, but ended in disaster.

"You don't know what it's like," said Victor, whose normal granite exterior was starting to show signs of cracking. "Even the best training in the world doesn't prepare you for the adrenaline. Every noise feels like the words of death sent to welcome you, every movement feels like your last. The darkness was everywhere that night, and time was running out for our planned exit. We were due to leave via a basement window on the ground floor, but as I reached the hall at the back of the house, I saw a light seep through the crack of the kitchen doorway. We trained our guns on the door, as still as possible, listening to the sound of movement on the other side as our brains somersaulted back to our contingency plans."

Victor choked under the weight of the memory, his still manacled hands placed together across his mouth.

"You will never be rid of that memory unless you make your peace with it," said Grace passively.

"Our training was very clear. If you believe you or the mission might be compromised you shoot first and explore later. It wasn't about survival for us, it was about anonymity. If we were captured or identified it would have created an international shit storm that would destroy our careers. I was young, I was keen to succeed, to prove myself. And I was first to act."

"And you fired."

"I shot a single bullet through the door and heard a body slump to the ground on the other side. When I opened the door, there she was."

"Who was she?"

"I found out much later that it was the diplomat's teenage daughter, she was about sixteen. My shot had struck her in the temple, it was instant, but…if I'd just opened the door. If I'd ignored my training her death would have been avoided."

"And how long did it take before you started acting strangely."

"A week, maybe longer. Every time I saw a door I had to check and check again that no one was behind it. At first I thought it would pass, but over time I became more and more agitated that my instincts were lying to me. I continued checking, three times before I was satisfied."

"You followed your orders. It was the process that was wrong, not you."

"The process didn't pull the trigger, did it? I did. Killing is easy when the person in the firing line is a criminal or an enemy of the state, but this girl was neither. Just an innocent, unfortunate bystander."

VICTORY

Victor slumped to the floor and buried his head in his navel to conceal his face from his own shame.

"Nash was innocent, too. He never asked for any of this. He was just always in the wrong place at the wrong time."

"I was following orders."

"I'm starting to see a nasty habit forming."

"I did what I had to."

"No, you were told to shoot the Clerk, not Nash. Why did you want the old man dead?"

"Because Byron commanded it. My whole career has been centred on discipline, following the leader."

"The Minister who you were trying to protect? It was Byron T. Casey, wasn't it?"

Victor nodded.

"Granddad didn't make good choices," replied Grace, reflecting how her own fleshy genetics were entwined with his. "And now because the Devil is walking in his place you feel a sense of accountability to him, or worse, a sense of fear as to what he can do to you."

Victor nodded again.

"What does he want you to do next?" asked Grace.

"He wants me to assassinate God," replied Victor.

"Then that is what you must do."

Victor stared at her in surprise, his brain rewinding the answer to ensure he'd heard it clearly. "What? You want me to do it, too?"

"In the not too distant future I will need someone who can handle a gun. Someone who can take the type of shot you fired at Nash this afternoon. If you agree to take that shot you will put things right, I promise you. Then you will be rid of him and your problem. Join me. There is still a future for you to make the right choice."

"But he is always with me. You cannot shake off the Devil that easily."

"No, you can't," came Byron's angry response.

"He's here!"

VICTORY

"Give him up, Victor."

"I can't."

"Tell her that I will soon destroy everyone and everything she loves."

Victor relayed the message.

"There is nothing that I love. Remind him, if you would, that my soul is incapable of it."

Victor felt like a divorce lawyer, relaying messages between a separating married couple who flatly refused to speak to each other directly.

"Victor, I need you to return to me immediately. We have work to do."

"He wants me to return to him."

"Don't go. Help us."

"I can't."

"Quite right. There is still so much pain that I can cause you, Victor Serpo. Loved ones I can still punish, memories I can tarnish, history rewritten," growled Byron over the telepathy connection.

"Yes, sir."

"Victor, do you know what 'grace' is?"

"I can't do this, I have made an allegiance."

"People of faith believe that grace is the love and mercy given by God because He desired us to have it, not necessarily because of anything we have done to deserve it. Well, God, by His actions, has given Grace to the world. By creating Emorfed He unintentionally created me. Grace is the salvation of sinners. I'm offering you that now, even though you may not deserve it. I do so because I believe you have yet to make your true mark on this world."

"I do not deserve your grace…but I gladly receive it," said Victor as kindness returned to his face. "What would you have me do?"

"You will pay a terrible price for this."

"I think it might be best if I write down what I want you to do," replied Grace in order to conceal her instructions from prying ears.

VICTORY

*****

Nash's body, covered by a shabby grey blanket, was being wheeled out of the Consulate office when Grace returned to the others. Scrumpy was slumped in the corner of the room red-faced and weeping uncontrollably. Rogier Hoffstetter had left with the corpse to arrange repatriation. The Clerk greeted the young girl with a gentle hug that felt honest but uneasy.

"Did you find who did it?"

"Yes."

"I was surprised to see you were suddenly missing from the room. There are powers inside you that I was not aware of."

"I only use them when it's completely necessary."

"And it will be again," said the Clerk.

"What do we do next?"

"Our coalition, the human race's meagre response to their own blindness, will march out and stand tall. I doubt it will be enough. Neither Baltazaar nor Satan will go quietly. They have little to lose. They will gather their forces and look to start all over again. We must travel to the old lands, the place of my birth, and there the end will come. If we are lucky other help may come."

Grace nodded in passive confirmation of her own part in what must happen. She'd known it for some time. It was the only way. She watched Scrumpy from the corner of her eye hugging his knees and rocking back and forward hysterically. His grief for a man who was no more a relation to him than she was, was palpable. Worse was to come for him. A shiver of guilt ran through her. It came from nowhere. It was an impossible instinct that had no place inside her. She ignored it: this was no time to evolve.

"What's the boy's connection to all this?" asked the Clerk aware of Grace's focus.

"It is nothing more than a fluke."

"I don't believe in them," replied the Clerk, frowning as he eased his elderly frame back into one of the chairs. "Who is he?"

"He's my adopted brother."

"And his real parents, who are they?"

"No one knows."

CHAPTER SEVENTEEN

SLEEP, PRAISE, REPENT

Roger and his friends had become quite used to their surroundings by the time Gary decided to put in an appearance. When his soul finally made its circuitous route from space to the glass bulb within the Soul Catcher it did so with a dull popping noise. Unlike the other animals, Gary's soul crawled around the edges, occasionally stopping completely for a celestial breather. The normal properties of a gas included such characteristics as low density, low viscosity and an ability to rapidly diffuse from one area to another due to something called Graham's Law.

When Mr. Graham first devised his law of diffusion he probably failed to consider testing how the equation might work if a gas existed that was one part emotional energy and one part sloth. Gases that act normally don't need to be coaxed out of a large, open nozzle with the assistance of a suction pump. When Gary's soul had finally been retrieved and placed inside a silk vessol it took several hours before the soul filled up all available space.

"Why."

"It's a good question," replied Wormwood sternly.

"Didn't."

"You have to be a bit patient, otherwise you might jump to conclusions," said Vicky.

"You."

"Anytime today, Gary," said Roger impatiently.

"Wait."

SLEEP, PRAISE, REPENT

"We constantly are," said Elsie with a giggle.

"For...me?"

"Because, Gary, waiting for you is comparable in speed and excitement to waiting for grass to grow."

Wormwood had heard enough. Not only was it inconceivable they were here, it was more than a little annoying. And it was definitely not his responsibility. The quicker he got rid of them, the sooner he could return to the mindless tedium he'd got so used to. After all, there was a class system. Everyone knew their place, and angelic mobility wasn't easily attained. Much to his consternation. Every time he'd requested a promotion he'd been given the same lame fob-offs. Eventually he'd given up applying completely. As a substitute to promotion he'd chosen belligerence and bitterness. He wasn't in a position to say whether it was a good substitute.

"Can we go and see him now?" said Abe, as excited as a five-year-old queuing up to see Santa, or at least to see a man who'd been paid minimal sums of money to pretend to be Santa based on the simple qualifications of being over fifty and owning a weathered face.

"See who?" asked Wormwood.

"God of course. May His grace illuminate His followers as they praise His purity."

"I think you'll be disappointed," said Wormwood.

"How can God be a disappointment?"

Wormwood considered for a moment why he was arguing when his central objective was to move these oddities to any place that was out of earshot and sight. Bitterness was as natural to him as illnesses were to a hypochondriac. It didn't matter what anyone else said, Wormwood was hard-wired to disagree. This had led the others, like Muriel, to believe that he thought very differently from the rest of them. Just some of his assertions and alternatives to recognised logic included that: God is actually a three-foot midget with a speech impediment; stars are just reflections from the world around us; and cling film is the most ridiculous invention in the history of humankind because it has the unique ability of clinging to everything other than the object you're trying to cover.

"I guess disappointments depend on expectations," Wormwood added. "And as you appear to have extremely high expectations I was just trying to soften the landing. I'd be more than happy to escort you there if you'd like to find out?"

"Definitely."

"I wonder if he will be as amazing as me?" said Roger. Even though Roger had now been to three of the four universes, it still hadn't deterred him from believing that he was the centre of all of them.

"Follow me," said Wormwood.

"Hold on, we just need to tie up the sloth."

"Not this time," said Abe with uncharacteristic aggression. "I'm not meeting my Lord with a mammal attached to my gut. God might mistake me for a kangaroo. It's not happening."

"Gary, it looks like you're going to have to walk."

"Fine."

They'd already left before his mouth had pronounced the F.

Wormwood guided them off the grass meadow and down onto a chalky, gravelled street. The white-domed houses were squeezed into every patch of available space, jumbled up with all the precision of a shanty town, each building identical to the next with the exception of the religious symbol that adorned the roof. Each had an entrance no more than five feet high and was sealed with a plain piece of wood to act as a door. They all had a solitary window, round and empty of glass, allowing wind, rain and wasps easy access. Not that they suspected snow was likely to be a very regular occurrence here.

They peered through the window of the nearest home where a crumpled-looking occupier sat bobbing continually in a tatty, old rocking chair. The silk of its vessol was grey and faded. There was no light inside the room other than that provided by the outside world. It was the same in every window they looked through. It was an odd sensation to be watching these 'people', seemingly restricted to their homes like animals in a zoo.

"What's wrong with them?" whispered Vicky.

"Wrong with them? There's nothing wrong with them," said Wormwood, annoyed by the accusation.

"Then why don't they move, or come outside for some fresh air or react when the gibbon jumps in front of the window and shouts 'boo' at them?"

"They're just old. Some of them have been here for thousands of years. The youngest amongst them is already about a thousand years old and stopped going to Communion about a century ago."

"Why don't they just pass over if they've had enough?" asked Vicky.

"They can't," replied Wormwood.

"You mean they're like that for eternity. Like vegetables."

"Of course. It's their reward for an unbending faith in God."

"That's not a reward, it's a sentence. They're prisoners in their own bodies. Why doesn't someone do something for them?"

"Do what?"

"Something to stop the suffering."

"But they're dead. There's not really another station on the line after this one," replied Wormwood.

"Of course there is," said Roger, opening the door of the nearest house and inviting himself in.

"What's he doing?"

"I'm not even sure he knows," said Vicky.

Roger approached the elderly woman, whose rocking chair was moving despite the fact that she was asleep. At the side of the chair a series of cogs and pulleys were attached to a small motor that kept the chair oscillating at an even pace. A gauge described

SLEEP, PRAISE, REPENT

three speed settings: sleep, praise and repent. Almost without thought Roger turned it from its current setting of sleep to repent.

One of the gears made a cranking groan as it engaged the belt for the first time in a generation. The motor mustered up as much power as its batteries would allow, and transferred the resulting energy to the gear with a jerk. The chair's speed increased. It quickly became clear why the setting was called repent. It was the internal feeling of guilt most people felt when they engaged it. Most people didn't include self-obsessed, sociopathic lions of course.

The chair was now moving at such a speed it was hard to make out the features of the person sitting in it. The old woman was starting to stir from her sleep, but not, sadly, before the chair catapulted her violently forward and through the open window. She landed on the chalky path in a crumpled heap. The shock of moving from sleep mode to repent mode in such a small time frame was evident on her face, a face that had spent much of the last three centuries with its eyes closed. She looked out at the world, gave a silent groan and the silk vessol ripped open at the frayed seams. Pop.

Out flew the light blue energy. It didn't have far to go. It would have been quicker for it to walk than be attracted to the Soul Catcher by the usual means.

"There you go," said Roger. "Piece of piss. They just need a push."

"Congratulations," said Wormwood in mock praise. "All you've done is move her from here to over there."

"You're welcome," replied Roger, walking away with his shoulders arched in victory.

"Has he always been like this or does he work on it?" asked Wormwood.

"I'd say it was a lot of both," replied Vicky.

SLEEP, PRAISE, REPENT

They continued tracking the path around the buildings, moving further into the city and closer to the centre.

"Why do they have different symbols on top?" asked Abe who'd been captivated with the variety of metal motifs on the summit of each house.

"It tells us which religion they believe in."

"My God is a Christian," said Abe resolutely.

"And his god," said Wormwood, pointing at an old man through the nearest window, "is Krishna."

"And you let him in!" said Abe.

"Of course. Positive is positive. It's only humans who have these warped ideas about which god they follow. It's perverse, really: more people in the history of mankind have died through religious war because no faction could agree which god was best, when all along no one was right."

"Why bother with the symbols, then?" said Vicky.

"Because even when they got here they couldn't leave their disputes behind them. They only wanted to associate with people of their own faith. Stupid, really."

"I only want to be next to those with crosses on," said Abe. "Religious freedom is a basic human right."

"I agree," replied Wormwood poignantly. "But if I'm not mistaken you are in fact some unspecified breed of cow."

"He's an ox," chirped Elsie. "I've checked, no testicles."

"It makes no difference really, as you won't be living in one of these houses anyway."

"I wouldn't want to," said Vicky sternly. "Too many ethnic minorities around here. I want to be near my own kind."

"Just with the other racists, then. Got it," replied Wormwood, pretending to make a note in an invisible notepad.

Vicky added angels to the groups who offended her.

SLEEP, PRAISE, REPENT

"You don't really get a choice where you end up. Ultimately he'll decide," said Wormwood, closing the conversation off for hopefully the rest of the journey.

The track wriggled its way around the chaotically positioned houses until the gradient slowly grew steeper. The closer they advanced on the centre, the less houses blocked their way. This wasn't what they were expecting. If God lived in the centre, why weren't the houses built closer to him? It was as if they were trying to stay away from him.

The dusty path ceased at the foot of the hill and was replaced by a series of stone slabs dropped at intervals up the bank. And as they climbed, the singing increased in volume. Towards the top it wasn't only loud, it was also decidedly tuneless. A crowd of angels had formed a conga line and were circling the building in an endless rotation. Their song, a rather loose description, had a repetitive chorus line that was immediately irritating, like a once-beloved pop song which had languished in the charts for so long, everyone, including the original composer, hated it.

"Holy, holy, holy is the Lord of hosts; the whole earth is full of His glory!" Quickly followed by and repeated endlessly by, "Holy, holy, holy is the Lord of hosts; the whole earth is full of His glory!"

"Who are they?" asked Abe with excitement.

"Bloody Seraphim."

"They're only celebrating God's glory," said Abe.

"Yes, but you've only heard it once, haven't you? They've been singing that same line since the dawn of time. Over and bloody over again. They've no idea what's been happening because no one can get them to stop. Oi, Seraphim. It's all over, you know. Bugger off!"

"Holy, holy, holy is the Lord of hosts; the whole earth is full of His glory!" came the response. A few of them turned their backs as they sang and the one at the end of the conga delivered a rude hand gesture as they circled past.

SLEEP, PRAISE, REPENT

"What's a Seraphim?" asked Elsie as she was hastily erecting a tripwire for their next rotation.

"They're in the first-sphere angelic choir. You can't get higher than them, if they'd let you, of course. It's an extremely difficult club to break into. Tried many times myself, but if your face doesn't fit, that's it."

"What are you, then?" said Roger.

"Third-sphere principality choir."

"Shame. What's it like being lower-class?" asked Roger with no hint of empathy in his tone.

"It's not like that at all. We don't have a hierarchy as such."

"What do you do, then?"

"Mainly jobs for the other angels," he replied.

"We got rid of all that back at Hell. Made everyone exactly the same. It's working perfectly," said Roger, who clearly had his eyes shut the last time he walked through level one.

A bunch of Seraphim toppled over as the first in line tripped over the wire recently placed there by Elsie. With barely a missed beat their singing continued.

"Holy, holy, holy is the Lord of hosts; the whole earth is full of His glory!"

"Oh, do shut up."

"Sorry," said Abe, who almost without conscious thought was singing along with the others.

"Come on. Let's get you inside and then I can go home."

They waited patiently for a gap in the conga line and then crossed over to the front of the building. Huge pillars of white marble kept the roof in the air hundreds of metres above them and was the only thing that separated the interior and exterior of the structure. On the other side of the pillars a hall stretched into the distance. At the far end a statue dominated the room and they walked slowly towards it.

The statue sat upon a marble throne lacking in any overexpressive detail. In one hand a dagger was held aloft above its head, and in the other hand, which lay on its lap, was a bird. All of it was chiselled from one almighty piece of pure white marble.

"Is that...a pigeon?" said Abe.

"No, it's a dove," replied Wormwood.

"You sure?" added Vicky. "He looks really familiar."

"What does it mean?" asked Elsie.

"How should I know? I'm third choir, remember," he scowled at Roger.

Although they'd been initially drawn to the bird, the most intriguing characteristics were further up the statue. It had no face. It had a head, yes. But nothing in the way of descriptive facial features whatsoever. It wasn't a woman, or a man, or young or old, fat or thin. It was just a huge, faceless figure holding court over an empty hall.

"Where's the face?" said Abe desperately.

"He doesn't have one."

"I can assure you He does. I've seen plenty of pictures of Him. Old, white hair, big muscles, charismatic and beautiful."

"Says who?" asked Wormwood.

"Every church I've ever been in."

"All guessing, then, aren't they? I've already told you, God is not associated with any particular religion. If you want Him to be an old dude, or a woman, or have six arms or wear a funny hat, that's entirely up to you. Close your eyes and be at peace with your own personal image of God. It'll be wrong but whatever gets you through the night."

"I'm not listening to this rubbish any longer," said Abe. "Oh Lord, I am hear to praise You. My love is pure and I repent my sins. Please accept me into Paradise."

"Oh, alright, then," came a booming voice that echoed through the cavernous room.

CHAPTER EIGHTEEN

FALSE IDOLS

Shortly after, a loud unidentified voice echoed around the hall, Abe fainted. It was all too much for him. Since the early days of Sunday school he'd studiously analysed the Bible and had taken a rather literal view of its stories and messages. Only now was that being challenged. The Book of Revelation might need to be rewritten based on his own personal experiences of the last few hours. After all, Paradise was not quite as he'd expected it. A faceless god, multiple faiths, very little exultation outside of the Seraphim, and motorised rocking chairs.

And then the voice.

It didn't sound like God. It had a lisp for a start.

Abe came back to life courtesy of a series of silky slaps to his snoot, mostly administered by the gibbon long after the ox had regained consciousness.

"My Lord, forgive my lack of purity," said Abe.

"Why are you here?" came the voice.

"We have come to offer praise and much rejoicing," replied Abe.

"He has," said Vicky. "I don't really like gods."

"SILENCE!" boomed the response.

When the voice spoke it was accompanied by a series of rather low-budget pyrotechnics. Here and there a flash of light and a puff of smoke would materialise in order to distract the animals from their own senses. A light from the roof shone down on the statue's head to form an unnatural halo. The gibbon snuck off to see how it all worked.

FALSE IDOLS

"Why are you here?" it repeated.

"You'd better ask the lion," said Abe.

"I don't have to explain myself. I'm Sir Roger Montague, third Earl of Norfolk. I do whatever I want."

"I could strike you down with a lightning bolt in a heartbeat."

"Bring it on. I've survived no less than thirteen lightning strikes in my life. Three on the same day."

"Can I go now?" said Wormwood, with no desire to witness an argument between two megalomaniacs.

"Yes. Go back to your duties. The rest of you can explain why you are here."

"Is that a speech impediment?" asked Vicky.

"I'm God, how dare you insult me in that way? I'm perfect."

"Then why did you just pronounce it 'west' instead of 'rest'?"

"It's got an accent on it. That's how you pronounce it."

"No it isn't."

"Look, this is getting us nowhere. What I want to know is…" The voice was momentarily distracted and its volume sank a notch. "What are you doing in here? Get out: this is a restricted area."

The noise of light squabbling rustled through the room as two unknown participants wrestled for control.

"Owwww….this is GOD! You're all DOOMED!" came a more familiar voice. "Hey, this is fun, you should all have a go."

The animals searched around the side of the statue to find a door slightly ajar at the base of the marble. One by one they moved inside to discover the workings of a small recording studio. Desks with intricately labelled buttons and colourful faders stretched across one wall. Screens presented pictures from various corners of Heaven, including one that portrayed the vast hall they'd just left. A microphone

FALSE IDOLS

hung from the ceiling covered in a black mesh. Wearing headphones and spinning on a swivel chair sat Elsie, holding a dwarfish figure in a headlock.

"Let go of me, you ape."

"I'm a gibbon!" she replied, squeezing his neck more fiercely.

"What's going on here?" said Abe. "You're not God."

"Well spotted, genius. Tell your monkey to let me go."

Elsie was torn between strangling him further or setting all the faders to different positions so no one knew how it all worked. In the end the second motivation won and she released her grip.

The midget fell to the floor. Whether he'd always been a midget was debatable. Either an extensive age span had conspired to shrink him to his current three-foot stature, or he was just a really old midget. His back was hunched in an arc, weighed down by the wispy clumps of white hair that dangled from his elongated, fleshy earlobes. His head struggled to hold itself upright, stopping him from talking to anything other than the marbled floor. Poking out of his hump were two shrivelled wings that wouldn't have looked out of place on a small frozen poussin.

"Exactly as I predicted," announced Roger in what was a now familiar way of stating his own self-importance and inner belief. "It's just like the Wizard of Oz pretending to be huge but actually everything being tricks and illusions. I remember the filming of it like it was yesterday."

"You weren't in *The Wizard of Oz*," said Vicky.

"I think you'll find the lion in it…was me."

"Even though it was filmed a long time ago, when you were in fact…a cat, or possibly even an astrocat!"

"How do you explain my Oscar award, then? Tell me that."

Almost as slowly as the sloth travelled, the old midget angel crept quietly towards the door.

FALSE IDOLS

"Not so fast," said Abe. "Explain yourself. Where's God?"

"Where He's always been, down on Earth fixing the human race. It's been a thousand years since we've had new arrivals, I wasn't prepared for your entrance. I left the door open: it does get a bit stuffy in here with all the heat and smoke bombs."

"But surely God can be everywhere and anywhere. He's three people after all, Father, Son and Holy Ghost. They can't all be away from home," said Abe almost desperately. All this time waiting to get here, only to find that God had gone out.

"Wrong," insisted the midget angel. "Where do you get these spurious thoughts of what God is? You've no idea at all. Think of God like water."

"Water?" said Abe.

"Yes. Water can be ice, steam or liquid. Your father, son and Holy Ghost doesn't mean there are literally three of God, more that God can take three different forms. Sometimes He's a spirit, other times a man, and infrequently a big fuck-off storm."

"And which one is He now?"

"Well, how should I know? Haven't seen him for an eternity. Last I heard He was in spirit form floating around the cosmos keeping an eye out for those that have plotted against Him. Humans have shot their bolt, I'm afraid. If they hadn't lost interest He wouldn't be so pissed off about it. Anyway you didn't answer my question: why are you here?"

"We escaped Hell, and ended up here," replied Abe. "We thought it might be better here, but I'm starting to doubt everything I've ever believed in."

"Sucks, doesn't it?" replied the tiny angel.

"But if God isn't here why do you pretend to be Him?"

"It's all about keeping order. If people already believe the con, then why not string them along a little longer so they do what you want them to? I saw you

FALSE IDOLS

on the screens approaching the temple and wanted to keep up appearances."

Up on the walls multiple moving pictures in grainy black and white pixels showed a variety of scenes from the world they inhabited. The inside of the temple was now empty, as was the view of the outside, at least until the Seraphim made another pass. The domed houses would easily have doubled as a ghost town or idle film set, and the Soul Catcher looked equally dormant. A library packed full of massive books clinging to shelves for dear life and surrounding a large, dead oak tree was seen in another. The final screen was a far more interesting channel.

"Who's that?" said the crusty, old midget pointing up at the final screen.

A sloth was standing on top of a large vat holding a football-sized lump of metal in both hands. Captivated by its wonder, he was slowly turning it around in his paws as the metal flowed across the surface.

"Oh him. That's just Gary," said Vicky. "Don't worry, he won't get far."

"I'm not bothered where he goes, but I demand to know what he's doing with the singularity."

*****

"Are you sure about this?" asked Ian.

"Absolutely," replied Asmodeus.

On the small, green hillock, directly below the trapdoor that led out of level zero, the remaining senior demons had gathered to make their move. Of the many that had first journeyed here to retrieve John's soul, few remained. Most of the others had come to some sticky end the last time they attempted to escape from the very same spot.

They clambered up the rope ladder in turn, silently and on alert. The lake at the top was empty and the trapdoor unlocked. Much had changed on level one since their last visit, the most noticeable being the two

FALSE IDOLS

demons that had been bound, gagged and strung up with cheese wire to the ceiling above. A cotton beard and a shabby, wooden hat lay on the floor beneath them. Just below them a drunken mob of lesser demons were burning placards in a makeshift incinerator.

Asmodeus felt that this was as good a time as any to break out his three heads, always a sure-fire way of scaring the shit out of the minions.

"ENOUGH!" he roared.

The fire in the incinerator reacted faster than the demons. It flickered, shrank and shivered, before being completely extinguished by the sheer force of his presence.

"Take them down," he added, pointing to the demons above his head.

Almost instantly the lesser demons remembered what they'd been bred for. Being shouted at. The fire in their hearts sparked, connecting to a past memory of the true pleasures of being demons that they had so easily substituted for false highs and easily attained vices. With the efficiency of a Japanese train schedule they'd released Red and Fluffy and lined up in perfect squadrons waiting for their next brief. Enamel demons, wooden versions, stone ones, metal types of all dominions collected in teams, doing their best to speed up the recuperation from their lingering hangovers.

"What's all this about?" said Asmodeus.

"They rebelled again, sir," replied Red, weeping a little. "Nothing was ever good enough."

"Right, listen up. The time has come to replace the chaos with order once more. Too long have we allowed Sandy and his shadows to suppress us. It is time to take back Hell," announced Asmodeus.

"Great," said Fluffy, more than a little relieved to be going back to level ten to offer pedicures to overpampered plastic madmen. "What's the plan?"

"We don't have one," said Asmodeus confidently.

FALSE IDOLS

"Um, come again."

"We don't have a plan."

"How are we going to know what to do, then?"

"You're not. Do whatever you want. Make it up as you go along."

"What genius came up with that?" said Red insolently.

"He did," said Asmodeus, pointing at Ian.

The demons all turned their attentions to a cross-eyed, white plastic pigeon who'd picked up the wooden hat and cotton beard and was busy trying both of them on.

"You're kidding, right! What happened to you lot down there: have you been brainwashed?"

"Quite possibly," replied Asmodeus. "We decided that the best way to deal with chaos was…more chaos. Now I want you to open all of the cells on this level straight away."

The demons continued to gawp vacantly.

"Hurry up."

"But won't all the 'patients' get out?"

"Yes. Look how bored they are, it's about time they stretched their legs and did something useful."

Drinking alcohol has many wonderful side effects. It can make you feel more confident, more attractive and even more compliant in the face of a ridiculous suggestion. If a sober person was asked to traverse a one-foot-wide plank over a raging river, or shave a rude symbol in their hair, or eat nineteen boiled eggs in a minute, the expected response would come in the form of raised fingers or vigorous head shake. Ask a drunk person and they'll boldly brag, through slurred words, that they are perfectly capable of doing all three at the same time. It was lucky, then, that at least half of the lesser demons were still drunk and saw Asmodeus's request as an interesting dare, rather than a stern command. They marched on the cells, brandishing master keys while immaturely sniggering to one another.

FALSE IDOLS

This was the biggest level in Hell and it had the most inmates. The oval cliffs, that housed the myriad of small, excavated, cave-like cells, ran around the stagnant lake in both directions further into the distance than anyone's eyesight. The process of releasing the convicts was necessarily slow. After all, they could not all ascend to the higher levels at the same time.

The frightened and bleary-eyed vessols struggled to move their frail limbs, cramped from a death spent in a six-foot-square cell since their first arrival. In the time between now and then they'd grown rather accustomed to their fate. At least the routine was clear in the era of B.S. Each inmate had their own keeper, a demon assigned to their section, who would visit once a day to deliver the unique punishment needed to cleanse their soul. And that was it for the day. Twenty-four hours before the next delivery. They'd never ever seen any of their peers being given a chance to 'stretch their legs'. And now all of them were.

When you knew what to expect, and it was always bad, your demeanour was hard-wired for it to continue. Whatever the reason for this current turn of events, it would only be ferociously disappointing. When a few hundred had congregated, wheezing and aching from the short journey, Asmodeus addressed the crowd.

"This is not a reprieve. You are not being returned to your loved ones."

Most of the crowd of plastic figures nodded knowingly. One or two of them looked crestfallen. It wasn't only negative souls that occupied level one. Even if you had been destined to come here in the first place, the fact that you were on this level meant you were only fractionally balanced on the negative spectrum. But some weren't meant to be here at all. This place had been receiving positive souls ever since Heaven had seen fit to turn off their Soul Catcher. And the occasional neutral soul came here even before that.

FALSE IDOLS

"Who's bored?" asked Asmodeus.

A few hundred struggled to raise their arms.

"And who's had enough of all this, ready to pass over and put all this pain and suffering behind them?"

Even more raised their hands.

"Then it's your lucky day. Those of you who are happy the way things are, and perversely enjoy the suffering and torture, please feel free to return to your cells."

About half a dozen trotted off back the way they'd come, either because they'd learned not to trust demons, which wasn't really surprising, or because they were just weird masochists.

"The rest of you can have one final chance to enjoy yourselves. Roam freely, see the sights, go for a walk, play hopscotch, fight each other, set fire to something, eat a rock, do whatever takes your fancy."

They looked at him in frozen confusion. What trick was this?

A bald, fat vessol with varicose veins and a fake scar where a pacemaker would have been in life, tentatively raised his hand.

"Yes, what's your name?"

"Herb Campbell."

"You have a question?"

"Yes. You said we can do anything, right?"

"Totally. The more random, the better."

"Ok, thanks," replied Herb, who immediate walked off in the direction of the 'Twilight Alehouse' pub that had been such a favourite amongst the lesser demons.

"Any other questions? No. Good. Can I recommend some of you give level twelve a visit. Excellent views."

CHAPTER NINETEEN

RUN RABBIT RUN

The darkness was ever present. It consumed everything other than time itself. It besieged all the senses like a fortress and spread like a cancer through every cell of his indescribable body. Submerged by its fearsome grip, it twitched in the fluid that surrounded it and very slowly, day by day, it grew. Imperceptibly at first, no more than a collection of cells making each other's acquaintance for the first time, uncertain as to each other's designated functions or motives.

Emotions swam freely in the spacious underground swimming pool, searching hopelessly for the protection of the shallow end. A strange mixture of panic and excitement combined in search of the water's edge, perfecting their butterfly stroke as they went. As his body expanded it grew four appendages, which thrashed at the fluid with new vigour, forcing it to flow outwards in search of more space. Alongside, also competing in the world's darkest aquatics competition, other creatures wriggled erratically for an advantage. The waves of fluid were held in place by a soft membrane barrier that kept them from cascading out of their cocoon and onto the metaphorical podium.

The freedom of movement was soon forced into retreat by the ever-reducing space around them. Squeezed together, body on top of body, the air above the water became claustrophobic and threatening. And soon that, too, would run out. Somewhere in the deep recesses of a brain yet to fully develop, he knew what was happening to him, even if he didn't know exactly where it was happening.

This series of events had not come about by accident.

It had been a conscious and organised journey from one existence to another. The past, a blurry concussion that had left many of the fine details behind, clung onto what it did remember in case the fluid washed it away permanently. He forced them to dance in his head, repeating them over and over as if cramming for an important examination. His mouth moved as he mimed a mantra over and over. Just two words, repeated obsessively.

His emotions, constrained and confused, jostled with each other in anticipation of what would come first: his suffocation in a watery tomb, or a release into the unknown. The other bodies, pushing up amongst his, lined up in anticipation of being the first to find out. They battled for supremacy over the ever-decreasing space, pushing desperately against the smooth outer membrane of their prison for a weak spot and an escape route.

And then came the flood.

The fluid cascaded away from them in a hurry. The darkness stayed put, frightened to meet the gloomy light that was occasionally released from outside their cocoon. The membrane convulsed powerfully against them in regular spasms as one by one the bodies in the queue slipped out of sight. Finally, as all the bodies left and the space was freed up, he was alone.

At the end of his tomb a thin shaft of dull light would occasionally open and tempt him to move forward. When he didn't, some greater force decided to go to plan B. Fear reared inside him. Did he want to leave? He'd been comfortable here, certain at least that he was away from harm. Now the unknowns were beckoning him to greet them.

He had little choice in the matter.

RUN RABBIT RUN

His head, forced through a hole poorly designed for such a large object, was the first bodypart to experience what was to meet him outside. Through the hole the stale atmosphere struck his face as he struggled to release his eyes from the sticky ooze that covered him. A moment later his body, clearly anxious about being left behind, attempted to overtake his head in being the first to escape. The pressure on his flesh and bones intensified, and with one final, painful squelch he hit the dusty ground. All of him, that was, apart from an elasticated part that seemed to snap with a twang. He never did find it again.

He lay there for a moment panting for oxygen, his lungs wheezing desperately to acclimatise to breathing through air rather than water. His eyelids struggled to open as the external pressure and viscosity of the ooze fought against it. Eventually his eyelids won the struggle and the wonderful sensation of sight, revealed through a narrow slit, framed his first vision of a new life. He wish he'd kept them shut. In front of him, as he peered harder, were two brown legs covered with sticky hair, a white, puffy tail saluting the air, and underneath it all was something...unspeakable.

"Urgh...arghhh!" screamed Nash as he stopped trying to focus on the tired and messy rear end of a rather knackered rabbit.

Even though the process of pushing nine babies out of her rear end had significantly tired her, she still had enough maternal instinct to show concern that one of them had apparently just screamed in a foreign accent. While she licked the other eight babies, who were fighting one another for their first drink, squirming over her body like a mass of tadpoles escaping from frogspawn, she kept a watchful eye on their much larger sibling.

Any instinct of thirst left Nash immediately. Which was odd because he had always been the first to get the drinks in. He hopped away from the brood who were packed inside an excavated dusty hole no bigger than a family suitcase. Eight pinky blobs hunted for the only thing that mattered. He needed to establish what was going on in a way that didn't result in him being forced to suck a rabbit's nipple. He stretched out his muscles and bones to ease the pain from a significant period of the time spent wet and cramped. The slime, that had impeded his sight, covered the rest of his body. As he did his best to remove it, he noticed a number of alarming changes to how he remembered himself.

On the side of his head, dampening the effectiveness of his hearing, two floppy ears drooped irritatingly against his face. Whilst his hearing had been somewhat disabled, his smell was ten times more effective than he remembered it, thanks to a nose that no longer came in three dimensions and was covered in small, hairy aerials. In contrast to his eight siblings, who were as naked as a Playboy bunny, the fur had already grown on his skin. At the back-end, providing no obvious benefit whatsoever, was a white, fluffy pom-pom that moved of its own accord, seemingly unattached to any synapse to his brain.

"Fuck," said Nash. "Not a rabbit."

His emotions had been desperate to avoid death, but not like this. He forced his emotions to rearrange his memories into an order that made sense and that could help him come to terms with what had happened. There was a lot more sense to it than he expected.

The Limpet Syndrome is normally a surprise to those who trigger it. It comes as a subconscious and unplanned struggle to survive and, as such, it usually takes the subject an age to work out what they are, where they are, and why it all happened. Following the Clerk's global message of 'don't die', the situation had changed. People went into the process willingly and conscious of the outcome. They knew that they would be reincarnated and they knew why. That didn't mean that everything about the transformation and the

RUN RABBIT RUN

two different states was retained, but it was a great deal easier.

Nash walked through his memories as if trying to navigate a library ledger in order to find an important reference document. The bullet had come out of the blue. It burrowed deep into his skin, flesh and vital organs without the slightest hint it had been on its way. The air was squeezed from his body as the force of the strike pushed him backwards and downwards. Fear ejected all other emotions from his mind, refusing to give hope, panic or resilience any airtime. Blood gushed from the wound, his brain faltered, and oxygen no longer felt at home in his lungs. Before consciousness gave way to the attack on his vital signs a final voice seemed to halt the process.

Don't die.

The message was clear.

As death froze he was able to make the final paranormal arrangements to hold it off permanently. Then came the darkness. Then the fluid. Then the slow growth as his soul readjusted to an alien physical design. Death had been cheated and now life would just have to get on with it once more.

But what sort of life would it be? He'd witnessed Ian and Sandy in this predicament and they didn't seem to enjoy it much. Although to be fair, they were being hunted by John at the time, under the false pretence that their existence threatened the fabric of the Universe. Like them, he would have to live like this until death came for him again. But would that be enough? Grace and Scrumpy were now on their own, heading for an inescapable conflict with gods, supported by the smallest coalition of forces in the history of human conflict.

He watched as his brothers and sisters eagerly drank their mother's milk, none seemingly interested in any other stimulus. Behind him a passageway led out of the burrow into more pleasant and lighter conditions. Fragile and undernourished, he forced his hind legs to summon up the lactic acid necessary to complete the journey. The tunnel, shorter than he'd expected, opened up onto a small copse of trees that sheltered him from the pattering rain bouncing off the leaves above.

A handful of larger rabbits were casually hopping amongst the undergrowth in search of vegetation, not wishing to move into more open and dangerous parts of their world. How many of them were like him? he thought. The 'don't die' policy had been in place for months and according to the papers Limbo had slowed. Countless humans like him had morphed and were scattered across the world, frightened and leaderless. There must be hundreds of thousands by now.

What if they could be gathered? What if survival wasn't reliant on a coalition of countries, but a coalition of species? Perhaps then he could still play his part in what was to come next.

"Does anyone here speak English by any chance?" Nash shouted through squeaky rabbit vocal cords not yet prepared for it.

A bunch of rabbits briefly stopped munching and looked up, before quickly returning to their lunch.

*****

The view from level twelve was as good as Asmodeus had promised. The other levels gave the same view in almost all directions. Stone, fire, metal and other vessels experiencing their own unique dose of horror became a little boring after a while. Here you could see stars. Billions of them. A hemisphere of stunning cosmic wonders, only slightly tarnished by the translucent window standing in between. Comets streaked past the window like massive fireworks, their tails glittering like tinsel as they faded into the distance. Indigo gas clouds from distant stars in the final steps of death, or the first toward rebirth, painted the skyline with exotic colours. And that was just what you could see through the window.

There were plenty of sights to witness closer to the ground for any would-be touring vessel on one last excursion before the end. There were the remaining glass vases sitting idle on their makeshift shelves, the heavy metal boxes floating statically in the air, and the collection of beautifully intricate pieces of furniture once crafted for a line of senior demons. These were all notable highlights for those willing to take the risk. Plus, for the bolder, braver visitor, there was a group of slightly surprised megalomaniacs trying to work out what was going on.

Many of the recently released vessels from level one had taken Asmodeus's advice to see what all the fuss was about. The lift would take about a dozen of them at regular intervals. And the more that took it, the more others wanted to follow. There were already a hundred or so milling around the lift shaft by the time the shadows had realised it wasn't a one-off.

"Is this your doing?!" shouted Silica to Brimstone, who looked just as confused and annoyed as everyone else.

"Absolutely not. It's taken me a lifetime of toil and sweat to put them in their cells. Why would I let them out again?"

"This is John's doing, then," replied the small, sandy ball of anger.

"How was I to know what he'd do?" replied John innocently.

"What do you mean 'he'?"

Amongst the mass of shabby and gormless-looking plastic ex-prisoners, who represented all shapes, sizes and demographics, were a pair of spindly white feet. Ian didn't really know what to do with them. Even chaos was difficult to second-guess. Like many of the vessels, he'd decided to go with the flow, forgetting that he had in fact seen the views from level twelve on more than one occasion. As the vessels started to spread out to explore, allowing more of their kind to gain access, Silica's patience ran out.

"Boys, it's lunchtime!"

The dictators didn't need to be told twice. A shadow soul had an insatiable thirst for emotional energy and it was a long time since their last binge. They'd already consumed their hosts, squatting in their bodies until the next victim came by. Now they marched on the newcomers, picking out those that might satisfy their hunger. Each soul they consumed was welded to an ever-increasing mass of blue energy, until finally full they'd retreat back inside the vessols of those who'd once resided on level ten, the very worst of human history.

Brimstone watched as the vessol of General Tito approached a lanky, level-one citizen distracted by the world around him. It stalked the ground behind him like a puma waiting for the right moment to strike. Then it came. A ferocious ball of energy burst through the valve of Tito's vessol, leaving the flaccid shell of his body on the floor to be retrieved once the feeding was over. The shadow wrapped around its prey and, before anyone could say 'he's behind you,' it was drawn inside its victim by a powerful force of suction. Twenty seconds later, after the vessol had convulsed on the spot like a witch doctor's spiritual dance, the energy shot out again, leaving a prosthetic bodysuit on the ground like a winkle picked from its redundant shell.

This massacre continued unabated as the shadows gorged on a free takeaway feast mistakenly delivered to the wrong address. Ian watched in horror. This wasn't how it was meant to be. Chaos was meant to be the answer, not a massacre.

"Stop!" he screamed.

Ian succeeded only in gaining the wrong type of attention. Silica moved forward, licking his lips. He'd had pigeon for starter and was getting the taste for it.

RUN RABBIT RUN

"Run, you idiot!" shouted Brimstone as he predicted the last thirty seconds of Ian's existence.

Just as Silica was about to strike, the lift doors swung open once more, but this time it was not full of tourists. Out marched the cavalry: Asmodeus, Primordial, Aqua, Gold, Bitumen, Fungus, and Silver, the demonic equivalent of the Magnificent Seven. Although there were eight. Mr. Virus spread out across the room unnoticed by everyone. Level twelve was their home, and they were taking it back. This unexpected arrival seemed to momentarily halt Silica's progress, but another event stopped it for good.

Idi Amin was choking.

The former Ugandan leader always did have a healthy appetite. He was one of the larger of the vessols that had found a place around Silica's table, obesely fat from a lifetime of gluttony for food and destruction. He'd been one of the first to scoff from the mobile buffet. It was on his fourth or fifth course when things had gone a little wrong. Rather than devour the soul within his victim, it appeared to be fighting back. The vessol of an elderly woman was smiling as the shadow combined with her soul. After much stomach rumbling the vessol burst down the seams and all that remained of both of them was a placid, blue aftertaste that floated meekly into the air and out of the window.

"What's happening?" demanded Silica, a newly found sense of fear rushing through his body.

The dictators continued, undeterred by their colleague's demise. They listened to no one. Dictators took what they wanted and when they wanted it. A lifetime of hearing the sycophantic praise from a myriad of minions too scared to tell their masters the truth, was coming home to roost. What had happened to Amin wouldn't happen to them. They were all-powerful, infallible and, as it turned out, quite digestible. In short succession, Pol Pot, Stalin and Franco had all picked the wrong dessert course and the resulting indigestion was floating out of the Universe forever.

"Stop, you idiots. It's a trap!" screamed Silica.

"Brilliant. Ian, you're a genius."

"Am I?" replied Ian, not really sure how his genius worked. "I thought the whole plan was just a gazebo effect."

"You mean placebo effect, right?"

"Do I?"

"Yes."

"I didn't know vessols had placebos in them."

"They don't. You've brought us something better, some of these vessols are neutral. The shadows are playing an afterlife version of Russian roulette, and they're losing. They don't know which of the vessels are good to eat and which one's aren't. If they get it wrong it's the end for them. Look, there goes another one."

In their arrogant belief that it wouldn't happen to them, murderous maniacs were popping like balloons all around them. Even Silica's desperate pleas weren't having much of an impact. When only a handful of them remained, the senior demons saw it as their opportunity to enter the fray. And whatever powers they still had to create fear and panic were being brandished and used to the full.

Primordial and Aqua both used their liquid forms to spill over the floor and flow under their enemy's feet, either washing them away from the crowd or covering them in ooze to disorientate their senses. The smell of detritus washed around them as small microorganisms from Primordial's moist skin infested anyone they came into contact with. The dictators ripped at their vessols to remove the multi-legged squatters with minimal success.

Brimstone, delighted to rejoin his brethren, was throwing lava grenades into the crowd whilst laughing uncontrollably and pointing out his next victim. When his finger of doom settled on a victim their facial expressions turned inside out. They knew what was coming. Brimstone had been bottling up a lot of anger and resentment through the service of former masters and the flood gates had well and truly disintegrated. Mr. Bitumen was supporting Brimstone's firestorm by feeding it with regular lumps of highly combustible fuel.

Mr. Gold and Mr. Silver had formed an impressive tag team. Each of them using the malleability of their metal bodies to spread themselves over huge areas to create barriers to constrain the shadows into a smaller and smaller area like the wings of a police cordon controlling an unruly crowd. Fungus looked inactive, but was in fact concentrating hard on giving everyone Thrush.

But none of this rampaging retribution from the demons was even close to the terrifying attacks coming from Asmodeus. When he adopted this demeanour his natural state was anger. All three heads were acting in unison, directing his forces towards their foes while breathing fire down on them with more ferocity than a disgruntled dragon. The mighty winged lion, which supported his body, swooped down on its enemies grabbing the now flaming plastic of their vessels in his massive black hairy arms before launching them into the distance, where Gold or Silver would push them back for more.

The enemy had had enough. As the space ran out faster than their resolve, they searched for an escape route. There was only one. All other directions would lead to destruction. Fixed to the floor was a thick, metal chain which stretched a hundred metres in the air before it came to an end at a metal cube.

And in their panic they climbed.

"I wouldn't like to be in that box," said Ian who had been sitting on the stone floor enjoying the show.

John knew who only too well. *"Things have just got a lot worse for poor old Sandy."*

RUN RABBIT RUN

A strange emotion surged inside Ian like a rattlesnake. He tried in vain to suppress it, but stubbornly it bobbed back up again. Every moment of his life had featured a cocktail of good intentions and regular disappointments. He took no credit for the victory that was unfolding in front of him. He'd been asked to be random and chance had put in a welcomed appearance. He was tired of his life revolving around chance and fate, unorganised outcomes that were guided by some other power rather than himself. Just for once, one pure and simple moment in life, he wanted to use skill and see if it proved lucky.

The unfamiliar emotion desperately tried to get his attention and change his belief. It hijacked all other considerations spinning around his mind and demanded to be taken seriously. It knew Sandy had done Ian wrong:, there was no deceit in its intentions. But it wasn't about Sandy now. It was about Ian. It was about time he stood up for himself for once and showed his true character. Like a coiled spring Ian burst out of his position.

"Where are you going?" said John, who forgot that he was everywhere and could just wait and see.

Ian flew with precision and poise to the metal box before the shadows reached it. At the very same time the senior demons were in the process of severing the chain from its anchor. Through a combination of fire and brimstone, both from Brimstone, the chain was being melted, chopped and strangled. The huge links of metal buckled under the pressure and heat until, inevitably, the weakest link broke.

The chains weren't just there for aesthetic effect. The boxes were so close to the outer atmosphere that without the connection they would be dragged out of the window and sucked into space, an event that they were all about to witness for the very first time. The box, suddenly untethered from the metal that held back physics, shot into the air and out through the window. It was shortly followed by the remaining shadow dictators still clinging nervously to the length of chain. The metal hit the window and evaporated. The dictators' vessols expanded and popped, releasing their shadows into the air. There they were consumed and destroyed by the constant stream of neutral energy that seeped out from the passing over of a thousand other vessols that occurred continuously on the other levels. Emorfed had finally caught up with them again.

The vessols of two pigeons slowly increased in size before the expansion had no room left to fill. They simultaneously popped, but, unlike the shadows, their souls lingered for a second before a new force connected and they disappeared from sight.

CHAPTER TWENTY

HOLY LAND

Scrumpy hadn't uttered a single legitimate word in the past forty-eight hours, which in normal circumstances might have been quite welcome to those who lived with him. He loved talking because he loved finding out how things worked and exploring the wonders of the world through both places and people. That's how eight-year-olds are supposed to act. His mind, sharp as a razor blade, could easily jump from one subject to the next, sometimes when you were in the middle of the explanation to a previous question, and often to something totally unrelated.

On the islands, education and the modern world had mostly passed him by. The modern world being a place thirty miles across a stretch of ocean that lay between his paradise and the mainland. Education being the little building on Tresco that lay between him and adventure. Adventure would usually win. What he lost in formal teaching he made up for through inquisition. He didn't hate learning, he just didn't want to sit still at the same time. That was the main state you had to adopt in school. He wanted the world to be his classroom and everyone in it to be his teacher.

But even his streetwise foundations hadn't prepared him for what he'd witnessed in New York. How could it? You can't learn grief. You have to experience it to fully understand its impact. The heart-crushing, soul-shattering, tear-inducing, life-changing pain of losing someone close to you who could never be replaced,

HOLY LAND

only mourned until hopefully their memory might settle in your own behaviour, their legacy secured through you.

Since the age of two, the people he loved had always been around him, or at least could be contacted by the wonders of modern technology. He'd videophoned his two mothers on Bryher, and Faith in London, every day since he'd left their protection. But no technology was available to reach Nash. There was no signal where he'd gone.

And to add to the sense of confusion, his grief was being interrupted by yet another plane journey, another country and another task. The only feasible response was to shut down and cry until some semblance of normality resumed, even though the sheer thought of it seemed impossible. Grace had tried clumsily to comfort him, but only managed to say all the wrong things. The elderly gentleman, who seemed to have surrogated himself to their group in Nash's place, had a tendency to just stare and tut loudly. It was his grief to shoulder, and like everything else in his life he'd find a way to learn how to tame it, eventually.

Two days after Nash's death they arrived in 'Lesbian', or at least that's what Scrumpy thought it was called. He was quickly corrected. Lebanon was hot. It was a dry, dusty hot that you couldn't escape from however much you tried. Here the concept of air conditioning involved taking the air out for a personal training session. In stark contrast to their last location, more people drove cattle than cars, and you could count the number of skyscrapers on one set of fingers. This was Byblos, home to a mostly seafaring population with a strong ancestry.

It was a beautifully serene town that clung to the shoreline of the Mediterranean in a dark, edgy country desperate to throw off the shackles of its history and break new ground. The townspeople bustled frantically through the narrow streets as if their speed of movement was being recommended and recorded by the authorities. Disputes clung to conversational clifftops, never quite falling, but always shouting uncomfortably at the possibility. There was an unspoken tension that filled an otherwise peaceful-looking backdrop. The Clerk, Grace and Scrumpy found their way to the marina, where terracotta roofs encircled the waterfront and shabby, barely buoyant tourist boats carrying unstable, white garden furniture bobbed in the calm sea.

"What do you think, Scrumpy?" said the Clerk as they stood on the harbour wall looking out at the vast Mediterranean Sea.

His shoulders shrugged weakly.

"This is the oldest continuously inhabited city in the world. Since the Phoenicians first settled here five thousand years, ago people have been fighting over this city. Everyone from the Romans to the Crusaders to the Nazis have fought for the ancient walls that encircle the old town."

Scrumpy's head continued the futile escape into his neck.

"Your sister tells me you like adventurers and history: I thought you'd like it here?"

More silence.

"Why are we here?" asked Grace.

"Because of ancient history, and one soon to be made. It will happen near here. The war to end all wars. Just north, in the deserts, there they will gather and we will be waiting, ready for the endgame."

"You know this place, don't you?" said Grace, noticing the Clerk's all too familiar knowledge of his surroundings and a sense of nostalgia that clung to him like a tight-fitting sweater.

"Yes. Do you see that ruin up on the hill there?" He pointed to the left side of the marina and up onto a raised clifftop. "That is the site of the original town. The foundations of the citadel still stand, but there was a civilisation even before that was built. No buildings exist that remember it, though. When it was safe I remember coming down the hill here in my younger days to forage for food or attempt to catch a fish or two with nothing more than my bare hands."

"You were born here."

"Yes, Grace. This is my home town, although it is some considerable time since I last saw it. Much of what we stand on didn't exist back then. The walls of the old town were a sanctuary from the constant attacks from those that jealously coveted what we had built over millennia, desperate for what we created here."

"What was it that they wanted?"

"Humanity. This is the birthplace of civilisation, society, religious thought, intelligent debate, commerce and, at one time, harmony. There were many Phoenician heroes born here whose songs we sang in tribute."

Grace was standing at the epicentre of human evolution and yet she'd never felt more out of place. Despite the suffocating heat, a chill ran through her veins to warn her away from some unseen disaster charging down the high street. Stone walls showed off their battle scars like overconfident strippers, trapped witnesses to too much death and conflict. The atmosphere screamed with a sense of foreboding and its number one fan was a foreign white-haired girl.

Scrumpy could feel something, too. He couldn't put his finger on what it was, but he knew what it was saying. Go home.

"I miss home," said Scrumpy, eyes rubbed raw and bottom lip still wobbling as frequently as the waves hit the dock.

"We all want that," said the Clerk. "But without you two there will be no homes to return to."

"I miss Nash, he always knew what to do."

"You know Nash isn't gone, don't you?" said the Clerk.

Scrumpy looked up, fighting the conjoined emotions of hope and deceit. If this was a trick he wasn't in the mood for it.

"No one can die anymore, Scrumpy. They only have two basic choices. Limbo or the Limpet Syndrome. I believe Nash chose the latter."

"What do you mean?" asked Scrumpy, breathing his first question in days.

"I mean he walks, swims or flies amongst the animals. Along with probably a million others by now."

"Isn't that painful?"

"Uncomfortable rather than painful, I'd imagine."

"And what has he become?"

"Sadly, I don't know. But they can speak English, or the language of their birth, so you may well find out, if you're lucky."

A plan started to hatch inside the scruffy-haired youngster. "What will happen to them in the end?"

"That depends how the war goes. If we win, someone will have to put them back. If we lose, there will be no need."

In the close vicinity a number of creatures went about their daily routines. A seagull was perched on a sailing mast, a couple of lizards chased each other over the clay-coloured, drystone wall, and a donkey was tied up against a house, waiting for the cart it was attached to to be loaded.

"Seagull, are you Nash!?" shouted Scrumpy, receiving no reply.

He scurried over to the wall.

"Lizards, are any of you Nash?" Both scurried off with other business before they'd even fully heard the question.

"Scrumpy, I'm sure Nash will talk if he sees you," said the Clerk from a distance as Scrumpy rushed up to the donkey.

HOLY LAND

"Are you Nash?" he asked the sad-looking creature, who'd spent much of the day trekking around the city as Byblos's answer to a home removal firm.

"No, I'm Pat. Please kill me!"

*****

Gary the sloth caressed the ball of metal with the love and care of a new mother cradling a baby. Its swirling metal flowed evocatively in his hands, desperate to pass its message to its lucky new owner. There was nothing much to see, but there was much to feel. A deep sense of longing and loss oozed invisibly up the sloth's arms and into its silken-clad head. It had much information to download but was struggling with its host's processing speed.

Gary's trance was broken by two separate noises.

The first would be enough to wake the dead, or at least the thousands of souls sitting idly in their rocking chairs on their perpetual 'sleep' setting. An air-raid siren was blasting an annoying and monotonous shrill from every building big and small. Its impact was Biblical.

The second noise was more familiar and localised, but no less annoying to those who'd heard it before. Not wanting to be seen to drop down the egomaniac pecking order, Roger was standing below him shouting.

"Gary, that's mine!"

Of course it wasn't. This round, smooth, mystical ball of wonder belonged to everyone. But it had chosen Gary to provide its voice.

"It...chosen...me," he said dreamily.

"Gary, why don't you come down?" said Vicky who'd grown quite attached to this strange creature, quite against her own prejudicial instincts.

The sloth, sitting astride a large vat, his legs hanging in the air, nodded his agreement. Slowly and steadily he descended, careful to protect his precious cargo as he climbed down to meet them. All the while the loud air-raid siren was still shattering the peace around them. When he reached the ground the midget angel arched his battered body towards him, hands outstretched.

"Give it to me, please," he said sternly.

"No."

"Why not?"

"I…can't," replied Gary.

"Come on, lad, this is serious. You can't just pick up a singularity and refuse to give it back."

"Sorry to interrupt," said Abe from the crowd. "What's a singularity?"

"The start of something new."

The midget went into a rather dull and detailed description of how a singularity was the fuse that propelled new life into space and time. The monologue was strewn with highly complex scientific rhetoric to confuddle even the most talented professors. Outside of Roger, who nodded regularly and threw in the odd disagreement to the facts being presented, no one understood a single word of it. They weren't really listening because it was totally bewildering as to why, here in Heaven, a member of staff was promoting the idea that this small, metal ball was responsible for creating life in the universe. Abe's will power could take no more.

"STOP!" he shouted over the noise of the monotonous droning of the siren. "I don't buy any of it. I want to see the real Heaven. The big bang, singularities, the creation of life through some barely understandable notion, it's all BULLSHIT! If this is responsible for everything we see, where does God fit in? Tell me that. How is this place even here?"

"I never said 'this' singularity was responsible for life around us. I said it was a singularity with the potential to do so. And as to where God fits in, well, He created this place and is linked, as we all are, to the original singularity."

HOLY LAND

"I can't believe how dull some people are," boasted Roger. "It's all a piece of piss."

"Are you saying there's some truth that links both science and religion in the story of creation?" asked Vicky.

"Yes, of course," said the midget.

"But if a singularity was responsible for the start of the universe, where did this one come from?"

"Hell," said Gary, still fondling the ball with a look of bewildered pleasure on his face.

"So that's where it went," said Vicky. "We saw it float out of the Soul Catcher when the shadows ripped it apart. Like us, it had nowhere else to go but here."

"Indeed, and we now have the advantage, and I'd like it back please."

The midget walked forward and attempted to wrestle the metal out of the sloth's hands. It wouldn't budge. Gary made no effort to withhold it, it just didn't want to be removed. The wizened angel struggled with the joint exertion of remaining upright and playing tug of war with an unhelpful sloth. Eventually he changed tactics.

"Ox, tell him to give it back or unspeakable things will be done to you and your ridiculous friends."

Abe was in no mood to be threatened. The solid foundations of faith, created around him for as long as he could remember, were a house that had just had its roof blown clean off. The walls of his belief were slowly collapsing under the weight of his hefty expectations. They splintered on the ground in dust and unleashed his deeply suppressed anger.

"Fuck you, midget!" he shouted violently. "This is my family and no one fucks with them!"

With that, he charged. The resulting impact of ox head against angel body resulted in the latter being quite some distance away, clutching his back and shouting profanities. The rest stared at the ox with a new sense of respect and just a touch of wariness.

"I."

HOLY LAND

Everyone took a breath and watched the sloth.
"Think."
"What?" said Elsie.
"We've."
Everyone nodded encouragingly.
"Outstayed."
"Always go with short sentences, single words are best," offered Vicky.
"Our."
"I'm bored already. I have a brilliant idea, you'll love it. Best one I've ever had," shouted Roger.
"SHUT UP!"
"Welcome."

Gary's timing, slow though it was, was perfect. Out of every white-domed house crawled a procession of old and knackered souls, each wearing a brand new outfit. Light danced off the surface of their costumes as they joined a long line of colleagues all marching towards them. At the head was a familiar face, with an equally familiar expression.

"Wormwood, what's happening?"
"Don't you hear it?"
"What?"
"The siren?"
"Yes, but we thought it might be a fire drill that no one could be arsed to notice, because frankly they're all so miserable that burning to death might be a welcomed change of scene," said Elsie.
"We've been summoned," replied Wormwood. "At least some of us have. Sadly, I'll be left here with the bloody Seraphim for company."
"Summoned where?" said Abe.
"To Baltazaar. To Earth. To war."

CHAPTER TWENTY-ONE

THE DEVIL IS IN THE DETAIL

Depression had hit epidemic proportions on Neutopia since the construction of the Soul Catcher. Playing constant rounds of I-Spy was only one of the triggers. Almost all of the Accountants had been affected by it in one way or another. Only Accountant A appeared to be holding it at bay.

Depression is a debilitating illness with the ability to paralyse those that suffer from it. It can fester inside us, waiting for its chance to strike, or it can be delivered by an external rift suddenly ripping a hole in life. Every patient can suffer uniquely different symptoms and many of the rumoured treatments may, or may not, make a markable difference. On Neutopia, the race of Accountants had evolved at an alarming rate in the first three months of their existence. This evolution had included mental illness but not, sadly, more than one way of treating it.

And that one size fits all was no silver bullet.

Not all non-sufferers are unsympathetic to those with depression. But Accountant A wasn't one of them. If he couldn't see it, then it wasn't happening. If one of the Accountant's legs had fallen off he would have been as caring as a district nurse, but if one of them complained of feeling 'down' or even mildly suicidal his response was always the same. 'Pull yourself together.' This has never been effective. No depression sufferer will ever hear that statement and

THE DEVIL IS IN THE DETAIL

respond, 'Oh, why didn't I think of that? Thanks for the advice, I feel much better now.'

The cause of the illness which infected the group of paper people was not difficult to identify. Their purpose for being alive was being questioned. When they were busy and motivated, clear in deed and thought, their outlook was consumed by a feeling of worthfulness. A vision had been presented to them of a future where they would guard over and protect those souls that reached them. They'd waited patiently to welcome the first with joy and reverence. But none had come. Each passing sunrise arrived with eager expectation and set with rejection and disappointment. As each day left its anonymous mark, the latter was all they felt as they ploughed on with each new one, hoping for better.

They were Accountants that were accountable for nothing more than their own distress. Accountant A did his best to keep their spirits up with all the empathy of a lump hammer massaging a light bulb.

"Listen up, I've come up with some team-building exercises."

A troubled groan hung in the air. Accountant Z, whose disappointment trumped most others as a result of still being disfigured and dealing with massive self-confidence issues, continued to administer paper cuts in an origami version of self-harm.

"What's the point?" said Accountant M, whose swan-like neck now drooped somewhere close to the ground.

"Cheer you up, keep you busy," said Accountant A.

"I refer you back to my last reply."

"There's no point moping around all day again, is there? I have a brilliant game we can play. You have to work as a team to build a tower out of grass and sap. Tallest wins, one hour."

"I'm still going with my first response," said M.

"It'll test your teamwork."

THE DEVIL IS IN THE DETAIL

"But we don't have a team. There's nothing to do. What you're suggesting is that we practise something we're never going to use in real life because there's NOTHING to do."

"Have you tried I-Spy?"

A lump of tree sap hit him on the back of his elongated neck and slid down to the ground.

"I suppose that's a yes."

"It's pointless," replied Accountant M. "I wish that ball had never come here."

A number of paper characters nodded in agreement.

"Without David-SYNTAX-ERROR-John none of us would be alive. We should be thankful."

"We should throw him in the quarry where he belongs," said Accountant M, hitting on a group activity that would be much more satisfying than building a pointless tower. "Let's do that."

The swan pulled itself from the floor and encouraged as many as the others to join his mob rule. Accountant A rushed to the Soul Catcher to protect his pride and joy. But the machine would not go quietly. The constant energy source streamed into the atmosphere from the funnel, collecting nothing as it always did. Until today. As the mob marched on it, two blue clouds circled in space at the end of the chimney and with a gurgle were sucked into the giant papier-mâché box. A message flashed on the console.

"We've got something!" screamed A in excitement. "I told you they'd come."

The mood of the mob was tempered slightly by this unexpected announcement, and they crowded around the terminal to see the message.

Two names flashed on-screen.

"What do we do now?" asked Accountant M.

"I'll ask," replied Accountant A.

David-SYNTAX-John typed his answer. 'Get the vessols ready.'

"What's one of them?"

'A body to place the soul inside,' came the response.

THE DEVIL IS IN THE DETAIL

"What do they look like?"

'In this instance you need to make two papier-mâché pigeons.'

*****

Byron contemplated his next move. War was coming and wars were not normally won alone. Even the Spartans had had three hundred, and despite the stories of heroism, they still lost eventually. One individual would not be enough. Baltazaar would certainly not fight on his own, if he personally fought at all.

Who could he recruit? Victor had abandoned him and access to Hell had been broken. That left only one option. Humans would have to come to Byron's aid.

It had been a long time since he'd meddled in their affairs directly. Could he still do it? The unused skills of corruption and persuasion had been left dormant as his other talents had been cultivated. Centuries had been spent confined to Laslow's temperamental and ageing frame, waiting patiently for the right time to strike and relocate. Even before that, he'd done little in the way of manipulation since the unfortunate situation with the Priest of Byblos. Before that, it had all came so easily to him.

All he'd ever needed to do was to work out which buttons to press in the human psyche. Wealth, power, desire, revenge, victory, self-discovery, notoriety and fear could all be examined and extracted to identify which one would open the door to their soul. Humans hadn't moved away from these desires over time. They might have been upgraded slightly to reflect the materialistic modern world, but it still boiled down to the same things. Thanks to the failure of Emorfed, at least one frailty lived inside every citizen and each could be reached because of it. All he had to do was make the call.

Most would be easy to affect. But there was always a risk. What if he failed again? What if one of them

THE DEVIL IS IN THE DETAIL

turned the tables on him just like the Priest had, a mistake which still stalked him today, one thousand and more years later? And what had become of him and his son? Was he still safely tucked away in a metal cask on level twelve as his father continued to wait in vain for his return? Maybe it was time to check.

*****

Relative normality had returned to Hell. Granted, it was going to take them a long time to round up all the residence and forcibly return them to their cells. A vigorous, deep clean would be needed on level one to remove the theme park of vice that had been erected there, before a process of satanic therapy could be administered on the lesser demons to remove any remaining substance addictions. A new use for the now empty level ten would be needed until the human race produced a new breed of mass-murdering idiots. It wouldn't take long. That's if they ever repaired their Soul Catcher.

There were many empty thrones around the table as the senior demons settled in position for a board meeting. More than half had failed to return or were missing in action. But importantly for those who had, there was not a pigeon in sight. Asmodeus stretched out at the head of the table, sporting a contented grin. If only the Devil could see him now, the victor and saviour of his domain, all troubles resolved.

Almost all.

"What about me, then?"

"Oh, for fuck's sake," grumbled Asmodeus, almost falling backwards off his throne as he rocked gently on it. "You're not still here, are you, John?"

"Afraid so."

"But why?"

"You have no Soul Catcher so none of us are arriving or leaving in the foreseeable future."

THE DEVIL IS IN THE DETAIL

"You just don't get it, John, do you?" the first words that Noir had uttered for ages, happy for John to take the dark matter stage for a while. *"I said you can go ANYWHERE."*

"I know, I have been."

"There's more than one universe to explore," added Noir.

"You mean I can go beyond the window?"

"You already are beyond it, John, you just don't know you are. You haven't connected with it yet."

John was filled with a new sense of adventure. If he wanted to he could visit old haunts, his homeland, his mother, his friends and even, if he chose, support the deeds of others. No longer would he be forced to roll his boulder up the hill, he might even visit the other Universes in pursuit of answers to the ultimate question. Who he was. He needed no second invitation. Meditating quietly to himself, he reached out in search of the way.

"There, easy, isn't it?" said Noir.

Noir was the only one who heard John's reply. The other demons placed their hands to their ears as a shrill noise of ringing pierced their eardrums. Someone was making a call, and only one of them was missing.

"Prince of Darkness, we have retaken Hell, all is well," said Asmodeus in greeting.

"I'll be the judge of that," replied Byron, *"I am very disappointed in how you, Asmodeus, have been running things there."*

"But your excellence, the circumstances have been unique to say the least."

"But not everyone panicked like you. Thanks to Mr. Brimstone at least someone was able to contribute."

Mr. Brimstone sat internally smiling to himself. Only he had survived the exodus of the senior demons. Only he had made contact with Satan to keep him abreast of progress. And only he had had to suffer at the hands of the shadows. It was rare for him to be

THE DEVIL IS IN THE DETAIL

singled out for praise, so he might as well enjoy it while it lasted.

"We were all involved in restoring order," said Asmodeus nervously. "It was a team effort."

"You have had your chance, Asmodeus. It's time someone else did. Mr. Brimstone, will you take the job?"

"Uh…what job?" asked Brimstone, not really following.

"The main job. Ruler in absentia."

"You want me to do Asmodeus's job?"

"It's not his anymore."

"Well, yes. I'm sure I could make a difference, lead a new era here, sir."

"Then it is yours. Asmodeus, move seats."

"But sir…"

"Does he get to keep the scary suit?" asked Brimstone.

"That's not part of the job, it's part of me," replied Asmodeus, aggressively still rooted to his seat for dear life.

"Chop chop, Asmodeus, and while you're on your feet there's something else you can do for me."

"Of course, Master," he replied, shuffling himself onto the ground.

"The Priest's son, is he still safe?"

Asmodeus stared up at the nearest box above the table. Its exterior looked different from the others, significantly older, made of a different material and sealed by rivets rather than welded edges. The sides were less uniform than the other boxes, curving inwards as if a power was sucking in the walls.

"Looks good," replied Asmodeus.

"Bring him down," ordered Byron.

With the collective effort of the remaining demons the box was lowered and hit the ground with a clang. Mr. Gold disappeared to locate a crowbar, the end of which was forced between the metal plates as it fought to keep its contents secret. The collective pressure

THE DEVIL IS IN THE DETAIL

from the demons was too much, and eventually the door buckled open and the air was sucked in. It was empty. Not even a flaccid, empty vessel was lying on the floor, discarded when the recipient had succumbed to their own solitude.

"There's no one inside!"

"What?"

"It doesn't look like there ever was," replied Asmodeus.

"Don't you remember putting him in there?" said Byron.

"No, not really. It was a thousand years ago, and that's just by Earth time."

"What is going on here?" said Byron.

"I think I can explain."

"Protocols please. I don't know who's speaking," said Satan, confused by this new voice.

"No one has ever been in there," said Noir, more familiar than most to places undiscoverable by the standard senses.

"Where is he, then?" barked Byron.

"The person destined for that box was processed very differently."

"Who is speaking? Name yourself."

"It's just Mr. Noir," replied Asmodeus casually.

"Who the fuck is he?"

"A demon you made from dark matter," replied Brimstone. "You probably don't remember him because he doesn't interact very much."

There was a pause so long that everyone tapped their ears to check whether they'd been cut off.

"I didn't make a demon out of dark matter," replied Byron.

"Then, if he's not a demon, what is he?" said Asmodeus to the others all looking perplexed around the table.

*****

THE DEVIL IS IN THE DETAIL

Scrumpy continued to dash around the city of Byblos interrogating animals in the vain hope that one of them was Nash. And as long as he stayed within view, Grace was very happy to let him do it. She understood that some humans needed hope, even if the probabilities involved had more noughts at the end than a googolplex. Sitting in a cafe drinking a rather pungent cup of coffee, Grace wanted to know more about the city.

"What year were you born here?" asked Grace.

"I'm not certain," replied the Clerk. "Definitely after the Romans. Why?"

"There's something I was wondering," said Grace.

"What's that?"

"Why this city? Why you?"

"The second question is simple. Satan offered me a deal and I foolishly took it."

"But how did you end up lasting for so long. Surely the Devil should have taken your soul from you as part of the deal."

"I fought back," said the Clerk. "I knew my life wasn't immediately threatened because I was very old and he took pleasure in taking souls from the less long lived. When the Devil showed me his vision it pictured a place of liquid metal deep underground. I travelled relentlessly to find it."

"Limbo?"

"Yes. I was weak of body but strong of mind, and I forced death to come back later. Through much personal danger I finally located it. I watched the streaks of blue electricity escape from a narrow glacial fissure deep in the heart of the mountains. What I know now, but didn't at the time, was that the Celestium had only recently been planted there. When I got to it, it was maybe the size of a small church. I couldn't get in, as much as I tried."

"What did you do?"

"I got down onto my knees and prayed."

"Really? After all that had happened to you. Why?"

THE DEVIL IS IN THE DETAIL

"Satan's vision, as horrifying to me as it was, clearly showed how the unique make-up of the human soul worked and proved one thing. If Hell existed, then so did Heaven. In my prayer I used this knowledge to highlight a weakness that I saw in the system. If Limbo had been stolen from the 'third way' to stop souls reaching it and to manage all souls for their onward journey, what would they do with the neutral ones? If they weren't sent there, then where?"

"Neutopia."

"Is that what's it called?" checked the Clerk.

"Yes."

"It's your Universe, Grace. The place you need to open."

"Did anyone answer your prayer?"

"Oh yes. Baltazaar was most displeased with Satan's behaviour and the deal that he'd struck with me, but was even more disturbed by what I knew about neutral souls. He invited me in and I started to work for him. You had a second question, I believe, about this city?"

Grace nodded.

"This isn't just where I was born. It was where he was born, too. God protects the King. Baltazaar in the Phoenician language."

CHAPTER TWENTY-TWO

THE MIRACLE MAKER

Heaven had a profound impact on the reincarnates in many interesting and unexpected ways. It was unclear whether this was due to Heaven being not how it was 'described in the brochure' or because, frankly, any break from Hell was a welcomed one. It was touch-and-go as to whether this change would lead to a lasting improvement in their overall characters, or was as fleeting as a holiday romance.

Whatever the reasons, both Elsie and Vicky were noticeably more restrained in their separate talents of prank and prejudice. Vicky was growing more tolerant of those around her, particularly ox, gibbons and sloths. It would take more than an epiphany to change her views on lions, however. Elsie, on the other hand, was seeing a different viewpoint, the one from the side of the person or creature she'd just embarrassed. In this place, pranks didn't feel as funny, like the joy had suffered a bypass over the years.

Abe, whose only ambition in life and death had been to praise the Lord, had experienced his epiphany. He'd not enjoyed it very much. The Teflon-coated image of God's magnificence, that he'd long held to be true, had shattered into tiny pieces. A plethora of souls from uncompromising faiths mingled together in small collective gangs, God was masquerading as an irritable midget, and almost everyone looked miserable. A great build-up of almost unbreakable conviction was being unshackled like a vicious dog. Love made way for anger. A thirst for retribution was

THE MIRACLE MAKER

accelerating towards the exits and directed at all those who'd ever convinced Abe that faith in the Almighty was the only true path.

Gary, on the other hand, was more at peace than ever, which was an impossible concept to accept as he wore a demeanour of almost constant unconsciousness. This historic reputation for slowness did have consequences. People didn't tend to wait for him. They got bored, irritated, exasperated and eventually got... off. Gary would usually follow in their wake some distance behind, hoping not to lose their trail. Finding the singularity hadn't changed him physically. But mentally he felt a new sense of confidence and a security from the singularity's desire to stay with him. It wasn't in a rush to jettison him in a search of a quicker high. It had made a connection and felt at home.

While for some the visit had done much to suppress the weaknesses inside them, for Roger the reverse was true. To his knowledge, and as far as he would believe, even if you told him differently, the five of them were the only creatures in history to see both sides of the theological fence. Surely that made them special. Destiny had finally recognised his sizeable contribution to human progress and they, no, he, had been chosen for this great honour. It was just the beginning. Now there was a war, and wars needed heroes. And not just any hero. One with karate skills.

The long line of angels that moved up the street looked like an OAPs' Christmas party had just started playing the conga line music. If this was all Baltazaar had for soldiers, he was in trouble. Deep trouble. They watched as the line crawled past the Soul Catcher and into the distance.

"Hey, Wormwood," shouted Vicky, "Aren't they going back via the Soul Catcher?"

Wormwood stopped ticking names off his clipboard and counted to five in his head, a recognised tactic for reducing irritation. His job had always been 'front of

… house', Heaven's bright and friendly welcoming party, ready to shake your hand and make you feel at home. He'd heard every pointless question in the book and yet they seemed to invent new ones every year. These questions were his specialist subject, but continuing to answer them with good grace took more than a little constraint.

"They can't use it."

"Why not?"

"We switched it off, didn't we?"

"Can't you switch it back on?" said Elsie.

"No point. If we sent them that way they would all get stuck in Limbo with the other undesignated souls," offered Wormwood, barely looking up from his notes.

"So, how are they going to get back, then?" enquired Abe.

"There's another way."

Vicky beckoned the other animals with four or five of her silken legs, only to find that Roger had already joined the fragile, angelic queue marching off towards the outer wall. Impatiently he was queue-jumping at every opportunity. Either he was at the front leading or nothing at all. The rest joined the melee, Abe once again acting as trusty steed for both Gary and his new luggage.

Walking isn't a uniform activity. Some people walk slowly and some walk fast. Leg span, destination and ability to shut off distractions are all part of the walking equation. But if you believe it's the lowest speed setting available, then you're wrong. Just below walking is a state of motion that is barely susceptible to the human eye. It's called faffing, and its purpose is to reach the desired destination in the slowest possible time frame. On a Saturday afternoon every shopping mall and high street in the land would provide all the evidence needed to see it in action. It was one notch up from sloth.

The angels faffed. It might have been their age, or their lack of practice in achieving the recognised

THE MIRACLE MAKER

walking pace, or the silken arthritis settling in their joints, or the realisation that they'd forgotten what the world outside of their domes looked like, or possibly a combination of all of them. If the war was soon, they were more than likely to miss it. This group attribute meant it wasn't long before Roger and the others reached the front of the queue.

At the walls of the kingdom they came to a halt. Over the top of the wall, thirty feet above their heads, the entwined black brambles, as thick as a lumberjack's forearms, fought with themselves to locate a route to the ground. The brambles were not the only life behind the wall if the disturbing noises they heard were anything to go on. A choir of angry voices, growling their own unique take on punk music, vibrated through the brickwork.

"Welcome to the wild," said Wormwood, turning to the angels, but finding only the five reincarnates had so far made it as far as the wall. In the distance the conga line continued its endless crusade.

"What's over there?" said Elsie. It was the first time in her life that she had no motivation for a joke or banter. Something behind the wall was making her uneasy.

"The exit," said Wormwood coldly, showing no anxiety as to what might greet them on the other side.

A small, wooden door with a reinforced metal frame, supporting numerous heavy padlocks, stood between them and the wild. Wormwood produced a large ring of keys and set about unlocking each one. When the last one fell to the ground the metal frame slid to the side and the door sprang inwards with a squeal. When the door came to rest the squealing continued.

It was coming from the gibbon.

Elsie dropped to the ground, hands over her head, eyes closed and mouth stretched to its limits. When her lungs ran out of air and the fears of being brutally murdered had subsided by the reality, she opened one eye. The door didn't, as she'd feared, open into the tyrannical danger expected on the other side. Instead it led into a walled tunnel, well lit and secure.

"Got you," said Wormwood, pointing at the gibbon. "You didn't think I was mad enough to actually go into the wild, did you?"

"Where does it go?" asked Vicky.

"Don't tell her, it's clearly obvious," replied Roger, walking straight into the tunnel with characteristic arrogance.

The tunnel was just wide enough for two people to walk side by side, but not high enough to support a sloth riding an ox. Gary was forced to lie down, clutching Abe with one hand and the singularity with the other. As they reached the other end of the tunnel it opened into a room that was separated down the middle by a thick sheet of glass. On their side was relative calm, but on the other a thick, black smoke wafted against the smooth, clear partition. Two doorways stood at the end of each compartment.

In each a familiar, thin veil blocked their view through to the other side. Like the window that surrounded Hell, this paranormal membrane had the effect of distorting the world on the other side of it.

"Right, then, Mr. Lion, as you're SO clever, you can explain what it is?" said Wormwood, who'd waited for the exact moment when he might show Roger for what he really was. A massive liar.

"Well, it's obvious isn't it? Even a stupid person could understand it. In fact, I'm not sure there's any point me wasting my amazing intelligence on this lot. They just don't have the capacity for my genius."

"Don't be shy, impress us with this stunning ability of yours."

Roger pretended to analyse the rooms in front of him, never in doubt of his capacity to understand, or his ability to bullshit his way to an answer if he couldn't.

"It's a transmogrifier!"

THE MIRACLE MAKER

"Lucky bastard. That was a guess, wasn't it?"

"No. I'm just amazing."

"What's one of those?" asked Abe.

"We call it the Miracle Maker and it replaces objects from one dimension to another by transferring them through a crack in the fabric of space. It can swap particles and energy sources from here to somewhere else. The problem is it can only swap things of an opposite and equal mass and scale."

"It's all about Newton, really," said Roger. "I learned all about that when I was an astronaut."

The others, for the first time in their relatively short history of knowing Roger, were starting to believe he might be telling the truth, about some things at least.

"How did it get here?" said Elsie, standing as far away from the glass pane as possible, still in fear of what might be lurking on the other side.

"Baltazaar built it. The Soul Catcher can easily move a soul across the cosmos, but this can move any item, but only in one direction. It was easy enough to use the Soul Catcher to farm Emorfed and collect it, but we couldn't use it to transport the substance down to Earth. That's what this machine was built for."

"And what's on that side?" said Elsie, pointing across the room in fear.

"That room is designed to capture the objects that come back in place of what is sent. Because Emorfed is neutral, it generally brought back water, all thanks to the efforts of one Dominic Lightower and his water treatment plant. But other, more positive objects have brought us some rather difficult neighbours. When the angels go through they'll bring back some pretty nasty shit. We'll have to reinforce the walls, although part of me wants the wild to break through and eat all the Seraphim."

Into the room emerged the more spritely angels from the front of the queue. They paid little attention to the scene around them or the fate that might greet them. They'd been summoned and they would do their unwavering duty without quibble or quarrel. Anything had to be better than sleeping in a rocking chair for eternity while you prayed that someone might engage 'praise' mode.

Before their ultimate passage through the veil, a series of steps had to be run through. Firstly each one stepped onto a set of scales that recorded their weight in beautifully old-school analogue detail. Next, a machine was wrapped around an arm, air being pumped furiously for a moment into an inflatable device that took a soul pressure reading from within the silken vessol. Finally, the angel's silk of armour, recently exchanged from their more comfortable onesies, were tested for vulnerabilities by a device that looked no more sophisticated than a pump for inflating car tyres. Wormwood would then use all the vital statistics to work out the answer to a complicated equation on a pad of paper. That sum was then used to pull a cord with a weight on it to indicate the score on a scale to the left of the exit.

Then off they faffed. One step and gone. A moment later something angry and dangerous would arrive on the other side of the glass. If they were lucky, whatever it was panicked and rushed out of the tunnel that connected that room to the world of the wild. If they weren't so lucky, a monstrous face would cut through the smoke and press its features up against the glass. The angels were good, so the transfer would bring the bad…and sometimes the ugly.

A continuous line of angels left their room to be replaced by another monster on the other side. Once the exchange was complete it was permanent. The angels were leaving for the last time. If they died in the war any remaining soul would be consumed by Limbo, and if they didn't, they'd be stuck on Earth. Heaven's purity was being watered down in front of their eyes every time an angel stepped into the Miracle Maker. And it was making Abe angry.

THE MIRACLE MAKER

"That's the last straw!" he bellowed. "You can't do this. This is Heaven, not some theme park for a world of dangerous creatures and criminals. STOP RIGHT NOW!"

"Don't worry, miracles work in mysterious ways. Anyway, it's well below my paid grade to stop it. If they'd given me my promotion, then maybe I'd be more inclined to give a shit. But I'm not," replied Wormwood.

That was it. The fuse blew. Shaking Gary to the floor, Abe reared up on his hind legs and started kicking wildly in front of him. Berserker-style he crashed around the room like a testicle-deficient bull in a china shop. Angels were knocked over, apparatus was broken, and the glass cracked as a mad ox screamed like an overexcited banshee. Wormwood held his ground determined to show how a lifetime of ambivalence could be a powerful weapon.

It wasn't.

A double-footed kick struck him squarely between the eyes. A wobble, then a stumble and then the fall, backwards straight through the Miracle Maker. A mighty rumble echoed back on the other side of the glass a few moments later. Something huge had replaced Wormwood and it wasn't satisfied with what might be out in the wild. Two gigantic, hairy, grey fists struck the glass repeatedly. It sent Elsie over the edge. Without hesitation she made a beeline for the exit door. Pop: she was gone.

The angels had decided faffing was overrated. Discovering a new standard of speed, a steady line of silken-winged OAPs were squabbling to jump the queue. All checks were dispensed with as they dived or jumped or pushed their way through the shimmering portal.

"I think I'm ready to leave," said Vicky urgently.

"Right behind you," replied Abe, panting furiously from his overexertion and feeling a little worried about

THE MIRACLE MAKER

his sudden anger issues. A small pop was soon followed by a bigger one.

The sloth looked up from his singularity. He'd been left again: forgotten or abandoned, it added up to the same thing. He wondered whether he'd even bother following them this time. He had the comfort of the singularity, still clinging to his paws for sanctuary. He thought that going through the portal would only lead to more trouble. The lion would wrap it up in glittery paper and call it an adventure, but sooner or later a disaster would befall them and they'd be on the run again. Not this time: he'd take his chances here.

"Seize him!" shouted the midget, bursting through the tunnel and knocking a number of panic-stricken geriatric soldiers out of his way.

He'd brought some friends. Two muscly bodyguards, as wide as they were tall and barely small enough to exit the tunnel in one piece, stood on either side of the midget. In an attempt to reduce the embarrassment of his stature, the midget was failing to use his wings to float at a more menacing height. The heavies moved on the sloth to retrieve what was rightfully theirs.

"I can't let you do that," said Roger, leaping between them and holding his arms out in protection.

"Who the hell do you think you are!?" shouted the midget furiously.

"I'll tell you who I am. I am Sir Roger Montague, the third Earl of Norfolk, Oscar-winner, moon explorer, ninja black belt, strategic juggernaut, legend and, most importantly, friend."

The departing angels had dispensed with the required and precise measurements needed to safely ride the Miracle Maker and the consequences were becoming clear. The commotion on the other side of the glass was rising. Indescribable beasts were mauling the glass, eager to see if anything more interesting than the wild was on the other side. All it took was a small crack to form and one mighty swing or push.

The glass gave way and shattered on the floor around them. Black smoke billowed through and was backed up by a bout of terror. Whatever had been on the other side was soon out of focus. Two further pops echoed, and Roger and Gary were gone. Neither of them wanted to see what would be brought back in exchange for Roger.

CHAPTER TWENTY-THREE

DARK CLOUDS

The Accountants were now leading experts in the mystical process of making first-class papier mâché. This was none of your primary-school quality. There were no errant newspaper cuttings peeping out from behind poorly painted, misshapen monstrosities. There were no bumps or blemishes where the layering had been rushed to get the last-minute homework finished. Everything they made was perfectly assembled and almost lifelike. While the quality of the craft was unrivalled, they did have a slight problem with design. This emanated from an encyclopaedic lack of knowledge in almost everything.

Art is influenced by what we see and experience in the environment around us. It moulds our inner spirit, drives our emotions, tugs at our heartstrings before being released naked and vulnerable for the world to judge it. Art has to be personal. Not everyone will understand it and not everyone will like it. But that doesn't mean it isn't art. The Accountants were not built for this perspective. They lacked both the internal talent and a rich environment to draw inspiration from. What they saw around them was limited and certainly not inspiring. Square mountains, angled landscapes, regimental fields of grass and absolutely no pigeons.

And no imagination to fill in the gaps.

The Accountants existed because the Celestium rolled over them. And the only life in the metal ball was the remains of one neutral soul: logical, exact, numerical and totally boring. In fact, all the guardians that maintained the three universes were produced this way. Celestium injected life into an inanimate object that had no right or biology in which to carry it out. What came from this miracle, kicking and screaming on the other side, would always be defined by the ingredients that were introduced to the melting pot. What goes in is likely to come out. If your intention is to make a chilli con carne, you can't throw in apples, flour, butter and sugar and hope for the best. You can call it a chilli con carne if you want, but that doesn't stop it being an apple crumble.

Telling an Accountant to make papier-mâché pigeons, without showing them a picture or describing them in detail or injecting some artistic force to support the execution, doesn't guarantee they'll make them accurately. Quite the opposite. In the end they called them pigeons, but they might as well have called them apple crumbles.

"He can't see, can he?" said Accountant J, flapping his wings nervously.

"Who?" said Accountant M.

"David-SYNTAX ERROR-John."

"Nah, doubt it."

"And Accountant A hasn't seen one either?"

"He can't have. He's only a fraction of a second older than we are, and as far as I know they aren't found naturally on Neutopia."

"So we're in the clear, then?"

"I think so. Let's find out."

The swan and the paper plane shuffled forward to the machine and attached their bodged offerings to the end of a paper valve. They nodded to Accountant A, who was hovering by the control panel, waiting to punch in the commands. There wasn't a lot of obvious indication that the instructions typed into the control panel had taken effect. The box wasn't see-through and it didn't move in a way that demonstrated its activity or the forces that might be taking place inside. After a little head scratching and debate as to whether anything had happened at all, the papier mâché in the valve started moving.

And screaming.

The recipient stumbled forward, pulling free of its housing and trying desperately to keep control of its body movements. Of course Sandy had been used to having wings for some time, just not this many. Learning to fly with two had been challenge enough, but seven was a whole new ball game, particularly as his tail was now split into several individual sections and was sporting a great clump of additional bulk. Several stumpy legs finally settled on the ground and his soul got used to its new home.

"What the fuck is this?!" he screamed desperately through what he hoped and imagined might pass as a mouth.

"It's a pigeon vessol," replied Accountant M, nervously looking around for moral support and group affirmation.

"Yes, it definitely is," added J, nodding furiously in a way that made him lift off the ground.

"Then where's my beak and where's my plump bosom?"

"I think the beak is around the back there, near the fifth wing."

"There are only supposed to be two of them. And why am I so white?"

"You can have it in any colour you like…as long as it's white," replied Accountant A, rushing forward excitedly, arms outstretched to greet Neutopia's very first official resident. Minutes later the population reached two. Both were pigeons, both were white, and neither had any resemblance to each other.

*****

In the Northern Bekaa region, a few dozen miles south of the city of Hermal, the coalition forces had gathered on a piece of parched empty wilderness. On one side

DARK CLOUDS

the mountain range of Mount Lebanon dissected the country like the raised fault line of an overactive tectonic plate. Below the mountain's slopes the River Assi struggled to flow with any purpose through the barren and tired landscape. Other than on the banks of the river, where hardy plants and thick bushes eked out a meagre existence, little more than beige grass grew on the plains. Scattered rocks left by some errant geological chess game lay in permanent checkmate on the dust and sand. Dunes held their positions like sandy warriors, thriving as little else could.

On one of the only flat and open parts of the desert, a makeshift compound had been erected from aluminium sheets and was partly filled with military paraphernalia. This had mostly been donated by the Swiss forces, the only serious faction of an otherwise pointless coalition. The Swiss Army, having presumably read the list of other countries they'd be fighting alongside, had overprepared for the conflict. They clearly weren't expecting much support. Tanks, mobile rocket launchers, ten thousand ground troops and a sense of discipline sadly lacking elsewhere were all stockpiled in every available part of the compound.

A coalition is a fusion of more than one group working in allegiance with another towards the same goal. It's only a tiny step from fusion to confusion, which was a much more accurate description for the four countries who'd volunteered. The forces of Djibouti were miles behind the sophistication of the Swiss, but would still be more reliable than the others. They'd brought approximately three thousand infantry soldiers and a few land vehicles, and were, at least to the untrained eye, identifiable as actual soldiers. That statement could not be made about the other coalition partners.

The Suriname National Army consisted of about a thousand troops, all of whom looked like they were heading for a military-themed fancy dress party. Their equipment included one knackered old jeep first commissioned in nineteen fifty-seven and a single helicopter that might even get off the ground if enough care and attention were lovingly applied. This conflict would be a very different one from what they were used to. They'd grown up on guerrilla rather than 'all-out' warfare. Small skirmishes that involved less than a dozen soldiers at a time, mostly hidden down a hole with the dual advantages of surprise and a well-thrown grenade. 'Charge!' and 'Fire!' were not commands they were used to following: those were two words likely to get yourself killed before the enemy.

Their participation itself had been one terrible mistake. When the translator had unplugged her headset during the UN Special Council, leaving the country's diplomat to fend for himself, he'd inadvertently put his hand up when they were looking for volunteers. They were not, as he found out later to his cost, voting on what time they'd finish for dinner.

The most incongruous and out of place group were those representing the Republic of Nauru. They stuck out as different for several reasons. Not only did Nauru lack an official capital city, it was also part of a select group of nations that had no recognised army. But something as trifling as that wasn't going to stop them playing their part in the survival of mankind, and the Clerk was more than happy to include them. All nine of them.

The military inventory that they *didn't* bring was quite something to behold. No tanks, no rockets, no guns, no armoured personal carriers, no helicopters, no generals, no grenades, no shiny, pointed spears, no scare-inducing war dances, no face paint and no tents. They brought lunch, and some very cheap home-made grass skirts.

This was the first time in their living memories that they couldn't see the sea from any given position. It was customary for them to find such a view in every direction they faced, a realisation of living on a group of small islands in the middle of the Pacific Ocean,

DARK CLOUDS

hundreds of kilometres from any other land mass. They tried sleeping on the bare rocks with nothing other than a grass skirt and muscles for padding, but they just couldn't get comfy. Instead they'd decided to relocate to the banks of the river several miles away, clutching an alien-looking device they were told was called a walkie-talkie, and instructed to keep it on at all times just in case the coalition needed nine unprepared, angry-looking, semi-naked soldiers to tip the balance in their favour.

Grace, Scrumpy, the Clerk and Rogier Hoffstetter had been gifted a scruffy aluminium shed inside the compound as their base. A couple of weeks had passed since they'd arrived to help co-ordinate the camp and welcome the new recruits. Little had happened in those weeks and so far no sign of the opposition had been identified on the highly complex surveillance equipment.

To fill the time, Scrumpy was still interrogating anything that wasn't human, but had a pulse and hair, in his search for Nash. It kept him busy and, more importantly, out of trouble. There would be a time when Grace would need to find more suitable protection for him, but for now she welcomed his company. The Clerk's health and well-being were much more of a concern.

The old man had visibly weakened since their first meeting several months ago. His life force seemed to be ebbing away with each morning as if his internal batteries were on their last legs. The Clerk knew what the problem was. Other than being older than some of the geography their camp was built on, his soul no longer had the protection of a wall of Celestium, and it was starting to weaken in the face of life itself. He'd stolen more time than he'd deserved and eventually it would run out. But hopefully not for a few weeks at least.

"Why have you brought everyone here?" asked Grace, as she sat on the ground in front of their lodgings watching the sun hang in the cloudless sky.

"Because this is where it happened."

"Where what happened?"

"Where gods discovered what they were, and what they weren't."

Grace sat silently and the Clerk could see the puzzle forming in her placid facial expression.

"Grace, do you believe that God created the universe?"

"No. There's no evidence for such a thing, and I believe in the provable laws of physics."

"And yet you yourself are a god: you introduced yourself as such when we first met. If gods did not make the universe, then what is the point of having them?"

"I guess humans need hope?"

"Indeed. Gods exist because people need answers. But gods are not defined by what people think or believe about them, they exist in their own right. Their histories run very differently from what humans have documented in books, and they use their powers not as their followers expect. They are a strange concoction of both real and imagined constructs of human storytelling. In the early days, when the Phoenicians walked these plains, they were worshipped because they were different. Their deeds and stories grew and developed their own myth. It's not that difficult to understand why some humans worship alcohol or materialism as their source of relief. Humans need something to hide behind because the truth would strip them bare."

"Why can't gods just live with humans side by side?"

"Because if they did that, my dear girl, they'd have to admit defeat. The fear of failure can be a dangerous adversary. Baltazaar and Satan are equal and opposites of the same coin, mutations of the soul that came into

DARK CLOUDS

existence, I believe, around the same time in order to create balance in the collective mass of soul energy. They had a power over humans because they could summon miracles and live longer than others. And when they did die they could move around freely as spirits, invincible souls, able to connect to the energy that runs through all of us. As you know, they can speak through it and travel to the universes that harness it. They built their fortresses there and breathed life into inanimate objects who were instructed to manage and control their worlds. And most of all they fought between themselves over souls, knowing that neither could win in a fight against the other – a status quo. The only victory, with an outcome that did not threaten their own existence, was over humans."

"How do you know all this?"

"Because I watched it unfold."

"I don't think you've told me the whole story of who you are and what part you've played in all this."

"I am and always have been a preacher. A man of faith. At first a man who had faith in a god I believed in. Afterwards, I found a faith in the need for human will power and self-determination. I was first known as the Priest of Byblos, then in Limbo the Cleric and with the passage of time, history changed my name to the Clerk. I have survived for one reason, to witness the endgame, and if possible to understand the fate of my own son."

"You had a son? Who is he?"

"Neither he nor I know, but I hope I will get a chance to work that out before the end."

Grace watched as grey clouds started to drift into the sky from the left- and right-hand sides of the horizon. These clouds would normally be forced to empty their contents as they hit the mountains and the pressure was forced to change. Not these ones.

"Do you have a plan?" said the Clerk.

"Yes," replied Grace.

DARK CLOUDS

"And how do you feel about what needs to be done?"

"I feel nothing. It's the only option, but it won't be easy."

"And when you get there, you'll know what to do?"

"If it is there, then I will turn it on. Will you look after Scrumpy for me?"

"There's not much time left for me, but while I still have it I will protect him."

A soldier approached them with a semi-automatic rifle held firmly in both hands. Behind him, more troops hurried into formation as if some unseen battle was unfolding around them. Until now everything had remained still and quiet as no signs of the enemy had been registered. Now something was happening.

"You must come with me," said the soldier, his face severe and unfriendly.

"Yes, of course," said Rogier calmly. "Who wants to see us?"

"Byron."

Grace looked at the Clerk and calmly got to her feet. She'd expected some trickery from him and it was always going to be necessary for them to get close to Byron.

Scrumpy was just returning to the compound as Grace, the Clerk and Rogier were led away with guns pointed towards them. They were escorted into a number of all-terrain vehicles and driven with speed into the distance, accompanied on foot by the entire compound of their coalition troops. He hid behind the aluminium sheet wall to avoid detection. What was going on? Were they going into battle already? Something deep within his instincts told him something was wrong. Quietly he scurried towards the river.

CHAPTER TWENTY-FOUR

SMALL BIRDS CHIRPING AT DAWN

Focus is difficult at the best of times. The world is crammed full of so many opportunities, there is almost too much choice. Too much choice breeds prevarication, which in turn gives rise to a sense of paralysis as our torn anxiety struggles to make the right decision. As a result those great opportunities are ignored and are substituted by sitting on your arse eating potato chips and watching reality TV. It's just a lot easier on body and brain.

There are people with amazing levels of will power. You'll see them at six o'clock in the morning pounding the streets with gadgets strapped to their arms as they attempt to break yesterday morning's personal best. They mock the rest of us with their external aura of 'look at me I'm making the most of my life'. They'll boldly, and falsely, tell you how much energy they have and why life is amazing, while all the time suppressing their secret internal misery. No one runs for fun. Period. If anyone tells you otherwise, they're lying.

Even though focus can be overrated, John was pleading for it to make a guest appearance for one night only. When you were everywhere, it was hard to concentrate. The energy-sapping meditation would only work for so long. If a supernova exploded somewhere in your peripheral vision it was pretty hard not to check it out. Just like the promise of reality television, it was often all show and no substance. After the disappointment he'd have to retrace his metaphysical steps and work out what his priorities were.

Concentration had at least assisted him in connecting to parts of his state that existed on the other side of the window. As he broke through metaphorical and physical barriers, a euphoria flooded over him more powerful than any since a life long forgotten. He felt free from the confines of his personal prison, even making it as far as the Earth before he'd lost his focus. Competing forces both directing him both towards and away from everything. There on Earth, right now, something vital was about to begin, and he felt an obligation to book a front-row seat. While all the time some external power was trying to stop him hearing the answers he hoped might be revealed.

Where, though, on Earth would it happen? He knew it would have to be a place of significance to all the important actors in the show. He focused on Limbo. It stretched across much of the Alpine mountain range but appeared dormant. Inside he felt an army of blue souls struggling to confine themselves within its walls. Whatever was happening, it wasn't here, at least not at the moment.

He stopped searching and started thinking. He was Sisyphus, boulder in constant motion up and down the mountainside. But what did the stone represent? What was he being punished for? He delved further into his memories to replay some vital remnant of history stored away in a dusty, creaky drawer marked 'forgotten'. In his forced vision a stone cairn sitting incongruously on a dusty plain materialised. The scene expanded outwards to the foreground and framed a long, jagged mountain range where a river hugged its roots like moss clinging to a drystone wall. And there it was. Some distance below him as clear as day in his foresight.

SMALL BIRDS CHIRPING AT DAWN

On the sun-soaked plain of semi-desert, three separate groups of soldiers were amassing for some great battle. On one side ten thousand soldiers encircled a small clearing where four figures were in conversation. Only one of them was familiar to him. It was the Clerk. But why was he there?

Up on the side of the mountain, on the other side of the plain, were a collection of characters all sporting rather puny wings that stuck out of their backs. A man in a hat was holding court in the centre. Then finally down on the banks of the river nine semi-naked men looked like they'd just opened the world's most remote and disorganised zoo. Whatever was about to happen, it was happening here and John needed to know what it was. It was about time to see if he could be everywhere at the same time and do what no man had ever achieved: multitasking.

*****

The mountains of the Middle East are a perfect place to hide from the authorities. A myriad of cave networks ran through a vast area, where few law-abiding civilians ever wished to venture. Here the worst of mankind sought sanctuary. Thieves, terrorist groups and enemies of the state all used the rugged terrain to escape the prying eyes of government law enforcement. Against this camouflage the most likely danger would come from a silent drone strike, and only then if you were stupid enough to wander outside for a cigarette or some fresh air.

A group of twenty or so miscreants, sporting long beards, characteristic keffiyeh headwear and gowns that were not suited to the thirty-five-plus degrees of heat, had gathered in a cave a hundred feet or so from where the sunlight only just managed to gatecrash the gloom. A strategy meeting was in full swing when it first started. It was certainly more dangerous than a drone strike and more unexpected than one of these people converting to Catholicism.

"If we approach the city from the sea, they'll never expect it," said a man wearing sunglasses. He appeared to be looking at no one in particular, the fashion statement being more important than the eye contact.

"The sea route is too difficult. The infidels will suspect something," came a riposte.

"Excuse me," said a third voice who was fidgeting against the bare and craggy rocks of the cave wall, "I don't do boats."

"What's wrong with boats, Hamid?"

"I'm allergic."

"We are frightened of nothing, brother."

"Apart from boats," added Hamid pointedly.

"Not boats. Not nothing. Allah is in our hearts and he will give us the strength we need in this life and the next. A thousand thanks."

"Remind me, Sayid, why are we targeting Byblos again?" said the boat hater to the man in glasses.

"How many times do we have to go over this? If you weren't my brother, Hamid, I'd suspect you were a CIA imposter. Byblos has been infested by…" – he spat on the ground – "…foreign scum. They parade through our streets enjoying their holidays, buying our goods and investing in our economy. Scum!"

"Scum!" echoed a number of others in harmony.

"That doesn't sound a very good reason to blow them up, Sayid."

"Oh, and what would you do, then? Take them all for a nice chat over a coffee and try to explain to them what we're fighting about until they convert to Islam!?"

"I like the idea of coffee: we haven't tried that, to be fair, but I think the main issue in that plan is we haven't actually agreed what we're fighting for. Remember, it was point five on yesterday's agenda and none of us could agree. In the end everyone went out on the mountainside and shot some goats to pass the time."

"You want a plan? It's simple. We hate Westerners, that's enough, isn't it?"

"It's a bit loose as far as strategic intent goes, don't you think?"

"Ok, we hate any Westerners who...don't have facial hair."

"Oh, that's much more sensible. We only hate you if you're non-Muslim and have recently shaved."

"Look, stop confusing things. We're not here to talk about why, only how. Understand? Any other points you want to raise, Hamid?"

"Yes, why do we always have to hide in caves? It's doing nothing for my backache and it's really affecting Mohammad's asthma."

Mohammad spluttered on cue and it echoed around for a good minute or so.

"Backache, asthma, boat allergies. We are freedom fighters. We live so we can die for our cause, nothing else matters. Allahu Akb..."

A powerful popping sound echoed around the chamber as Sayid evaporated into thin air before he'd finished his sentence. In the spot where he'd been sitting he was replaced by a tall, blond man with huge biceps and a highly disgruntled demeanour. Despite the shock, the others kept their composure and were soon training several Kalashnikovs on their uninvited guest.

"Typical," grumbled Wormwood.

"CIA!" shouted one of the aggressors through a scarf that muffled his words.

"More like CoE," replied Wormwood.

"Where is Sayid? How did you find us, foreign dog? Talk or die."

"I'd love to explain, but I'm not sure you'll be here long enough to hear the answer."

Pop. Another one was gone. Pop. And another.

SMALL BIRDS CHIRPING AT DAWN

The human popcorn machine reached critical temperature and soon the cave was consumed by the rattle of angels arriving and terrorists leaving.

Pop. Pop. Pop.

Wormwood was no longer staring down the barrel of several semi-automatic weapons. They, along with the people holding them, were now exploring the 'wild' on the other side of Heaven's wall where beast and badness lived in a constant state of disagreement. Standing in their place were a cat, a tarantula, an ox and a gibbon, all sporting wings.

"Come on, you lot," said Wormwood. "Let's see what's going on here."

They left the cave and ventured out onto the slopes of the mountain where they found they were not the only ones who'd arrived. At least a hundred decrepit-looking silkened OAPs were standing in a shallow valley between the mountains, watching the proclamations of an equally elderly gentleman wearing a white Panama hat.

"Who's that?" asked Elsie.

"A wrong 'un. I don't like men in hats," said Vicky. "Something deeply suspicious about them."

"I think that's Baltazaar," said Wormwood. "It's been a while since we saw him in human form, but it certainly feels like him."

"Who's Baltazaar?" asked Abe quietly.

"Well for the purposes of this situation and your own personal desire, mister ox, he's God."

"God!" said Abe. "God doesn't wear a hat."

"He does today."

The elderly preacher tipped his hat back slightly to allow him a better view of his troops. Leaning on his walking stick for support, he cleared his throat.

"Welcome."

No one responded.

"You have been summoned, which means Heaven has been compromised. There is no way back. This will be your last stand. Here in this valley we will enforce the endgame and the universe will be renewed. We may be outnumbered, but our advantage will not be numerical. You, my angels, should not be here. You are not mortal and therein lies our real advantage. Take what skills you have with you into battle."

"I'm amazing at kung fu!" Roger shouted from the crowd.

"I will return here once I have met with our enemy. In the meantime ready yourself for war."

After a brief pause, the weather congregated around him to lift Baltazaar up on a breeze and carry him down the valley with ease.

"Show off," said Roger rather too loudly. "I can do that. Piece of piss."

*****

Byron sat on top of the stone cairn as he watched them approach. Ten thousand troops designed to fight against him were now in his control. It had been rather too easy. Every one of those troops had been corrupted by the same desire. Survival. The coalition was a shambles and Byron had offered them a way out. Fight with him, and live. Fight against him, and don't. He'd only had to melt five or six of them before he'd got his point across.

Now they were bringing him his foes without him lifting a finger. Who needed Victor when you had ten thousand gun-touting converts? Whatever Baltazaar managed to summon would be no match for guns, tanks and bombs. And his greatest weapon was the small girl walking towards him. Only two small, unknown factors niggled against his obvious victory. The dual revelations that not only was the Clerk's son unaccounted for, but there was also a demon in Hell he knew nothing about. Whoever this Mr. Noir was, he was most definitely not a demon. Which meant there was only one thing he could be.

The soldiers led their captives up to the cairn and only Rogier didn't know who it was they were facing.

"I demand you give me back my army," beseeched the Swiss Premier in uncustomary forcefulness.

"They're not yours anymore. It's simply a case of psychology. You want them to fight with a bunch of ill-prepared misfits and I want them to fight with a man who's capable, and extremely willing, to melt those misfits before they get within rifle range. It's not a hard decision, really."

"What do you want, Byron?" asked Grace calmly.

"I want to repair what has been broken. I want vengeance."

"Against who?"

"Him," he said, pointing at the Clerk, "and the rest of humanity."

The Clerk edged forward, the energy squeezing from every cell in his body from the effort. The wind ruffled through what remained of his hair. It whipped in circular gusts around the cairn before a clap of thunder placed Baltazaar in the centre of them like a magician's spectacular entrance. Storms were absent, the polarities of the three gods beautifully balancing each other out. He doffed his hat in silent welcome and waited for the Clerk's speech, eager to see what he might learn.

"It wasn't me that concocted the deal," said the Clerk. "You were responsible for that."

"You tricked me," said Byron.

"And now you know how it feels," replied the Clerk.

"He tricked us both," said Baltazaar. "You showed him a vision, Byron, and it caused him to preach against us. It started a revolution against religion. He started to turn humans against us."

"How?" said Byron.

"Because I knew you had no way of dealing with neutral souls, and if I could create some you would need a solution," said the Clerk. "After you showed me my vision, I went to Limbo and explained to Baltazaar what you were doing. He offered my sanctuary."

"Is that true?" asked Byron.

"Yes," said Baltazaar. "I gave him a job."

"Why?"

"Because it would piss you off and he said he had a plan for dealing with the neutrals. It was the Clerk who suggested building the court and judging over the neutral souls that came there."

"But you didn't tell me it was his idea when you asked me to agree to it, did you?" said Byron.

"No."

"He tricked you into creating the twelve because he knew that his own son was preaching a message to create more neutral souls. Without him, they would have been an anomaly, a one-in-a-million occurrence!" exclaimed Byron.

"Without you, you mean," said the Clerk defiantly. "It was your deal, wasn't it? You were desperate for a decent competition, weren't you? I gave it to you, even though you weren't aware until now."

"Humans have reduced our influence and they must be punished," said Baltazaar.

"Why should they worship the two of you? You're nothing but freaks of nature. Mutations of the soul. You did not create humans and you have no authority to destroy them," said the Clerk.

"Quite right," said Baltazaar. "But we know what did create the Universes and how it can be reversed. The endgame only needs a spark."

"Over my dead body," said Byron, squaring up to Baltazaar for the first time in his life. "I'm not ready to go. You will put things back as they were or I will destroy you."

"You know that's impossible. You really think your illustrious crony Victor can just shoot me?"

"I think you'll find he's my crony now," said Grace.

"It doesn't matter who he belongs to, no bullet can destroy me," bragged Baltazaar.

"What I want to know most of all is what happened to your son," said Byron to the Clerk.

"I wish I knew. I'm guessing he's not where you thought he was."

"No," said Byron. "He apparently never was. How can that be?"

"Because when you took his life he had already cleansed his soul of all negative and positive influence. He was neutral when you took him and that means he only had one place to go."

"But your jury in Limbo would have judged him and sent him on. So he must have gone to Heaven instead, then."

"That depends," said the Clerk.

"On what?" said Byron and Baltazaar together.

"If you remember, Baltazaar, when I suggested the court I recommended that you use the first neutrals to arrive as the jury."

"John," replied Byron. "No wonder he's been such a pain in the arse all this time."

"It makes no difference," snorted Baltazaar. "John and David are gone and nothing remains of the twelve. They are dead and can no longer hurt us."

"Well, that's not quite true," said the Clerk. "Grace here is John's daughter, born to a mother who was under the influence of Emorfed. It produced a mutated neutral soul. Or a god if you want to give it a label. Another unintended consequence of your desire to subdue mankind, Baltazaar. By the way, I think Byron may have been keeping that information from you."

A sudden force ten gale crashed through the gathering, knocking most people off their feet as an angry curse reverberated through their bones. Baltazaar's anger overflowed as he sent balls of thunder crashing down on the soldiers from every finger. Bodies were flung into the air like rag dolls.

"STOP!"

SMALL BIRDS CHIRPING AT DAWN

And everyone did.

*****

Finally Scrumpy was engaged in what he enjoyed doing most. Adventures. The world was waiting to be explored and an enemy was there to be defeated. And this time it was real. In the past, pirates had been vanquished in his mind alone, imperial soldiers defeated by the might of his imagination, monsters destroyed by whatever weapons he could pretend to yield. It was useful training for what would come over the next few days.

The enemy had taken his sister prisoner and only he would be the hero. But he'd need more than an overactive imagination. He needed weapons, allies and a bloody good plan. Sadly, the first two had seemingly walked off with the captives, and the third was very much a work in progress. Escape first, plan later was the order of the day.

When he reached the banks of the Assi River he found a small, empty camp consisting of an extinguished fire and a few discarded fishing rods. A wooden boat had been fashioned out of twigs and reeds and was floating on an eddy, calmly tethered to the bank. In the distance the noise of the camp's returning occupants padded along the riverside.

Nine burly Pacific Islanders, wearing simple headpieces and sporting less clothing than a newborn baby, walked in single file along the beige grass bank. Their faces were set to a permanent grin as if their brains hadn't felt it necessary to communicate to the rest of its body that they might actually be in a war zone. They smiled even more when they saw the curly-haired body standing alone in their camp.

The largest of their kind marched forward, picked him up by the ears and threw him into the air, only to catch him again before his limbs were crushed by the ground. The others clapped along madly as if they knew what was going on. They didn't.

"Me, Chief Uinirau. It means 'small birds chirping at dawn'. Welcome."

"Me, Scrumpy…um…which means…'mighty apples produce sore head'. What are you doing here?"

"We fight. We ready for great battle."

The eight others clapped again but showed no obvious sign they understood any of the limited English that Chief Uinirau was uttering.

"I want to fight, but I'm too small. Not sure what help I'll be."

"In Nauru mightiest tree grow from smallest seed. Size of heart more important than size of body."

"I've only got an eight-year-old's heart, it's probably not that big either."

"Heart not organ, heart is will, is courage, is confidence."

"I should be ok, then. I've taken on loads of pirates in my time," he said puffing out his chest and smiling ruefully at the sky. "This enemy is different, though. And they've taken my sister."

"Girls not fight. On Nauru we protect girls."

"Well, she is a god so I'm not sure she needs much protection."

"Girl not a god. God invisible voice in the air that comes from ball of shiny metal," said Uinirau.

"If you say so. Don't you get cold?" asked Scrumpy, suddenly realising how inappropriate it was for an eight-year-old boy to be surrounded by nine broadly naked men. Nash would definitely not have approved.

"Clothes for battle."

"Armour, shields, helmets, that sort of thing?" said Scrumpy.

"Grass skirts."

"Not much though, is it? You might get shot in the nipple."

"Fear not, Chief Scrumpy, Nauru people have tough skin and mighty army to bring us victory."

SMALL BIRDS CHIRPING AT DAWN

Scrumpy scanned, from the waist up at least, the nine bulky, some might suggest even rather overweight, middle-aged Polynesians. They were neither mighty nor definable as an army. Plucky, but not an army.

"I'm not sure nine counts as an army, Uinirau."

"Nine! No, many more."

Uinirau placed his fingers to his lips and produced the loudest whistle Scrumpy had ever heard. It bounced off the mountain walls and carried for miles. After about a minute of this deafening shrill he stopped.

"Wow," said Scrumpy excitedly. "I'm going to need you to teach me that."

"Yup yup."

"What was it for?"

"Army."

In the distance a massive swarm of bodies was moving in all directions to join forces. Some strolled down the slopes of mountainside, some floated down the river, others walked from the plains and here and there heads popped out of holes in the ground. Creatures on four legs, two legs, no legs, swam, walked and flew towards the camp. There were thousands of them: bears, dogs, badgers, rhinos, buffalo, squirrels, vultures, eagles, a German Shepherd and from every other branch of the animal kingdom. And at the front, leading them all, was a small, brown rabbit with big, floppy ears.

"Where did they come from?" asked Scrumpy.

"All over. They come to fight," answered Uinirau.

"How do you know?" asked Scrumpy curiously.

"Told us."

"You mean they can all talk?"

"Yup yup."

CHAPTER TWENTY-FIVE

THE SLOTH AND THE SINGULARITY

Darkness settled on the plains for one last calm night before the storm burst. Tomorrow the amassed forces would be unleashed against each other, and no discerning bookmaker would even contemplate offering odds on who'd win. In the gloom of dusk a man in black settled down for the evening in a makeshift trench. Next to it stood a dune high enough to see the battle from, but low enough to avoid any attention which might come his way.

He checked and cleaned his SVLK long-range sniper's rifle. It was a sophisticated weapon. As long as the marksman was competent enough, it was capable of hitting an object as far as three kilometres away. And fortunately he could make that shot dancing the American Smooth and half-drunk.

Victor removed the folded piece of paper containing the instructions of what was required of him. Once he read it his position and mission would be compromised. Removing a lighter from his rucksack, he ran his thumb over the flint. It sparked, the mechanism as hesitant as he was to go through with the action. He thumbed it more confidently and the gas lit the end. He placed the paper into its flame and in moments its sooty remains floated into the night sky. He didn't need to read it. He knew what to do.

*****

THE SLOTH AND THE SINGULARITY

The unexpected vocal appearance had led to chaos on the cairn and a scattering on all sides. Baltazaar shot off into the evening on the back of a strong tailwind. Grace, the Clerk and Rogier commandeered one of the Swiss tanks, which had earlier been removed from the compound along with the entire Swiss Army. In the confusion of Baltazaar's strop, that had claimed the first casualties of war, they'd slipped not so quietly back to the compound. There they were alone. Their army had shrunk from ten thousand to three, unless of course they could get hold of the Nauru with the walkie-talkie. Tomorrow they'd have to face up to battle with or without an army. Since their return there had been no sign of Scrumpy, just one more thing to worry about.

"Clerk, I think it's time you got back to Limbo," said Grace. "You'll not survive much longer without its protection."

"You're probably right," he replied. "I can feel the life force slipping from me with every breath. I was hoping to see the endgame for myself, but I'll have to leave humanity's fate in your hands."

"If all goes to plan you'll still be needed in Limbo. And so will John."

"After all these years at least I know where my son is. If only I'd known when I saw him in Limbo before his trial. I said at the time even his mother wouldn't recognise him. How right I was. He's had so many faces I'm not sure he would recognise his original self either."

"Will you take Scrumpy with you?" asked Grace. "I don't want him in the middle of all of this. His moment is still to come."

"Of course, if we can find him, that is."

Night-time was in full swing. Only the light from a couple of torches illuminated the now deserted makeshift barracks. The only sounds to break the deafening silence were the gentle beat of their hearts

THE SLOTH AND THE SINGULARITY

and the rhythmic hum from the wings of nocturnal insects dodging around the torchlight like a poorly organised rave. They settled for a breather on the tank's painted camouflage where, to their own and lasting surprise, they combusted into dust. Grace watched these apparently unintended suicides with interest. She placed her hand on the tank's shell to see what was causing it, only to find it was almost too hot to touch. Things did get hot here, but not usually at night when the combination of sun and sand were doused by the night's sky.

The tank glowed red for a moment and then disappeared with a sizeable pop.

Grace was the only one who didn't jump. Unusual though this was, there would be a logical explanation. Although at times like this logic did look like a bit of an arse. Substituted in place of the tank was a silky-winged sloth clutching a silver-coloured metal football. On the face of it, when you're due to go into battle the next day and your only military equipment was the tank, it seemed like a pretty disappointing exchange.

"Hello," said Grace, contemplating another unfathomable puzzle. Rogier and the Clerk shook off the initial shock and came to join her.

"Hello," said Gary.

"What are you doing here?"

"Trans...mog...ri...fi...cation."

"Where's my tank?" demanded Rogier sternly.

The sloth shrugged.

The tank was being put to good use. A group of Islamic fundamentalists were delighted with its unexpected arrival and were already test-driving it into a wall covered in brambles, much to the concern and irritation of one grumpy, short-arsed angel on the other side.

"And what's that you're holding?" asked the Clerk, taking a keen interest in the object and the way it was being protected by the creature.

THE SLOTH AND THE SINGULARITY

"What?"

They waited.

"This?" said Gary pulling the ball closer to his chest in slow motion.

"It's."

"It's what?" asked the Clerk, interrupting and not yet familiar with Gary's unique communication style.

"MINE," snapped the sloth.

"You know what it looks like, don't you?" said Rogier to the Clerk.

"Gary's."

"That's what I was thinking," replied the Clerk.

"Singularity."

"A singularity!" said Grace in confusion. "You can't just hold a singularity. They're impossibly dense and filled with enough energy and matter to create a big bang. Plus they have no discernible volume, that's why they are called a singularity."

"That's."

A snail made decent progress across the ground.

"Why…"

Rogier gave an encouraging hurry-up signal. Even the Swiss Parliament made decisions quicker than this.

"I'm…"

"What?" said all three in unison.

"So…slow."

The Clerk signalled to Grace to join him for a quiet word away from the sloth's earshot.

"Grace, this is most irregular. This object shouldn't be here. If I'm not mistaken it's made of Celestium and is probably one of few pieces in the known cosmos."

"But he called it a singularity," said Grace totally befuddled. "The same thing that triggered the big bang thirteen billion years ago. How can it be made of Celestium?"

"Maybe there's a connection. Perhaps there is more to this metal than meets the eye. We know it can expand, we know it absorbs energy and can be

THE SLOTH AND THE SINGULARITY

absorbed by the right type of soul. Only ones that are not balanced correctly, that is, like John's, or Baltazaar's or Satan's or…yours. We know there was a piece at the centre of every Universe except this one. That's why Satan stole the piece from the 'third way' and brought it here in order that humans wouldn't find it. This piece must have come from Heaven or Hell. Probably from one of their Soul Catchers. This might just be the bargaining chip we need."

"To stop the war?" said Grace.

"Or win it," answered the Clerk. "Gary, which Soul Catcher did you take this from, Heaven or Hell?"

"Neither," replied Gary correctly.

"Then where did you get it from?"

"Heaven."

"That makes no sense at all. It came from Heaven but not from their Soul Catcher."

"I think I can answer this one," said John, who'd been listening to multiple conversations around the world, but found this one the most interesting.

"Who keeps doing that?" said Rogier, holding his heart to stop it popping out of his chest again.

"Keeps doing it? I think that was the first," said John, uncertain as to why Rogier was so familiar with a voice from thin air. *"I'm John, and there's only one of me…or at most two."*

"But do you have to butt in like that when we're not expecting it?"

"I can't exactly give you a nudge or a wink beforehand can I."

"What about a subtle signal?"

"Ok, next time I'll cough first."

"What do you know, John?" asked the Clerk.

"When the Soul Catcher in Hell was ripped apart by the shadow souls, a ball of metal similar to that one rose from the machine and disappeared out of the window into space. It must have been drawn to the nearest Universe."

THE SLOTH AND THE SINGULARITY

"A ball of metal also came out of David when he was killed on Tresco by Baltazaar," said Grace.

"David entered Limbo like few others can, walked straight through the metal. His soul must have absorbed some of the Celestium."

"What would happen if David triggered the Limpet Syndrome for a third time?" asked John, thinking about what he would have done in David's position.

"It would have torn his soul apart and jettisoned whatever was left into the galaxy. That's only a guess, mind. I've not heard of anyone triggering it that many times before."

"That explains a lot. But if there was Celestium inside him, where would it go?"

"The third way. The very place that Baltazaar was trying to stop him going. Of course, without knowing it he sent David there and left the real god, Grace, to fight on."

"I think I need to have a look at this singularity," said Grace, approaching the protective sloth.

Gary did his best to run away, not that anyone noticed. In his mind he was at a sprint when she finally caught up with him. Others, like the midget, had already attempted to forcibly remove the object from him. No matter how hard they'd tried, the singularity clung to Gary like a limpet. Grace, though, had no desire to remove it, she just wanted to touch it. As her hands came to rest on the sides where there weren't sloth paws, the metal reacted. Imperceptibly it explored her fingers, its liquid structure analysing the flesh and the soul within it.

After a few moments of connection between her soul and the ball, Grace let go and moved away. Gary smiled at her and bowed. An action that was completed sometime around dawn.

*****

THE SLOTH AND THE SINGULARITY

"Wake up!" shouted Roger at the top of his voice. "It's hero time!"

"Oh do fuck off," replied Vicky, stirring from an uncomfortable dream that had involved being held captive by a bunch of terrorists dressed as rodents and wielding feather dusters.

"We're going to war, and I'm going to be amazing at it. Get up."

Roger had been busy this morning. He'd already fashioned a rather feeble helmet out of a bandana left by one of the last residents of the cave, buffed his wings shiny, and was wielding what can only be described as a lasso in one paw.

"Do we really have to fight with this lot?" said Abe. "I mean, are they on the side of the righteous?"

"Who said anything about fighting with the angels?" replied Roger.

"Whose side are we on, then?" asked Elsie.

"Ours."

"What?"

"The four of us will fight together for ourselves."

"Against who?" asked Vicky. "We don't even know who we're up against or what the fight is about."

"It doesn't matter," said Roger.

"Roger, war has been a thing for as long as man has had something to fight about. And in all that time there hasn't been a single incident of war where an army has gone into battle without knowing who they're fighting!"

This was true. Wars were as much a part of human existence as wings were part of an effective jumbo jet. The first wars were simple affairs based on minor squabbles that began with such remarks as 'They've got more food than us,' or 'I want to have sex with their women,' or 'Who threw that stone?' They were generally over pretty quickly. Either someone ran away, or they got tired of hitting each other with bits of trec.

THE SLOTH AND THE SINGULARITY

The length of wars could be plotted on a bell-shaped curve. At first they were over quickly, then as opposite foes discovered simple but crude weapons, they got longer. Because no one had superior weapons they lasted for decades until no one could quite remember what they were fighting about in the first place. Religion usually. Recently wars could be over in a matter of seconds. Just one big button to press. In all of this pattern, Vicky was right: everyone always knew who they were fighting even if they couldn't remember why.

"We're going to fight anyone who gets in our way," answered Roger.

"He's properly gone over the edge this time," said Elsie.

"In the way of what?" said Abe.

"Protecting our friend. The five of us have been on this journey together from the start and no one will be left behind."

They immediately recognised what he meant. They'd always left Gary behind with little care for his welfare, always more interested in their own. It had taken the least likely of their gang to show the most important of qualities, friendship. The five of them were, after all, separated by so many differences in their beliefs, personalities and prejudices that only one thing really united them. Each other.

"You're right, Roger. What's your plan?"

"Spectacular."

"I wasn't looking for a review," said Vicky. "I wanted the details."

"When the angels advance into battle just stay close to me and I'll show you the AMAZING plan, the best plan you've ever seen," said Roger, padding out of the cave and into the sunlight that rose over the plain.

"He's actually got no idea what the plan is, has he?" said Abe solemnly.

"Not sure he ever does," replied Vicky.

CHAPTER TWENTY- SIX

THE BATTLE OF GODS

Sunrise arrived with the same relentless regularity that it did each and every morning. The grey clouds loitering in the low atmosphere could do nothing to stop its march. Occasional shards of sunlight pierced through their shield and momentarily shone like spotlights on the ground. Tomorrow it would happen all over again like clockwork. Whether any of the three armies amassed under it would bear witness would become evident the next time it rose from the east.

Grace strode confidently out of the compound. If she'd prepared for the battle it certainly wouldn't have been evident in a 'spot the difference' competition. She wore no armour, carried no weapon and did nothing to hide her position or intentions. To her left was a middle-aged man in a suit who looked like he was walking to a job interview. To her right, being pulled along on a small cart with wheels attached to each corner, was a sloth holding a metal ball looking like nothing you've ever seen. This might break records for the shortest involvement in a war by any army ever.

Marching towards them across from the opposite side of the plain was the first battalion of the Swiss Army. They weren't the best fighting force the world had to offer, but perfectly capable of defeating an eleven-year-old girl, a public official and an almost static sloth. They'd dispensed with the need for heavy artillery. The missiles were primed and waiting if the unthinkable happened, but for now they just sent

THE BATTLE OF GODS

forward a thousand of their best men. The forces of Suriname and Djibouti were kept in reserve, very deep reserves at that.

On the other side of them, descending gingerly down the mountainside, was a fashion show from the fifties, although it wasn't clear which century. Silken vessols, which fluttered slightly as the wind breezed through their lightweight bodies, advanced, seemingly more interested in the three of them than the military might of Byron's army. Who could blame them?

Byron stood some distance behind his soldiers on top of the stone cairn that balanced on top of the dune. Baltazaar watched his winged assailants from the safety of a craggy outcrop on the other side of the battlefield. Grace only had one plan and that required that both of them were drawn into battle. Her coalition of three would have to hold off the oncoming troops until they saw fit to join in. As she was desperately trying to contemplate how that could be achieved other than stopping time, which would only delay the situation, a long, loud whistle pierced the air behind them.

In the distance, behind a large dust cloud that blocked the horizon, something massive was getting closer. The dust was soon replaced by a long line of creatures running to their aid. In front, nine Polynesians were defying their natural bulk by keeping pace with a curly-haired boy riding a horse and holding a rabbit. Closely following behind was the thunderous noise of hooves, paws and wings.

"Hello, sis," said Scrumpy as he drew up next to her.

"Scrumpy! I wondered where you'd got to."

"I brought you an army."

"So I can see," she said as more and more animals joined the throng. "They're all reincarnates, aren't they?"

"No. Nine of them are big blokes from a little island called Narnia."

THE BATTLE OF GODS

"Nauru," offered Chief Uinirau in correction.

"And I found a friend," added Scrumpy, holding up the rabbit.

"Hello, Grace."

"Nash. You managed to hear my message before you died."

"I did. It's not quite what I'd have chosen, but beggars can't be choosers."

"Why are you here?" asked Grace.

"When I changed form I could remember everything that we were working towards. I knew I needed to do something to help."

"Did you do all of this?" said Grace, pointing at the thousands of mammals collected around her.

"Yes. There are just so many of us out there now. Every one of them was keen to put humanity back on track, even if humans aren't willing to. We're here to fight for you, Grace. We're here to make things right again."

"You might just give me the time that I need."

"This the girl god?" said Chief Uinirau, looking at her suspiciously.

"Yes," replied Scrumpy.

"She do miracles?"

"I've asked her to, but no."

"What about invisible man in sky?"

"Oh, we've got one of those, too," replied Grace.

"In that case, Chief Uinirau and his army at your command."

"Me, too!" shouted Scrumpy.

"Not you," replied Grace.

"What! I've brought you an army. I'm their leader."

"You're an eight-year-old boy who's too important to me to lose in battle. Chief Uinirau take our army to the battlefront. I'll join you once I've spoken with Scrumpy. Nash, you can stay here, too."

Chief Uinirau gave another of his customary whistles and the hairy and feathered reincarnates followed him at a walking pace towards the enemy.

THE BATTLE OF GODS

"Scrumpy, you must leave this place."

"Why?"

"Because I don't want you to see what will happen to me."

"What are you planning?" said Nash.

"I must make a choice between saving gods and humans. You are my only family and I love you."

"Love us?" said Nash from behind prickly whiskers. "Grace, you're neutral and love is a positive emotion."

"I don't think love has anything to do with the soul. I think love has a force of its own. Even the most wicked person can show their love for someone. Is it not also rational to protect those that you love. I will protect you and the rest of mankind, but I cannot stay with you."

"What do you mean?" asked Scrumpy, trying to follow Grace's train of thought but struggling with all the soppy sentiment.

"I won't be coming back from the battle. I'm the only one who can stop it and there is only one way it can be done."

"You can't leave us," said Scrumpy. "I don't want to be on my own."

"You're not alone, Scrumpy. The Clerk and Nash will look after you and soon you'll have another companion, if all goes well."

"What about the battle? I brought all of these animals here, I can't leave them to fight alone," said Nash.

"They have their own scores to settle."

"But what will happen to you?" said Nash.

"I'm a god, and gods have certain duties to take care of. We'll see each other again, onc day."

Scrumpy dismounted the horse and flung himself at his sister. Hugging wasn't really her thing. She didn't really understand how it worked and what it was for. But she recognised that others gained warmth and comfort from it and so she did her best to engage in it. Nash was hopping around her feet doing his best to join in by flapping his big ears against her ankles. When it felt like the moment had gone on long enough, Grace pulled out and a tear ran down her cheek.

"You must go now, the Clerk doesn't have long to live. Get him back to Limbo and help him get what he needs."

They watched as she walked casually off to join the new coalition without glancing back again.

*****

If you absolutely have to watch a war at close range then the best place to be is where John was. Everywhere other than physically involved. There wasn't a documentary maker in the world that wouldn't envy the camera angles that John could get. He could see the battle from an aerial position, from within the melee, from the left flank, right flank and, even if the motivation took him, on the shoulders of a sloth on wheels. John watched everything unfold, waiting for the right moment to make an appearance.

The first wave of attacks came from Chief Uinirau. His command of English might have been less than perfect, but his instincts were on top form. When the animals got close enough to assess what they were up against it seemed a sensible move to advance on the geriatric angels, rather than the highly weaponised Swiss Army. After all, they appeared to be slow, unarmed and lacking in spirit.

The birds of prey were sent first, dive-bombing the first line of angels that had made it down onto the plain. Owls, eagles, crows and anything that had flight rained down on them to peck away at their soft armour. The angels' only response was to complain aggressively about the bird shit falling on their best 'battle suits' and to swat their arms aimlessly into the air. Little serious damage was done in this first wave.

THE BATTLE OF GODS

The silken vessels were a lot more robust than they looked.

Wormwood, who was at the front of the pack and one of the only ones not wearing a vessol, did his best to look interested, even though he wasn't in the slightest. The only resistance came from four unusual-looking angels who were screaming berserker fashion and charging out of the pack. John watched as they threw stones at owls, tripped up other angels, and shouted 'GARY!' at the top of their voices.

The second wave came from the Swiss. Realising that the angels were not putting up much of a fight, and noticing the reincarnates had weakened themselves by making the first move, Byron sent in his soldiers. The first battalion advanced on foot and when they were in a suitable position their general announced the command to fire. It only took one shot.

Animals are born with an inbuilt fear of death. The options for snuffing it were everywhere. It might come from a larger animal of the same breed desperate to prove it was bigger and stronger than you, or it might come from something with bigger teeth further up the food chain. But often it came from man. In the deep recesses of the mammal's brain the sound of a gunshot had the immediate and impulsive reaction of sending the animal into hasty retreat. Not all of them, though, in the same direction.

The battlefront was starting to resemble the mass escape from a safari park. Reincarnates bolted in every direction, before switching tack with each further gun fired. Were they running into danger or away from it? A couple of rhinos with poor sense of direction bolted right into the first line of the Swiss Army, launching a number of them perpendicularly into the air. A couple of rhino-shaped lines severed the unit down the middle.

In the hysteria of gunshots and panicking zebras a German Shepherd totally lost it. Its only impulse was to maim whatever it could shake, which just happened

THE BATTLE OF GODS

to be a few of the angels that had got close enough to the battle. Once he'd got his teeth jammed into their silk vessols, had shaken them repeatedly around his head, and discarded them into the air, they came apart at the seams with an almighty rip.

Once an angel was out of its vessol, all that was left was a short burst of energy with nowhere else to go. The soul was spent but the energy at least still had life left in it, for about three seconds at least. The energy burst outwards like a broken balloon, taking any angel within two metres' proximity with it. And so this chain of events continued like a well-placed domino race up the hillside.

The chaos and gunfire continued, but Chief Uinirau wasn't done. Small fights were breaking out in every available space across the vast expanse of barren desert. The Swiss Army were out of formation, firing madly at anything that moved. The use of any of the more destructive weapons would only result in a partial destruction of their own forces. Uinirau directed a squadron of otters and squirrels down one flank and sent the insects in on the other.

Shooting a rhino was fairly straightforward as long as you got it from a distance. Rabbits and other small mammals were more of a challenge, but you were happy if they came close in so you got an easier shot. But not even Victor could take out a wasp with a rifle.

No one likes wasps at the best of times. They have a habit of ruining BBQs by pissing in everyone's beer and squatting on your beautifully cooked lamb kebab. No suitable deterrent has ever been invented for mitigating against the little sods. Their only purpose in life is to annoy humans, which is why they make perfect paratroopers. John watched a large platoon of Swiss soldiers running in circles while swatting the air and firing indiscriminately, often into their own colleagues.

John never once felt like getting involved. Against all the odds the coalition of beasts was winning

THE BATTLE OF GODS

against the well-heeled professionals and the less-heeled angels. In the centre of it all, Grace, Rogier and Gary continued to walk slowly towards the cairn where Byron was watching the battle, and his advantage, fall apart. When the three of them reached a visible distance from Byron, Gary raised a round, silver object into the air.

*****

Baltazaar watched the battle from the mountainside a safe distance away. It was clear his side were losing, just as he'd planned it. The angels were never more than a distraction, a way of deflecting attention from him and drawing forces away from Byron. The minor battles could go on for as long as necessary. Any deaths would merely advance his agenda of human destruction. The angels wouldn't be going back the way they came, and it was essential they all came to a sticky end.

What was needed now was a new plan. Limbo had evidently stopped expanding as more humans opted for reincarnation. Many of those that had were here, and hopefully a few might be dispatched through the natural selection of battle. But the genie was out of the bottle. Word of mouth wasn't something that could easily be stopped. It had become an exponential chain reaction, like seeing a thousand reflections of yourself in a mirror. But humankind must still end if gods were to regain control. And that would never be possible if the third way was open. If Grace was killed, that possibility became more likely. Only another big bang could avoid it.

Down on the battlefield a collection of geriatric angels were acting as mini-hand grenades as one by one their vessels were being disrupted and the small explosions were wiping out anything in their vicinity. A horde of creatures were rampaging in chaotic formation in all directions on the instructions of a semi-naked giant pointing what looked like a large piece of hollowed-out bamboo cane. And there in the middle of it all were three figures advancing on what remained of the Swiss forces. The sun glinted off the surface of a shiny object raised up high by one of them. Was that what he thought it was?

"Time's running out."

"I wondered when you might make an appearance," replied Baltazaar calmly.

"You know what that is, don't you?"

"It looks like a singularity."

"Yes. And you know what that means, don't you?"

"Not if I get to it first."

"Your reign will soon be over. Like every other so-called god that has gone before you, there is no substitute for the real thing."

"I'll decide when it's over. I'll decide what happens next. For over five thousand years I have manipulated the direction of human life and death. I have built a domain and managed the afterlife. I have changed the path of evolution itself and not even you can stop me."

"We'll see, won't we? I've been watching it for over thirteen billion years. I'm tired. It's John's turn now."

*****

Before Byron and Baltazaar could reach Grace and her companions, four significant others beat them to it. Roger, leading from the front as always, had dispatched all in his path as they'd made a beeline for their velocity-challenged friend. Angels, animals and panic-stricken Swiss infantrymen had all scarpered as the four misfits had charged down the mountainside, across the plain and within sight of the cairn on the dune. In their minds the two characters standing either side of the sloth must be holding him prisoner.

"Let him go!" shouted Roger at the top of his voice.

"They're," started Gary.

"Who are you?" said Rogier.

"On."

"Freedom fighters!"

"Our."

"But you're made of silk and your wings don't work."

"Side."

"Do you want some?" growled the ox, still unable to control the bouts of anger that appeared to come instantly the moment someone looked at him in the wrong way or spoke in an overly aggressive tone.

"What do you mean they're on our side, Gary?" said Vicky.

"We are! I'm Rogier, President of Switzerland."

"That's not how you pronounce it," said Roger.

"Not how you pronounce what?"

"It's R-O-G-E-R, not Rogier," said the lion indignantly. "And you can't possibly be a president."

"Yes, I am!"

"You've just made it up to make yourself sound more important."

"And he should know," whispered Vicky under her breath.

"Gary is holding something rather important," said Grace, speaking for the first time in what was an unexpected twist of events. They'd double their force in number, but not, by the looks of it, in talent. "Very soon two rather annoyed omnipotent beings are about to come down here to take it from him."

"Well, that's not happening," said Roger.

"No, it's not," replied Grace. "But we do need them here. If you want to survive what is about to happen I suggest you encourage your friend here to hand it over to me and retreat as quickly as you can."

Gary shook his head and drew the ball of metal further into his abdomen like he was protecting a fragile vase.

"No. If Gary won't part with it then we won't part with him."

"Then you are most welcome. Rogier, you have given more than anyone could ask of you, I think you should go back and join Chief Uinirau."

"I just said I'm not going anywhere," repeated the lion.

"She's talking to me," said Rogier.

"Good. We only need one Roger, I bet you don't even know how to do a double roundhouse kick?"

"He'll be in good company then," added Vicky.

"Thank you, Rogier. If you see my brother, help him as best as you can."

"Good luck, Grace."

"She doesn't need luck, she's got us. It'll be a piece of piss."

CHAPTER TWENTY-SEVEN

SHOOT

Simultaneously Byron and Baltazaar swept into the midst of their group. Byron arrived in a burst of fire, the flames whipping round them and causing the air to scorch their throats. His face had aged since yesterday's meeting as if the weight of his inner age had seeped through his soul and into his flesh. Wrinkles dug across his skin, and his eyes burnt with the energy of a fire's dying embers.

Baltazaar circled through the air and landed with a thud on the ground on the other side of them. The ubiquitous Panama hat could be seen floating away on the gusts of wind left in his wake, a lost artefact of a persona soon to be changed forever, one way or another. Both advanced with their hands outstretched towards Gary and his precious cargo. Immediately the four other animals encircled the sloth protectively.

The battle continued in the background unabated, but in this small patch of dusty, rock-strewn ground an unseen serenity surrounded them. John watched it intently from his front-row pew. Grace was the only one whose demeanour remained consistent. The means of the gathering may have been different than she'd imagined, but the scene was exactly as she'd planned it.

"I'm going to give you a choice," she said, looking left and right to ensure that both of her peers knew she was addressing them.

"You don't get to make the rules," said Baltazaar.

"That doesn't seem to have stopped you in the past."

SHOOT

"How dare you speak to me like that! You know nothing of divinity. We are gods. We do as we want."

"You may call yourself gods, but you are not godly. You may have an advantage over humans, but that does not give you the right to change them," replied Grace.

"Not all of us have done that," added Byron. "I have been trying to preserve humanity."

"For your own gains. You just want their energy to fuel your own hunger. Baltazaar's deceit has, until recently, been to your own advantage."

"That's hardly my fault, is it?"

"You offered the Priest a deal, though, didn't you? You lit the fuse of humanity's corruption."

"I'm on your side, Grace: he wants the singularity to renew the Universe, he wants to start over again with a new big bang."

"And you want it to, for honourable reasons, I'm sure."

"The singularity belongs to Hell, it must go back there so we can ensure those who deserve damnation are given it."

"But who does deserve it? Many have been sent there who didn't, and many more because of your own personal interference. The afterlife must no longer be divided by the haves and have-nots."

"True!" shouted Roger. "I did nothing wrong my whole life, but I still ended up there."

Byron stared for a moment at the puffed-up lion, attempting to familiarise himself with the soul under the silken surface.

"Ah, Roger. I remember you. I'm sure he's told you a tale or two. What's his angle this time? King of Sweden, inventor of the hearing aid, world's strongest man. Roger, lying is a negative emotion, I'm afraid. There's no conspiracy as to where you ended up."

"But all that is true…other than the bit about being the King of Sweden, I never said that."

"I don't think it's important," replied Elsie who was feeling as nervous now as when she was standing next to the Miracle Maker.

"I actually said I was the Emperor of Sweden."

"You spoke of a choice, Grace, let's hear it," said Baltazaar, edging closer to the sloth all the time.

"Go home, both of you. Head back to the dominions you've built and care for those that exist there. Millions of souls still need your care and attention, they deserve better. You still have the opportunity to repair the damage you have created."

Byron and Baltazaar looked at each other for a moment and then burst into fits of laughter. Both had borrowed bodies that were in elderly states of health, and the convulsions from their deep belly laughter were doing nothing to keep their souls safely inside. The others watched with confusion as tears rolled down their cheeks and the colour in their faces turned a rosy shade of pink.

If anyone knew a good joke when she heard one, it was Elsie. Granted, she was often the exponent of the joke and likely to be the main one laughing. "I don't get it."

"It's funny," said Byron wheezing for breath, "because even if we could go back, which we can't, why would we want to bother with them? Those souls are broken. There's no fun to be had there."

"Then you give me no choice," said Grace.

"Look, just give me the singularity," pleaded Baltazaar, "let me make the world a better place. Grace, you can be a part of it, you are not like these mortal fools. We can work together."

"I don't think that's very logical."

"Logical? What in life is logical these days?"

"This is."

*****

SHOOT

The cross hairs focused in on the group. The weather conditions were benign and his heart rate was level. Through the sights of his rifle a group of figures stood together. In the centre, Victor could make out the shiny sphere concealed by hairy arms holding it close. It was a difficult shot but certainly make-able. Moving the sights to the right slightly, there was nothing to obscure the line of sight to Byron. How he'd love to make that shot and rid his mind of the incessant backchat.

On the other side, an elderly gentleman leaning on a cane was moving forward towards the sloth. If he took what he wanted the time for action may be gone forever. Byron had wanted him to kill this man, but that plan had changed. Baltazaar had never personally done him damage or tried, as Byron had, to manipulate his mind. They'd certainly had some choice words in the past. On the yacht in Monaco he certainly got in the way, but only to stop Byron, not to stop him.

His finger hovered over the trigger.

The battle had largely ignored him in his hidden position in the sandy dunes on the perimeter of conflict. A few errant wasps had been a little irritating and a number of petrified soldiers had gone through his dune without even noticing his presence, such was his ability to go unnoticed. The battle would soon be over without anyone knowing that he was the one to fire the shot that would finish it.

It needed to happen soon. There would only be one chance. Everyone had to be in place, exactly as they were now through the powerful scopes of his sniper rifle. All he needed was the signal. Who knew what would happen to him then? Would he feel the sense of renewal he was promised by rectifying his mistakes? And if he did, what would he do then? A lifetime in the service of others would end and he'd have to discover new meaning. Could he live a normal life like everyday people. Retirement seemed like a valid

SHOOT

option to avoid it. Anything to gain some sort of inner peace.

He moved the sights fractionally from one target to the next.

"Now, Victor."

He lined up the shot and squeezed assertively on the trigger.

*****

Grace placed her fingers to her lips. The scene around her froze. She couldn't move from her position in case she forgot the exact spot to return to. The bullet was in the air somewhere between Victor and them and must finish at its intended target, and there was no way of telling which direction he was firing it from.

This moment was for her. One last chance to take in the world and those in it. She'd imagined having people around her. Certainly Byron and Baltazaar were where she wanted them. But at her side were five of the strangest characters she'd ever met. An angry, previously religious ox, a protective lion with a fondness for exaggeration, a nervous gibbon, a liberal spider, and right in the middle of all of them the most unexpected creature of all. A sloth with a singularity. The key to drawing the gods in.

And what's more, unlike all but four nations of the world, they were willing to stand and fight for what they believed in. Not for nation or religion or their breed, but for friendship, love and the principles of right and wrong. She couldn't have chosen it any better if she'd tried.

"I'm proud of you, Grace," said John.

For the first time in her life Grace was a little startled. Everything was usually so predictable. Whatever John had become, this proved he could break the rules of science, and that would be one final puzzle to solve before the end.

"I didn't know you could do this, John."

"I'm learning as I go. I guess if I'm able to define space, time comes as a two-for-one deal."

Grace fell silent. She'd imagined this moment to be a solitary one and not one to share with someone who she knew little about other than the fact that she probably shared a healthy dose of DNA, or at the very least some paranormal input.

"What's the matter?"

"I've been building up to this moment. Even though I've only known about my role for a short time, the puzzle has always been with me. I've solved the puzzle, but I need to put the last piece in place."

"The simplest things can sometimes be the hardest."

Grace closed her eyes and visualised a question quite alien to her rational behaviour. "What does it feel like?"

"Death? It's hard to say. I don't recall any pain as such. Fear more than pain. Fear of the unknown, of a destination untrodden. I've spent so much of my existence dead, I've sort of become used to it."

"I don't fear it. I know where I will end up."

"Where?"

"Home."

"Well, that's good, isn't it?"

"Yes, but I still fear that when I leave I will no longer be able to help others."

"You don't owe anyone, Grace."

"I owe you."

"What do you owe me?"

"I was responsible for running you over. And you are responsible for my creation and saving my family."

"Don't worry about me, there's nothing you can do."

"I think there's still hope for you."

"For me? No. I'm Sisyphus! I'm not sure I know how to live life anymore, let alone figure out a way of achieving it. Part of me is in a different universe, and

SHOOT

the rest of me appears to be in all of them. You'd need a hell of a net to scoop me up."

"When you're done here, go to Limbo. I think there just might be a way…if you want to, of course. I think the only other option for you might be bad for the rest of us."

"What do you mean?"

"I figured it out sometime ago. When the sloth turned up with the singularity there was only one answer to it. You'll figure it out before too long and you'll have to make a choice. For now I have to make mine."

Grace replaced her finger on her lips.

*****

"Don't you at least have some scissors?" demanded Sandy, wobbling around uncontrollably from the weight of having more wings than a family of bees.

"Scissors?" replied Accountant A.

"You must know what they are! Anything sharp at all so I can hack a few of these off."

"The rocks are pretty sharp," said Accountant M. "Lots of edges and angles."

"You're our very first guest, pleased to meet you," said Accountant A, stretching a paper hand out in what he hoped was the correct greeting. The others followed suit, copying as ever to avoid embarrassment. Not quite knowing what to shake, everyone grabbed a chunk of Sandy's wings and started giving him the avian bumps.

"Stop," grumbled Sandy. "Wherever this is, I hate it."

"I like it," said Ian, who had been hobbling around the Soul Catcher and taking in all three of the significant tourist attractions.

"What do you know? You're an idiot."

"That's nice. Saved you from Hell and you're still being unkind."

SHOOT

"How do you two know each other?" asked Accountant M casually.

"He's my servant," said Sandy.

"We don't have servants here," replied Accountant A. "This is a world for only those with neutral souls. There can be no possession. Accountant J, make a note about that one."

"Er…with what?"

"Um…improvise."

Accountant J flew off into the distance to 'improvise' which would likely consist of using its nose-cone to make markings on the sand, soon to be removed by the strong winds that constantly buffeted the world.

"I'll have you know," said Sandy in the grandiose fashion he'd become accustomed to using, "I used to run Hell. I'm a big deal."

Accountant A indicated for the rest to huddle together in discussion out of earshot from the disfigured birds. After much rustling of bodies and whispering they seemed to come to an agreement. Accountant A returned to speak to Sandy.

"We like this one," he said, pointing at Ian, "but you're a wrong 'un. We manage this world and our rules state no intimidation of any kind."

"I thought you said we were the first. How can you have the rules already if no one has ever come here?"

"We just decided on them now."

"You can't just make it up as you go along!"

"Of course we can. We're Accountants, rules and regulations are what we do best."

"I'm not putting up with this," said Sandy.

"You've no choice. You can't stay here anyway. It would upset the balance and atmosphere for the other residents."

"But there's only Ian here! And he's a simpleton who wouldn't know an atmosphere if you took it away from him, that's how little oxygen his brain needs."

"Oh, he's doing it again," said M.

SHOOT

"I know," said A. "Something must have gone wrong, we're definitely only meant to be receiving the neutral ones."

"We'll have to return him."

"What do you mean, return me!?"

"Can the machine do that?" said M, totalling ignoring Sandy's remonstrations.

"Let's ask David-SYNTAX ERROR-John."

"Who?" shouted Sandy. "Ian, I demand that you stop them doing whatever it is that they intend to do."

Ian remained motionless. Possibly because his body still didn't function with the desired level of dexterity, and probably because he'd decided he was no longer following orders. These Accountants were nice to him, they recognised him for what he was and more importantly, what Sandy was. Maybe this was the ideal place for him. A non-judgmental, simple and fair society that saw you for what you were. Accepted your failings as well as your talents, as limited as they might be.

"Not this time, Sandy."

"If I didn't have so many wings, I'd give you a proper kicking."

Accountant A typed a question into the computer terminal to establish whether in fact their Soul Catcher had a reverse gear.

'Yes. Press the 'backspace' button,' came the typed reply. But hurry up as there's another soul incoming.'

"Marvellous," said A to the others. "We have another one coming in. Better get another vessol made."

"What shape?"

"Improvise."

"We're pretty good at apple crumbles," replied M.

"Right, fine. The rest of you, go get the wrong 'un."

Fifteen of the more mobile and traditionally limbed of the Accountants circled around Sandy in all directions. In his attempt to bolt from the lynching, he tried to co-ordinate his seven wings, but only succeeded in flying in a manic figure of eight formation just marginally off the ground. The Accountants soon got hold of him and dragged him back to the machine. They attached his paper valve to the machine and Accountant A pressed what he hoped was the backspace button.

Sandy's vessol fell to the ground and the energy was sucked into the machine. It coincided with a large flash of white light from outside of the atmosphere of the planet. A silver ball no bigger than a tennis ball broke through the window and flew down the chimney. The machine rattled ferociously.

"Right. Time to go to work," said a softly spoken voice that hung on the wind.

CHAPTER TWENTY-EIGHT

GODSEND

A huge crater now occupied the space where a cairn of stones once stood on a dune. It was ostensibly still there, it had just turned itself inside out. The clouds, which had in an instant descended from nowhere, had now dissipated and the blue sky let the sun beat down on the battlefield. The column of fire that had joined the party at the same time as the clouds, stretching up into the air for miles, was just a smouldering mist that clung to the ground like a poorly managed school science experiment.

The battle had, to all intents and purposes, ceased the moment the crater emptied its rocky contents far and wide across the plain like an unexpected meteor shower. The different fighting forces had either stopped to watch, or simply stopped existing altogether. Those angels that hadn't already detonated themselves, either were struck by falling debris or made an even wiser decision to commit soulicide. In the main this involved gaining the attention of a boisterous German Shepherd or standing close to someone who had.

The Swiss forces stopped because they weren't altogether sure what they were fighting for anymore. The implanted suggestion, that had lingered in the front brain of every man and woman, had cleared like a fast-working acne cream. They were even more bewildered when some of them found they were in the process of fighting an otter or a squadron of sparrows. Rogier Hoffstetter was soon on hand to offer some

GODSEND

explanation before he, and many others, headed for the centre of all the action: the fallout from the huge explosion that had just ripped through the countryside.

Chief Uinirau and the eight other Nauruan probably had the hardest of jobs at that moment. Getting the message over to their unique army, when all their soldiers wanted to do was bite, sting or scratch, irrespective of whether there was a big, windy fire crater or not. Uinirau did his whistle command which was usually so effective and gathered about seventy-five percent of them to him. Whatever he tried, he was never getting the wasps back. They were less compliant than cats. Plus if you came back as a wasp you were probably a loathsome individual that no one was likely to miss.

Uinirau strode purposely towards the crater where Rogier was trying to cut his way through the smoke to identify survivors. Scraps of silk with fine gold thread were scattered here and there along with a few smouldering wings. As he'd suspected nothing had survived the catastrophic blast that had occurred here.

"Where, girl god?" asked Chief Uinirau as he cast a long, bulky shadow into the hundred-metre-wide abyss.

"Gone," replied Rogier solemnly. "Along with everyone else."

"How that?"

"I'm not sure."

"I think I can help you with that," came a voice casually over their shoulders. A man dressed in black and holding a long, thin gun case strolled up alongside them and examined his handiwork. The shot had been perfectly fired, but not even he was prepared for the pyrotechnic aftermath.

"Who you?" said the Chief, aiming his hollow bamboo towards the newcomer with aggression.

"I'm Victor Serpo. And I just ended the war."

"By shooting Grace!" said Rogier. "You bastard. Chief, finish him."

GODSEND

Uinirau swung his bamboo around his body and brought it swiftly down in the place where Victor had been moments earlier. With effortless precision the assassin skipped to the side, disarmed his aggressor, and threw the bamboo pole into the steaming pit.

"I'm British Secret Service, you're just an overweight fisherman and on this occasion I'm going to spare you. Too many have already perished through misunderstanding. I'm on your side and I only shot her because she wanted me to."

"What? Why would she want that?" said Rogier.

"Because she knew it was the only way to remove the other two."

"Uinirau not understand."

"It's quite simple really. While Grace, Byron and Baltazaar are in the same place their souls are in balance and little harm can come to them. But Grace knew that if she was removed from the equation, while they were standing only a few feet away from each other, the resulting combination of forces would be catastrophic. I've seen what happens when they're separated by only a hundred feet, and Monaco is still cleaning up the mess."

"So what happened to Baltazaar and Byron?"

"I'd imagine they're no more. When their energy fused together they cancelled each other out. And the explosion and the crater you see in front of you are the side effect."

"What about the others?"

"What others?"

"The weird bunch that turned up at the end. There was a sloth holding a silver ball of metal."

"Yes, I did wonder what that was. Grace never mentioned it to me. I suspect they got caught in the blast."

"Poor things. The least we can do is honour their sacrifice," said Rogier, turning around to see if any of his troops were suitably equipped to carry out a salvage operation.

GODSEND

Watching them in the distance was a large, blond man wearing a Swiss Army uniform at least two sizes too small for him. Rogier waved him over. After several rounds of pointing to himself and then to Rogier, the soldier seemed to understand the request and shuffled slowly over to the crater's edge.

"What's your name, soldier?"

"My name?"

"Yes, it can't be that hard, can it?"

"Um...Peter," came the uncertain reply.

"What regiment are you in?"

"Third sphere," said the man.

"Why does your shirt say '4th Mechanised Division', then?" asked Rogier.

"Oh so it does...I must be suffering from shell-shock, sir."

"You should be suffering from a lack of legs by the look of your trousers: they've got two bloody big bullet holes in them, yet your legs appear to be completely unharmed."

"Yes...I dodged them."

"What after the bullets pierced your trousers you managed to move quickly enough so they didn't go through your actual legs!"

"Um...yes. Anyway you wanted something, sir?"

"Yes," replied Rogier, remembering his initial request. "Go down into the hole please and bring back whatever remains you can find. They'll mainly be bits of silk. Also look out for a ball of metal."

"If I must," came the slightly irritable reply. As he bounded into the hole, legs certainly none the worse for their miraculous escape, Rogier again stopped him.

"What's wrong with your back?"

"Nothing."

"There are two bulges on either side of your shoulder blades!"

"Oh...really. That'll be kyphosis."

"What's that?"

"I'm a modern-day hunchback, sir."

"But one of them just twitched, is that normal?"

"Oh yes…very."

The muscular soldier moved from place to place gathering up what was left of five rather well-travelled reincarnates. There was a surprising amount of them. The seams were all frayed and broken but you could certainly make out the udder of an ox or the odd spider leg if you looked hard enough. When he returned to the observers he dropped the remains on the floor in a heap.

"Thank you, soldier. No sign of the metal ball, then?"

"No, you won't be seeing that again."

"Why do you say that?"

"Um…just a guess, sir. I have absolutely no idea what it is, what it does and where it has gone," replied the soldier rapidly, while desperately trying to avoid any eye contact.

"Hmmm. There's something rather odd about you, Private. You've probably got a big future. Return to your regiment and tell your commanding officer to give you a promotion."

"Really! Oh, sir, what can I say? I've waited so long to hear those words. It really is an honour to serve your country. I'll go over there straight away. Thank you, thank you again."

Wormwood practically sprinted off into the distance. It had taken him about half an hour of false participation in the Swiss Army to get a promotion, some five thousand years quicker than the efforts he'd put in to get a promotion as an angel.

"What will you do now, Victor?" said Rogier.

"I'm not sure. I guess I'm unemployed for the first time in my life."

"We always need men of your calibre in our Secret Service, if you'd like to apply."

"Are you sure?"

"Yes. Do you have references?"

"Ah. That might be tricky."

GODSEND

"Why?"

"My last two employers have just gone up in a ball of flames!"

*****

Limbo's northern meridian nestled on the banks of the Thun, a two-mile-wide lake that used to split two mountain ranges. Now it split one mountain range to the north and the ominous metal sphere to the south. Limbo's growth had been static in recent months, much to the relief of the people that lived and worked in the nearby town of Interlaken. Everything south of the pretty Alpine town was now hidden under liquid metal. The Eiger, Jungfrau, Aletsch Glacier and several thousand cows were all presumably inside somewhere.

The Clerk rested his body on a large rock that kept the lake from flowing onto the footpath and allowed his lungs to fill with fresh mountain air. It had been a struggle to get here. Not logistically. That had involved a series of fairly simple flights from Beirut to Zurich. Nash had been a little irritated to be placed in the hold with all the other animals, but accepted it for the greater good. The real struggle had been the Clerk's energy levels. His internal reserves had long been running on empty, and like a non-functioning television remote there was only so many times you could rub the batteries to keep it working.

Soon it would run out and he'd finally pass on.

Once he entered Limbo, as he planned, its protective power would conceal him from death once more. But soon it, too, would be reduced to nothing, and with it, him. One final action needed to write the end of his own personal story. The endgame as he'd designed it.

"That thing is huge!" said Scrumpy as he climbed up onto rocks to see if he could see the top. He couldn't.

"It's a lot smaller than it would have been, if it wasn't for all our efforts. This is where you would have ended up, Nash, if you'd not made alternative arrangements."

"I think I'd rather be inside a rabbit than inside that. It's intimidating," said Nash as he hopped around the banks of the lake mowing up bits of grass. He'd still not got used to the taste of it, but any alternatives had given him terrible flatulence. "How many souls do you think are in there?"

"Tens of thousands, I should think. All flying around desperately trying to work out what's happened to them. The sheer pressure of their proximity to each other may have created a number of interesting mongrels, but let's hope not."

"So, when do we go in!?" said Scrumpy excitedly.

"Oh you're not going in. Just me."

"Why just you? I've already missed out on a war and now I'm missing out on another adventure."

"Because the afterlife has another purpose for you. Mine is almost finished."

"What are you going in there for?" asked Nash.

"To die…and to find John."

"But John isn't in there!" said Nash. "Usually he's somewhere near me, or so I usually find at least."

"Ahem," came an over exaggerated cough out of the air. *"He's right,"*

"What was that!" said Nash nervously.

"I was told I needed to cough before speaking, settles the nerves apparently."

"It really doesn't."

"Sorry, there's no pleasing some people. In truth I guess I'm inside Limbo as much as I am everywhere else."

"John, you've been in the wardrobe to find a vessol more than once: didn't you recognise your true self in the past?" asked the Clerk.

"No. I don't remember that face anymore."

"Well, I do," said the Clerk. "I would never forget the face of my son."

"What?"

GODSEND

"When I first started working there I waited patiently to see you arrive, John. Every day I observed the vessels that had been sent from the Tailor into me. Every day I tried to guess which one was you. Hoping that you had done what I'd asked of you and become neutral. Unknown to me, you had, I just never recognised you. I'm sorry."

"Why?"

"All of this has happened because of me, John. In my stupidity I struck a deal with the Devil and dragged you into all of this. You've been paying the price ever since. I've lived a long life whilst you have lived fifty and many more deaths. If I'm going to make amends I have to try to find a way to give you back what I took from you."

"How can you possibly do that? I'm in so many pieces."

"If I can find the vessel that looks like you then the rest will be down to Grace."

"Grace, where is she?" asked Scrumpy desperately.

"Doing her job."

"What good is an empty, plastic vessol going to be?"

"It won't be empty for long," said the Clerk.

"What's a vessol?" said Scrumpy.

The Clerk briefly explained how the souls were normally placed inside, either here or in Hell, to hold the soul. The explanation wasn't long enough for Scrumpy, who had a million questions and no empathy for the Clerk's imminent death.

"Why plastic, though?" said Scrumpy.

"They haven't always been. Once they were made of balsawood, but mobility was much harder and everyone kept complaining about splinters."

"How did the plastic ones come about, then?"

"That's another story," said the Clerk, "and not one for now, I'm afraid."

"What did you mean, it won't be empty for long?" asked John.

"Soon you'll see Limbo shrink, and when it does, you'll need to focus all of your attention on the interior. Once there I'll show you what to do."

"I'll try, but I haven't really perfected my cosmic yoga yet."

"Your life depends upon it. That is…if you want to take it back."

"And what do we do?" asked Nash, hoping that there might be some action to help him regain the ability to order a pint without the ignominy of being a foot tall and having a fluffy tail.

"All you and Scrumpy need to do is wait."

"For what?" Scrumpy responded excitedly. "Explosions, quests, adventure…"

"Yes, quite possibly," replied the Clerk mysteriously. "You'll know when it happens."

"Ohhhh, exciting!"

"It is time I left."

The Clerk sought help to raise himself off his makeshift seat. Ancient bones creaked into position for one last time. One last walk into a place that had been home for most of his existence. Wheezing with the effort, he took a few steps forward and placed his hand on the metal. It swam around his fingers, analysing the owner to check eligibility for entry. Soon the metal had consumed his right hand in friendly welcome. The Clerk took one last look at his companions and stepped forward and out of sight.

CHAPTER TWENTY-NINE

NEUTOPIA

The first recorded expletive ever used on Neutopia was uttered shortly after an unknown voice came out of thin air. The word was 'fuck' and the culprit was Ian Noble, an indescribable seven-winged papier-mâché freak. The word became popular almost immediately. Accountants were fast learners. In the days to come the word was being used in almost any context when something surprising, disappointing, irritating, contentious, amusing or painful happened. Sometimes it was even used accidentally as a substitute for silence.

It wasn't really their fault. They could only learn from those around them, and as Ian was the first to arrive they learned more from him than most. As long as it was within the Accountants rapidly and recently expanded rule book about how things here should be, it was fine. In their mind 'fuck' wasn't rude, it was just another noun or verb, depending on the sentence they wanted to use.

Ian could be forgiven for uttering said expletive. He'd been in places where invisible people suddenly started talking to you without warning, and on most occasions it would be followed by some deep level of disappointment or pain. When this one spoke he just couldn't help himself, particularly as there was more than one reason for his swearing.

Not only had the voice made an unexpected entrance, Sandy had also made an unexpected exit.

The round silver ball that had catapulted into the box at the same moment Sandy had been added to it, was now the only object inside when they opened the door. Sandy was gone and truthfully nobody was that sad about it.

"Take the ball to the computer," said the mystery voice as Accountant A examined it, much like he had when David-SYNTAX-John had first caught his attention. The two objects were identical in every way.

"Where are you talking from?" said Accountant M.

"Up here."

"Up where? I can't see you."

"You won't. I'm sort of everywhere."

"Well, that's not very fair, is it? What are you doing here anyway?" said Accountant A.

"I belong here. This is my world, you see. I'm the third coming, and at last I have come."

Accountant A threw himself to the floor so that his head was millimetres from the ground as if he was pretending to vacuum up atoms. Most of the others did likewise, although this was much easier for Accountant J, who spent most of his life somewhere near the ground anyway. Accountant Z rolled about as ever, unable to control a body that only knew chaos theory.

"Oh fuck," said Accountant M, cottoning on to the new lingo quicker than most. "Does that mean we don't have to do what Accountant A tells us anymore?"

"No. He's still in charge."

"Fuck," said M coldly as he joined the others in multidirectional homage.

"I'm Grace, and we have much work to do here."

A muffled answer came in response.

"There's no need to offer me your praise. There'll be none of that here."

"What would you ask of us?" said A now that his face was partially lifted from the ground.

NEUTOPIA

"Very shortly you'll receive some new arrivals. You'll need to build more vessols."

"How many?" asked M.

"A few hundred..."

"Fine."

"...thousand," finished Grace.

"Fuck."

"That's impossible," said J, "there isn't enough time."

"Don't worry about that. Your time doesn't work the same way as Earth's does."

"What shapes?"

"Mainly humanoid, but if you could do me an ox, spider, lion, gibbon and sloth first, I'd be most thankful."

"What are they?" whispered J.

"Apple crumbles," said A.

"Oh fuck it!" said M.

"You heard her, let's get building," added A. "One hundred thousand."

"Fuckety fuck fuckers," replied M, although none of the Accountants could translate whether this was a good reaction or not.

*****

The Clerk had never seen Limbo like this before. For starters there were several mountains occupying the centre, there was a strong smell of cow manure, and every available space was taken by a cloud of blue electricity. He'd eventually have to climb the peaks in order to find the white valve that offered exit from this monolith. But first he needed a vessol. And not just any vessol.

The Tailor's room had always been located off the main chamber to the west edge of the sphere. With a renewed energy gifted by the protection of Celestium on his soul, he followed the circumference of the wall in a clockwise direction. Throughout his walk souls would fly over to him in either curiosity or desperation. They'd been here for months. Each of their unique energies colliding together to share virtual experiences with one another. They could not affect the Clerk's soul, but they certainly did their best to get in his way.

After several hours of hiking he found what only he was capable of recognising, a section of the wall that looked a clone of any other section. There was no door through to the waiting room or the Tailor's. It had been designed to reduce any chance that a soul might try to escape from the exit chamber or their own trial. The Clerk instinctively stepped forward and was once again consumed by the silver liquid. On the other side the waiting room was not where he'd left it.

The chalk line that he'd drawn after first realising that the structure was on the move was miles away from him. The small, plastic chairs were all piled up against the wall, trapped by Limbo's movement. Through the only other door it was a similar picture in the tailor'd room. The wardrobe, as vast as it was, had been crumpled from the disruption and several of the vessols had fallen from their hangers and were lying on the floor. Several were so damaged they'd never be used by occupants again.

The Clerk entered what was left of the wardrobe and focused on the side which had the vessels wearing suits with male faces. He knew how far the line went, but he'd never been to the back before. Every vessel here had been made to order. They did not represent every living person that came here, instead they were intended to be a generic mould of ninety-five percent of the human genetic spectrum. You didn't have to pick the one that most looked like you, but if you did the features had been designed so you'd find something close enough to your own memory.

He looked through them for hours. It was important he got the decision right: it was the least he could do. Even the slightest discrepancy in appearance was rejected. Eyes slightly too close together, nope. Earlobes too small, nope. Hair colour too light, not good enough. And then, towards the very back of the wardrobe but still nowhere near the end, he found it.

"Hello, John."

He lifted the vessel from its hanger and checked for any damage that might have been done by a previous occupant. He folded it carefully and hung it over his arm. Now for the long walk to find the exit valve.

It took two days of continual walking to scale the peaks by the easiest possible route. The north face of the Eiger was the shortest, but being immortal didn't make him Anderl Heckmair. Instead he reached the glacier at the top by following the tourist train track that meandered up through the mountains. Other than the souls and cowpats it was pretty easily. Finally his walk took him across the glacier and down into the crevice where Limbo once lived permanently hidden.

Above his head, thousands of feet in the air, he could just about make out the white plastic funnel. Eventually he'd have to secure the vessel he'd just picked out onto it, but it would be impossible unless he could get it closer.

"Well, Grace," he said. "I hope you're ready."

At his feet a lever poked out of the ground. It was pointing to the left where in large letters carved on the floor it read 'negative'. He grabbed the lever with both hands and dragged it into the central position, not as far as the label on the other side that said 'positive'. The funnel above him lit up brightly and with a whoosh of energy the nearest blue clouds started to rush towards it, fighting each other to be the first to escape.

*****

There wasn't a conveyor belt in Neutopia, but everyone there could appreciate why the invention had been welcomed so excitedly in Hell when they'd first built one. Thousands of paper vessels were piled in every available location and the only way of getting them to the Soul Catcher was to walk over and get one. This was easily achievable if souls arrived as rarely as the first few did. It became a little trickier if they entered one after the other without a pause.

Accountant A had devised a solution that involved everyone except him. He called it his conglomerate of effort. Accountant M had suggested calling it a 'chain', but that had not won enough votes. If you were the leader, people tended to vote for you, even if you didn't have the right or best answer.

Everyone in the conglomerate of effort passed a vessel to the next person, and they did likewise, and so on until the last one attached it to the valve. And boy, did they have to move quickly. Thousands of them had arrived already. Each soul as bemused as the last as they were fitted into some strange modern art form that the Accountants repeatedly referred to as vessels. That was about all the direction the new arrivals were given, and in the absence of anything instructional they just found somewhere to sit down and avoid looking untidy.

Any notion of depression washed out of the Accountants instantly: they were just too busy to worry. It might return in due course, but for now they had purpose and it was knackering. After what felt like a never-ending period of hard work, Grace brought everything to a halt.

"That should do it for a while," announced Grace. *"Turn the machine off: we need to make a switch."*

"A switch?" asked A, unused to taking orders, particularly ones he didn't understand.

"Yes, we need to take David out of the machine and put the new piece of Celestium in."

"But why?"

"Because David is going home."

"Reverse again?"

"Exactly."

NEUTOPIA

Accountant A, quite the expert now in using the Soul Catcher but still some levels away from the likes of Mr. Brimstone, turned the machine off and brought the conglomerate of effort to a standstill. Tea breaks weren't big in Neutopia, but whoever ended up inventing them would be a hero.

Accountant A carefully removed David and replaced him with the ball that had arrived just before Grace did. When that ball was in place the computer screen started typing obscenities at him.

'Bastards. Traitors. Papery twats.'

"Um, Grace, something is wrong with this ball, it seems to be angry with me."

"Well, you had something in the machine when it first arrived, didn't you? It is Celestium, it likes to absorb souls."

"The wrong 'un," said Accountant A knowingly.

"It's only what he deserves," said Ian, who was never far from the computer terminal fascinated by its workings.

Ian gave the others a full and detailed version of Sandy's journey from politician to pigeon to master of Hell.

"Sounds like Sandy has got what he always wanted, power. It might not be the power he was after, but he will now be the power that brings those souls to us, and you, Ian, will care for him and the Soul Catcher. That is the job I am assigning you because I trust you."

"Thank you," said Ian, pride filling many of his unnecessary paper parts and joining a strange smile that would take some time to shift.

"I need to talk to you about those special vessels I asked for," said Grace.

"Not up to your liking?" said Accountant A.

"Not up to the brief, I'm afraid. The lion has three tails and more legs than the spider. Ian, I wonder if you could help out on this one. After all, you spent some time with them, I believe."

"Oh…they're not coming here, are they?"

"Yes."

"Can't you just leave the lion behind?"

"Oh, no. He's as much of a hero as the others," insisted Grace.

CHAPTER THIRTY

PITCH DARK

"It's shrinking!" shouted Scrumpy who'd been keeping an eager eye out for any perceptible movement of the vast sphere.

He was right. But this was no gradual creep like the vast glacier living deep within its guts. It was moving faster than they could keep up with. Within a minute of Scrumpy's announcement and Nash acknowledging it, the sphere had revealed a two-lane arterial road and a bank of spruce trees. Nash hopped across the road in the knowledge that no one would have waited patiently for the road to clear over the last month. They chased after the perpetual retreat of the outer wall as it sped up through the forest, leaving ancient trees to shake off their enforced hibernation.

"John," hollered Scrumpy through cupped hands quite pointlessly. "It's started, it's time."

"I see it…from every angle."

It wasn't just the reduction that he could see. The reason for its rapid shrinkage was also visible. At the top of the enlarged structure a continuous stream of blue energy was being fired away at incredible speeds from the top. The imprisoned souls were on the move. It was impossible to pick out any individual one because they left in such numbers, leaving a pulse of energy from sphere to space, shimmering and erratic in its wake.

Before long, the speed of contraction and the steepness of the hill beat the young boy and his rabbit, and they were forced to watch Limbo as it moved away from them like a blanket of rainfall. Undeterred they kept moving to track its progress from the brow of the hill. When they reached it they could see Limbo disappearing into the distance.

"Now John! Before it gets away from you."

"I'm everywhere, Scrumpy!"

"Oh, right. That's weird, though, isn't it?"

"Quite!"

"Are you in Belgium?"

"Yep."

"My old house on the Bryher?"

"Yep. I can see Fiona and Violet sitting very happily in their garden holding hands."

"What about the rings of Saturn?"

"Yes...everywhere..."

"Behind the fridge?"

"Yes," said John, seeing no sign that this pattern might come to a natural conclusion of enlightenment. *"I think you might be right, Scrumpy. I'd better get on with it."*

"Right you are."

"It's been good knowing you, John. We'll follow the trail until we see it disappear. If you have a choice about your next move, can I ask you that it doesn't involve me," pleaded Nash.

"I'll do my best. It's not always that easy to choose, you know."

John closed off his consciousness from any external stimuli as best as he could. In many ways he was attempting to re-create the first moments he'd spent in this form when he found himself on level zero. Then he thought it would be impossible to move out into space and time the way he had. Now he had to concentrate on pulling all of himself into one ever-decreasing sphere of metal.

The meditation drew him closer in, concentrating his existence into a smaller and smaller space. First Europe. Then Switzerland. And finally the canton of Bern. The effort had a sizeable impact, not only on

PITCH DARK

John, who felt heavy and slow, but also on the landscape around him. The water of the lake buckled and shifted, causing sailing boats to rock and even stop in unconventional ways. Trees bent over so that their branches tickled the bottom of their trunks unaided by the elements. A number of cars disappeared completely from a small village nearby as they were cloaked by unknown forces of space static.

Scrumpy and Nash quickened their pace, but it was no good. They were in the centre of John's cosmic maelstrom. Their feet moved faster than the land vanished beneath them as they found themselves inexplicably chasing down the vast, metal dome shrinking into the background.

The concentration in John's mind was intense. Every ounce of effort moved his mass from one Russian doll to the next smallest as his emotions and memories pressed down on each other. He'd only experienced it once before when he'd spent an elongated period of time in the Soul Catcher after his exorcism. Just as he had then, his memories and experiences were being woven into a surreal amalgamation from fifty identities long forgotten. Nothing now made any sense other than the need to make one last push for Limbo. Placing the disturbing visions to one side, he dug deep for one final step. It was so close now. Within touching distance.

"Don't do it, John."

John was shaken from his inner trance and expanded away from his target.

"Have you ever prayed, John? In all the lives that you have occupied have you ever sat and desperately pleaded for help from a higher power?"

"Yes."

"And did anyone answer you?"

"No," answered John.

"And do you know why?"

"No."

PITCH DARK

"The highest powers don't really interact, unless it's absolutely necessary, and most of the time it isn't."

"Noir? What are you doing here?"

"Interacting for once, because this is one of those times when it is absolutely necessary."

"I don't have time for this," replied John. *"Limbo is shrinking fast and I must concentrate myself inside it before it disappears."*

"Which is why interaction is necessary. If you do go through with your plan, you won't be fulfilling your potential. You won't be finding the way."

"Find the way? That was you! All that time ago. I thought I was being told to find a way to survive, or to find a way to unlock the conspiracy of where all the souls went, or even the way to return Sandy and Ian back to Hell. But it wasn't any of them, was it?"

"No," replied Noir. *"Find the way was an instruction. It refers to your ability to renew the Universes. That was my message. To take my place in the regeneration of all that you see. A new beginning after the inevitable endgame."*

"I'm not with you," said John truthfully.

"I'm tired, John. I have watched evolution for thirteen billion years and it can get a little tedious. It is your turn now."

"What do you mean, my turn? You can't just to choose to start the Universes all over again."

"But you can."

"What?" said John.

"Just like me, you have also been through the Limpet Syndrome three times. As a result you have produced a singularity and moved over to another dimension, a dark matter existence that does not act like the rest of space and time. The darkness at the edge of darkness."

"I didn't produce a singularity. What are you on about?"

"But David did. A mutated soul like his, like yours, can move through the Celestium and absorb some of it

into themselves. The Limpet Syndrome can only keep you alive if you still have parts of your soul to cast off. He had nothing left to give and this is the result, you and him. A singularity and a spirit," said Noir.

"But how can those things restart the Universes?"

"Your singularity is on its way back here. If you don't join it, as you plan to, it will eventually start a chain reaction of expansion before it consumes everything in its path. Eventually shrinking down under an incredible weight, having consumed everything in space and time. Then the big bang will come. You'll be able to watch of course, it won't affect you, you'll be in the vacuum of nothingness that surrounds it. If you wait a while, couple of billion years should do it, you'll see the long, slow process of the Universes being formed again."

"Is that what happened to you?"

"Yes."

"What about Baltazaar and the Devil?"

"Gods, a name only branded on them by naive humans, came much later as a result of the development of human souls' evolving emotions. Once that started they were needed to manage the flow of those energies as they left their hosts. Sadly, they, too, ruined things through their desperate battle for dominance over each other. I'm pleased to see the back of them. It just makes all of this so much easier."

John was aware of Limbo retreating beyond the top of the Eiger mountain. Soon there would be nothing of it left.

"What's Limbo, then?" said John.

"It's a part of the last singularity. It was a single piece once, until Byron, Baltazaar and then David took pieces of it away to use in their Soul Catchers. Limbo and I go back a long way. The dawn of time, in fact."

"But what about all the people, won't they die?"

"Of course. Along with everything else. It's the way it has always been. But you, you'll be immortal, the

creator of everything around you. You can live forever...or just for one more life. It's your choice."

"I think I'd rather live just once well than forever in boredom and without interaction, thanks."

"It's your call, John. I can't make you do it. Just consider the opportunity."

"You don't know me at all. In fact, through all the confusion over who I am, I haven't forgotten what I am. I'm honest, fair, liberal and unselfish. Those are more important than an arbitrary name ironed onto the back of a jacket or illuminated on a computer screen. This world is worth saving, even though those who live in it may sometimes lack the grace to appreciate it."

"If you don't do it someone else will come along to fill the void. You can't stop it, it's inevitable."

"Let's just hope we can develop in others the same strengths we believe in."

"The world you want to build is sitting on a foundation of sand, John. There is much to mend. You have no exits for souls, no gods to govern the Universes, a mass of reincarnates running wild across the planet with no one to retrieve them, and a species who only sent four meagre countries to fight for their own survival."

"Then we will have to amplify the message, won't we? I'd love to chat but my window of opportunity is disappearing rapidly."

"It's your funeral, John."

"I've had many, one more won't matter."

John doubled his focus. He had to act fast. The target zone had reduced exponentially from the one he'd been aiming at just an hour ago. He would only get one chance. As his mass become denser and more uncomfortable, he felt himself being drawn closer in on the Celestium.

Inside its walls the Clerk was waiting for the signal to place the vessol he'd chosen onto the valve of the funnel.

PITCH DARK

"I'm ready," said John's deep and distorted voice.

The light of the pyres, which had burnt continually at four points around the cavernous metal ever since Limbo's construction, were extinguished and the room was plunged into pitch darkness.

CHAPTER THIRTY-ONE

PLASTIC MAN

"Surely you can do better than this," said Roger.

"Believe me it took a great deal of effort to get it right," replied Ian who was pretty pleased with his efforts overall.

"But it isn't right!"

"What's wrong with it? Did I get the mane wrong, or the paws perhaps."

"It's made of paper," said Roger. "It's not meant to be made of paper."

"You didn't complain when it was made of silk, though, did you?" offered Vicky.

"No, because I look amazing in silk. In paper I look like a cardboard lion that's been left out in the rain."

"Stop complaining," said Abe. "You're one of only five creatures to visit all four Universes…and in a period of just over a week, I might add. You're very, very special!"

"Doh…I've been telling you that all along, haven't I?!"

"You know we still haven't kept up our part of the deal, though," said Elsie.

"What do you mean?" asked Vicky.

"Gary, he's still not here, is he? We've left him behind again."

"You don't need to worry," added Ian. "He beat you to it."

"What do you mean?" asked Elsie.

"He was the first to arrive."

"Rubbish," remarked Roger, "I am always first, it's in the rules."

"Not here it isn't," said Accountant A, who knew the rules better than most as he was the main one making them up.

"So where is he, then, if he's already here?" asked Abe.

"Gone for a run," said Ian, pointing to a vast plain that once had a lot more white grass on it.

Over in the distance they could see a streak of dust approaching at a phenomenal speed. It reached them moments later. It was Gary, and there wasn't a bead of sweat to be seen on him.

"Alright, you lot, you took your time, didn't you?"

"What the fu…"

"Oh, it seems the singularity exploding may have rubbed off on me a bit. See you later: just off to do a couple more laps of the planet."

Before they could respond, or ask more questions, the sloth was speeding towards the horizon.

"Ian, it's time to set the machine up for David's return," said Grace calmly. *"Please pop him into the machine for me."*

"Of course. Consider it done."

"I'd like to make a complaint," said Roger holding a solitary paw in the air.

"What can I do for you, Roger?"

"Where's my super power."

"Sorry?"

"If Gary got one, then rest of us should, too."

"But you already have so many!"

"True, but you can't really max out on super powers."

"You're not looking hard enough, Roger. You have also gained from the explosion."

"Have I?" said the lion, showing self-doubt for the first time in his life.

"Oh yes. You're a very different creature than you were. If you look hard enough, deep under the surface, you'll find your super power."

"Oh God, please tell me it's humility," said Vicky.

*****

Limbo had returned to its more familiar dimensions. The white cone was now accessible just above the Clerk's head. Grace had succeeded in turning on the new Soul Catcher, and now all the souls had been rehoused. Soon Limbo would fall in on itself, lacking the energy to hold up its foundations. But first, for the plan to work, something had to arrive. And so far it hadn't.

"What now?" said John's booming and slow voice from around the darkness.

"I just have to place the vessol on the cone and wait for David, your neutral part to return."

"Where from?"

"Neutopia. If all has gone to plan, Grace now manages a new exit for the afterlife."

"But what about all the other souls?"

"They will all go there. Heaven and Hell can no longer be accessed, so Grace will have to look after all of them."

"And what will happen when David arrives?"

"You'll get another chance at life, John."

"But what do I do with it?"

"Live it. You don't have to keep pushing the rock up the hill. Let it go."

"You know I had a choice to be immortal, but I think you can only live if you know your own mortality. I need to find a purpose in the time I have left."

"The endgame has only been delayed, John. If you want a purpose, then find a way to stop it for good. You have much to do and limited time. I don't know how long you'll last in this hybrid. But there is someone who is desperate to help you."

PLASTIC MAN

"Who?"

"The boy. He can carry on the work after you."

"And what about you?"

"Me. Oh I'm an expert on endgames, it's about time I saw my own. This is it, I'm afraid. You won't see me again, it is time that I made my peace with the afterlife."

"Be at peace. I forgive you, by the way."

"Forgive me?"

"You made a mistake, but you have put it right and that's all anyone can ask."

"And it's that message you must take to the world, John."

The darkness of the room was lit up by something entering the top of the funnel and trying to force its way in but with nothing to trap it. The light illuminated the sphere and demonstrated just how much of Limbo was left, barely more than a small bungalow.

The Clerk attached the vessol. "I hope you like what I've picked out for you."

*****

Nash and Scrumpy watched from the viewing platform as Limbo shrank back into the cracks in the ice. A small ball floated past their heads and shot down into the fissure to join it.

"What do you think has happened to John?" asked Scrumpy.

"I've no idea. Maybe you should go and find out?"

"You mean…you want me to go down there!"

"Well, it's not going to be easy for me to do it."

"Finally it's my turn to have the adventure. Thanks, Nash."

"Just be careful."

Scrumpy didn't really understand what the word 'careful' meant. When you were eight and full of energy, careful didn't really come into it. This was his moment. After all the travelling, all the watching others take centre stage, finally he got to be part of the fun. And this was his sort of fun, too. Climbing, jumping and sliding into a dark hole with any number of possibilities.

Within seconds, Scrumpy was out of sight. The bottom was a thousand feet down and he had to navigate a series of icy chimneys and rocky slabs. Not once did he struggle, skipping from one overhang to the next. Even when it got dark it only inspired his progress. A shrinking, white light was the only beacon to guide him. As he got closer to it, it was almost extinguished.

His feet hit the unsteady surface of the ground after no more than thirty minutes of descent. There was no longer a trace of the metal sphere that they'd followed all the way from Lake Thun. All that was left was a dim glow in the distance. He ran towards it, excited to discover what it was.

"John!" he shouted, hoping to discover if the plan had worked. He wasn't confident.

The source of the dull light came from a man wearing a suit. He stood static, his head forced backwards so he was looking up into the sky. His body didn't look natural, like a shop mannequin had been given a spray job. It looked as if someone had erected a statue in homage to a historic moment in human endeavour. He watched it for a moment to see what would happen, before his confidence returned to normal and he approached it.

He placed a hand onto the figure's arm. It was warm but with a plastic feel to it. The skin was hardened as if in some way it had been reinforced.

And then the arm moved.

Scrumpy jumped backwards in fright. "Who are you?"

The man's eyes opened and for the first time since a bullet pierced his chest he looked out onto the world with real eyes. His hands instinctively reached for his face to check they were real and familiarise himself with features he'd not seen or touched in fifty lifetimes. Was it real? Was this who he really was?

"I don't know," came the answer to Scrumpy's question. "I've been so many people."

"How do you feel?"

"Alive."

"I'd say that was good, then."

"How do I look?" he asked.

"Good. A little rigid but otherwise good."

"I feel…well, it doesn't matter how I feel…it's enough that I can. The air on my face, the stone beneath my feet, the warmth of my body."

"How did it happen?" asked Scrumpy.

"As Limbo reduced to nothing a ball entered the vessol the Clerk had picked and everything was sucked into it, including me. There was a moment of silence when the world stopped and then you arrived."

"Then you must be John."

"I think you're right, although anything is better than being Sisyphus."

*****

It took them a lot longer to remove themselves from the heart of the Alps than it had for Scrumpy to get down into it. John's body was slow to adjust to its new surroundings and some of the climb was tricky even for Scrumpy. They worked as a team, helping each other find the best hand- or footholds to use. As the outside world drew closer and the cold wind rattled around them, John started to feel the excitement rise within him. He was about to re-enter the world. When they reached the top, Nash was waiting nervously.

"You found him."

"I found someone," replied Scrumpy.

Nash watched as a man clambered over the edge of the fissure and squirmed his way onto the snowy ground of the glacier, which was seemingly

PLASTIC MAN

undamaged from its stint inside Limbo. His body was not made of flesh and bone, but plastic and metal. But one thing was for certain, if this was John Hewson, then he was very much alive.

"Welcome back, John," said Nash, feeling an immediate connection with a man he'd had first-hand experience of.

"How do you know I'm John," said the man.

"Because I have been closer to you than most. I have shared your memories and emotions. Part of your soul lay on me for a time, if you remember. I'd know you anywhere."

"But do I look like me?"

"How should I know? I never saw you, did I? And I don't think it really matters what you look like. It only matters how you are and what you do."

"I guess you're right."

"So is that it?" said Scrumpy. "Everything is back to normal? No more adventures left to have?"

John looked at the brown rabbit with the big, floppy ears some distance below him. "Not quite."

CHAPTER THIRTY-TWO

MATTERS OF LIFE AND DEATH

This was the second time that Rogier Hoffstetter had spoken at the United Nations and this time he stood confidently at the rostrum. When you'd fought gods, narrowly escaped assassination and met creatures from across the universes, nothing much fazed you. Down to his left, Victor Serpo stood protectively, Rogier's personal security guard. He'd returned to his attire of black clothes and looked much trimmer than he had.

There were some other friendly faces in the crowd. Sitting across two of the blue and cream leather seats, still wearing less clothes than suitable, was the newly elected diplomat for the Republic of Nauru. Chief Uinirau waved excitedly, still unclear to the conventions needed in the chamber. In a front row VIP seat was a young body whose hair had been forced into a neater and less frantic style. On his lap sat a brown rabbit looking serious.

All around them worried and irritated faces stared up at the President of Switzerland. They were about to be given another lecture and this time there would be no pretending to sleep. A short video had been played to them before Rogier took the stage. It was a montage of videos from the war, taken from Swiss headcams. It also included a series of interviews with reincarnates in the style of famous celebrities appealing for charity donations. There was no hiding from the truth this time. But that didn't mean they would act.

MATTERS OF LIFE AND DEATH

"Ladies and gentlemen. You know why you are here. It is time I introduced you to someone that none of have you have ever met, but all of you owe. You owe him your thanks and gratitude. Without him, none of this would be here. Everything you hold dear would be gone. He has occupied many bodies and worn many faces. But only he knows who he truly is. He's decided to go by the name John Hewson and he has an important message for you."

Rogier was brief and to the point. This wasn't his moment, it was John's. After all he'd made a choice which had saved every person in the room and he'd earned the right to explain why and demand more. John stood up and made his way slowly to the rostrum. His body moved clumsily as his plastic body lacked the flexibility of those around him. He inhaled through the small, plastic valve that sat in the back of his throat.

"Death is easy, it's life that's hard."

He paused for the message to sink in.

"Death can be achieved in an instant. There are a thousand ways to do it. Turning the lights out on life is just one sharp left turn whilst driving on the motorway. But then what? Do you think it'll get any better after that? Do you think your problems will be solved? I've been dead a lot, I know how it feels. Life, on the other hand, is much more challenging. It's not enough just to live, the human race now must decide how to live."

The auditorium hung on his every word.

"Some months ago my father spoke in this very room and told you 'don't die.' It was an important message that helped to slow the endgame. It resulted in tens of thousands of people triggering the Limpet Syndrome, some of which you saw in the video earlier. Their existence does not threaten us, they must live in harmony with humans until their time runs out. At that stage I and my associates," he looked down and offered a heavy plastic wink at Scrumpy and

Nash, "will ensure they find the exit door to the afterlife."

Scrumpy stood up and bowed to the room quite unexpectedly. This new assignment meant his whole life was now an adventure. No school, no sitting still, and lots and lots of travelling the world. And all he had to do was to utter a strange chant every time a reincarnate met their end.

Sat either side of him, looking completely out of place in their strangely informal attire, sat Fiona and Violet on a rare visit from the peace of Bryher Island. Their combined expressions were a mixture of pride and terror. Here was their adopted child taking plaudits from a room of dignitaries before he was let loose into the world with a plastic man and a rabbit. In many ways their approach to his upbringing and their own life experiences had seeped into every part of the young boy. After all an undercover journalist and a animal welfare protestor were interesting role models.

They were not the only ones to make the trip to New York for this historic moment. Faith sat in the front row nursing a rabbit on her lap. She'd lost a sex crazed partner and gained a sex crazed rabbit. How ironic it was that Nash had ended up with such a familiar mindset. Faith looked somewhat relieved by these new circumstances. She was not an adventurer by nature and yearned only for a quiet life to rebuild her own future.

She had though lost a daughter, even though she'd spent much of Grace's life distant and unsupportive. The pride of her achievements was tinged with a sense of lose that no connection was possible now, in life or death. As she considered her own next steps, John outlined his.

"Recently I was offered a choice. The choice was simple. Live forever or try to change mankind. I chose the harder of the two because life isn't about the easy or straightforward. It isn't about the everyday chores or minor victories. It's not about the moments of joy or the times of challenge. Life, life is about the trials and tribulations. It's about how you react to the disasters. It's about the principles of what you stand for. I'm not the only one who you owe for the opportunity to live for these things. Grace Foster-Stokes also stood for what was right. She made the ultimate sacrifice."

A tear welled up in his eye at the thought of what Grace had unselfishly done for mankind.

"We as a species must stop trying to find the quick fix or shortcut. We must suspend our need for easy answers and false hope. We must give up our individual selfishness and find a collective will to support each other, irrespective of our differences."

John paused again. Every seat was taken and in every one of them a pair of eyes maintained contact with him.

"Each one of you, and every single person on this planet that you represent, must now realise that death is easy. My father gave you a message. 'Don't die.' My message is this. Life is really difficult. Treasure it. Go out and live it, because one day it won't be there anymore. Mankind might not get another chance. The next person who is offered the choice I was given might not make the same decision. So go and live… and try not to fuck it up."

THE END...

COMING IN 2019

'THE END OF THE WORLD IS….NIGH!'

Sign up to the newsletter
www.tonymoyle.com/contact/

Printed in Great Britain
by Amazon